until you loved me

Also by Brenda Novak

NO ONE BUT YOU
FINDING OUR FOREVER
THE SECRETS SHE KEPT
A WINTER WEDDING
THE SECRET SISTER
THIS HEART OF MINE
THE HEART OF CHRISTMAS
COME HOME TO ME
TAKE ME HOME FOR CHRISTMAS
HOME TO WHISKEY CREEK
WHEN SUMMER COMES
WHEN SNOW FALLS
WHEN LIGHTNING STRIKES
IN CLOSE
IN SECONDS
INSIDE
KILLER HEAT
BODY HEAT
WHITE HEAT
THE PERFECT MURDER
THE PERFECT LIAR
THE PERFECT COUPLE
WATCH ME
STOP ME
TRUST ME
DEAD RIGHT
DEAD GIVEAWAY
DEAD SILENCE
COLD FEET
TAKING THE HEAT
EVERY WAKING MOMENT

And look for Brenda Novak's next Silver Springs novel

RIGHT WHERE WE BELONG

available soon from MIRA Books.

brenda novak

until you loved me

mira

Recycling programs for this product may not exist in your area.

ISBN-13: 978-0-7783-3102-5

Until You Loved Me

For questions and comments about the quality of this book, please contact us at CustomerService@Harlequin.com.

www.BookClubbish.com

Printed in U.S.A.

Dear Reader,

Welcome to Silver Springs, population 5,000! I love writing this new series, mostly because I enjoy working with wounded heroes, and the boys' ranch at the edge of my fictional Southern California town (located about ninety minutes northwest of Los Angeles) supplies many of those. Hudson King, the hero of this novel, was abandoned the day he was born—in Bel Air, of all places, one of the richest areas in the state. No one can say who left him or why, but his fortunes have changed dramatically over the years. He's no longer an unwanted orphan. As one of the most gifted quarterbacks in the NFL, he's achieved what most men can only dream about. He has *everything*. Almost. He still craves answers, has to find the person or people who left him to die all those years ago so he can learn *why*. Problem is...what he finds out makes him wish he'd never solved the mystery. Good thing he has just the person to stand in his corner with scientist Ellie Fisher...

I love to hear from my readers. If you're on Facebook, you can find me at www.Facebook.com/brendanovakauthor. You might even be interested in joining my online book group, which consists of over 6,000 book fanatics! We have so many fun things going on—group T-shirts and sweatshirts, personalized and autographed bookmarks, monthly "professional reader boxes," a birthday program, an annual "in person" event, a commemorative pin for anyone who's read more than fifty Novak novels, and more! You can learn all about it on my website (www.brendanovak.com). Just click on the Book Group page (which is where you can also find the link to sign up). And while you're there, be sure to add your name to my mailing list. I'd love to be able to notify you of sales, new books and other news.

To happily-ever-after...

Brenda Novak

until you loved me

To my husband, who's listened and offered feedback
as I've read every single one of the sixty novels I've written aloud to him.
(Sometimes he's heard them two or three times!)
That's what a real hero is like.

PROLOGUE

Wincing against the glare of the sun that slanted through his front windshield, the man drove slowly through Bel Air, California. There was so much money in this area. He couldn't even afford to pay the rent on his dumpy one-bedroom apartment and yet these people owned estates that sprawled over half an acre. Didn't seem fair.

The baby he'd put in the seat next to him—only a few hours old and wrapped in a tattered blanket—began to squirm. It wasn't in a carrier; he didn't own one. He wasn't about to spend good money on something he wouldn't need.

"Don't you cry," he muttered under his breath. "Don't you *dare* cry." He couldn't tolerate that sound—it was like nails scraping down a chalkboard. He had to get rid of the child before it started to make noise. Noise would draw too much attention.

He'd intended to take it to the far corner house. He'd been to that mansion twice before and thought the woman who lived there might be empathetic enough to take in an abandoned baby. But the needy infant was already waking up, so he pulled over immediately, looked both ways on the quiet summer street and grabbed the squirming bundle.

It took only a few seconds to stash the newborn under the closest privacy hedge. He didn't dare go any closer to the house surrounded by that hedge, couldn't waste the time or he'd risk being seen. The neighborhood was quiet in midafternoon, but there were always service people coming and going…

He heard the baby start to fuss, which only made him move faster. After jumping back into his vehicle, he took off.

CHAPTER ONE

Thirty-two years later

"You look miserable."

Ellie Fisher forced a smile for her oldest friend. "What? No, I'm not miserable at all!" She had to shout over the music pulsing through the air and reverberating off the walls and ceiling. She'd never understood why, in a place designed for singles to meet and become acquainted, the music had to be so loud. A hundred twenty decibels made it almost impossible to have a conversation and *had* to be damaging their hearing, but she didn't say that. She knew how Amy, her friend since early childhood, and Amy's friend Leslie, whom she'd just met tonight, would react. Besides, after the emotional trauma she'd been through in the past week, she wouldn't have felt much better anywhere else. "I'm having a great time!"

Amy pursed her lips. "*Sure* you are."

After being inseparable in grade school, she and Amy had grown apart in middle school and taken very different paths. Amy had been the stereotypical cheerleader—popular, outgoing and fun—and had opted for cosmetology school instead of college. She now worked at an expensive hair boutique in Brickell, a neighborhood in downtown Miami. Ellie had never received the same amount of attention, especially from boys, but until recently she hadn't cared about that. She'd always preferred her studies to parties, had been her high school valedictorian and was accepted into Yale, where she'd done her undergraduate as well as postgraduate work. Since leaving school, she'd been determined to overcome the immunology challenges associated with finding a cure for diabetes—her favorite aunt had lost a leg to the dreaded disease—and now she worked at one of the foremost research facilities in the world, which just happened to be here in Miami, where she'd been born. But thanks to that early bond, she and Amy would always be friends. Ellie had never been more grateful for her than during the past week, since Amy was the one who'd been there when Ellie's world fell apart.

"It's true." Ellie glanced from Amy to Leslie as if to say "Here we are, sitting at a tiny table in one of South Beach's most popular nightclubs. What's not to love?"

Amy rolled her eyes. "I know you too well to believe that. But I'm not letting you cut out early, so don't start checking the time on your phone. I've invited a couple of friends to come and meet you, remember?"

Ellie remembered, but Amy hadn't mentioned any names. Ellie got the impression it was because she didn't know which friend would show up—that she'd simply gone through her male clients and other contacts and invited anyone who might be available. "I wasn't checking the time," Ellie said.

Amy scowled. "I saw you!"

"I was looking to see if my parents texted me! They should've arrived in Paris by now." Ellie wished she'd gone with them, but by the time her life had imploded, they'd had their travel plans in place, and it'd been too late to get a plane ticket. They'd be teaching in France for the next year, though. Once she finished the clinical trials she was working on, she hoped to fly over and meet up with them. Now that she wouldn't be going on her honeymoon, she had enough vacation days to stay for three weeks. Surely visiting Paris would provide a better distraction. Hanging out with Amy didn't seem to be helping.

"Your parents will be fine," Amy said. "You need to loosen up, have a few drinks and start dancing. Forget about everything, including that bastard Don *and* the man he cheated on you with."

Ellie didn't think she could get drunk enough to forget about Don. Three days ago, she'd caught him in bed with Leonardo Stubner, a member of the administration staff where they worked. She'd have to face them both—as she had on Wednesday, Thursday and today—when she returned to the Banting Diabetes Center on Monday. And that wasn't the worst of it. Since her shocking discovery, he and Leo had come out of the closet and declared their love for each other, adding another level of humiliation to her suffering by making it all public. Half of their coworkers felt so sorry about the pressure they'd been under to hide their sexuality that they were praising them for having the courage to finally make "the big reveal." The other half, those who were critical of their deception, didn't dare speak out for fear of being accused of being unsympathetic, homophobic or both. One way or the other, almost everyone she knew was talking about Ellie and her situation and forming an opinion.

After hearing what Amy had just said, Leslie leaned forward, finally showing a spark of interest in Ellie. "Your fiancé cheated on you with another *man*?"

Ellie squirmed under Leslie's horrified regard. When Amy had said they were taking Ellie out to get her mind off a broken engagement, Leslie had barely reacted. But the circumstances of her failed relationship made Ellie that much more pathetic. When Ellie caught her fiancé with his "best friend," whom he'd known since college—Don was the one who got Leo hired at the BDC—she'd also come face-to-face with the realization that all the "golfing" trips the two had taken since she and Don started dating hadn't been as innocent as she'd been led to believe.

The one man who'd told her he wanted to spend forever with her hadn't really been attracted to her in the first place. He'd been using her as a cover so he wouldn't become estranged from his ultrareligious parents.

That hurt more than her lost dream of having a family.

But the fact that she was ill at ease in a nightclub wasn't Don's fault. She'd never felt comfortable in large groups, didn't consider herself particularly adept at the kind of social interaction they required. She'd been too devoted to getting her PhD in biomedical engineering—and following that with a postdoctoral fellowship at the BDC, where she'd met Don, a fellow scientist—to have much time for clubbing, so she'd had little experience.

She shouldn't have let Amy drag her here, she decided as she gazed around. But maybe one of Amy's friends would show up and make her feel like less of a loser. Nothing else had worked since Don's betrayal, so she forced herself to hold out hope. If she didn't make *some* effort to recover and move on, even if it resulted in only a very short rebound relationship, she'd die an old maid, as her grandmother would've put it. That had never seemed more of a possibility than now. Her thirtieth birthday loomed ahead, but instead of planning her wedding, as she'd anticipated, she'd be doing all she could to continue her research while bumping into her ex-fiancé *and* his lover on a daily basis.

A man from across the room came toward them. With his sandy-colored hair swept up off his forehead, he was attractive in a frat-boy way—well built and preppy, which was a look she found attractive.

"Mind if I join you?" he asked.

Frat Boy immediately singled out Amy—not that Ellie could blame him. Dressed in a short, tight-fitting black dress, six-inch stilettos and smoky makeup with bright red lipstick, Amy oozed sex appeal. So did Leslie, for that matter. Due mainly to

Amy's insistence, even Ellie had had a complete makeover and was dressed in a similar fashion, except her dress was white and dipped low in the back instead of the front—the only concession Amy would allow Ellie's natural modesty.

"You need to get laid. That's what you need," her friend had said when she'd balked at wearing the skimpy lingerie she had on under her dress or complained about the height of the heels Amy had pressed on her. If someone *did* ask her to dance, she'd probably turn an ankle, which was hardly conducive to hooking up later. Then her first Brazilian would definitely not be worth the shocking pain.

Amy looked Frat Boy up and down before widening her smile. "Sure. It'll save me the trouble of searching for you when I'm ready to leave."

He obviously liked that response. Ellie had to admit it was evocative. She almost brought up the notes app on her phone so she could jot it down—except she was fairly certain that line wouldn't come off so smoothly if *she* ever attempted to use it. Flirting sounded silly coming from her. She loved sarcasm, had always traded put-downs with her father, but she doubted that talent would impress other men.

With some effort because of the throng of people who filled the club, the man located a chair and dragged it over before introducing himself as Manny. He made small talk for a few minutes. Then he waved over his friend, a shorter, stockier version of himself, who'd been getting drinks at the bar.

Manny explained that they were both commercial real estate agents with a local firm and introduced his friend as Nick. Nick focused on Leslie, since Manny already had dibs on Amy, making Ellie the third wheel she'd expect to be in a situation like that. She tried to contribute to the conversation but found herself peeking at her phone when Amy wasn't looking. Not only was she uncomfortable, she was bored. But if she tried to get a taxi, Amy would remind her of the "friends" who were coming to meet her.

As the two couples got up to dance, leaving Ellie alone at the table, she let out a long sigh and flagged down a waitress. "Bring me three shots of vodka," she said.

Maybe if she forced herself to get buzzed, the rest of the night would pass in a merciful blur. The alcohol wasn't good for her liver. As a scientist, she couldn't help acknowledging that. But as far as she was concerned, it was vital for her poor aching heart.

Hudson King loved women, probably even more than most men did, but he didn't trust them. He'd gotten his name from the intersection of Hudson and King, two streets in Los Angeles's exclusive Bel Air community, where he'd been abandoned and hidden under a privacy hedge as a newborn, so he figured he'd come by that lack of trust honestly. If he couldn't rely on his own mother to nurture and protect him when he was completely helpless, well...that didn't start him off on the most secure path. Even once he'd been found, hungry, cold and near death, screaming at the top of his lungs, his life hadn't improved for quite some time.

Of course, he'd been such an angry and unruly kid, he was undoubtedly to blame for some of the hurdles he'd faced growing up. He'd made things more difficult than they had to be. He'd had more than one foster family make that clear—before sending him back to the orphanage.

Fortunately, with his foster days long behind him, he'd buried most of the anger that had caused him to act out. Or maybe he just controlled it better these days. Some people claimed he played football with a chip on his shoulder—that his upbringing contributed to the toughness and determination he displayed on the field—and that could be true. Sometimes it felt as if he did have a demon driving him when he was out there, making him push himself as far as possible. Perhaps he was trying to prove that he *did* matter, that he was important, that he had something to contribute. Several sports commentators had made the suggestion, but whether those commentators had any idea what they were talking about, Hudson couldn't say. He refused to go to a psychologist, didn't see the point. No one could change the past.

Either way, once he was sent to high school at New Horizons Boys Ranch in Silver Springs, California, where it became apparent that he could throw a football, his fortunes had changed. After that, he was named First Team All American in college. Now, as starting quarterback for the Los Angeles Devils, he'd been named MVP once, played in the pro bowl three years running and had a Super Bowl ring on his finger. In other words, he had everything a man could want—a successful career, more money than he could spend and more attention than he knew what to do with.

Not that he enjoyed the attention. For the most part, he considered fame a drawback. Being in the spotlight proved to some of the families who'd decided he was too hard to handle that he might've been worth the effort. But it made his little problem with women that much worse. How could he trust them when they had all that incentive to target and mislead him? Getting involved with the wrong girl could result in false accusations of rape or physical abuse, lies about his personal life or other unwelcome publicity, even an intentional effort to get pregnant in the hopes of scoring a big payday. He'd seen that sort of thing happen too many times with other professional athletes, which was why he typically avoided the party scene. He wasn't stupid enough to fall into *that* trap.

So, as he sat back and accepted his second drink at Envy in South Beach, he had to ask himself why he'd let his new sports agent, Teague Upton, talk him into coming to a club. He supposed it was the fact that Teague's younger brother, Devon, was with them, making it two votes in favor to his one opposed. Still, he could've nixed the outing. These days, he usually got his way when he demanded it. But since his former agent had retired, Hudson had recently signed with Teague, and Teague lived in Miami and was proud of the city and eager to show him around. Besides, the game Hudson had flown in for didn't take place until Sunday, so boredom was a factor. Since Bruiser, his closest friend on the team, wasn't arriving until tomorrow due to a family commitment, and the rest of the Devils were going to a strip club tonight, loneliness played a role, too—not that Hudson would ever admit it. He was the guy perceived as "having it all." Why destroy such a pleasant illusion? Being that guy was certainly an improvement over the unwanted burden he'd been as a child.

Besides, the owner of Envy had been very accommodating. Because Hudson didn't want to be signing autographs all night, the club owner had made arrangements with Teague to let them in through the back and had provided them with a private booth in the far corner, where it was so dark it'd be tough to recognize *anyone*. From his vantage point, Hudson couldn't see the entire dance floor—and only a small part of the lighted bar—but he could observe most of what was happening, at least in the immediate vicinity. That trumped hanging out alone in his hotel room, even if the skimpy dresses and curvy bodies of the women created a certain amount of sexual frustration he had little hope of satisfying. The strip club would've been far worse...

"Hudson, did you hear me?"

Hudson lowered the hurricane he'd ordered so he could respond to Teague's younger brother. Teague himself had already found a woman to his liking and was hanging out with her closer to the bar. "What'd you say?"

"What do you think of *that* little hottie?" Devon jerked his head toward a buxom blonde gyrating against some skinny, well-dressed dude.

"Not bad," Hudson said. But he wasn't all that impressed by the blonde. He was far more intrigued by the woman he'd been surreptitiously watching since he arrived. Slender, with black hair swept up and away from an oval face, she wasn't as pretty as some of the other women he'd seen tonight, but she wasn't nearly as plastic, either. She seemed oddly wholesome, given the setting. The poise with which she held herself told him she deserved more attention than she was receiving. At times, she even seemed slightly bewildered, as if she didn't understand all the frenetic activity around her, let alone thrive on it. She'd just ordered three shots and downed them all—without anyone cheering her on or clapping to encourage her, which wasn't how most party girls did it. Then, while her friends were still off dancing, she'd gotten rid of the evidence and ordered something that looked like a peach margarita.

"Man, I'd like to get me some of that," Devon was saying about the blonde.

"Go talk to her." Hudson hoped to be left alone, so he could study the mystery woman at the table nearby without interruption or distraction.

"Can I tell her I'm with you?" Since Devon laughed as he spoke, Hudson knew he was joking, but he made his position clear, anyway.

"No. Don't tell *anyone* I'm here. That would mean I'd have to leave, and I'm enjoying myself at the moment."

"You are? You didn't even want to come."

"I'm glad I did."

"You're not doing anything except having a drink..."

At least he was having a drink around other people, could have some fun vicariously. "That's good enough," he said. "For now."

"Man, you could change that so easily. All you'd have to do is crook your finger, and you could have any woman in here."

Probably not *any* woman, but more than his fair share. That was part of the problem. Hudson never knew if the women he met were interested in *him* or his celebrity. "Fame isn't all it's cracked up to be."

Devon's expression said he was far from convinced. "Are you

kidding me, man? I'd give anything to be you. I'd have a different model in my bed every night."

Hudson didn't live that way. He hadn't slept with anyone since his girlfriend broke up with him nearly two years ago. He hadn't planned on remaining celibate for such an extended period; he just hadn't found anyone to replace Melody. Not only did he prefer to avoid certain risks, like getting scammed, he didn't believe it was ethical to set someone up for disappointment. People like him, who struggled to fall in love, should come with a warning label. That was the reason he and Melody had gone their separate ways after seven years. She'd come to the conclusion that he'd never be willing to hand over his heart—could never trust enough to let go of it—and she wasn't interested in anything less. She wanted to marry, settle down and have a family.

He respected her for cutting him off and had realized since then that she was right. He'd stuck with her as long as he had because she was comfortable and safe, not because he felt any great passion.

Still, it was difficult not to call her, especially when he needed the comfort, softness and sexual release a woman could provide. Only his desire to protect her from getting hurt again, since the breakup had been so hard on her, kept him from relapsing.

"I refuse to be that big a fool," he told Devon.

Teague's little brother leaned closer. "What'd you say?"

"Nothing." Devon wouldn't understand Hudson's reluctance to churn through women even if he tried to explain it. Part of it was Devon's age. At twenty-four, nothing sounded better than sex with as many girls as possible. Hudson had felt the same way eight years ago. Only his peculiar background, and that trust issue, had kept him from acting on his baser impulses. Also, he'd achieved early success through college football at UCLA and already had something to protect when he was twenty-four.

"So why don't you approach her?" Hudson pressed, gesturing toward the blonde.

Devon took another sip of his drink. "Think I should?"

The song had ended and she was walking off toward a table on her own. "What do you have to lose? She might shut you down, but then you'll move on to someone else, right?"

Freshly empowered, Devon put down his glass and slid out of the booth. "Good point. Okay. Here I go."

As soon as he left, Hudson donned the sunglasses he kept in his shirt pocket—he was already wearing a ball cap—and called over the waitress.

Fortunately, she was so busy she barely looked at him, so the disguise seemed unnecessary, but he wasn't taking any chances.

"What can I get for you?"

"That woman over there—what's she drinking?" He pointed at the lone figure he found so intriguing. He didn't have to worry about her seeing the gesture, since she had yet to look over at him.

The waitress cast a glance in the direction he'd indicated. "I'd guess a peach margarita."

Just as he'd thought. "She needs a fresh one. Will you take care of it?"

"Of course."

"Thanks." He handed her a twenty. "Keep the change."

CHAPTER TWO

When the waitress brought Ellie another drink and explained that a gentleman in a booth not too far away had sent it, she almost refused it, especially when she twisted around and saw that he was wearing sunglasses. What kind of guy was so clueless or affected that he wore sunglasses in a dimly lit bar, especially at nighttime?

She found that behavior slightly ridiculous, but what she could see of the rest of him was appealing. A snug-fitting T-shirt revealed broad shoulders, a solid chest and well-muscled biceps. He seemed tall, even though he was sitting down, and his face wasn't unattractive. Matter of fact, she liked the square shape of his jaw and the strength of his chin. Don had a weak chin, now that she thought of it—not that she meant to. This guy looked like someone who might be in the military, a pleasant association since she'd always admired the men and women who fought to keep America free.

Besides, she'd come here to take her mind off her troubles, hadn't she? It wasn't as if her girlfriends were doing much to help. Every time they came back to the table to check on her, the two men they'd met would drag them off again.

So, after taking the drink from the waitress, she lifted it high to show her gratitude to the man who'd purchased it for her. If some stranger wearing sunglasses in a bar wanted to buy her a drink, let him, she told herself. At least she was starting to relax, to enjoy herself. No doubt the alcohol could take full credit for that. She still felt like crying whenever she thought of Don. But she *wouldn't* think of Don. Like everyone else here at Envy, she'd lose herself in the strobe lights, the music and this fresh margarita.

The woman didn't seem to recognize him. She gave him a smile that said "Thanks, but I'm not interested."

Hudson wasn't used to that reaction. Maybe he'd underestimated the power of a pair of sunglasses. Right now his Ray-Bans seemed to be acting a little like Harry Potter's invisibility cloak.

Or was it possible that she *did* realize who he was but simply didn't care for football players?

Either way, now that he'd seen her more clearly, he was interested in engaging her again. She was pretty and had an abundance of creamy skin to go with that rich, dark hair.

As soon as she finished her drink, he sent over another one—which she sent back without a moment's hesitation. He could hear her explaining to the waitress that, while she was grateful, she'd had enough. Something about not being irresponsible, which confirmed his first impression. She wasn't the typical clubber.

When she turned and waved—her way of being polite, thanking him in spite of her refusal to accept the drink—he waved back. Surely, once she got a good look, she'd recognize him. Usually buying a drink for a girl meant she'd be on his lap by now.

This one merely returned to watching the dance floor.

Hudson didn't want to venture out of the booth, but he did want to talk to this woman, and she wasn't coming to him. Even more intrigued, simply because she didn't seem excited about meeting him, he hauled himself out of the booth and eyed her as he approached her table.

Since he came mostly from behind, he startled her when he folded himself into the chair closest to hers. *Now she'll figure out who I am*, he told himself. But it was apparent that she had no clue when she introduced herself as Ellie and asked for his name.

Did he *have* to reveal who he was? He liked blending in for a change. Liked being no different than anyone else. He considered making up a fake identity but couldn't bring himself to go that far. "Hudson." He felt certain *that* would rip away his anonymity—his name wasn't common—but it didn't seem to change anything.

"To what do I owe this pleasure?" she asked.

She wasn't being coy. She really didn't care if he joined her or not. He could tell. "Looked like you could use some company. That's all."

She thought that over for a moment, then nodded as if she agreed. "I guess I could. Beats sitting here alone, in any case." She extended her hand. "Nice to meet you."

"Same here," he said as they shook.

"Do you live in Miami?"

He wondered if she was being facetious. Could this be for real? Everyone knew he played for Los Angeles, so chances were slim that he'd live clear across the country. But after studying her expression, he decided his first assessment had been correct. She had no idea who he was. "No. Just visiting," he said. "You?"

"Born and raised in Doral. Now I rent a house in Cooper City."

"Which is..."

"A suburb not too far from here."

He gestured at her empty glass. "You turned away my drink. It's not too late if you're regretting that decision."

"No. Alcohol is *so* unhealthy. I've had enough."

"Isn't a little alcohol supposed to be good for you?"

He was teasing, but she took him seriously. "You mean red

wine. They say that, but you're killing brain cells in order to help your heart. Doesn't make a lot of sense. If you're exercising and eating right, you're better off without it."

He held the hurricane he'd brought over loosely in one hand. Since he was into health and fitness himself—he had to be if he wanted to remain at his physical peak—her words didn't fall as flat as they might have. He was used to hearing cautions like that from his various trainers. "What are you, some sort of doctor?"

"Scientist, but I specialize in immunology, so I have a solid understanding of how the body works." She tucked a strand of hair that'd fallen from her messy bun behind one ear. "How long will you be in town?"

"A few days."

"Are you here for work or play?"

"Um, I came to play," he said, which was technically true. He just didn't add that play for him *was* work.

"Have you ever been here before?"

"Couple of times." He spoke dismissively, hoping to minimize the fact that he came here every two or three years to play the Dolphins.

"And? How do you like it?"

"It's nice." He took in her innocent-looking eyes and wide, expressive mouth. He found her attractive in a girl-next-door way. "To be honest, now that I've met you, I'm starting to like it even better," he said with a grin that came naturally to him for a change. He hadn't had an encounter like this—one that didn't begin with some fawning statement about his looks, football ability or fame—in quite some time. The normalcy this woman offered felt like a life preserver, one he could grab to save himself from drowning in a sea of cynicism.

When her gaze cut to the dance floor, as if she might panic and go find her friends, he thought he'd come on too strong. But then the tension in her body eased. "After the week I've had, that's good to hear. Even if you *are* wearing sunglasses."

"Excuse me?"

She leaned closer. "Isn't it a little dark for those?"

He nearly laughed when it registered that she was embarrassed for him. "My eyes are sensitive to the strobe lights." That was the only outright lie he'd told her so far, and it wasn't a big one—nothing she could get too angry about if or when she learned who he was.

"Oh. I guess that makes sense, then."

Afraid her friends would return and recognize him, he checked the dance floor himself.

Luckily, he saw nothing to suggest impending discovery. "What was so terrible about your week?" he asked.

"Nothing I care to discuss," she replied promptly.

"Is that why you were knocking back those shots? You're trying to forget?"

Her expression filled with chagrin. "You saw that?"

"I found it a bit curious that you were doing it alone when it's more fun with the support of a group."

She shrugged. "Desperate circumstances call for desperate measures."

He liked the delicate curve of her neck and her small, slender hands, which were devoid of the fake nails so many women wore, suggesting she possessed a certain practicality. "That bad, huh?"

"That bad."

Stretching out his legs, he crossed them at the ankles. "Won't you give me a hint about what went wrong? Did you lose your job? Get some bad news?"

The darkness of his sunglasses made it difficult for him to determine the color of her eyes, but he admired the thick fringe of lashes that showcased them. He was almost certain they were blue…

"I *wish* that's all it was," she said.

"What could be worse?" He hoped he wasn't putting his foot

in his mouth, that she hadn't recently been diagnosed with cancer or some other disease. He'd feel foolish for pushing the issue then. But he figured that couldn't be it. She'd said it was worse than "getting bad news."

"I caught my fiancé in bed with another man."

He froze with his drink halfway to his lips. "You did say *man*…"

"Yes. His 'best friend' from college. Apparently they've been together for some time."

He put down his drink. "Wow. That sucks."

"You have no idea. Speaking of *sucking*, what I saw will forever be etched on my brain."

Hudson grimaced. He was no homophobe. As far as he was concerned, people had a right to live as they saw fit. He'd be the first person to fight for that. He just found nothing appealing about having sex with another man, so the image she'd created in his mind made him cringe. "Are you *sure* you wouldn't like another drink?"

"I'm sure. I didn't really come to drink. Well, I guess I did. But only because I was looking for some sort of diversion. I'm tired of seeing the whole incident over and over in my head."

He considered asking her to dance. That would be a diversion, wouldn't it? He craved *some* excuse to put his hands on her. It'd been so long since he'd held a woman against him—and this one seemed different, refreshing.

He didn't dare take the risk of exposing his identity, however. At six foot five, his height was enough to draw attention. Once someone really looked at him, the jig would be up in spite of the dark glasses.

"The music's so loud in here. Why don't we go out and walk along the water, where we can talk?" he asked.

He'd probably made his move too soon, but he didn't have a lot of time. If *her* friends didn't come back, *his* would…

She seemed uncertain, so he lifted his hands to indicate that he hadn't meant to put any pressure on her. "Or, provided you're willing, I could get your number and take you out tomorrow night." If it came to that, Teague could arrange for some private place where they could dine without being gawked at or interrupted.

She checked the time on her phone. "It's only eleven-thirty."

"What does that mean?"

"I don't think they're going to show."

He felt his eyebrows go up. "Who?"

"My friend's been expecting a few others to join us."

"So..."

"I'll take that walk with you," she said. "Otherwise, I could be sitting here for another two hours."

"Great." Maybe that wasn't the most exuberant response he'd ever received, but a yes was a yes. He stood and offered her his hand, and felt his pulse spike with hope the second her fingers curled through his.

The moon hung low in the sky, so big and full it appeared to sit on the water. Ellie thought it could almost be mistaken for another planet. "That has to be the most beautiful sight I've ever seen," she said to Hudson, tugging on his hand to get him to stop long enough to let her stand and gaze at it.

"It's gorgeous, all right," he murmured, but he wasn't looking at the moon. He was staring at *her.* She'd had his undivided attention ever since they left the club. Maybe it was the alcohol, but he was having quite an effect on her. Now that he'd removed his sunglasses and she could see his whole face, she had to admit that he wasn't only large and well built but also stunningly attractive. She'd never had a more handsome man take an interest in her.

"Did you know that our moon is unique in the whole solar system?" she asked.

His gaze moved down to her lips before returning to her eyes. "No. What's unique about it?"

He wasn't thinking about the moon; she could tell. He was thinking about touching her, kissing her. That possibility made her heart race and her knees go weak, which was crazy. She'd just been totally eviscerated, in an emotional sense, by Don. And yet…the warmth of Hudson's hand, the glint of his teeth when he gave her that sexy grin of his and the deep timbre of his voice seemed to bury all that pain and disappointment—and make her feel like she was flying.

She swallowed hard before continuing. "It's disproportionately large, for one thing. If it wasn't, it wouldn't have sufficient gravity to hold the Earth steady on its orbital axis. That's what keeps our climate relatively stable."

"Interesting," he said as his hand slid up her arm.

Ellie felt goose bumps break out on her skin. "And it didn't form from leftover clouds of dust and gas, like most other moons," she added breathlessly. "Astronomers believe there was a-another planet that collided with Earth nearly four billion years ago."

His hand climbed higher. "Is that so?"

"Fortunately—" she cleared her throat "—it was just a glancing blow, or the Earth would've been destroyed."

"How tragic."

"Instead, the collision ripped off a huge chunk of the Earth's crust, which began to orbit around us."

"Eventually becoming our moon."

"Yes." She tried to keep her eyes on the huge white disk they were discussing. She was afraid she'd lose the small grip she still had on reality if she looked up into his face. They'd been walking along the beach, shoes off, for over two hours, talking about anything and everything except the mundane details of their lives. As they left the club, they'd agreed to forgo the usual small talk. Since they lived across the country from each other and would probably never meet again, there didn't seem to be any point. But Hudson's physical appeal and the excitement she was feeling were difficult to ignore.

"You know a lot about everything—except TV, sports, movies and any other part of popular culture," he teased.

She opened her mouth to defend herself, but he was right. She was always involved in a book or an experiment. Anyway, she didn't get the chance to say anything. He blocked out the moon by moving in front of it. Then his head came down and his mouth very gently met hers.

Ellie told herself to step back. She didn't even know this man. But the conversation they'd had for the past two hours had been so easy and companionable. And the way he made her *feel*! She'd never had such an immediate, visceral reaction to anyone.

A tremor of excitement rolled from her head to her toes as his big hands moved up her back, pressing her against him as he parted her lips.

Ellie heard a groan—and realized the sound had come from her. She'd never been kissed quite so well. He wasn't overpowering her, wasn't forcing his tongue down her throat. He was tasting her and inviting her to taste him, with such expertise she felt she could trust him to treat her just as she wanted to be treated.

Before long, her head was spinning, and she couldn't blame it on the shots she'd downed at the bar. She'd sobered up quite a bit since they left. She got the impression that Hudson had been biding his time, waiting until she was capable of knowing what she wanted and what she didn't. She respected him for that. But his kiss was as intoxicating as any liquor, maybe more so.

When Ellie woke up, she knew exactly where she was. She just couldn't explain the behavior that had led to finding herself in Hudson's bed. It was so out of character.

She held her breath, listening to the steady sound of his. He was still asleep, thank God. Not only had they made love three times, they'd slept in each other's arms. Why? Sure, she'd been hurt by Don's pretense and, when she'd texted Amy to tell her she'd met someone and would find her own way home, Amy had jokingly responded that she deserved a little revenge sex. From a birth control angle, she'd been prepared for it. Leslie had shoved a fistful of condoms in her purse—and in Amy's purse, too—before they'd arrived at the club. But the hours Ellie had spent with Hudson weren't about her broken engagement. After he kissed her that first time, she hadn't thought of Don once. Hudson had obliterated him…and everything else. She'd never been tempted to describe someone she knew personally as virile—that wasn't a word that came to mind very often—but it fit Hudson. He was so perfect in every regard that there were moments she suspected Amy had set her up.

Maybe she had, Ellie thought, as she went over the sequence of events in her mind. Maybe Ellie would return to her regular life and learn that one of Amy's friends had shown up, after all. Hudson. And that he'd only pretended to believe she was a complete stranger as a favor to Amy, to help rebuild Ellie's self-esteem and teach her there were other men, other options.

If that was the case, she'd certainly fallen for it—not that she found *that* very flattering. Either way, though, she was encouraged. He'd charmed her to the point that she'd forgotten how pathetic her real life was and just…lived in the moment. There was something to be said for that. The whole night had been magical, including the time they'd spent on the beach. Once, when she tossed her shoes aside and darted into the surf, he'd followed and plucked her out with one arm to save her from a particularly large wave. After that, the water had crashed into *him*. Somehow, he'd remained steady in spite of that. Then, soaked to his thighs, he'd carried her out, and they'd fallen onto the sand, laughing.

Smiling at the memory, she raised her head. Sure enough, she'd spent the night with the handsome stranger from the bar. He was only inches away, covered by a sheet, but she knew he was naked underneath. How had she let it go that far? When he said he'd kept her out too late and offered to call a cab, she'd agreed. It was only after the taxi arrived, and he'd pressed her up against the car and kissed her for the second time—a deep, openmouthed kiss—that things went a little crazy. As with the first kiss, her head had started to spin and her heart had started to pound. But instead of letting him pull away, she'd grown bolder. When he'd finally opened the door to put her in the back seat, she'd been so hungry for more that she'd pulled him in with her. And instead of giving the driver her address, she'd whispered to Hudson that she wanted to know what it felt like to have sex with a man who truly desired her. A man who wasn't attracted to someone else. And he'd immediately barked out the name of his hotel.

Ten minutes later, they were hurrying to his room like randy teenagers making sure they left nothing unexplored on prom night. But Ellie hadn't been invited to prom. She'd established too much of a reputation as a bookworm by then, and that wasn't the sort of girl who got many dates. So she felt she owed herself the experience. And as reckless as her behavior had been, she couldn't bring herself to regret being with him. She'd never been shallow. To her mind, Don, with his narrow shoulders and weak chin, proved that. But Hudson… Wow! His body was a work of art—strong, sinewy and ideally proportioned.

She couldn't help glancing down to where she knew she'd find other parts that were decidedly impressive. Even in that regard, he was far superior to anyone she'd ever known.

A fresh wave of heat flowed through her as she remembered how masterfully he'd taken charge of her body. He'd quickly found all her most sensitive parts, adapted to every sound or movement she made—read her easily—and made her vibrate with pleasure.

She covered her mouth at the memory of how she'd cried out at her first climax. She was embarrassed by that, and by the way she'd climbed on top of him later.

She had to get out of here, she decided. She didn't want to

face him. Before last night, she'd had sex with only two other men, both of whom had been long-term boyfriends, not strangers. So the question remained—how had she stepped outside her overly cautious, preoccupied-with-other-things self and let go like that? Made love with such wanton abandon?

She had no idea, but she couldn't pretend that she hadn't discovered how good connecting with a man she highly desired could be.

Ellie was afraid she'd wake Hudson as she slipped out of bed. It had to be morning. But with the drapes closed to block out incoming light and the alarm clock turned away from the bed, she couldn't tell.

Thankfully, Hudson didn't even stir.

As soon as she could move freely, without fear of bumping into him or causing the bed to shake, she hurried to pull on the skimpy white dress that lay in a small heap on the floor. While she was now glad of the Brazilian Amy had forced her to get—and the lingerie—she hated having nothing modest to put on. Anyone who saw her leaving such an expensive hotel would probably assume she was a high-priced hooker.

At least Amy would be proud that she'd quit being so conservative, that she'd actually cut loose...

She tried to take solace in that as she jotted her phone number on the pad by the phone. She thought Hudson might want to see her again. He'd seemed to have a good time, too. But after pausing to take one final look at him—the well-muscled arm flung out across a pillow, the tousle of dark curls against the white of the linens and those big, broad shoulders—she went back, quietly tore off the paper and shoved it in her purse. She didn't want to risk having him *not* call. She'd been through too much, and it was still too recent. Besides, he lived across the country, so there was no reason to take the risk. It wasn't as if what they'd started here could really go anywhere.

Last night had been a grand and memorable adventure.

She was going to leave it at that.

CHAPTER THREE

The constant buzzing of his phone, vibrating from the pocket of his discarded pants, woke Hudson. He lifted his head so he could turn the alarm clock around to face him before dropping back onto the pillow. It was after noon. How had he slept so late? He was usually an early riser, couldn't lie in past seven or eight even if he wanted to.

Only after he'd had a few seconds to regain full consciousness did he remember that he'd had a woman with him last night—a sweet, smart woman who'd made him laugh on the beach and given him a wild ride in bed afterward. *That* was why he'd been able to sleep so late. He hadn't sacked out until almost dawn—and only after significant physical exertion. That workout had been the good kind, too, the kind he'd been craving for some time, which had to be why he'd scarcely moved since. Satisfaction. At last.

He reached out, searching for Ellie's warm body next to him. Maybe the fun didn't have to be over, he thought. But she wasn't there.

His phone stopped vibrating as he shoved himself into a sitting position and squinted to see in the dark room. He had a suite at the Four Seasons, so the fact that she wasn't in the bedroom didn't necessarily mean she was gone. She could be in one of the bathrooms or the dining or living area.

He didn't hear any noise, however—nothing to indicate he had company.

Why would she leave so soon? Without even giving him her number or pinning him down on when he might be interested in getting together again?

"Ellie?" he called.

No answer.

He got up and pulled on his boxers before opening the drapes to let in the sun. Then he walked through the whole suite.

As he'd begun to suspect, it was empty. And her clothes and purse weren't anywhere to be found.

Had she gone out to get them some breakfast?

Hudson would've been happy to order room service if she'd told him she was hungry...

If she *had* stepped out for food, she might've left him a note to say she'd be back. He checked the desk, but there was nothing on the pad by the phone.

Returning to the bed, he held the pillow she'd used to his nose. He could smell her perfume. That was the only trace left of her.

His phone started to vibrate again. Disappointed that the woman he'd met and liked had walked out on him without so much as a goodbye—when she knew he still had a day or two in Miami—he picked up his pants and dug his phone out of the front pocket. As he did, he felt a small burst of hope and thought maybe she was calling. Until he remembered that she didn't know who he was. They hadn't exchanged numbers; they hadn't even exchanged last names!

Before she left, she could've gotten his phone out of his pants and called herself to capture his number. He'd had other women help themselves. But it would have been locked since he hadn't used it recently. Besides, she didn't seem the type. If he was being honest, that was partly why he'd been attracted to her. She wasn't as aggressive as some of the other women he'd met since launching his career. So he wasn't surprised to find that his caller was just Teague.

With a sigh, he hit the talk button. "'Lo?"

"There you are!" Teague said. "Jeez, I've called you at least ten times. Where the heck have you been?"

"What do you mean, where have I been? I was up late. I've been sleeping. Why? What's the emergency?"

"No emergency. Just checking in. I was afraid you were unhappy when you left last night. I would've left with you if you'd told me you were going. I tried texting you, but after that cryptic message you sent me—'Leaving, see you tomorrow'—I got nothing."

"I didn't expect you to leave the club. I was having a good time without you." The last thing he'd wanted was for Teague to catch up with him and ruin his fun. In addition to his fear of being recognized, that was why he'd made up an excuse to Ellie that they needed to slip out the back and only texted Teague once he was safely away. Otherwise, he knew his agent would have come running.

Crazy thing was, there were a million reasons last night shouldn't have happened the way it did. And yet everything had worked out.

He'd never forget the moment Ellie pulled him into that cab. It had taken her so long to warm up to him that he hadn't expected it. He'd spent several hours, both before and after that, with a woman who had no clue he was a professional athlete, let alone the starting quarterback for the Los Angeles Devils. And just as he'd suspected, taking his celebrity out of the mix had made their interaction so much more genuine. For once, he could be confident that the person he was with had no ulterior motives, that she honestly liked him for him.

"You were having *fun*?" Teague said in surprise. "Sitting in that booth alone? No, we shouldn't have left you. We knew you weren't that big on—"

"Teague!" he broke in.

"What?"

"I left with someone, brought her here to the hotel."

There was a slight pause. "*You did?* How? I didn't even see you talk to anyone."

"Well, you weren't watching me the whole night."

"You were in that damn booth every time I checked."

"There was a woman by the name of Ellie sitting nearby. We hit it off."

"Just like that?"

"Not quite as fast as it sounds, but yeah."

"She a football fan?"

"Don't know. She didn't recognize me. That's what made it so enjoyable."

Teague grunted as if he was struggling to process that. "You didn't tell her who you were?"

"No."

"And she couldn't figure it out for herself?"

Hudson could hear the skepticism. He remembered feeling the same disbelief at first—waiting for her to put two and two together. "Guess not. She doesn't watch sports. Which isn't too big a shock, I suppose. She's a scientist."

"Interesting. I feel a lot better, then. Glad you had a great time."

He did have a great time, and then he'd slept like a baby, something he'd been unable to do for months. He'd been too worried about Aaron Stapleton, one of the boys he mentored at New Horizons Boys Ranch, the behavior-focused boarding school he'd attended himself from his sophomore to senior year. The kid had been diagnosed with bladder cancer six months ago and was going through a second round of chemo, which made him deathly ill, and he didn't have any parental support. Hudson was terrified that the treatments wouldn't be as effective as they needed to be, that he'd lose the one person he'd felt he could trust with a big piece of his heart.

But he didn't want to obsess about that while he was in Miami. He'd be home soon—in time for Aaron's next appointment. "I'm glad I met her," he said.

"So…where is she now?" Teague asked. "If you're talking this openly, she must not be close by…"

He crossed over to the window and peered at the ground twenty-two stories below. He thought maybe he'd see her getting into a cab, but none of the people he could make out were wearing that killer white dress. "She's gone—left before I woke up."

"Well, that's good!"

"Good?" he echoed, surprised by the relief in his agent's voice.

"At least you didn't have to come up with a way to get rid of her or face any awkward goodbyes."

"I guess." He supposed that was lucky, since he wasn't looking for anything permanent.

He'd gotten what he wanted, he told himself. He'd had an incredible encounter with a woman he was really attracted to, and it had led to some of the best sex of his life. Even better, he'd done it all anonymously, so there'd be no blowback, no upsetting recriminations for not falling in love, no requests for money or other favors, no unexpected information about his love life showing up in the press. He hadn't even had to give Ellie his autograph.

He should have been relieved, happy, ready to move forward from here.

So…why was he hoping she'd come back?

Ellie sat at a sidewalk café not far from where she'd been shopping and pushed her new sunglasses higher on her nose. After getting home and showering, she'd gone to the Shops at Mary Brickell Village and purchased quite a few clothes, including a black sheath cocktail dress, since she didn't own one, some more lingerie—she'd gone a little crazy there, considering the prices—and a pair of Dolce & Gabbana sunglasses. She wasn't sure why she was reacting to her night with Hudson by going on a shopping spree. Sleeping with him had been too self-indulgent already! But he'd made her feel so attractive and desirable that she was still running wild and free. Staying busy kept her from thinking too much about her actions. So there was that. And now that the wedding was off, she wouldn't have to help her parents finance the reception or pay for her honeymoon to the Seychelles (Don didn't have the savings, which meant she was carrying the financial burden). Although the venue had already been booked and she'd lost a couple thousand dollars in deposits when she canceled, that was only a fraction of what the whole thing would've cost, so she'd still have extra money to play with.

She counted the bags she had with her—she'd brought them into the restaurant so she wouldn't have to walk all the way to her car—and felt a moment's panic. Maybe she'd spent too much...

No. She refused to regret what she'd done today, any more than last night. She might as well start enjoying life. She wasn't getting any younger, and now that she wasn't getting married, either, she had only herself to please.

Should she go to the Seychelles without Don?

She'd been looking forward to seeing that part of the world.

She imagined what it might be like to spend two weeks on the islands by herself. If she could find another man like Hudson, it would be worth the time and money—

"There you are."

At the sound of Amy's voice, Ellie turned to see her friend weaving through the tables as she came onto the patio. Ellie was relieved she hadn't brought Leslie. She hadn't cared for Leslie all that much.

"Whoa! Look at you!" Amy stopped to gape at the evidence of how Ellie had spent her day. "I see you've been having fun."

"Other than the stuff you convinced me to buy for last night, I haven't been shopping in ages. I was too busy saving up for the wedding. But now… I figured I might as well splurge."

"Those are some great brands." She took her seat across from Ellie. Amy had called several times to talk about last night. Rather than answer her friend's questions over the phone, she'd simply invited Amy to join her for an early dinner. Amy's salon was close to the restaurant, so it was convenient, and meeting up allowed Ellie to postpone returning home, where she'd have to face her regular life.

"Are those new sunglasses?" Amy asked.

"Yeah. How do you like them?"

"They're stylish. You look amazing."

"Thanks."

A waitress came to greet them and ask for their drink order.

"So…what happened last night?" Amy asked once they were alone. "I assumed you were joking when you texted me about leaving with someone, but I went by your place on my way home, and you weren't there. Kind of scared me, to tell you the truth. I was afraid I'd contributed to something that put you in a tricky spot—or worse."

When Ellie felt herself blush, Amy's eyes narrowed in suspicion. "What? Don't tell me you *did* go home with someone!"

"Yes."

"Who?"

"Some guy at the bar."

"*Some* guy? You don't know his name?"

"Hudson." Ellie watched carefully for Amy's reaction. "Does that ring a bell?"

There was no recognition. Either Amy was the best actress

in the world, or she wasn't behind Hudson's picking up Ellie. "No. Why would it?"

"I thought maybe he was a friend of yours."

"I've never met anyone by that name."

"Then it happened naturally." Ellie found that hard to believe. There'd been prettier girls at the club. Ones with more curves, too—and gregarious personalities. Why hadn't Hudson chosen one of them?

Amy's smile spread wide. "Tell me about it!"

Ellie waited until their server had returned with their water and they'd placed their dinner order. Then she explained how Hudson had bought her a drink, joined her at the table and asked her to go for a walk.

"You went out on the beach with him."

"For a couple of hours. I thought that should be safe. There weren't a lot of people around that time of night, but I could've gotten someone's attention if anything felt...off."

"You must've felt safe."

She remembered how he'd saved her from a tumble beneath the inky black waves. "Completely."

"So then you agreed to go home with him?"

"After a couple of hours we wound up at his hotel. And it wasn't just any hotel, either. He must be a high-powered businessman or someone else with money, because he had the most luxurious suite I've ever seen. I've *never* stayed in a place like that. There were these expensive perfumed soaps, you know? I almost put them in my purse. I doubt he would've noticed since it was obvious he hadn't even been in the extra bathroom."

"You should've done it."

"Probably. Anyway, the towels were thicker than any I've ever felt, and there were monogrammed robes with slippers in the closet. It was pretty impressive."

"Wow. So he was good-looking *and* rich."

"Yes. And he had other assets, too."

Gripping the sides of the table, Amy leaned forward. "Are you talking about what I think you're talking about? You didn't actually sleep with him, did you?"

Ellie felt her face heat even more.

"You *did*?" Amy gasped.

She nodded. "And it was absolutely incredible."

Amy's jaw dropped as she fell back in her seat. "I can't believe it. So he was normal? Didn't do anything that made him seem weird or made you uncomfortable?"

"No. I've never been touched like that. It was the best night of my life."

"Wow!" Amy leaned forward again. "Going home with a stranger doesn't always work out so well. I hope you understand that."

"Good thing. Otherwise, I'd go clubbing every night."

"I've never seen you like this," she said with a laugh.

"I've never *been* like this."

"It was that good."

"Better than good. But I don't have a lot of experience. So maybe it was just better than Don." She stopped for a second, remembering her boyfriend before Don, and changed her mind. "No. Anyone would think that was about the best sex can be."

Amy acted as if she didn't know what to say. "You could knock me over with a feather right now."

"I was shocked myself. I never dreamed I was capable of being that reckless."

"Speaking of *reckless*..." She lowered her voice. "Please tell me you used protection."

Ellie glanced around to make sure no one was listening. "Of course. We used the condoms Leslie shoved in my purse."

"Condoms...plural?"

Ellie cleared her throat. "He, uh, recovered quickly."

"Whoa. Okay, but...he didn't have any birth control of his own?"

"None. We would've had to stop and buy some if Leslie hadn't given me those, so it worked out perfectly."

"And here I thought it was more of a joke when she gave us those. I certainly didn't use the ones she shoved in my purse, but she got a kick out of making you blush. She told me she's never met anyone who can still turn red over things like that." She clasped her hands together on the table. "But back to your… experience last night. What man goes to a club and picks up a girl without having any condoms?"

A man wearing sunglasses, which was also odd, but she didn't mention that part. "He's traveling. I guess he didn't expect to need birth control while he was here."

"That makes him seem even better. Obviously he wasn't cruising the club just hoping to get laid." Her expression turned pouty. "I wish I could've at least caught a glimpse of him."

"You didn't see us because we slipped out the back."

"Why would you do that?"

She shrugged. "He said it was too crowded in front."

"And no one tried to stop you?"

"He's pretty tall and imposing, and he moves with…authority. I don't think there are too many people who'd dare get in his way."

"There are guys who get *paid* to do that. They're called bouncers, remember? You can't walk out the back of a club."

"I'm not sure what to tell you. Hudson spoke to some guy, and the big man guarding the back door let us out."

"Hudson, huh?" Amy pulled out her smartphone. "Hudson who? Let's see if we can find him on social media."

"I don't know his last name."

She raised her eyebrows. "Why not?"

"We weren't focused on that sort of thing."

"Isn't that basic?"

"It is, but…" Almost as soon as they'd walked out of Envy, they'd agreed *not* to talk about their families or their work, the two things most people droned on and on about when they first became acquainted. It seemed a little strange now, although it hadn't then.

"But what?"

"He said he was tired of repeating all the same stuff, and you know me—I've never been much for small talk. In this case, there didn't seem to be any point in going through the motions. He'd already told me he wouldn't be in town for long. We both knew we weren't starting a relationship, that once he left, we'd probably never see each other again. That changes your expectations."

"You said you spent two hours on the beach."

"We did."

"You must've talked about something!"

"We talked about philosophy, politics, religion. Even certain mysterious phenomena he saw on a TV program last week where they used satellites to spot odd structures on earth."

"You talked about philosophy, politics, religion and *science*?"

"Yeah. You know, how the universe was created, and the fact that Venus was a sister planet to Earth at one time and might've fostered life before a runaway greenhouse effect turned it into an oven. Whether we're looking at something similar on Earth."

She shook her head. "Only you."

"What's that supposed to mean? It was fine. We agreed on politics and religion."

"You told him you believe in evolution."

"Of course! I told him the evidence for it is *staggering*."

"Like I said, only you." She laughed as she moved so the waitress could deliver their salads. "Even drunk, you're talking about heavy subjects, risky subjects or subjects most other people don't know much about."

"He knew plenty." Ellie had been surprised that Hudson was so intelligent. Not because she was arrogant about her own IQ.

She just didn't think it was all that common for one man to have so much going for him.

A text came in. Her parents were safely in Paris, said they were jet-lagged but would check in later. Relieved to know they were okay, because it stabilized her world after a crazy twenty-four hours, Ellie was about to put away her phone and start on her salad when she got another text—this one from Don.

Hey, I was wondering if tonight would be a good time to come by and get the rest of my things.

She stared down at those words. They seemed so impersonal, the kind of thing he'd say to any old friend. Only four days ago, this was the man she'd been planning to *marry*, to spend the rest of her life with. And now he was coming to get his CDs, his sweater, his cat, who'd been living at her house since they typically spent more time there, and a few pans he'd left. Her life had changed so abruptly and so completely.

"What is it?" Amy asked.

Attempting to mask her frown, Ellie glanced up. "Nothing."

"Come on. What is it? You were so happy a second ago."

"Don. He'd like to come by tonight."

Amy took a drink of water. "What for?"

"I have some of his things."

"Are you going to let him?"

"Why not?"

Amy blinked in surprise. "Last I heard you didn't want to see him. You said it was hard enough to run into him at work. But since you have no choice about that, why not put his stuff in your trunk and let him get it at the lab?"

"Because I can't put his cat in my trunk."

"He's taking Lulu?"

"Why wouldn't he?"

"You love that cat!"

"So does he."

"That's cruel."

"It is what it is. And why put it off? I might as well let him come tonight," she said and texted him her response. That's fine. I'll be home after seven.

"You don't think he'll bring Leo…"

"He could. I doubt he's looking forward to facing me alone."

"He'd better not bring him." Amy stuffed a forkful of lettuce in her mouth and spoke around it. "I'm shocked you haven't destroyed what you have of his, to tell you the truth—except for Lulu, of course. Lulu's a great cat. You should keep her on principle."

Ellie hadn't even considered damaging his property or keeping his cat. She'd been too brokenhearted to be angry or vengeful. Would that come next? She'd lost something that was important to her—she still cared about Don, after all—and anger was part of the grieving process. But thanks to Hudson, she thought she might be able to skip that step. What she'd done last night, going to his hotel room, was impulsive and foolish, and yet she'd experienced emotions and sensations she'd never felt as strongly before. Those few hours in his arms had shown her that losing Don might not be the end of the world.

She'd never be Mrs. Donald White. She wouldn't be seeing Hudson again, either. But that didn't mean there wasn't something else out there for her—and maybe it was even better than the life she'd planned.

She slid her phone back in her purse and picked up her fork. "Somehow I'll get through this."

CHAPTER FOUR

"Did you like that?" Teague asked as they drove back from the Everglades tour he'd insisted they take.

"Loved it." In an effort to be convincing, Hudson spoke with more enthusiasm than usual. His new agent had been doing his best to show him a good time. Hudson wanted Teague to feel he'd succeeded, but he hadn't been very interested in the sight-seeing they'd done today. He hadn't been very interested in any-thing—not since Ellie left. He knew it was a strange reaction on his part, but he felt he might've lost something he should've taken a closer look at. She was so different from anyone else he'd dated—from anyone he'd ever met.

He suppressed a grin as he remembered the enthusiasm that had filled her voice when she talked about the moon. He'd never met anyone who viewed the universe and everything in it with such wonder. She didn't know what small talk was. If the sub-ject wasn't meaningful in some way, she had no interest in it, and nothing seemed to be off-limits. He'd never had a woman probe his religious and political beliefs so thoroughly, not on a first encounter.

That could've been offensive, but he hadn't been put off because she'd approached his opinions, especially on those subjects, with the respect and objectivity of a scholar, someone who was willing to take in new information and view things from a fresh perspective. He found nothing objectionable about that; he'd actually enjoyed the depth of their conversation.

She was questing and so damn smart—and yet she knew next to nothing about popular culture. Like the fact that he played professional football. His picture was on TV several times a week, especially during football season. His mug also appeared in practically every article written about the Los Angeles Devils. He'd feel guilty about not revealing himself if that weren't the case. But with so much exposure, he figured she'd stood more than a fair chance of recognizing him. The truth was readily apparent to almost everyone else. He couldn't walk through a restaurant without being stopped for an autograph.

Actually, maybe he should have felt a *little* bad for keeping his mouth shut on that subject. She wasn't like most people. She'd admitted she didn't watch much TV other than the Science Channel and knew next to nothing about sports. She hadn't even argued when he'd teased her about not keeping up with the latest movies, musicians or fashion trends. While she could tell him a great many details about humanoid fossils that were being excavated in South Africa or why the body's immune system responded to certain toxins or bacteria the way it did, she couldn't tell him which actors or movies had won an Oscar last year.

"What should we do tonight?" Teague asked. "Want to go back to Envy?"

Would Ellie return to the club? Hudson doubted it. She wasn't any more enamored with the bar scene than he was, wouldn't have been there in the first place if not for her friends. She'd told him they'd insisted she go because they thought it would get her mind off her broken engagement.

Besides, if she wanted to see him, she knew where he was staying. Truth be told, he was hoping she'd come back. "No."

"Why not, man?"

"I need to rest up for the game tomorrow."

"Gotcha. That's probably wise. Let's hope it's not true what they say…"

The salacious smile Teague shot him finally caught Hudson's undivided attention. "About what?"

He started laughing. "Women weakening legs."

"Even if we lose, last night was worth it," he muttered.

"Wow. Never dreamed I'd hear something like that come out of *your* mouth. You care more about winning than any athlete I know."

"Everyone cares about winning."

"Maybe you should've gotten her number."

"Maybe so." Too bad she hadn't given him the chance. He wasn't hiding that because of his ego. He just didn't feel like going into it. He was tired of making the effort to be social and couldn't wait to retreat into the hotel.

"You're up for contract next year, so…make sure you kick some Dolphin ass tomorrow. Okay, bud?"

Hudson didn't want to be reminded of his upcoming contract negotiations, didn't want to let what could happen get inside his head. It was one thing to play football with focus and purpose, another to play scared. Perhaps he was being superstitious, but he believed playing scared would get him hurt, and once he got hurt, he wouldn't be worth a damn—to anyone. It was football that had given him a life; he knew where he'd be without it. "Right. I'll be sure to do that."

As Teague pulled in to the hotel, Hudson gestured toward the valet section under the portico. "You can drop me there."

Teague checked the time on his expensive watch. "It's only seven. Don't you want me to come in with you? The restaurant here's good. We could grab a bite to eat before you turn in for the night."

"No, thanks. I'll order room service." A long soak in the jetted tub would help calm his mind and his body. The longer he remained in the league, the more banged up he became. The trick was not to let the aches and pains stop him from giving his best performance in every single game.

"Okay. I'll send up a bottle of wine."

"Don't bother. I won't be drinking tonight, either. But I appreciate the thought."

Teague leaned forward to look up at Hudson as he got out. "Everything okay?"

Hudson rested one hand on the top of the car. "Yeah. Everything's fine. Thanks for taking me out today. I'll see you after the game tomorrow."

"Hey, wait a sec. You seem… I don't know, kind of remote."

"Stop worrying," he said and shut the door. He'd told Teague he was fine, and he was. Sure, he was a little lonely, but he could be lonely in a crowd. He'd never been like everyone else, never had the close connections parents and siblings provided.

His team was his family, he told himself. Except eventually, they all went home to their real families.

Maybe it had been a mistake to bring Ellie to his hotel. Being with her had assuaged that deep ache, and since she'd left, he felt the isolation more acutely than ever.

Leo was with Don, all right. Ellie could see him from her front window. He was sitting in the passenger seat of her ex-fiancé's Chevy Volt when Don pulled into her drive at exactly seven o'clock.

"Punctual as ever." She liked that he was never late, but that was about all she liked these days. She'd hoped he'd have the courtesy to show up alone. Having Leo there, watching this exchange, made her feel they were both laughing at her. *You believed he loved you? Really?*

Don didn't approach the house right away. He sat in the car talking to Leo as though he wasn't looking forward to confronting her.

Once he got out, she whispered, "You can do this," to encourage herself and stooped to pick up Lulu, who'd just finished her dinner. The breakup had been difficult enough. Losing Lulu made it worse. Ellie had adopted Don's pet as *her* pet, too. But he'd never part with Lulu. Not only was the cat a British Shorthair, one of the most expensive breeds in the world, she'd been a Christmas gift to Don from his mother two years ago. Ellie had no right to keep her, wasn't even going to ask. She was just glad he hadn't come into the relationship with kids. If she felt this destroyed over an animal, she could only imagine how she'd feel if she had to say goodbye to a child.

Warning herself not to allow this encounter to turn into an argument—what was the point of angry recriminations at this juncture?—she mustered as much dignity as she could and opened the door.

"Hey." He wore a collared shirt, plaid shorts and sandals. He'd always been neat and clean and stylish. But he'd had someone other than Amy, who normally cut his hair, dye it black two days ago. Ellie thought he looked a little ridiculous, given the pale, almost-translucent shade of his skin and all those freckles.

Maybe Leo liked the new look.

She wished she could give Don a nonchalant hello, wished she could act as though he hadn't hurt her so badly, but she couldn't speak around the lump suddenly clogging her throat. So much for the mental exercises and clichés she'd employed to prepare for this moment. *Time heals all wounds. This, too, shall pass. Everything happens for a reason. If we were meant to be together, we'd still be together.* She couldn't gain any perspective on their breakup; it was too soon.

Doing her best to imitate a polite smile, since she couldn't conjure up a genuine one, she handed him his cat.

"Thanks for taking care of Lulu. You've been really kind to her."

Ellie had been kind to *him*, too. Loved him. Trusted him. Planned to spend the rest of her life with him. The scent of his cologne brought back memories of curling up next to him on the couch while they watched a movie, hugging him before he had to leave, sidling closer at work just to catch a whiff.

Afraid he'd realize she was battling tears, she bent to pick up the box of his things she'd put by the door, which included Lulu's feeding dish and cat toys. There was also a big sack of kitty litter she'd purchased so Lulu would have what she needed at both houses.

"Here, let me get that," Don said about the box. "Just a sec. I'll take Lulu out first."

Ordinarily, she would've followed him when he went to the car so he wouldn't have to return to the house. But she refused to approach Leo, who, on Thursday, had confided to Mary Jane Deets, a fellow scientist at the BDC, how distasteful Don had found it to sleep with her. How difficult it had been for both men to keep up the charade of friendship when she was the one who got to sleep with Don most nights.

Ellie wished Mary Jane had never mentioned that conversation. The last thing she wanted to hear was that making love to her had been an unpleasant chore. Sex required so much trust… She didn't easily expose her body *or* her most sensitive and private self, which was why what she'd done last night had been so earth-shattering. Only because she didn't know Hudson and would never see him again had she been able to let herself go.

The memory of his hands on her body helped her hold herself together. She had her own naughty secret. She wouldn't be gauche enough to confide what she'd done to anyone at work, so Don would never hear about it. But she'd enjoyed making love with Hudson far more than she'd ever enjoyed making love with her ex. So what if Don had left her bed and returned to Leo's? So what if they'd mocked her and laughed or said nasty things about how revolting it had been for him to touch her?

Fortunately, she managed to clear the lump from her throat by the time he came back.

"Thanks for gathering up all this stuff for me," he said.

"No problem," she responded. What other choice did she have? She wasn't about to let him back in her house.

He looked as though he had something more to say but wasn't sure how. So he took the box and stepped off the stoop.

Grateful she'd escaped with so little interaction, she started to close the door but paused when she heard her name.

"Leo and I would like you to know that we both feel terrible about how everything…you know…went down," Don said.

In the first place, that was a terrible pun. In the second, she didn't believe they felt bad. They both had places of their own and yet she'd caught them in *her* bed, simply because it was closer to work, more convenient for their tryst. That showed no respect, no concern for her at all. And now? They acted relieved, even *happy* that she'd provided the impetus for them both to come out. To be their true selves.

Everyone deserved that right. She had no problem with same-sex relationships; it was being used that bothered her. She felt duped, cheated. "Okay," she said. "Good luck to both of you."

"I mean it," he insisted. "You're a nice person. I know that."

Of course he did. That was why he'd felt so comfortable taking advantage of her. He knew she wasn't nearly as experienced when it came to romantic relationships as most other women her age. He'd preyed on that innocence and, somehow, she'd missed the obvious. "Thank you."

He seemed surprised that he wasn't eliciting more of a fight from her. There were so many things she wanted to say—and rightfully could say. But getting ugly wouldn't change anything.

Why make it possible for him to excuse his actions by claiming she was a bitch?

"I should've told you I was confused," he added.

She tried to hold her silence but couldn't let that go. "You weren't confused. You just didn't want your family to find out that you were really in love with Leo."

"I was confused about how to handle it," he clarified. "You don't understand how much pressure I was under to be something I'm not. At least try to understand that we were *both* victims."

Maybe that was true. As nice as his family was in so many ways, they had no business making him feel he was any less because of his sexual preferences. But she hadn't been a victim until he told her he loved her and asked her to be his wife. As far as she was concerned, this situation could've had one *less* victim if only he'd been honest with her. "You told me more than once that you'd like a family," she said.

He seemed startled by the change in subject. "I do!"

"Is that why you did it?" she asked. "Were you waiting for me to pump out a couple of kids before you revealed the truth?"

His eyebrows, dyed black like his hair, drew together. "No! How can you even think that?"

"Maybe because of the other lies you told me." And practically speaking, while a plan like that was reprehensible and totally unfair to her, it was a much less expensive way to have children than paying for a surrogate...

"I knew how much my parents would like you," he said.

"Your parents," she repeated. Wouldn't this have been the time to suggest *he'd* cared about her, at least a little?

"My whole family," he clarified.

The lump in her throat returned. Part of her desire to cry came from the usual hurt, but that wasn't all of it. Despite their faults, she especially loved his parents, had welcomed them into her heart. "I'll miss everyone," she admitted.

"That's the thing. You don't have to miss them. I'm hoping we can remain friends."

She shook her head. "I'm not sure I'm capable of that, Don. Not for a while, anyway."

"Take a couple of weeks, then. But you could still be part of my life, of my family's lives. To be honest, I think it would really help them accept Leo if they didn't have to give you up at the same time. My mom's having a big birthday party on the twenty-first. Why don't you join us like you normally would? We'll all three go together and explain that…that you understand the pressure I was under and sympathize with what I was going through, and—"

"You want *me* to help smooth things over with your folks?" she broke in, stunned. "Help them accept Leo?"

He didn't get a chance to answer before she rolled her eyes in disgust. "Unbelievable," she said and closed the door.

"Hey, man, don't beat yourself up. We'll get 'em next time."

Hudson could barely keep from snarling as his left guard rested a ham-like hand on his shoulder before leaving the locker room. Will Hart, or Bruiser, as they called him, was a nice guy and had quickly become Hudson's best friend since joining the team last spring. But Hudson wasn't in the mood to hear any placating bullshit. He'd played the worst game of his life, had thrown not one but *two* interceptions and faltered in the red zone when he should've been able to convert. Although he'd had a few bright spots—one was when he'd scored on a thirty-six-yard keeper, putting the Devils on top for a short time—that last interception had sealed their fate. They'd been favored to win by fourteen points and would have if their quarterback hadn't screwed up so badly.

A loud clang resounded in the now-empty room as he let his head fall back against the metal lockers. Why hadn't he taken the sack? If he hadn't tried to extend the play, to make something out of nothing, they might've won. He should never have thrown that last ball. He should've gone down and relied on his defense to ride out the final two minutes—a point the ESPN sports announcer had just made when she interviewed him, and she was right.

He could imagine what all the pundits would be saying in the next week. They'd question whether he'd been injured on the Dolphins' first blitz, when he took such a hard hit from lineman Hap Palmer. Whether, after ten years in the game, he was losing his edge. Whether he'd become a detriment to his team.

Lifting the sweat-soaked Devils T-shirt he wore under his pads while he played, he peeled back his football pants to stare down at the bruise forming on his hip. That hit *had* been hard, but he couldn't blame the injury for his poor performance. During the game, he'd had so much adrenaline pouring through him he'd barely felt the pain.

He regretted that was no longer the case. His hip felt like it was on fire.

"Fuck," he muttered, leaning forward and hanging his head. Not only was he upset by his performance, he was worried. When he hadn't been able to get hold of Aaron before the game, he'd called Aiyana Turner, the woman in charge of the boys ranch in Silver Springs. She'd told him Aaron wasn't doing well, that he couldn't keep any food down and was back in the hospital. She'd been scared—he could hear it in her voice—and that had scared him.

Would the news be even worse now?

He was afraid to find out, but he pulled his cell phone from his gym bag and called her, anyway. "Hey. How is he?"

"Better."

The pain in his hip eased a bit as he drew in a deep, hopeful breath. "Yeah?"

"They've got him on an IV to make sure he's getting the fluids he needs." Aaron, like Hudson, didn't have any parents, at least not reliable ones; Aaron had a mother in a halfway house somewhere. Aiyana did her best to look after him, the way she'd tried to look after Hudson when he'd been at New Horizons. With nearly three hundred students at the school, however, many of whom came from tragic situations—and eight boys she'd officially adopted over the years—one person could do only so much. That was the reason Hudson had finally purchased a home on the edge of Silver Springs three months ago, even though he already owned a place in LA—so during his off-seasons, he could mentor the boys at the ranch who needed someone most.

"Bet he loves having another needle in his arm," he said. The poor kid had been through so much...

"So far, I've convinced him not to tear it out," she said.

"Stubborn as he is, I'm sure that hasn't been easy."

"No. But we can talk later. He's sitting right here, asking for the phone."

"You're at the hospital?"

"Yeah. I had some things to do earlier, but I came back around three."

"Okay. Let me hear what he has to say."

Aaron didn't bother with hello. "Seriously, man? *Two* interceptions? What *happened*?"

The relief Hudson felt at the pique in Aaron's voice—irritation he wouldn't feel if he was *too* sick—put the loss, and his own poor performance, into perspective. Maybe the kid really was doing better. "Had a bad game, dude."

"I saw that. I hope you know you owe me twenty bucks."

Hudson straightened. "I do? Why?"

"I bet a friend the Devils were going to win, damn it!"

"Watch your language." Although he wasn't upset by a few curse words—he said and heard worse on a daily basis—he was the kid's mentor.

He couldn't inject any real sternness in his voice, though.

"*Damn?* You think that's a swear word?" Aaron asked.

Perhaps he *was* being a little ridiculous, but he had to send the right signals. "It *is* a swear word. And Aiyana's sitting there, too."

"She doesn't care."

"Yes, she does. Show some respect. You shouldn't be betting on games in the first place."

"Why not?" he demanded.

"Because you're not old enough to gamble!"

"But I may not live until my seventeenth birthday!"

Those words pulled Hudson back to reality, helped check his emotions. Aaron sounded better today, but what would tomorrow bring? "Don't say that. You're going to be fine."

"Chances are I *won't* be fine. You need to be prepared."

"I'm not listening to that."

"Just because you don't want to face it doesn't mean it doesn't exist. Sometimes I think *you're* more afraid of death than I am."

Hudson wasn't afraid of his *own* death, but he was afraid of Aaron's. He was more than afraid; he was terrified. "You're not going anywhere."

"If you say so. Anyway, about that twenty bucks…"

"Forget it. I'm not paying that."

"Why not? You're loaded."

Hudson had to smile. "Gambling often means losing. You need to learn what that's like so you'll think twice about doing it again."

"I wouldn't have to know that if you'd been yourself out there today. I still don't understand how you let the game get away from you. What was going through your mind when you threw that last pass, man? What did you think you were going to be able to do while you were falling backward?"

He'd been trying to take control of *something*—trying too hard, in retrospect—because he couldn't control what was happening to Aaron, couldn't even be with him when the boy needed to go to the hospital. "We all have bad days."

"Yeah, well, give me a heads-up when you're out of sync next time so I can bet on the opposite team, will ya?"

Hudson promised himself he'd never self-destruct in another game, especially one Aaron was watching. The boy needed something to smile about. Instead of giving him that, he'd panicked and let fear undermine his concentration. "You'll never get a call like that from me, because it's not going to happen again."

"Good. So when will you be home?"

"Team's flying out tonight at eleven-fifteen." They had a chartered flight via one of the major airlines, with the Boeing 757 reconfigured to contain half as many seats as usual. It even had eighteen beds to fit the large bodies typical of football players, plus massage therapists, big-screen TVs for gaming and a smorgasbord of food catered by a local restaurant.

But since they'd lost, the mood on this evening's flight would be subdued. Hudson wasn't looking forward to spending five hours cooped up in a plane with his teammates, especially since he was to blame for today's loss.

"Hey, are you going to get showered? The bus is waiting." Bruiser was back, all six feet eight inches and 370 pounds of him. No one else would dare try to roust Hudson. The fact that Hudson had done his interviews before he'd even taken off his uniform told them he was in no mood to be bothered.

"Be there in ten," he muttered.

Bruiser looked as though he was tempted to stay until Hudson proved his words by heading for the showers, but he didn't. After giving him a skeptical once-over, he left.

"Will I see you tomorrow?" Aaron asked on the phone.

Hudson returned to the conversation. "Yeah. I'll come by the hospital."

"No need. They're going to release me."

"When?"

"Tonight. Doctor said so. I'm gonna be okay, Hudson. For

now, anyway. So quit fretting like a little girl. It was just a bad reaction to the meds."

Chuckling at the "little girl" comment and ignoring the "for now," Hudson finally stood up and pulled off his shirt. "Then I'll come see you at New Horizons."

"Will you be up for the drive?"

The town of Silver Springs, population five thousand, was between ninety minutes and two hours northwest of LA, but once he broke free from the big-city traffic, the drive wasn't too bad. Hudson made it often. Ojai, where the hospital was located, wasn't much farther—if, for some reason, Aaron wasn't released as planned. "'Course I will."

"Maybe you should stay in the city and get some rest. You were hit pretty hard at the start of the game. I saw how slow you got up. And you don't have a lot of time to recover. You've got the 49ers next weekend."

Fortunately, that game was at home. The travel during the season was the biggest nuisance of Hudson's job. "I'll be fine," he said and believed that would be the case, as long as Aaron was, too.

After saying goodbye, he hung up and hurried over to the showers.

When he eventually boarded the bus, Hudson was mildly surprised that so many of his teammates made an effort to rally behind him. Once he'd returned from his interviews, they'd given him space, quietly showered, dressed and left the locker room, allowing him time to cope with his frustration and disappointment. But now they were offering their support.

"Anyone can have a bad game… No loss is due strictly to one guy… Hey, it's a team effort… We'll get our groove back… That was just four quarters. We still got plenty of season ahead of us… Don't worry about today, man. Next time, huh?"

As Hudson nodded at each encouragement, he promised himself he'd never let them down again.

CHAPTER FIVE

The next seven weeks were every bit as difficult as Ellie had feared. Initially, Don had been penitent enough to smile or try to speak to her as a friend might when they passed in the halls or had to interact at work, but he quickly grew resentful that she wasn't doing more to help his family adapt to his new lifestyle. Apparently they were still having a problem with his sexual orientation or they didn't like Leo or something. But Ellie wasn't trying to subvert him. She didn't feel it was her place to get involved. She had her own problems, was struggling to get over the rejection and adjust to a very different future than the one she'd planned.

Sadly, Don and Leo didn't see it that way. They shot her pouty, sullen looks whenever they were in the same meeting together, and they were in a lot of meetings since the entire staff gathered often to go over recent progress, set current priorities and discuss the merits of outside projects. Others in the room could feel the tension between them and would shift nervously—or worse, begin to whisper. Ellie always felt as though they were talking about her, because they probably were. *Poor Dr. Fisher.*

Can you imagine what it would be like to find your fiancé in bed with another man?

To make matters worse, with her parents away, she had nothing to do in the evenings. She was used to spending most of her leisure time with Don, Don's family or his cat (if he was "golfing" with Leo), and now all those people, as well as his pet, were out of her life. Although Amy invited her to go clubbing almost every weekend, so far she'd refused. She'd enjoyed that night at Envy—probably too much—but she wasn't looking for a repeat. She wasn't really the kind of person who did things like that, and she didn't want to leave herself vulnerable to what could go wrong if something similar were to happen again. She knew she was unlikely to enjoy another fairy-tale ending like the last one.

Instead, she tried to ignore the emptiness of her personal life by chasing her dream of finding a safe and reliable method to protect transplanted insulin-producing islet cells, so no one else would have to suffer the way her aunt had. As it stood now, without harsh immunosuppressant drugs, the immune system saw the cells as foreign and destroyed them. Finding a way around that was important if transplantation was ever to become a routine solution for diabetics.

So she told herself she didn't mind spending longer and longer hours at the lab. Not only did the challenge keep her focused, it gave her a purpose.

But on a Saturday evening at the end of October, she hit a wall. Too exhausted to continue, she forced herself to knock off at six. She was planning to treat herself to a grilled cheese sandwich and some chocolate-chip cookies while watching the first season of *Outlander.* Diane DeVry, who headed up the fundraising entity that supported the BDC, had brought in the first two seasons to share with her. And if *Outlander* didn't "sweep her away" as Diane promised it would, she had several medical journals she'd been meaning to read.

Content with her plans, she almost didn't answer the phone when Amy called as she was driving home. She was afraid her friend would once again try to press her into going to a club, and she wasn't interested.

She let it ring four times before she knocked over her purse trying to catch the call. She figured she'd be a fool to alienate Amy. Amy was the only friend she had left—other than her colleagues at the BDC, almost all of whom had families they went home to at night, worked the same crazy hours she did or sided with Don.

She turned into the driveway of her rental house as she answered.

"What are you doing tonight?" Amy asked.

Ellie thought it was terribly nice of her friend to continue to reach out. She probably would've given up by now were she in Amy's shoes. But Amy was far more persistent than she was. Thank goodness. Even if she didn't see Amy often, hearing from her brought Ellie some comfort. "You wouldn't approve," she said.

"You're still at work."

She pressed the button that activated her garage door. "It isn't *quite* as bad as that. Just got home."

"Wonderful. At least you can't tell me you're too busy saving the world to go out tonight."

"I don't want to go to a club, Amy."

"I was going to suggest a movie."

"You'd miss dressing up for Halloween to go to a movie?"

"I'll celebrate Halloween tomorrow night. Since it's on a Sunday, this is kind of a weird year, anyway."

"Then how about an *Outlander* marathon at my place?"

"You have *Outlander*?"

"Someone at work lent it to me, promised I'd like it."

"I've seen a few episodes and I've been meaning to watch the rest. It's impossible not to fall in love with the actor who plays James Fraser."

"That should be safe, then. I can't get hurt by a fictional character, right? Why don't you come over?"

A slight pause indicated that Amy was still trying to decide. "Do you have any food?"

"I'll soon have homemade chocolate-chip cookies."

"I'm in."

Ellie laughed. If Amy joined her tonight, she wouldn't be able to bail out and study, but she figured that was okay. She needed to at least *try* to stop her world from shrinking down to work and only work. "Great. What time will you get here?"

"Give me an hour."

"See you then."

Ellie turned off the engine, lowered the garage door and released her seat belt. Before she could go in, she needed to gather up everything that'd spilled onto the passenger seat when she knocked over her purse.

She picked up the pretty business card case her parents had given her when she landed her job at the BDC, as well as her keys to the lab, some lip gloss, a condom she had left over from the night she'd gone to Envy—she wasn't sure why she was keeping *that*—and a couple of tampons.

After a quick search between the seat and the console to check that she'd gotten everything, she was about to step out of the car when the purpose for those tampons registered. She hadn't used any feminine hygiene products in a while. Wasn't she due for a period?

She remained in her car as she counted back the days. Her last period was…before Don had broken up with her! Could that be true?

No! Or…maybe.

Her heart began to thump. Yes, it was true. She was late. And not by a mere few days. Her period had just ended when she caught Don in her bed with Leo. Perhaps she would've noticed that it had been a long time had she not been so caught up in trying to adjust to the radical changes in her life…

But…what did late mean? It wasn't so unusual, was it? Lots of things could cause a delay. Stress was one of them. Stress could wreak havoc on a body.

Except…it had never wreaked any havoc on hers. Not to the point that she'd skipped a period. She'd *always* been regular—so regular that she never paid much attention to her cycle. That part of her life was something she dealt with automatically. It wasn't as though she ever got cramps or a headache or anything else that made menstruating more than a minor annoyance.

But seven weeks! That was a significant delay, which hinted at a problem beyond stress.

"Oh, God." She broke into a cold sweat as the possibility of a pregnancy loomed in her mind.

She brought up the calendar on her smartphone. She'd learned about Don's affair with Leo on September 7. The hair appointment she'd had that same day confirmed that she couldn't have confused the date. She was staring at the notation for the appointment right now. Afterward, instead of heading straight back to the lab, she'd swung by her place to put a roast and some vegetables in the slow cooker. She'd thought it would be a nice surprise for Don if she had a hot meal ready when they got off work. But she'd come home to see *Leo's* car in her driveway. If it had been Don's car, she probably would've entered the condo calling out his name. Finding him here would've been unusual, since he was supposed to be at work, but not as unusual as seeing Leo's vehicle. So, wondering what was going on, she'd entered without making any noise. A sickening unease in the pit of her stomach suggested she was about to find something she wouldn't like, and that had proven true. Only moments after entering, she'd heard moaning—coming from her bedroom.

She cringed at the memory of how she'd slipped down the

hall. Although she didn't want to recall what she'd seen when she opened the door, it was that shocking incident that made it impossible to forget or confuse the date.

But…was she *sure* she hadn't had a period since?

Positive. She'd gone off the Pill two months earlier because she'd started to suffer from nausea and headaches and her doctor had recommended stopping it, at least for a while. She and Don had been using condoms since then. But they hadn't been together in that way for at least two weeks before she found him with Leo—well before her last period. She and Don had both been too intent on separate projects at work.

The only man she'd slept with after that was… Hudson.

Although her phone was going off again, she couldn't bring herself to even reach into her purse. She sat there, frozen in terror, scarcely breathing as she stared blankly at the bare wood studs of the garage walls. Surely, after everything she'd been through, she wasn't carrying a child. That wouldn't be fair. She'd slept with only three men in her life, and she was nearly thirty! And she'd had just that *one* one-night stand. Even then she'd used birth control. Hudson had worn one of the condoms Leslie had given her every time.

She was shaking as she withdrew her phone so she could access the internet. "How reliable are condoms?" she typed into Google and nibbled on her bottom lip while waiting for the links to appear. One website said that "male condoms" were "82–98 percent" effective. Another rated their effectiveness at 85 percent.

"Eighty-five," she mumbled, feeling shell-shocked. Eighty-five meant there was still a significant chance of pregnancy. Why didn't more people talk about the failures? Why did everyone act as though a condom was sufficient?

Her phone rang while she held it, startling her since she was already so jumpy. Amy. The call she'd missed had also come from Amy. No doubt her friend couldn't understand why she wasn't picking up; they'd just talked.

Closing her eyes, Ellie leaned against the headrest as she answered. "Hello?" she said, but the word came out so softly, so breathy, she wasn't sure Amy could hear her.

Amy paused before responding. "Hello?" she said, far more stridently than before. "Ellie? Is that you?"

"Yes, I'm here," Ellie replied, but she was holding her stomach with one hand.

"I was going to ask if you'd like me to pick up some takeout on my way over. But…you sound strange. Is something wrong?"

Ellie considered lying. She wanted to lie—to herself, too. But what good would it do to hide from the truth? She was too practical for that. If she was pregnant, a swollen belly would soon make it apparent to everyone. "Yes."

"Did you say *yes*?" she squawked.

"I—I'm afraid I'm about to throw up."

"Why? What's wrong? Do you think you might have the flu?"

"No. It's not that."

"Then what is it? You're scaring me!"

"Could you bring a pregnancy test when you come?"

"A *what*?"

Ellie couldn't repeat the request. She was beginning to hyperventilate, needed to focus on slowing her breathing. *That's it. Calm down. In and out. Everything will be okay…somehow.*

Fortunately, Amy caught on, even though Ellie couldn't clarify at the moment. "Holy shit! Did you say what I think you said?"

"Yeah, I did. Can you get one?"

"Of course. I'm on my way over right now."

CHAPTER SIX

Hudson was as busy as always during football season. He had two flights a week, some longer than others depending on their schedule, regular team practices, meetings with the coaches and managers, periodic medical checkups and physical therapy to keep his body patched up so he could make it through the season. And then there was interview after interview with the sports media, photography sessions for his various endorsements—even a commercial for a new sports drink—and numerous appearances for charity. He also spent hours watching game film so he could be prepared for whatever opponent he'd face next. That didn't leave him with a lot of free time, but he returned to Silver Springs as often as his schedule permitted, even if he could steal away only for a night and a day.

Fortunately, the doctors had adjusted Aaron's treatment. The new chemicals weren't as hard on his system, so he seemed okay for the time being. The more stable Aaron became, the better Hudson felt, and that seemed to be reflected in his game. Since Miami, the Devils hadn't lost. Hudson couldn't take all the credit. Some of his teammates had really stepped up—his front line in particular. They hadn't allowed more than a handful of sacks in the past six weeks. But he was having a good personal season, too, and felt they might have another shot at the Super Bowl.

"So this is the new abode?"

Hudson had just let Bruiser in through the front door of his home in Silver Springs. Like Hudson and the rest of the team, for the most part Bruiser lived in LA, and he had a wife and two-year-old kid. But his wife had taken their little girl to visit her mother in New York and was gone for a few days, so Bruiser had accompanied Hudson from LA. Bruiser had expressed an interest in getting involved in the type of mentoring Hudson was doing at New Horizons, so first thing Monday morning, Hudson was taking him over to the school. They'd be addressing the student body and encouraging the boys to put in the work necessary to fulfill their dreams. He and Bruiser were even planning to show up at football practice later in the day and help the coaches by running a few drills.

"Not bad, huh?" Hudson said as he tossed his keys on the granite counter.

Bruiser frowned as he took in the wooden floors, the high ceilings, the wainscoting and the ceiling fan in the expansive living room of the ranch house. Hudson hadn't bought the most expensive property in the area, but homes in the Ojai Valley weren't cheap, especially when they sat on chunks of land the size of this one. He needed the space to protect his privacy. He'd spent nearly $9.5 million for this fifteen-acre, 10,663 square-foot, four-bedroom, five-bath home with its accompanying view of the surrounding Topatopa Mountains.

"You could afford a lot better," Bruiser teased.

Hudson winked. "I love it here. You will, too. That's why I've asked the real estate agent who sold me this to show you some properties while you're in town."

Bruiser put down his duffel bag. "You went to the trouble, did you?"

Hudson slapped his broad back. "I did, brother. We're meeting her tomorrow."

Bruiser fingered the Fu Manchu mustache he'd grown this season; he'd said he wouldn't shave it off until they won the Super Bowl. "Not sure my wife's gonna be willing to move out here. I told you that."

"We'll see," he responded as if he wasn't worried in the least.

His friend's eyebrows rose. "You think you can convince her?"

"I do. Jacqueline's a real softy. Once she meets some of the boys and realizes what a difference you could make in their lives, she'll be all for spending the off-season here, at least for the next couple of years, until you have another baby or Brianne starts school."

"Maybe." He shrugged, relenting as easily as ever. Hudson had never met a nicer guy—not that he'd ever want to take Bruiser on when Bruiser was mad. Hudson had seen his friend pushed to that point only once, when a player from the opposing team nearly broke Hudson's leg with a late hit. Bruiser went after the dude, and it was all the refs could do to pull him off. From that day forward, everyone in the NFL knew that no one messed with Hudson if Bruiser was around to guard him. Hudson was Bruiser's quarterback, the man he defended, and he took that seriously. That was part of the reason they were doing so well this season. Hudson had been safe in the pocket, and that had resulted in a high percentage of completions.

"So…you got a beer?" Bruiser asked.

Maggie, the housekeeper Hudson had hired when he bought the house, kept the place clean and well-stocked. She lived in the guesthouse at the back corner of the property and made sure the gardeners did their job and the house was ready whenever Hudson decided to come home. Once he arrived, she stayed in her own place unless he was there for an extended visit and needed help with meals or laundry. He paid her a monthly salary whether she did much work at the main house or not, so she didn't mind that he preferred his privacy to having her wait on him. "I've got a fridge filled with Bud Light, Heineken, Sam Adams, you name it," he said. "Want to play a game of pool after we grab a cold one?"

"Only if you're ready to get your ass kicked."

Hudson grinned. He and Bruiser had never played before. Bruiser hadn't been on the team that long. They'd just grown close very quickly. And Hudson didn't have a table at his LA house. "Any chance you'd be willing to put your money where your mouth is?"

He could see Bruiser contemplating the possibilities. "Come on," Hudson said. "You're a betting man."

"Yeah, but I'd never bet against *you*," Bruiser finally grumbled, his expression leery.

"Too bad. I suck at pool," Hudson said and proved it by losing twice in a row.

"Shit," Bruiser drawled. "I should've taken that bet. I could be fleecing you right now."

Hudson rested his pool cue on the ground. "I'll give you another chance. We could play a third game. Put a thousand bucks on it."

Bruiser seemed tempted, then narrowed his eyes. "You think you're clever, don't you? Forget it. You're not sharking me."

Once Hudson started laughing, he almost couldn't stop—especially when Bruiser beat him a third time. "You *weren't* sharking me," his friend complained. "You *do* suck at pool. You're just damn good at mind games!"

Hudson cocked his head. "We could bet on a fourth match..."

"You little shit!" Although it took some effort, and they were both breathing heavily from the exertion of wrestling by the time it was over, Bruiser eventually managed to heft Hudson over one massive shoulder and carry him through the open doors of the game room to the patio beyond, where he proceeded to throw him in the pool.

"You were only able to do that because I let you," Hudson called out, laughing and wiping the water from his face as he surfaced.

"Yeah, yeah. I'm getting another beer." With a careless gesture, Bruiser went back inside. But he returned with a towel as well as two beers and sat on a nearby chair while Hudson dried off.

"It's nice out here," Bruiser said, gazing at the gold and lavender hues of the fading sun. "I could get used to this."

"Quiet, isn't it?"

"Yeah. Glad we have a bye this week. I like getting away from the city, especially midseason, when we're so busy. Sometimes, with all the traffic and the noise—everyone blathering on about their opinions, the phone ringing and the TV rattling the walls—it feels as if I can't hear myself think. But this…this is almost as though we put LA on pause."

Hudson dropped onto a lounge chair not far away. With an average high of eighty degrees in October, the weather was fairly mild in Silver Springs. But the temperature was dropping as night came on, and he was wet. Trying to conserve his body heat, he rubbed his head vigorously to dry his hair. He didn't want to catch a cold, but he also didn't want to go in. He, too, was enjoying sitting outdoors and watching the sunset. "You're not getting tired of the game, are you?" he asked.

"I could never get tired of the game," Bruiser replied. "But all the stuff that goes with it? Yeah. And I don't have to do half the shit you do. Don't know how you keep your sanity."

After wrapping the towel around his shoulders, Hudson popped the top off the beer Bruiser had brought out for him. "Other than New Horizons, work's all I've got. I prefer to stay busy."

Bruiser rested his elbows on his spread knees. “Any word from that private detective you hired a few weeks ago?”

Hudson wasn’t sure he wanted to talk about this, wasn’t sure why he’d ever confided in Bruiser about it. He was so conflicted about the whole thing, he hadn’t told anyone else, and it’d taken him years to make the decision. He’d been hoping Bruiser would talk him out of it, he supposed, show him how useless it was. But his friend hadn’t even tried. He’d been as hopeful as Hudson was sometimes tempted to be—and quietly supportive, like always.

“Not yet,” Hudson said. “I might call him off, to be honest. Drop the whole thing.”

“Why? You searched and searched the internet for the ideal guy. He has all those great reviews on his website, right? What can it hurt to let him do his job? See what he finds?”

“Chances are he won’t find anything. The police never could.”

“Then you’ll have to live with the past, but at least you tried.”

“What if it goes the other way? What if he solves it, comes up with an answer?”

Leaning back, Bruiser crossed his ankles. “You don’t have to act on the information unless you choose to.”

Hudson took a long pull on his beer. “Will I be able to stop myself? Sometimes it’s safer *not* to know.”

“The reality can’t be any worse than what you’re imagining.”

“Who says? It could be like Pandora’s box—better not to open it.” That was what had kept him from searching before. “Even if I track down whoever abandoned me, what will I say? ‘Thanks for nothing’? And because of my fame—and money—how will I know they’re being sincere if they say they’d like to be part of my life? I’m at the peak of my career. Almost everyone wants a piece of me.” But not always for the right reasons. That was why he missed the woman he’d met at Envy. He’d tried dating since but had been disappointed by his options. The brief flashes of attraction he'd experienced had been with women who hadn't come off as half as honest.

Bruiser's dark eyes blazed. "You have plenty to offer without the money and without the fame," he said as if he was angry Hudson would suggest otherwise.

"Maybe so. But we're talking about someone who left me to *die* under a hedge. What do you expect that type of person will want? Help paying the bills? A new car? Or connecting on a meaningful level?"

"Listen, I'm the last guy who'd ever want to see you get hurt."

Hudson grimaced. "I'm not saying I could get *hurt*, exactly."

"Oh, cut the macho bullshit," Bruiser said, waving him off. "It's me you're talking to. What you're after could be devastating, and I know it. That's what you're afraid of. Well, it's my job to protect you, and that doesn't disappear once we're off the field. You're like a brother to me. But you need to know what this PI might be able to tell you. You've needed to know for a long time—maybe always—to answer all the questions in your mind and put your issues to rest."

Hudson challenged him with a pointed glance. "My *issues*?"

Unrepentant, Bruiser grinned. "Yeah. You've got more than a few."

"That makes me feel better. Thanks."

At the unmistakable sarcasm, Bruiser lifted his beer. "You can always count on me to be honest."

"Now might be a good time to tell you I could've kicked your ass at billiards in at least three of those games. A guy doesn't own a table without being able to play."

Cursing and laughing at the same time, Bruiser shook his head. "I *knew* it. Least I didn't fall for your act."

Hudson tipped his drink in his friend's direction. "No, you didn't."

"Asshole."

"Back to the private detective," Hudson said. "Think of the

media circus if he *does* find my mother and word leaks out. How will I cope with that, in addition to everything else? The media's already all up in my business. They bring my background into every damn article. I saw one recently with my photo and the caption, 'The star quarterback who might never have been, if not for the pizza delivery boy who heard him crying.'" He stared down at the bottle he held. "Hell, I've had people coming out of the woodwork for years, claiming to be my long-lost relatives. I believed a few of them, too, but they never checked out. If I keep on pushing for answers, I'll be asking for more of the same."

"So? You're a celebrity, dude. You're going to deal with that. You need to know what happened that day."

Hudson used his left hand to comb some of the tangles out of his hair, which wasn't easy because of the chlorine. "*Why* do I need to know? That's what I keep asking myself. Why can't I leave it alone?"

"Curiosity? Closure? Only natural you'd want answers. Even if you fire this guy, I predict you'll hire him again—or someone else."

Whoever had left Hudson on the day of his birth obviously didn't want him. But somewhere, deep down, he was hoping there'd been a mistake. That he hadn't been thrown away as casually as it seemed. That his mother, and maybe his father, had been searching for him his whole life and somehow missed the media coverage of his background. That he had grandparents, aunts, uncles, cousins and maybe even siblings out there somewhere who hadn't been involved in the decision.

Question was, *why* had it happened? It must've been intentional. How could anyone leave a baby to die *by mistake*?

Because Hudson couldn't answer that, he was tempted to call off the investigator. The only thing that made him hope there might be more to the story, something to pursue, was the area in which he'd been found. Bel Air wasn't known for drugs or crime or abandoned babies. Part of the Platinum Triangle that included Beverly Hills and Holmby Hills, where the infamous Playboy mansion had recently sold for $100 million, it was a residential area that contained some of the most luxurious homes in Southern California. With large green privacy hedges surrounding most of the estates, only three roads leading in, and no sidewalks, there wasn't a lot of traffic. Had some spoiled rich girl gotten pregnant, hidden the fact from her parents, delivered in the bathroom and left the baby in that hedge for the gardeners or someone else to find in the morning?

That was the most likely explanation. But if so, whoever the girl was, she couldn't be related to any of the people living in the houses closest to where he'd been discovered, wrapped in a threadbare blanket. Thirty-two years ago, the mansion behind the hedge belonged to an eighty-year-old couple with one adult child who had a family but lived and worked in China. A lesbian couple owned the next closest house. They had a teenage son, but he managed to convince the police that he didn't know about any pregnant girl or newborn baby. The property across the street, kitty-corner, belonged to a divorced director who hadn't even been home at the time. His place had been closed up while he was on location, filming a movie in Alaska.

Hudson had a copy of the police file. He'd requested it soon after he entered the NFL. No one in the neighborhood had been able to offer a single clue as to who might've abandoned a baby at Hudson and King. That was why he'd been taken to Maryvale, Los Angeles's oldest children's charity, and farmed out to a foster home, his first of many—until he'd eventually been sent to New Horizons Boys Ranch. That was where he'd spent the final three years of his adolescence, before he was recruited to play for UCLA and started his football career.

"You're probably right," Hudson muttered. "I won't be able to let it go." Finished with his beer, he stood. "I guess I'm just a glutton for punishment."

★ ★ ★

"Are you going to be okay?"

Ellie looked up at Amy and groaned. Once she'd taken the pregnancy test and seen that telltale pink line, she'd stumbled to the couch and had been lying there ever since. Her arms and legs felt like they had fifty-pound weights attached. She didn't think she could possibly get up. "No."

Amy's face creased with worry as she perched on the chair nearby. "Being pregnant isn't the *worst* thing that could happen to you. I mean…you were talking about having a family a couple of months ago."

"I was engaged to be married a couple of months ago!" she said. "I thought I was ready to take the next step in my life. But now…" She shook her head in disbelief. How could this have happened after everything she'd been through since finding Don and Leo in her bed?

Amy stared down at her hands before raising her eyes again. "Are you sure it isn't Don's?"

"Yes, I'm sure," Ellie said. "I've had a period since the last time we had sex."

"That makes it easy to pinpoint the father, at least."

"True. Thank God for small mercies! Can you imagine what it would be like to carry a baby for nine months and not know who the father was? Not to mention, if there was any uncertainty along those lines, Don would be waiting in the wings for the better part of a *year*, hoping to celebrate with his new partner. I feel that's what he was hoping for from a relationship with me in the first place."

"I thought he wanted to use you as a front for his family."

"That, too. But he's always wanted kids, and he knows it'll be harder to have them with Leo than with me."

"Then you're lucky." Amy gave her an encouraging smile, but one look from Ellie made her smile wither. "Sorry," she mumbled.

"No problem," Ellie said, but she was still playing the injured party. She had a right to feel sorry for herself for a while. But there were a *few* bright spots. The fact that the baby belonged to Hudson was much luckier than he or she belonging to Don. Her relationship with her ex-fiancé and his new partner had become so hostile. She could only imagine how terrible it would be if she had to tell them she was pregnant. Trying to work out custody and support issues—all of it would have been a nightmare. Not to mention that a child would have bonded her and Don together for life just when she'd begun to think she'd been fortunate to get out when she did.

"So…you're positive you can trace this back to that one night at Envy."

Ellie detected a sheepish note in her friend's voice, probably because *she* was the one who'd taken Ellie to the club and goaded her to let loose for a change. "Yes. No question. Since it's not Don's, it has to be Hudson's. I've only been with the two of them in the last seven or eight years."

"Okay." She let her breath go in an audible sigh. "That solves a few other problems, then."

Ellie lifted her head. "Like what?"

"You'll have total control. You won't have to tell Hudson he's got a child."

"I *can't* tell him. I don't even know his last name!" And how was that a good thing? He had a right to know! She should've left her number that morning at the Four Seasons. He might not have called—but then it would've been *his* fault she couldn't make him aware that he was going to be a father. At the moment it felt like her fault…

"That's my point! You'll be able to keep the baby all to yourself without feeling guilty about it."

But she *did* feel guilty. That was the problem. And would keeping the baby all to herself truly be a positive thing? She alone would be responsible for the care and nurture of another human being. Her child would have only one parent. That wasn't unheard-of by any stretch of the imagination. Many single parents functioned fine and did a fabulous job. But could *she* handle that role—effectively enough that she wouldn't screw up the little person who'd be relying on her? She was so engrossed in her work. How would raising a child as a single mother affect her ability to succeed as a scientist and vice versa? "I'm not sure you're helping."

Amy got to her feet and began to pace. "I'm at a loss here. I don't want children—ever—so I feel really bad for you."

Ellie rolled her eyes. "Now I *know* you're not helping."

"I might be blundering around a bit, but I'm trying to find some way to reassure you. You *do* want children one day, right?"

"Yes. I've always wanted children—"

She threw up her hands. "There you go! This guarantees it."

Ellie had been feeling the ticking of her biological clock. That was one of the reasons her breakup with Don had been so painful. She wasn't great at getting out and meeting people, didn't hold out much hope of finding someone else in the next five or ten years. She didn't want to miss out on raising a family, but having a baby on her own wasn't something she'd ever considered. "Men have it so easy," she grumbled. Hudson had been able to enjoy their night together and fly home to wherever he lived without so much as a backward glance, and here she was, paying the price for that encounter. A baby would change *everything* in her life.

"It *isn't* fair," Amy agreed, pivoting at the other end of the living room. "But you have a good job with medical benefits. You'll be able to afford a child. And…once it's here, I'm sure you'll love him or her. Of course, there's all the misery you'll have to endure before then—the weight gain, the swollen ankles, the possibility of gestational diabetes, stretch marks, backaches and the excruciating delivery. God, I can't even imagine the delivery. You'll never be the same. But—"

She stopped, finally realizing that Ellie was glaring at her.

"Okay. I'll keep my mouth shut."

"Thank you."

Amy rubbed her palms on her jeans as she continued to pace, but she didn't hold her silence for very long. "I'm sorry, El," she blurted. "This sucks. I usually have an answer for everything, but even I don't know what to say to make *this* better."

Ellie closed her eyes. "You could say you'll help..."

"I *will* help. I may not want kids myself, but that doesn't mean I won't make a fabulous godmother and honorary aunt. I'd be perfect for the job, since I won't be busy raising a family of my own."

"I guess." Amy didn't strike Ellie as the godmother type, but she'd been a true friend, so maybe that wasn't a fair assessment.

"You don't sound totally convinced I'd be good with your kid," she said, her voice filled with suspicion.

Ellie would've laughed except she was too glum. She opened her eyes and stared down at her stomach. Although it was flat at the moment—her baby was only the size of a peanut, if that big—as the months passed she'd look like she'd swallowed a watermelon. That was coming. Too late to avoid it.

"I have no idea how to tell my parents about this," she said. "It'll ruin their year in Europe. They'll feel they need to come home to support me, even though they tried to complete their travel before I got married, let alone had children. I've totally screwed that up for them." She sniffed, unable to suppress the tears that suddenly welled up. They'd almost come home when she told them about Don, so she knew how they'd react to *this*. "What am I going to do?" She knew she was in real trouble if she was appealing to Amy, but who else could she turn to?

Amy came over, knelt by the couch and took her hand. "I'm guessing you won't want to hear this, but there are...things you can do to...to take care of this if you really don't want the baby. You don't *have* to go through with it."

"You're talking about an abortion."

"Yes. I'll go to the doctor with you."

Ellie snatched her hand away. "That's not for me. I spend my days trying to *save* lives. I could never… I mean, I don't judge anyone for the choices they make, but… You're right. I couldn't end the pregnancy."

"What about adoption?"

Ellie rubbed her forehead. "I can't see myself going in that direction, either. Like you said, I'm almost thirty. And I do want children eventually. Maybe this is my chance. Maybe it'll be my *only* chance. The timing isn't ideal, and it's been a shock, but… I'll get used to the idea, won't I?"

Amy peered at her more closely. "Will you?"

"Of course," she responded, wiping her eyes. Perhaps she wouldn't have any help caring for the baby, and no support from a financial perspective, but she also wouldn't have to send her son or daughter off to spend weekends with someone else. She wouldn't have to cope with the various romantic interests passing in and out of Don's or Hudson's lives, either, wouldn't have to argue with anyone about how she wanted to raise the child. Her parents were busy people, still active, but they'd be supportive. It wasn't as though she'd be *entirely* alone—once they got back.

"I feel like I got you into this," Amy said, wrinkling her nose in chagrin.

"You didn't get me into it, Aim. I'm an adult, responsible for my own behavior."

"You wouldn't even have gone to Envy if it wasn't for me."

"True, but you're not the one who pulled Hudson into the cab. I did that."

Amy reared back. "You did? You *pulled* him into the taxi with you?"

Ellie nodded. "Bottom line, I wanted to go to Hudson's hotel, wanted to sleep with him, or I wouldn't have done it."

Amy's chest lifted as she took a deep breath. "Okay. So this *is* entirely your problem."

When Ellie gasped, Amy gave her a devilish grin. "Kidding. I'll be here for you. We've always been there for each other, haven't we?"

"Yes." Ellie didn't understand how or why. They were such opposites, and yet it was always the other people in their lives who came and went. Case in point—she hadn't heard Amy mention Leslie in a month or more. "I can do this, can't I, Aim?"

"You can do *anything.*" Amy squeezed her arm. "That's part of the reason I've always admired you."

For once, Amy seemed to be in earnest. Slightly reassured, Ellie managed a watery smile. "Thank you."

"So are you going to call your parents?" she asked.

"No. I won't tell them for another five months. That way, they'll have enjoyed a big chunk of their trip before they're forced to decide whether or not to cut it short." She took Amy's hand. "Somehow I'll get through the next half year without them."

"The way you work, you could end up staying in the lab that long," Amy said, and they both laughed.

CHAPTER SEVEN

By mid-January Ellie was four months along and starting to show. She could easily cover the baby bump she saw in the mirror when she got out of the shower each morning with a big sweater over a pair of leggings. But instead of waiting until the last minute, she'd made the announcement at work a week ago that she was expecting, due on June 10.

Putting off the "big reveal" until the scandal of her breakup with Don could blow over had seemed wise, but in reality, the wait hadn't made speaking up any easier. She'd barely gotten out of the limelight and didn't want to step back into it.

Problem was, she also didn't like the idea of her fellow scientists or the rest of the staff noticing the curve of her belly and beginning to speculate about a pregnancy. She felt it would be smarter to get out in front of the rumors by revealing the truth herself. Then she wouldn't be so tempted to assume her coworkers were whispering behind her back. Once a secret was out in the open, it became far less tantalizing to the gossips.

Not surprisingly, Don didn't take the news well. She'd spoken up at the end of a staff meeting, had said she was "excited to announce" she'd met someone and, although this "someone" was no longer in her life, she was now pregnant. No one had ever heard her talk about another man, but most of her colleagues had applauded. That was the polite thing to do, since she was acting as if it was good news.

Although Leo hadn't been at the meeting, Don was, and, unlike the others, he didn't pretend to be pleased.

He'd stood there with his mouth agape. Then he'd come to her lab later in the day, before she left, to insist that *he* had to be the father. He'd been shocked—and not totally convinced—when she insisted she'd been telling the truth about another man.

He'd asked for details, but she'd refused to elaborate. She didn't want her child to feel any less loved because of the manner in which he or she was conceived, so Ellie didn't say too much. She had a right to her privacy. The only drawback to keeping things vague was that it made Don stay there and argue with her. He'd said he would've guessed if there was someone else so soon after him, that she'd done nothing except work. She then said she'd been totally clueless that there'd been someone else—for him—*while* he was with her. But he told her he was going to demand a paternity test once the baby was born. And she'd said she'd comply if it would put his mind at ease.

Her capitulation had thrown him. He'd expected her to refuse, but she had no reason to. She knew the baby wasn't his.

Agreeing to the paternity test didn't get him to back off completely, however. Now, anytime he saw her, his eyes followed her around the room as if he wished he had X-ray vision and could see the child she carried.

It was because of Don that she almost didn't go to Diane DeVry's Super Bowl party on January 23. Diane, who'd given her the *Outlander* DVDs the night Ellie learned about the pregnancy, had invited everyone from the BDC. That meant Don and Leo *could* come, but Ellie didn't think they would. Other than golf, neither one of them enjoyed sports. She couldn't remember ever watching a single game with Don.

Determined to get out and enjoy herself—she'd been cooped up in the lab far too much lately—she prepared some barbecue wings from a recipe she found online and took them over to Diane's house. Diane was married to the president and CEO of the Banting Diabetes Center Foundation, so they were on the fund-raising side together, and they had a lovely home in Doral with a huge deck and pool. Diane had shown Ellie several pictures when they were purchasing the property, so Ellie was eager to walk through it in person.

When she saw the cars lining the street, she felt a little overwhelmed. She'd made the announcement about her baby so recently, she knew she'd have to contend with a lot of questions and comments. Given the circumstances of her child's conception, that left her uneasy. But she didn't see Don's car—or Leo's, for that matter—so she felt she could handle the extra attention. After all, she had to let everyone react, get it over with.

After parking as close as she could, she carried her offering inside. The Super Bowl wasn't a big deal in her world—she didn't think she'd ever watched more than a few minutes of one—but Amy had met a man through the salon and gone to Vegas for the weekend. With her closest friend *and* her parents out of town, Ellie had been lonely. She figured this was as good an excuse as any to be with other people. The Los Angeles Devils were playing the Chicago Bears. She knew that much because it was on the invitation, but she didn't care who won. She was more interested in watching the commercials, since they were supposed to be some of the cleverest of the year.

"Ellie! I can't believe you came!" Diane exclaimed as she opened the door and took the Crock-Pot containing the wings.

"I told you I'd be here," Ellie said.

Diane didn't miss a beat. "I was afraid you'd change your mind and...go to work or something."

Ellie didn't have a chance to respond before Diane's husband stepped up to greet her. Diane was carrying the Crock-Pot to the island, anyway, which was filled with vegetable platters, cheese and crackers, guacamole and chips, Swedish meatballs, cookies, cupcakes and other sweets.

"Great to see you, Ellie."

She smiled. "Thanks, Dick."

He made a sweeping motion with one arm. "Come in, make yourself comfortable and, whenever you're ready, grab a drink and some food. Game hasn't started yet. We've got another half hour or so while they go through the usual pregame coverage."

She thanked him and, after chatting with several of the other scientists and staff—during which she assured everyone she was ecstatic at the prospect of becoming a mother—she loaded her plate. She'd just found a place to sit when she heard a voice that made the blood curdle in her veins.

"Wow! Nice house. I love it."

Don. Don and Leo had come. She'd barely had thirty minutes at the party without them. Struggling to conceal a grimace, she listened as everyone else welcomed them. She wasn't happy they were here, but she refused to rush out simply because they'd arrived. She'd been having a good time so far. Why let them ruin it?

Forcing herself to stand, she nodded rather than saying hello, but Don's eyes didn't skim over her and move on as they had with all the other guests. He stopped talking as soon as he saw her, and his gaze dropped to her belly, as it always did ever since she'd broken the news.

"What can I get you to drink?" The enthusiasm in Dick's voice sounded a bit fabricated when he addressed the newcomers, as if he was trying to stave off an awkward moment.

Leo answered that he'd like a glass of wine and drew Don farther into the kitchen.

Once they were out of her immediate sight, Ellie breathed a sigh of relief and, since she was no longer interested in food, focused on the TV for the first time. If she seemed engrossed in the game, which had started, she wouldn't be expected to socialize so much. She'd lost her desire to mill around and converse along with her hunger. Truth be told, for all her self-talk about staying, she was already looking for an excuse to leave.

She'd decided she'd try to stick it out until halftime when she saw a face that made her scream and jump off the sofa.

At her outburst, the room fell silent, except for the TV, and everyone turned to stare.

"You okay?" Dick asked.

"It's not the baby, is it?" Her boss, Carolyn Towers, who ran the Clinical Islet Transplant Program at the BDC, set her plate aside and hurried over. Carolyn was trying to get Ellie to sit down again, but Ellie couldn't move. She was stiff with shock and rooted to the spot.

"It's not the baby," she managed to say.

"What is it, then?" Carolyn asked.

She pointed at the handsome player on the sidelines who'd taken off his helmet on leaving the field. "I—I know that man."

"Of course you do, honey." Carolyn spoke gently, soothingly. "That's Hudson King, quarterback for the Los Angeles Devils. He's famous. *Everyone* knows him."

"No." She shook her head as though what she was seeing couldn't possibly be real. "I mean… I *know* him."

Dick moved closer. "Personally?"

"I met him at a club," she explained.

"And you didn't recognize him?" This came from Diane, who'd quit fussing with the food in the kitchen to find out what was going on.

Ellie couldn't quite process what she was seeing and hearing. She'd thought Hudson was gone from her life for good, forever lost. But no. Here he was, talking to another player on TV while the cameras rolled and an announcer described him as one of the best quarterbacks in the league.

"Ellie?"

Carolyn's voice came to her from what seemed to be a far distance. Carolyn was repeating a question. Ellie hadn't known who Hudson was when she met him at the club. She'd had no clue whatsoever. Why hadn't he said something? He must have realized she didn't recognize him. But even if he'd mentioned his last name, she doubted she could've identified him as a famous football player. She'd never paid any attention to sports, had too many other things on her mind that night—mainly her own misery and humiliation. "No," she replied. "And he never told me."

"Are you sure it was him?" Dick asked. "I mean… I think you'd know if you ran into one of the most famous quarterbacks on the planet."

"Even if you didn't, why would meeting him be a problem?" Diane bent to pick up the food Ellie had unwittingly dumped on the hardwood floor when she got up. "Famous or no, that man's as handsome as a man can be."

"*I'd* sure like to meet him," another female coworker piped up with a raucous laugh, but Ellie didn't bother turning to see who'd spoken.

"Yeah. He's handsome," she agreed. He was also good in bed. *She* should know. She'd spent an entire night with him—and wound up pregnant with his baby.

Belatedly realizing that she should help clean up the mess she'd made, she dropped to her knees. "I'm sorry," she said. "I didn't mean to ruin your party."

"Oh, stop. You haven't ruined anything. This'll wipe up easily enough." Diane caught her hands as she continued to help, then frowned. "Your fingers are ice-cold, Ellie. What's going on?"

"I shouldn't have come here. I—I'm not feeling very well."

Dick raised her gently to her feet while his wife finished picking up the food, and she began digging around in her purse for her keys.

Despite Leo's disapproval, which Ellie could feel rolling off him like a heat wave, Don stepped in front of her as she headed for the door. "Ellie, what's wrong?"

"Nothing." She skirted past him, hauling in a deep breath as soon as she stepped outside. The fresh air felt good, but she wasn't safely away quite yet. She knew when Don yelled her name that he was coming after her.

"Ellie, can we talk for a minute?" he asked, hurrying to catch up.

Ducking her head, she kept marching down the street. "No."

"Wait. I have a proposition for you, something I think you'll like."

Despite the way her heart hammered against her chest and her thoughts raced in her head, this caught her attention. "What is it?" she asked, whirling around to face him.

"Leo and I, we…we understand that it might be difficult for you to take care of a baby all on your own."

Where was he going with this? "The baby's *my* problem." She was about to walk off again, when he grabbed her arm.

"That's the thing. Your pregnancy doesn't have to be a problem at all. You couldn't have planned this, not with your folks out of town for the year."

"So?"

When she didn't argue, couldn't argue, he seemed to take courage. "I've always wanted children."

She lifted a hand to interrupt. "You can still have children, Don. Even if you don't use a surrogate, you could adopt."

"That's true, I guess, but adoption's an expensive process. Heck, it costs a lot of money just to rescue a dog these days."

Why did he insist on waylaying her? She wanted to leave, go home, turn on her TV and stare at Hudson when no one else was around to notice how deeply the sight of him affected her. She hadn't stopped thinking about him, not for one night. "That's the way things are." How did Don expect her to fix the system? "I—I can't change the world."

"I'm not asking you to change anything. I believe there's a

solution here that'd make us both happy. Rather than pay sixty to eighty thousand to get a surrogate, I'd prefer to give you that money. I mean, you could buy a house."

She brought one hand to her chest. "You're offering to pay me for my child? You want me to *sell* him or her to you?"

A pained expression appeared on his face. "No, no! That's not it at all. I'm saying if you're open to considering...placement options, Leo and I will do everything we can to be good parents. We'd *love* to have the baby—and we'd be generous with you in whatever way you needed."

"This isn't your child, Don. I've told you that before."

"Doesn't matter," he argued. "I hope it is, so I'll have some rights if you refuse my offer, but even if it's not, I'd like the opportunity to be part of this kid's life."

She pulled her arm from his grip. "No! Go back and enjoy the game with Leo."

Leo stood on the stoop, watching them. He'd come out shortly after Don. Ellie couldn't help wondering what Don's partner was thinking. Was he in agreement on this baby business? She couldn't see his expression clearly now that she was two houses down, but it looked as if he was wearing a dark scowl.

"Just keep that in mind," Don said. "If you decide you're not ready for a baby—and you'd like your child to have the stability of *two* loving parents—we're here. We're ready for that when... when maybe you're not."

He believed he and Leo could offer her child more than she could? Eager to strike back after all he'd done, she said, "There's no way. This baby belongs to Hudson King. Even if I wanted to, which I don't, I couldn't give the child away. He'd have to agree."

Don's eyebrows jerked together, becoming one giant slash above his blue eyes. "What are you talking about?"

What *was* she talking about? She'd spoken impetuously, allowed her desire to show him that she was more than his pathetic castoff take control. But she needed to keep her mouth shut, at least until she could decide what to do. "Nothing. Never mind."

As she turned to go for the second time, he caught her by the shoulder. "Are you telling me that Hudson King—*the* Hudson King of the Los Angeles Devils—is the father of your child? That's why you freaked out in there? You didn't even know he played football?"

"No. That's laughable. Of course I know who I slept with. I'm not feeling well, not making sense. I have to go." Pulling away, she ran to her car, got inside and locked the door. But Don didn't go back to the party. As she started the engine and punched the gas pedal, a quick glance in her rearview mirror showed him standing in the middle of the cul-de-sac, looking as stunned as she felt.

As soon as she got home, Ellie recorded the rest of the game. She watched it as it recorded, too, studied Hudson's every move. That was the man she'd met at Envy, all right. So much of that night suddenly made sense. Why he was hanging back on the periphery of the crowd when he could've been in the middle of everything. Why he was wearing sunglasses even though it was dark. Why he'd escorted her out the back door. Why he had such a magnificent warrior's body. And why he'd been in town in the first place. She'd signed on to the internet and called up the Devils' schedule. Sure enough, they'd played the Miami Dolphins the Sunday following her stay at the Four Seasons. The Devils had lost, but that was one of only three losses on the season.

How had she missed all the media coverage of this man? Amy always joked that she lived in a cave. This was embarrassing proof that she let far too many things escape her notice. She would've called Amy, but didn't want to interrupt her weekend in Vegas. She also didn't want whoever Amy was with to overhear what she needed to talk about. She regretted saying what she had to Don. He'd already left her three messages since she got home.

"Hudson's a professional athlete, Ellie. He probably has women in every city he plays in. Who knows how many kids. He won't care about you or your child, certainly won't want to take on the duties of a father. But I'm here to help. Call me, okay?"

Next message: "Ellie, you'd be crazy to tell King. Whatever happened between you must've been quick and dirty if you didn't even realize who he was. He won't be thrilled to have you pop up in his life again. Why not save yourself the rejection? What if he tries to take the baby away? Leo and I have a better solution. So will you please call me?"

Next message: "Ellie, pick up. Come on. I'd really like to talk to you. Leo and I have discussed everything, and he's hoping for a chance to assure you that he feels the same way I do. We'd both love to raise this child. We're nearly forty. It's the perfect time for us, the only thing we're missing."

"Why wouldn't I go for that? I live to make *you* happy," she muttered when she heard his last message and turned off her phone. She didn't need Don's interference. *She'd* decide the future of her baby, not him.

So...what *was* she going to do? Now that she knew who Hudson was, she could search online and learn all kinds of things about him. When she put his name in Google, she was presented with a list of articles dating back several years.

Most of the information was sports related—his stats, his responses to wins or losses, whether or not he'd been injured in a particular game and how long he might be out if he was. Some personal stuff came up, too, however—more than she would've wanted circulating about her if she was a public figure. She focused on one article in particular.

What's in a name?

Ask one of the best quarterbacks ever to play football. Hudson King was named after two cross streets in Bel Air, a ritzy Southern California neighborhood, where he was found hidden under a privacy hedge at less than a day old. No one knows who his parents are or why he was abandoned the day he was born. The police investigation turned up no legitimate leads…

"Wow, that's terrible," Ellie muttered, but it was obviously true. She discovered plenty of other articles to confirm his background. After going in and out of foster care for a number of years—and trying to steal a car when he was only fourteen—he'd been sent to a place called New Horizons Boys Ranch. Although Ellie wasn't familiar with boys ranches, she quickly learned that they were reformatory boarding schools for troubled teens. This one was in Southern California somewhere. It was at New Horizons that Hudson's athletic ability began to shine. Somehow he got his life turned around, went to UCLA, won the Heisman Trophy his senior year and entered the NFL. He'd been with the Devils ever since. Ellie read that he'd taken less from the Devils on his last contract than he could've gotten elsewhere so he could stay in California and the organization would still be able to get some experienced talent at receiver. He mentored many of the boys who went to his old high school and didn't want to leave the area.

The fact that he was so interested in the welfare of the students at New Horizons brought Ellie a degree of comfort. She had a good impression of him from the night they were together, but one night, especially one spent making love more than talking, didn't reveal a whole lot. He was largely an unknown to her.

She saw another article about his involvement in the school. The administrator, someone named Aiyana Turner, said he'd donated hundreds of thousands of dollars in scholarships and sporting equipment, so much that the football field at New Horizons had been renamed in his honor this year. Ms. Turner admitted he'd had a few brushes with the law when he was a kid, but she'd been quick to add that was all in the past.

Ellie touched her stomach. She'd gone four and a half months thinking this was her baby and hers alone, that her child's biological father would never be part of the picture. Seeing Hudson on TV had upended all of that. So what now? Did she dare keep the news to herself?

She was tempted. Her silence could eliminate several risky variables. What if Hudson wasn't as good as his service to New Horizons made him appear? What if he gave her nothing but grief? What if he demanded shared custody? They lived across the country from each other. She didn't want to be putting her child on a plane every other weekend.

She'd be much smarter to keep her mouth shut. But would that be fair? Didn't she owe it to Hudson to tell him? Beyond Hudson, what about her responsibility to the baby? Did she have the right to deny her child some kind of connection with the man who'd fathered him or her? Didn't common decency suggest she do everything possible to facilitate that relationship?

Fathers were important; they could make a big difference. Her own father was the parent who seemed to understand her and who'd nurtured her the most while she was growing up.

If Hudson didn't want to be involved, that decision should come from him. But how would she even approach him to find out? What would she say? "Excuse me, do you remember that night in Miami?" Chances were he wouldn't remember her at all. Professional athletes were notoriously promiscuous. She was probably just one of many women he'd been with in the past several months.

He won't be thrilled to have you pop up in his life again…

Don obviously agreed. But she wasn't going to let her ex-fiancé's skepticism get inside her head. Hudson hadn't even had any birth control with him.

On the other hand, that could mean he'd simply used it all…

She was about to watch the game for the second time, as if that might show her something she hadn't already seen, when she discovered a video clip on YouTube that held her spellbound.

It was part of a press conference, in which one intrepid reporter kept asking Hudson personal questions that should've been out of bounds, since those questions had nothing to do with what he was there to discuss, which was, of course, football.

"How do you feel being abandoned as a baby has figured into your view of life?" the reporter asked. "Would you say your history's made it more difficult for you to succeed as an individual?"

Ellie watched Hudson's eyes narrow as they focused more intently on the woman who'd asked that question. "Excuse me?"

Ellie was pretty sure that almost everyone else who'd received such a look would've slunk into the background. Not this girl. She repeated the question, loud and clear.

A muscle moved in Hudson's cheek, but then he grinned as if he was just a good old boy who didn't care much about anything. "I wouldn't consider it a *positive* thing," he joked. "No one wants to be discarded like trash. But that was thirty-two years ago. I've had plenty of time to get over it."

"The holidays are coming up," the woman said, going after him again. "Do you find that a particularly difficult time?"

Somehow, Hudson managed to keep his smile in place. He was acting the part of a big, tough football player, and he was doing it well. But Ellie had spotted an almost-imperceptible wince, knew that question had blasted a hole through him, even if the stupid reporter didn't. "I've got lots of family," he said. "They're just not related by blood."

"Have you ever done any of your own searching, hoping to find out who left you under that hedge?" she persisted.

Hudson responded as though he didn't hear her third question. He scanned the crowd and called on someone else. But since the first reporter had ventured beyond how the Devils were planning to prepare for the next game, or whether Hudson thought they had a serious Super Bowl bid this year, the next reporter couldn't seem to resist following her lead. "Would you want a relationship with your mother if she ever did step forward?"

"Looks like we're out of time," Hudson replied briskly, and Ellie nearly cheered when he stood, putting an end to the conference.

"Poor guy." With a sigh, she pushed her computer away and turned on her phone. She'd told herself she wouldn't call Amy, but she had to talk to someone about this, and her parents still didn't know she was pregnant. Whenever she spoke to them, she pretended nothing had changed since her breakup with Don, which meant she still had that daunting conversation ahead of her.

As soon as her phone powered up, she saw that Don had stopped calling but had been texting instead. Leave me alone, she wrote back.

Before she could reach Amy, however, another call came in, this one from Diane DeVry. Amy felt it would be rude not to answer, since she'd been so rattled when she left the Super Bowl party.

She pushed the talk button, hoping to reassure her colleague.

"Is it true, Ellie?" Diane demanded.

A sick feeling came over Ellie. This wasn't the question she'd been expecting. "Is what true?"

"Hudson King isn't the father of your baby, is he?"

Ellie dropped her head into her hand. Don had told Diane, had probably announced it to the whole party. *Why?* Why would he do that if he didn't even want her to tell Hudson? she asked herself.

But the answer was obvious. He couldn't resist. The news was too exciting *not* to share.

So...should she lie? Deny her child's paternity now before the news could spread throughout the BDC? Or should she admit the truth?

She had no choice, she decided. Not really. This affected two other lives; it wasn't something she could keep to herself indefinitely. She figured she might as well be honest from the start. She was going to have to tell Hudson, anyway.

"Yeah," she said. "It is."

CHAPTER EIGHT

Hudson's address was unlisted. Ellie couldn't find any way to contact him online—no PO box where she could send a letter or Facebook page where she could message him. She called the general number for the team, and a number that was published for his agent, but she didn't dare leave detailed messages, and her name wasn't enough to get a call back from either one. They probably thought she was yet another woman wanting to hook up with him. She was wondering what she should do next when the answer became clear. The boys ranch where Hudson helped out had a webpage that gave quite a bit of information, including the fact that it was located in a town of only five thousand people. Surely, in that small a community, someone should be able to reach him—or know someone who'd know someone who could. With football season over—the Devils had lost their Super Bowl bid to the Bears in overtime—she hoped he might live close to the boys ranch. One article she ran across mentioned that he'd purchased a property not far away. Even if he wasn't in town, she felt there was a strong possibility Aiyana Turner, the woman who ran the school, could pick up the phone and call him.

It took two weeks to arrange the travel, partly because she

had an ultrasound appointment she didn't want to miss—one at which she was supposed to learn the sex of her child. She was having a boy, which she'd already guessed. She'd been so sure, almost from the beginning, that she'd begun choosing the furniture and the exact shade of blue she wanted to paint her nursery. Confirmation of that somehow made it even more important he know his father, that he have his father as a role model, so she worked up the nerve, put in for the vacation days and, on February 10, flew to Los Angeles, where she rented a car and drove an hour and a half northwest to Silver Springs. She was so nervous that she couldn't focus on her surroundings. LA just looked like urban sprawl. As she got outside Ventura, however, she started noticing the bucolic countryside—something she hadn't previously associated with California. And she found Silver Springs quite appealing, with the rolling hills and mountains that seemed to hold the town in a cradle, the Spanish Colonial Revival architecture and the many mom-and-pop businesses in town. There wasn't a single chain store she could see, except for a couple of gas stations. She thought that was nice.

Although she stopped to rent a room at a place called The Mission Inn so she could freshen up after the five-hour flight and subsequent drive, she didn't hang out there for long. She'd gained three hours crossing the country and entering a new time zone, but she planned to hit New Horizons when she'd be most likely to find someone who could help her, and she assumed that would be before school ended. She didn't want to wait until tomorrow. She was set on delivering her message as soon as possible—getting it over with so she could sleep that night. Because of the way she'd been obsessing about telling her parents, how she'd juggle a child with her career and now, what to do about Hudson, she'd been losing weight in spite of the pregnancy, which didn't make her obstetrician happy.

Once she left the motel, she followed her GPS to the address listed on the New Horizons website. She found the school without any problem, but she was so agitated when she rolled under the wrought iron arch, reached the administration building and parked in guest parking that she stayed in the car for several minutes. She had no idea what she might encounter—how she'd be treated here, whether she'd see Hudson himself.

How many other women had made this trek? she wondered. Maybe the staff wouldn't think it was any big deal. She imagined them chuckling among themselves after she left. *"There goes another one."* But she chastised herself for judging Hudson according to a stereotype. The women he'd been with, even the number of illegitimate children he might've fathered—that was none of her business. *She* was the one who'd pulled him into the cab that fateful night in September; she could hardly accuse him of being a womanizer. And now that a pregnancy had resulted from their encounter, she needed to do the right thing, had to give Hudson the chance to know his child and be involved in that child's life. He should have the opportunity to choose.

After taking a deep breath, she climbed out. *It'll be over with soon.* Squaring her shoulders, she clung tightly to her purse as she strode to the stairs. Intent on watching her feet so she wouldn't trip in the gravel with her high-heeled boots, she nearly bumped into a tall, thickly built man with black hair and blue eyes approaching the same building.

"Sorry," she murmured as he caught her by the elbow to steady her.

"No problem," he said and held the door before following her inside.

She approached the reception desk only to glance around uncertainly when she didn't see anyone sitting behind it.

The man who'd walked in with her had moved toward a nearby office but, realizing there was no one to greet her, paused. "I guess Betty isn't back from her dentist appointment yet. I'm Elijah Turner. Maybe I can help. Are you here to apply for the music teacher position? Because I'm fairly certain those interviews are scheduled for tomorrow."

Elijah was coadministrator of the school and one of Aiyana's adopted sons. She'd read his bio on the website. "No, uh, no. I'm not here to interview. I was hoping to talk to Aiyana."

"My mother was in earlier. Let me check," he said and crossed over to the corner office.

Ellie curled her fingernails into her palms, but she didn't have to wait long. A moment later, he poked his head out and beckoned her toward him. "Come on back."

Here goes... Standing, Ellie picked some lint from her sweater to give herself an extra moment to overcome her nerves. Fortunately, she didn't think Elijah or anyone else could tell she was pregnant, not in what she was wearing today. She hadn't bought any maternity clothes, hadn't needed them yet. She was wearing her best-fitting jeans, unbuttoned at the top to accommodate her thickening waist, covered by a long black sweater. She'd chosen this outfit because it went so well with her new boots, but at the last minute, she worried that she might be dressed too casually. She felt she was already at a disadvantage; she didn't want Hudson, if she saw him, to wonder if he'd been blind to hit her up at the club in the first place.

As soon as Elijah showed her into the office, an attractive, petite woman looked up and smiled. Ellie guessed Aiyana was part Native American, what with her creamy, café au lait skin, the thick black braid down her back and the abundance of turquoise jewelry on her arms, fingers and neck. "Hello. I'm Aiyana Turner." Offering her hand, she came around a large desk. "What can I do for you?"

Elijah's footsteps moved slowly toward the common area. Ellie could tell he was hoping to learn her purpose before he left. No doubt he was curious. But she lowered her voice. "It's a—a private matter."

"I see." Aiyana fell silent until they heard the click of the door.

After her son was gone, she threaded her fingers together and propped her hands on her blotter. "Are you here because you have a loved one who might be a candidate for enrollment?"

"No. I was hoping you could put me in touch with Hudson King."

"Hudson," she repeated in surprise. "Are you a reporter or—"

"Not a reporter," she broke in. "I—I have something important to discuss with him. That's all."

"I see." Aiyana spoke slowly as if she was trying to decide how to respond. "You do realize there are a lot of people who try to reach Hudson through us."

"I didn't know that, but…it makes sense, I guess."

"That means we have to be very diligent about safeguarding his privacy. It wouldn't be fair to give his contact information to any stranger who stopped by."

"I understand. But I'm not looking for an autograph or a—a story. I'm not trying to sell him anything, either. We've met before, once. I'm only in town for a couple of days and…and I really need to speak to him while I'm here." She was being vague, but she wasn't willing to say more—not to anyone Hudson knew—until she'd broken the news to him personally.

"I see. I believe you. I do," Aiyana said. "Problem is…we aren't at liberty to reveal his contact information to *anyone*, not without his express permission. If you'd like to leave your name and number with me, however, I'll let him know you stopped by."

Ellie put her purse on her lap. "He's in town, then?"

"I'm afraid I can't reveal that, either. Silver Springs is too small."

Wow. They were even more protective of Hudson than she'd expected. Was it because Aiyana respected him? Or was she simply afraid to lose his patronage?

Ellie hoped it was the former. That indicated the father of her baby was likely a good person in addition to being talented in sports and physically gorgeous. "I understand." She reached into her purse and retrieved the note she'd written, just in case.

"If you could pass this along, I'd appreciate it." She stood as she handed the envelope across the desk. "I'm in room 103 at The Mission Inn. Tell him I'll stay there until the day after tomorrow. If I don't hear from him, I'll assume… I'll assume I've fulfilled my obligation."

"Which means…you'll leave town?"

"Yes. I'll have to leave early Saturday to catch my flight, since it's out of LAX."

"I'll make him aware of your time constraints."

"Thank you." Ellie offered her a brief smile before leaving the office. She told herself the meeting had gone as smoothly as she could have expected. At least she'd spoken to someone who could pass along a message—and seemed reliable enough to do so. But even after she reached her motel, the butterflies in her stomach made it impossible to eat the sandwich she'd picked up along the way, although she hadn't had anything since she left Miami other than a few pretzels. She couldn't sit down, either, couldn't stop moving. So she paced back and forth at the end of the two double beds in her room, rehearsing what she planned to say *if* Hudson bothered to contact her.

Maybe he wouldn't respond, she told herself. Maybe she'd spend two agonizing days waiting for some word from him, and it would never come.

That would be good, right? Then she could go on her way without any guilt.

She tried to convince herself. Part of her, the part that feared how he might react, would be relieved. But the rest of her wanted to see him again. After all, he'd fueled her fantasies for months.

When Hudson received Aiyana's text saying she needed to talk to him, he was leaving the doctor's office with Aaron. Aaron's last round of chemo was over. They were running tests to see if it had worked. He knew Aaron was worried about what those tests would reveal; so was he, since they'd had bad news before.

But they'd been laughing and joking with each other all afternoon. The kid was the bravest person Hudson had ever known. He was also a real smart-ass, which Hudson happened to enjoy.

Hudson waited until after they'd returned to the ranch and Aaron had gone up to his dorm room before he responded to Aiyana. He was afraid Aaron was what she wanted to talk about. That was what they usually talked about—Aaron or another one of the boys who needed something. But once he texted the school administrator to let her know he was in the parking lot and heading toward her office, she wrote back to say he should wait where he was, that she was coming from the science building and would meet him at his truck.

He leaned against the driver's door while he waited, waving at the various students who called out his name as they hurried to their after-school activities. He liked that they didn't make a big deal of his presence on campus. Although most were more than eager to do anything he invited them to do, they respected his personal space better than many adults. He was at the school often enough that they took his appearance in stride, which let him relax, be a normal person for a change.

He noticed Aiyana making her way toward him and straightened. He could tell by her expression that something was wrong. Her smile, always so warm and infectious, didn't reach her eyes.

"What is it?" he asked, tossing his keys from hand to hand.

"I don't know exactly," she replied.

"What do you mean? This isn't about Aaron…"

"No. A young woman—quite attractive—showed up here today, asking for you."

"A young woman."

"About your age, yes."

"And? Who was she?"

"She didn't give me her name. Just said she needed to talk to you. When I told her I couldn't share your contact information, she took this from her purse and told me to tell you that she'll be in room 103 at The Mission Inn until the day after tomorrow." She handed him an envelope with his name penned in a feminine script on the outside.

"That's it?"

"Pretty much."

"Ms. Turner! Ms. Turner! Are you coming to watch my debate?" Colin Green called out from near the English department.

"Of course," she called back.

"Hurry! It's about to start."

"I'll be there!"

When Aiyana returned her attention to Hudson, he raised the envelope in a salute. "Thanks for this." He began to get in his truck but she stopped him.

"Hudson?"

"Yeah?"

"I didn't get the impression she came for a social visit—an attempt to reconnect or anything like that. She seemed nervous. Said something about fulfilling her 'obligation,' so you might want to be prepared for the unexpected."

"I'm not worried," he said. "I haven't done anything that could come back to bite me." Whatever this was, it had to be some sort of mistake. Or maybe, even though Samuel Jones, the private investigator he'd hired, had checked in just last week to say he hadn't been able to find anything yet, this was a result of some stone he'd overturned. Most likely Hudson's mother was the one who'd abandoned him. Perhaps she'd made a friend or loved one promise not to reveal her identity until after she was dead, and now she was gone.

Had to be something like that, Hudson decided. He couldn't be in the kind of personal trouble Aiyana seemed to think. Very few single men were as circumspect as he was.

At his reassurance, her smile eased. "Great. I've been worried for you. Now, good luck with…whatever it is. I have to go see how well Colin defends his favorite president."

He told her goodbye and shut his door before tearing open the envelope. He expected the note inside to contain some news about his background—if not what he'd imagined, then something similar. Perhaps this was from a woman claiming to be related to someone who'd seen or heard something that day. Heck, it could even be someone claiming to be related to him. Wouldn't be the first time that'd happened. In the year following his first pro contract, he'd had three different women come forward, declaring they were his mother. One had been only twelve years older than he was. Another was in Pennsylvania the day he was born, and DNA had ruled out the third. DNA had ruled out a handful since then, too.

But the note didn't say anything like that.

> Hudson, this is Ellie Fisher, the woman you met at the nightclub (Envy) in Miami on September 10. I went to your hotel room with you at the Four Seasons.

She didn't have to get that specific. Ellie and Envy would've been enough. He hadn't forgotten her. *Couldn't* forget her. But the note went on.

> I'm sorry to surprise you like this. I'm sure you weren't expecting to hear from me. But I need to talk to you for a few minutes. Please call me.

She'd scrawled her number below her name, so he added it to his contacts. He'd wished, on several occasions, that he'd asked for a number or email address, some way to reach her before she could slip away. He would've requested her number; it just hadn't occurred to him to do that up front. He'd never had a woman run out on him like she did.

Feeling more excited than worried, he started his truck. Aiyana didn't understand the circumstances. Ellie had figured out who he was, or she wouldn't have been able to track him down. She probably hadn't been *nervous* when she met Aiyana so much as angry because she felt she'd been misled.

Before shifting into Reverse, he almost called Ellie's number to let her know he was on his way. He had his phone in his hand but changed his mind at the last second. Why call? Aiyana had told him where Ellie was staying.

He'd just go there.

CHAPTER NINE

The Mission Inn was the least expensive motel in town, but Hudson preferred it to the others. White, with a red tile roof, it was modeled after the twenty or so religious outposts built by the Spanish to expand Christianity in the late eighteenth century. It even had a bell tower, like the nearby Spanish mission he'd used as inspiration when he'd had to create a replica in fourth grade. Most California students had to build a miniature mission as part of the history curriculum in grade school, and he hadn't been any different. The memory stood out because that was the year he'd been placed in a home that had a mother who tried to support him in his schoolwork. If only she hadn't lost her sister in a car accident six months after he moved in, she might've kept him. Instead, she'd taken him back to the orphanage so she could cope with the adoption of her two nieces and one nephew.

Since becoming famous, he'd heard from a lot of his foster caregivers. They seemed to have very different memories of how they'd treated him than he did. But she'd been sweet—and she was the only one he now occasionally kept in contact with.

He had no trouble finding a parking space. Although Silver

Springs received its fair share of visitors, most came in spring, summer and fall. Today, other than a handful of cars, the lot sat empty.

It had been sunny when he left his house this morning, so he hadn't put on a coat over his long-sleeved golf shirt and the comfortable pair of faded jeans he'd worn, but the weather was turning chilly. They were in for another thunderstorm tonight. The past few days had been wet.

Room 103 was located right off the parking lot, not a far walk. He passed a rental car—economy—in front of her room and guessed it was what Ellie had driven, since there weren't any vehicles on either side for several slots.

Out of curiosity, he peered into the car but saw nothing other than the remains of a Starbucks tea drink in the cup holder and a leather jacket on the passenger seat.

A rush of expectation shot through him at the prospect of seeing the sexy, sweet, fun woman he'd met in Miami. When he knocked, he was already planning where he'd take her to dinner. He wasn't positive they'd hit it off the way they had back at Envy. That had been positively electric. But he felt certain they could get through a meal. And if that spark was still there? Who could say what might happen? He didn't think she should be *too* mad at him. After all, she was the one who'd left without so much as a goodbye.

The door opened almost immediately, as if she'd been standing behind it, waiting for him to arrive—and there she was, peering out at him through the opening.

"Wow. I thought I'd never see you again." He'd been worried he might not recognize her. For the most part, he'd seen her only in the dark. But she looked exactly as he remembered, maybe prettier.

"I thought the same."

He expected her to let go of the door and possibly greet him with a hug. He didn't feel that would be inappropriate, considering what had taken place between them. But she didn't even smile. She seemed flustered, worried, as Aiyana had said.

"Please, come in," she said, moving back to allow him room.

Hudson felt his own smile fade as he stepped across the threshold. Already this meeting wasn't going the way he'd imagined. "Look, if you're mad, I can explain."

"Explain?" she echoed.

"Why I didn't tell you who I am."

"Oh." She spoke in a throwaway manner, giving him the impression that couldn't have been further from her mind. "I admit I found it slightly...curious. Why *didn't* you tell me?"

"I didn't want that to influence what you were thinking or feeling. I preferred to be a regular guy for a change." Remembering the soft mound of her breast beneath his hand, he grinned. That first touch had been so intoxicating. It was one of his favorite memories.

But even then she didn't smile back. She shifted her gaze away as if she couldn't allow herself to be distracted. "Makes sense, I guess," she said.

That was easy, so easy it caused Hudson a moment of alarm. "You're *not* mad?"

"No."

If she wasn't upset that he'd hidden his identity, and she wasn't happy to see him, what was this about? "Aiyana said you have something to tell me."

Her hand went to her stomach, which drew his gaze lower. She looked as thin as ever, but the roundness he saw once she pressed the fabric against her body made his heart jump into his throat. "You're not—you're not here to tell me you're pregnant or anything, are you?"

She nodded, seemingly relieved that she hadn't had to be the one to say those words. "Yes, I'm afraid—" when her voice squeaked, she cleared her throat "—I'm afraid I am."

A red-hot rage poured through him. No. After what he'd

been through when he was young, rejected by his own mother right from the start, he'd promised himself he would not bring an unwanted child into the world. He'd been so careful, denied himself so many times. This could not be happening. "There has to be some mistake," he said. "We used protection. I *always* use protection."

She blew out an audible sigh. "I thought the same thing at first. Believe me, it came as a complete surprise when…when I didn't get my period the next month. I didn't even notice I was late—that's how unexpected it was. I was so caught up in my work and life in general that the dates got away from me. But then…well, I *did* notice. So I used one of those at-home pregnancy tests."

Hudson's chest had constricted to the point that he could scarcely breathe. "Those can be wrong," he croaked.

Her gaze skittered away. "That's true. Except this one wasn't. I've been to an ob-gyn since then. A blood test confirmed it, and I'm starting to show. There's no question."

Feeling as if someone had just kicked him in the stomach, he steadied himself by putting a hand to the wall. "Look, I'm really sorry that you…that you're in a difficult spot. I can give you some money, if that'll help. But…you're not carrying *my* baby."

She seemed taken aback. "Yes, I am," she insisted. "There's no confusion about that."

The fact that anyone would try to hold him responsible for something he'd gone to such pains to avoid made his muscles tense. "There has to be!"

She winced when he exploded, lifting her hands, palms out, as if beseeching him to remain calm. "I know this comes as a shock. I'm sorry about that. But can we… Can we talk through this without the emotion?"

"Without the emotion?" he repeated. "How am I *not* supposed to be upset? You're saying I've done the very thing I promised myself I'd never do."

She frowned. "I'm just letting you know what happened. I felt it was only right to make you aware that we…inadvertently created another human being."

"Of course. No doubt your motives in bringing me this *welcome* news are *completely* altruistic."

He knew she'd heard the sarcasm in his voice when she stiffened. "Please, if you'll hear me out—"

"What about that fiancé you told me about?" he broke in. "The one you said you caught cheating with another man?"

"What about him?"

"Was that just a clever story? A way to make me feel sorry for you?"

She looked bewildered. "No! Don is real."

"I hope so. Because if there really was a fiancé, I'm guessing you slept with him, too." Surely this line of reasoning would provide a rope he could use to climb out of the pit into which he'd fallen.

"Yes."

"Then this baby could also be his."

"Except we weren't intimate after my last period."

"Maybe the sperm lasted—that can happen. They can live inside a woman for several days."

"It was longer than several days."

"Then there has to be some other guy who did this," he insisted. "Who else have you slept with?"

She wrapped her arms around herself as if fighting a strong headwind. "No one! I haven't been with anyone else in seven years."

"Bullshit! That's not even normal."

Tears began to roll down her cheeks, but he refused to let that soften his heart. She'd played him so well, so perfectly. No way was he going to make this easy on her, not after what she'd done to him. She had no idea how strongly he felt about making sure two adults were ready for a child before creating one.

He saw her throat work as she struggled to swallow. "As weird as it may seem to you, I've only been with three men in my whole life. Two of them were long-term, steady boyfriends."

"You expect me to believe, after going to my hotel a couple of hours after we met, that I'm the *only* stranger you've ever slept with?"

She rocked back as if he'd slapped her. "Yes."

"And the one person you chose to do that with just happened to be a famous quarterback."

"Yes, I mean…no. It's not like you're making it sound. I didn't know you were a famous quarterback. I wasn't *targeting* you."

He moved forward the same distance as she'd moved back a moment earlier. "How do *I* know that?"

She seemed at a loss for words. "I—I guess you don't."

"Exactly. All I have is your word."

"You're the only person who could be the father." She stared up at him, imploring him to believe her, but he refused to be persuaded by that earnest, innocent-looking face. She'd suckered him once; he wouldn't let her do it a second time.

"You can be *that* specific?" he said. "Really?"

"You're not convinced."

"Is it any wonder? You set me up! Admit it!"

She'd been pale when he first came in; now she was white as a sheet. "No!"

"Stop lying!" He took another menacing step toward her, and she backed up even farther. "You recognized me all along, didn't you? You knew who I was. You were only pretending you didn't so you could get me in the sack, and I fell neatly into your trap."

"I wasn't trying to t-trap you!" she stammered, coming up against the wall.

"Then how do you explain that *you* were the one who provided the condoms that didn't work?"

She tried to slide away from him, but he propped a hand on either side of her face, confining her between his arms. "Tell me the truth," he said through gritted teeth. "You did this to me on purpose!"

The tears were coming faster now. "Of course I didn't! If you'll listen, I—I can explain the condoms. You see, my f-friend shoved those condoms in my purse that night as a—a joke."

"You told me that before we used them."

"Exactly. See? I never d-dreamed I'd really need them. But then I met you, and one thing led to another, and you didn't have any condoms yourself, and I had those and…" Her words dwindled as if she could tell by the murderous look on his face that she was only making him angrier. "Wait." She sniffed and dashed a hand across her wet cheeks in an attempt to compose herself. "This is getting out of control. I understand why you'd be tempted to—to think the worst. Some of the facts do seem odd. But let's wait until the baby's born. You can order a paternity test at that time, which would…which would prove I'm not lying."

"About the paternity."

"Isn't that all that matters at this point?"

"Hell, no!" he cried. "I won't let you make me accountable for an unwanted child entering this world. We're ending this pregnancy. Now." He knew it wasn't his decision. He wasn't even sure he was fully committed to what he'd just said. He'd never seriously considered what he'd do in a situation like this. But he couldn't stop himself from pretending he could take charge and do something about it.

"What?"

Slightly gratified by her panic, he pushed the bluff a little farther. "Get your jacket. We'll go to LA right now, find a clinic and take care of this. Then we can each go our separate ways."

More tears streaked down her cheeks. "You want me to get an abortion."

"You're smarter than you look."

Her hands covered her stomach in a protective motion. "It's too late. I'm in my second trimester."

He gaped at her. "What'd you say?"

"I'm twenty-two weeks. A pregnancy only lasts forty. That's over halfway."

"Of course!" Shoving a hand through his hair, he whirled away from her and began to pace. "That's why you waited so long to tell me. So I'd have no way out."

"That isn't true!"

"How else would you explain it?" he yelled, turning to face her again.

"I c-can't explain anything. You won't let me. You're too convinced I'm trying to—to screw you somehow. But I swear, I just figured out who you were two weeks ago. I was invited to a Super Bowl party and…and there you were. On TV."

"I've been in the Super Bowl before. How is it that you're the only person in America who missed it?"

"I don't give a damn about sports. I think it's stupid to pay millions of dollars to grown men who throw their bodies at each other! Why not do something that could really make a difference in life?"

Her retort infuriated him. He had to hit something, had to find an outlet for the frustration and disillusionment welling up inside him. After all the years he'd felt rejected and unwanted because someone had gotten his mother pregnant when she wasn't ready for a child, here he was, repeating the same damn cycle. "You didn't seem to mind what I did for a living when you seduced me!" he said as he slugged the wall.

She flinched and covered her head, as if he might strike her next. When he didn't advance, merely shook the pain from his hand, she blinked at the hole he'd put in the Sheetrock. "You need to leave," she said. "*Now.* Before I call the police."

"I haven't done anything that would warrant getting arrested! You're the one who scammed *me*! You set me up, got pregnant on purpose, and now you're here to…what? Collect a fat check? Is that what's coming next?" It was easier to focus on the support she'd require than all the rest of it. But he had plenty of money. He just didn't want to be responsible for creating a child under these circumstances. He'd told himself he'd never be that guy—and yet, because he'd met Ellie five months ago, here he was! There wasn't a worse way he could've let himself down.

She was beginning to tremble. "You're wrong. I'm not after your money. Listen, you—you're not the man I thought you were."

He agreed. That was what was killing him!

"I shouldn't have come here," she went on. "This whole thing, it was a mistake."

"Damn right it was a mistake. You went after the wrong guy." He closed the distance between them and bent his head to get in her face, even though he could tell she was terrified of him. "What did you think I'd do? Take it lying down? Let you ruin my life without so much as a whimper?"

"*Ruin your life?* I don't think a—a child has to ruin your life!"

She didn't understand, would never understand. If he ever had a kid, he didn't want to be a part-time dad; he wanted to be the father he'd never had. "Tell the truth!" he shouted. "You've been lying the whole time."

She was now crying so hard she had to gulp for breath. "Yes. That's it. I—I was lying. I'm *still* lying. You're fine. Nothing's going to get in the way of you living your life. You can leave. There's no baby."

Her sudden reversal shocked him. He felt as if she'd knocked the wind from him. As long as she'd been trying to plead her case, trying to convince him, he could fight her, vent his disappointment in the situation and himself. But what was he supposed to do now that she was no longer resisting? She'd taken back everything she'd said, given him the opportunity to leave as if this encounter had never taken place—and he was tempted.

He wanted to forget the whole thing, pretend he *didn't* know. But he could never do that, which meant he had no way out.

"Hey!"

They both turned to see that a man acting in some official capacity—Hudson guessed he was the motel manager—had opened the door and was poking his head in. "I've been getting complaints about the noise. Everything okay?"

Hudson nearly sent the guy away, but Ellie spoke before he could.

"No." She sidled toward the manager as if he was her salvation. "Everything *isn't* okay. I need you to call the police."

"Hudson King?" The man's face registered shock when he realized who'd been causing the commotion.

"This isn't what it appears to be," Hudson said. "We're not fighting, exactly. Not physically, anyway. And I'll pay for the Sheetrock." He pulled several bills from his pocket, way more than the repairs could ever cost, and tossed them on the bed.

"I'm more worried about her than the wall," the guy said.

Hudson raised his hands. "I haven't hurt her. Tell him I haven't hurt you."

"He h-hasn't hurt me," she admitted, sniffing and wiping her wet cheeks. "But he could. I want him gone. This is *my* room, and he's no longer welcome in it."

"What?" Hudson said. How dare she act like the injured party? So he'd raised his voice a little. Look what she'd done to him!

"If you leave this minute, we'll just forget this ever happened," she said. "Otherwise—"

"Wait." Hudson scrubbed his face with one hand. She was still going with the "drop everything" approach. But he couldn't do that, not now. "We still need to talk. Nothing's been resolved."

"Yes, it has," she said. "I'm done. I did what I felt was right, and you didn't want to hear it, so...we'll leave it there."

A new surge of frustration made him feel he was all tied up

in knots. So now she was cutting him out? She came here, devastated him, and then…it was goodbye? "But—"

"Mr. King?" The motel manager interrupted before he could argue with her.

"Don't call the cops!" Hudson lifted a warning finger. "I'm sorry for the noise, but I haven't done anything except put a hole in the wall, which I've paid for."

"I understand. I'm glad you're taking care of it. But you're causing a disruption. And, let's face it, you're awfully angry. I can tell your poor girlfriend's scared to death."

Girlfriend? That made Hudson want to punch the wall again. "I'd never hurt her or any other woman!" He was irritated that anyone would even suggest it, but neither attempted to reassure him. Hudson got the impression they didn't fully believe him, which only twisted him up worse.

"If you leave, there'll be no need to get anyone else involved," the motel manager said as he gathered the money and backed away again. "Let's just… Let's just get you out of here, okay? Look at her. She's shaking like a leaf."

Hudson couldn't help feeling a little shocked when he looked at her objectively. She did seem frightened. He hadn't done anything *too* bad, but he realized then that they were reacting to what he *could've* done. She didn't trust him any more than he trusted her. "She brought this on herself," he muttered, but he was no longer so sure. That sudden denial of hers at the end, when she'd been saying anything just to mollify him and get him to leave, had stolen the fire from his anger. What if, despite all the unlikely circumstances—including the fact that she'd provided the faulty birth control—this really was just one of those things? A surprise that no one had planned?

Maybe, the night they met, she hadn't known the condoms weren't reliable. Maybe she'd been as innocent as she claimed. If that was the case, he shouldn't have accused her, shouldn't have shaken her up. But he didn't know *what* to think. The realization that he was now facing the very mistake he'd tried his hardest to avoid made him nauseated.

So what should he do? He felt as if she'd driven him into the turf better than any lineman he'd ever faced. His head was swimming so badly he couldn't get his bearings.

"This way," the manager coaxed him. "Come on, now. I don't want any trouble."

Hudson couldn't let him call the police. He knew what the media would make of the fact that he'd acted badly with a woman in a motel room. They'd exaggerate everything, paint this little incident as much worse than it was, and then he'd be like all the other guys who'd given professional football players a bad name. He'd sworn he'd never do anything like that—which was why he conceded. "There's not going to be any trouble. Look, I'm leaving."

The motel manager backed out of the door as soon as Hudson reached it. The man seemed as scared as Ellie. Given that, Hudson had to admire the way he continued to insist.

At the last second, Hudson stopped and turned to Ellie. He felt he should say something. This had gone so badly. "I'll call you later, when…when I've had a chance to calm down, okay?"

"No, don't bother," she said. "I don't ever want to hear from you again."

CHAPTER TEN

Ellie couldn't pack fast enough. She was getting out of Silver Springs right away. She'd delivered the news. Hudson could pretend it wasn't true if he wanted to. She was fine with that. She just hated that coming here had ruined her image of him. Otherwise, she could've continued to remember their time together fondly.

After she pulled her small suitcase off the bed, she nearly fell herself. She didn't have her normal strength, needed to eat. She opened the wrapping on the sandwich she'd bought earlier and shoved a bite in her mouth, then checked outside to see if the coast was clear.

Hudson seemed to be gone. The motel manager was just walking back from having seen him off. Since he was coming to her door, probably to follow up and make sure she was okay, she stepped out and rolled her suitcase to her rental car.

"You're leaving?" he asked as he watched.

"As soon as possible," she responded.

"But I have you down for two nights."

She wasn't about to let that stop her. "Credit me what you can. Keep the rest." If she couldn't change her plane reservations, she might have to pay for a motel in Los Angeles, but she didn't care if she ended up paying twice. Anything was preferable to staying here.

He frowned and shoved his hands in his pockets as she went back inside the room to get her computer, her purse and the rest of her food. "For what it's worth, I'm really surprised by Hudson's behavior," he said when she came out with the rest of her things. "I've never heard of him being violent with anyone—least of all a woman or a child. Most everyone around here sings his praises, especially Aiyana out at New Horizons."

"Of course Aiyana loves him. He gives her a lot of money for the school."

"Yeah, but he also spends a lot of time out there, helping the boys."

"That's nice of him," she said, but there was no true admiration in her voice or her heart. All she could think about was the cold, hard look on his face when he'd advanced on her, and how decisively he'd talked about driving her to LA to get an abortion. This baby had already become real to her. Just last week she'd felt the first butterfly-like movement in her womb—proof of life—and had been contemplating names. Heck, she'd even started preparing the extra bedroom in her home as a nursery. What had ever possessed her to make this trip?

She'd been delusional, she decided, too honest for her own good and far too optimistic about the type of man she'd gotten involved with.

The manager told her he could credit her for one night. She thanked him, and that was it. As she pulled out of the parking lot, she said a silent *good riddance* to Hudson and the upsetting encounter they'd had. She was going back to her peaceful, steady life. Maybe it wasn't exciting, but at least she wasn't subjected to the whims of a pompous, overbearing professional football player. Once he understood that she didn't expect anything from him—even support for their child—he'd forget about her.

She hoped.

Hudson felt terrible.

He felt terrible about bringing a child into a less-than-ideal situation, and that the child might feel the repercussions.

He felt terrible that he'd blamed Ellie for lying, if she wasn't. (He still wasn't quite sure about that; their encounter in September had been so unusual.)

He felt terrible for acting like a belligerent bully in front of her and the motel manager of The Mission Inn. They had to think he was some kind of monster.

Bottom line, he hadn't felt worse in a long, long time.

"Shit," he muttered as he prowled around his house. He needed to go back to the motel, needed to talk to Ellie again. She wouldn't be happy to see him, but he'd behave much better this time, be more diplomatic. To begin with, he'd set his doubts aside in favor of trying to solve the problem at hand. And that was...what to do about the baby? He'd have a paternity test conducted once the child was born—to be absolutely sure—but Ellie was so certain he was the father that he suspected she was right. They hadn't made love only once. They'd made love three times, which raised the chances, and each encounter had been gloriously messy and primal and uninhibited. He hadn't noticed a leaking or broken condom, but that would be easy to miss. It wasn't as though he'd ever turned on the lights to examine what they'd used. He'd just gone into the bathroom and gotten rid of it.

So...he needed to look at this situation as if he *hadn't* been duped. He needed to take a deep breath and wrap his head around a different future than the one he'd envisioned for himself. He'd be a father before he became a husband. He couldn't escape that now, so he had to figure out a way to accept it. But as if that wasn't bad enough, his child would arrive in four months. He had very little time to prepare mentally or emotionally and, even worse, he or she would live clear across the country.

How could he be a decent father if he saw the kid only every couple of months?

He had no answer for that.

"Shit," he said again. He'd been cursing ever since he'd met up with Ellie today. If something like this *had* to happen, why couldn't he have gotten some local girl pregnant?

After everything he'd done to avoid getting *anyone* pregnant! All the nights he'd spent in his hotel room when his teammates were entertaining prostitutes down the hall. All the craziness he'd avoided when various friends had invited him to Vegas—and he'd called it a night when the groupies showed up. This wasn't fair, he thought, then stopped himself. He couldn't go back down that road. That would only rile him up again.

Once he was calm enough to stop pacing, he was tempted to go to bed, pull the pillow over his head and not wake up for several days. But Ellie was in town only for tomorrow. He had to deal with this problem while she was still here.

Remembering something about her that he wanted to check out, he went into his office, where he'd left his laptop. When they'd met, she'd said she was a scientist specializing in immunology. And when they'd talked later, she'd made that seem believable, with everything she knew about the moon and the stars, even the tides. She was educated, and someone as educated as she was would be unlikely to try to trap him with a pregnancy. Someone like Ellie could earn her own living. Besides, how would she have known he was going to be at Envy in the first place?

Now that his more rational self seemed to be making a comeback, he glanced at the note Ellie had left with Aiyana to make sure he spelled her last name correctly as he typed it into a Google search. Although he didn't expect anything too detailed or revealing to pop up, he didn't have to sift through several pages to find a link. The very first one took him to the webpage for the Banting Diabetes Center, where she worked. He knew that because he found her picture on the staff page, along with her bio.

> Ellie P. Fisher, PhD, is pursuing a postdoctoral fellowship at the Cell Transplant Center at the Banting Diabetes Center, working in the fields of cellular therapies, immunoengineering and tolerance induction for the cure of type 1 diabetes.

There she was. If only he'd had her last name, he could've tracked her down months ago. She really didn't seem like a woman who'd sabotage a condom in order to get pregnant. That kind of person typically wasn't a respected scientist. That made him feel less cheated, but it also made him feel like an ass. If she *didn't* trick him, she must've been as surprised and unprepared for the pregnancy as he was. Winding up in bed together wasn't all her fault. Sure, she was the one who'd pulled him into that taxi, but he'd been more than happy to let her. He was the one who'd pressed her up against the car and kissed her, wasn't he?

Wincing as he remembered punching a hole in the wall of her motel room, he stared down at his swollen knuckles. "Shit," he grumbled again and, with a deep sigh, forced himself to get up and find his phone.

He'd put Ellie into his contacts, so it wasn't hard to bring up her number. He considered calling her but decided she might be more receptive to a text, since that was less intrusive.

Hey, it's Hudson. I'm sorry for how I behaved, he wrote. I won't ever treat you that way again.

No response.

Can we talk? he wrote.

She ignored that, too. He spent the next two hours moving

restlessly through the house, trying to decide whether he should give up on the texts and call. He'd just made the decision to go ahead when he finally got an answer from her.

We have nothing to talk about. I don't want anything from you. No money. No support. Nothing. You're free to go on with your life as if you never heard from me.

"Oh, hell," he muttered and scratched his neck as he considered his own response.

I didn't mean to sound stingy. I'll help, of course. You know I can afford it. This isn't about the money. It was never about the money. I was…taken off guard.

I honestly don't need you, came her reply. I can take care of myself and the baby. No worries. Have a good life.

"Have a good life?" He raked his fingers through his hair, which he'd been doing quite a bit. I'm going to ignore that, since I know you're mad and I deserve it. But, seriously, I won't stick you with all the expenses, he wrote.

Nothing.

I'll be generous, he added. He meant that, but he was also hoping to entice her to reenter the conversation.

Sadly, it didn't work. And when he tried to call her, she wouldn't pick up.

After he'd tried her another five times, she broke down and texted him again.

Please quit harassing me, or I'll change my number. It was a mistake to give it to you. I had no idea you were abusive when I did that.

I'm not abusive! You just…took me by surprise.

Do you think I was happy when I first got the news?

I'm sure you weren't. I feel bad about that now. I'll apologize again, if that will help.

Like I said, don't bother. I've seen all I need to see.

He felt a moment's panic.

So you're cutting me off from the baby?

If you'd like to see the baby, you can send a letter to my place of employment at the Banting Diabetes Center after June 10. I'm not due until then. You'll find the address online.

I have rights, you know, he wrote, but he could tell that wasn't the direction to go, either, because she wouldn't respond to him at all after that.

Hudson doubted he'd ever had a worse night's sleep. As the wind and rain from the storm he'd been expecting lashed the house, he'd forced himself to leave Ellie alone so she'd have a chance to recover from their argument, but it hadn't been easy to sit back and do nothing. He craved some form of resolution. He knew he couldn't push her too hard. God forbid she got it in her head that he *was* really harassing her. A public scandal would only make this worse. It was going to be difficult to keep a lid on what was happening as things stood.

He got up at first light—didn't see any point in continuing to toss and turn—and stared out the kitchen window to see that the rain had stopped. As he made coffee, he repeatedly checked his phone. She had to answer him sometime, didn't she?

Apparently not, he realized as the minutes dragged by. Maybe she'd even blocked him…

Hello? he texted. Will you please meet with me today?

At last he heard a ding, but he wasn't happy with what he read. Write the BDC after June 10.

He wouldn't wait that long. He was going over there to confront her. She *had* to talk to him. But he needed to be smarter this time. He figured he'd go to the office first and ask the manager to accompany him to her door. With someone else there, chances were she'd give him a few minutes. Once he convinced her that he wouldn't go ballistic again, maybe she'd let him in. Worst case, he hoped to work out a six-months-on/six-months-off arrangement. He hated the idea of missing half his child's life. For him, stability was everything, since it was what he'd never had. But splitting each year meant he could take the baby in the winter, after football season ended and he wasn't so busy.

Getting his keys, he rushed out of the house. But then he made himself go back and shower and shave. He had to look civil, unthreatening, presentable. He even splashed on some cologne.

There, he thought as he studied himself in the mirror. He didn't appear dangerous. Other than his bloodshot eyes and the tightness of his jaw, evidence that he'd had a rough night, he simply looked like the jock he was supposed to be.

"Here's hoping," he said and grabbed the card Ellie had given Aiyana. He thought it might help him convince the motel manager that she'd come to Silver Springs planning to meet with him.

"What do you mean, she's not here?"

The same manager Hudson had met yesterday—Monty, according to his name tag—was manning the front desk. "What I said. She cut out right after you left."

Hudson's heart sank. "But I need to talk to her."

Monty made a clicking sound with his tongue. "I'd say it's best you leave her alone."

Like hell. She was carrying his kid. "Did she mention where she was going?"

"Back to Miami, I guess," he said with a shrug. "That's where she's from. I told her I'd have to charge her for the stay, but she didn't care. I did credit one night," he added, as if that mattered to anyone besides Ellie.

"She lives in Cooper City." She'd told him that much at the club. "Can you give me her address?"

"Sorry, no. I'm not allowed to give out that kind of information."

The keys in Hudson's hand dug into his fingers as he tightened his grip on them. "But you did take a copy of her driver's license."

"Of course. That's standard operating procedure."

"So you could call that up on the computer—and you could easily give me her address."

His eyes widened. "Except I can't, like I said."

"Why not? Who would know?"

The guy seemed flustered. "I would! What if I gave you her address and she ends up getting beaten or...or murdered? I wouldn't want to be responsible for the next Nicole Simpson!"

He must've acted even crazier yesterday than he remembered—or this guy had one hell of an imagination. "That's ridiculous. I would never hurt her or anyone else," he snapped and stormed out. He didn't need the manager. He could get that information easily enough from his private investigator. And he proved it. After one phone call and an hour's wait, he had what he was looking for.

CHAPTER ELEVEN

Ellie couldn't change her flight, not without significant added expense. It was cheaper to get a motel room until she could leave town, so that was what she did.

Since she was in LA, she told herself she'd do a little sightseeing on her free day. Forget Hudson; enjoy herself. But she never made it out of the room. She couldn't stop crying. She wasn't even sure what she was crying over. That was the weird thing. She just couldn't shut off the waterworks, not with pregnancy hormones working against her.

Once the worst of her crying jag was over, she spoke to Amy, who was anxious to hear how her meeting with Hudson had gone.

Amy wasn't too happy once she learned. She called him a big jerk and used several other choice words. But she ended the conversation with an optimistic "You don't need him."

Although Ellie agreed, she wasn't entirely convinced she was rid of Hudson for good. That last line he'd texted her—*I have rights, you know*—made her uneasy, which was probably why she hadn't mentioned that part of their exchange to Amy, hadn't mentioned anything that had happened after he left her motel room.

Hoping he'd forget about her and the baby, that everything

would be okay despite the terrible choice she'd made to alert him, Ellie decided to look forward and not back. But she was still depressed the next day, especially on the flight home, when she came down with a headache and chills. She tried to convince herself it was only morning sickness, especially when the nausea kicked in. But she hadn't experienced much of that so far, and morning sickness was supposed to ease in the second trimester, not suddenly appear.

By the time her plane landed in Miami, she was afraid she was getting the flu.

"You can make it," she groaned as she hurried to catch the bus that would take her to long-term parking, where she'd left her car.

"You okay, miss?"

She'd just sat down, closed her eyes and rested her head on the back of the seat. She hadn't paid the bus driver much attention when she handed him her carry-on, but judging by the concern in his voice, he'd noticed that she wasn't looking well. She wasn't feeling well, either.

Forcing her eyelids open, she attempted to reassure him. "I'll be fine," she said and slid over to make room for other passengers.

The repeated jerk of the bus as it started and stopped several times nearly caused Ellie to throw up.

Somehow, miraculously, she managed to hang on to the small dinner she'd had on her layover in Houston and considered herself lucky when she reached her car without an embarrassing incident.

After tossing her luggage in the trunk, she took off, eager for the privacy and comfort of her home. It was getting late—nearly eleven—and the flight had been long and crowded, with a child kicking the back of her seat. She couldn't wait to fall into her own bed.

When she arrived, she left her key in the door and didn't even bother to turn on the lights. She was in too much of a hurry to reach the bathroom. But as she dashed across the floor, she tripped over a pair of long legs that weren't supposed to be there and hit her head on the corner of the coffee table.

"Ouch!" she cried at the blinding pain. "Don? What the hell are you doing in my house?"

A male voice responded, but it didn't belong to her ex-fiancé. "Holy shit! Are you okay?"

Hudson. Her brain registered his identity as he jumped up and lifted her to her feet. "I'm sorry."

While attempting to rub the pain from her temple, she encountered a wet substance that had to be blood. "What are you doing here, hiding out in the dark?" she asked as she staggered over to flip on the light.

He squinted against the sudden brightness but looked positively mortified when he saw her wound. "Yikes! Are you okay?"

"No, I'm not okay!" She scowled as she pressed her palm to her aching head. "What were you trying to do to me?"

"I wasn't trying to do anything to you! I came to talk. But you weren't here, and I fell asleep while I was waiting. I had no idea it'd grown dark or that you'd gotten home or anything else until…until you fell."

But she'd left him in California the day before yesterday. What was he doing in Miami? "How'd you beat me across the country?"

"When I went back to the inn, and you were gone, I made arrangements to leave as soon as possible. Took the first direct flight, which left at dawn this morning."

Her flight hadn't left until one. And, trying to save money, she'd accepted an itinerary that included a layover. That was how he'd beaten her. But there were still a lot of other things that didn't make sense. They hadn't even known each other's last name until three days ago. And here he was, sleeping *in her house*! "How'd you get my address?"

He didn't answer right away.

"Hello?" she prompted.

"It's called a reverse directory," he muttered.

"A *what*?"

"On the internet."

She was fairly sure her address wasn't anywhere on the internet, but she didn't argue. She'd never attempted to look it up, so she figured there could be a site out there. In this day and age, there seemed to be no privacy, so that wouldn't be entirely surprising. "You haven't explained how you got inside my *locked* house."

"That wasn't hard, either."

She stared down at the blood she'd gotten on her fingers from touching the cut on her temple. *"You broke in?"*

"No! Of course not. That would be illegal. I used the key under the rock by the back door." He tilted his head to catch her attention, since she was still a little dazed. "That's not a smart place to hide a spare, by the way. Just because it's in the back doesn't mean no one'll look there."

"Obviously, if you found it," she said. "But…you had no right to help yourself, to…to invade my personal space."

"I *had* to resort to this! We need to talk, and you won't answer when I text or call!"

"That should tell you something." She swayed on her feet. He reached out to steady her, but she moved back and used the wall instead.

"It does tell me something—just not what I want to hear." He grinned, turning on the old quarterback charm.

His smile was so alluring, Ellie looked away before she could be caught in its tractor beam. "Do you always get what you want?"

His grin took on a wicked slant. "Usually."

"I can't believe I flew clear across the country to create my own nightmare," she complained. "That's par for the course this year, I suppose."

"Don't be *too* hard on yourself," he said, his expression sheepish. "I'm not as bad as I seem."

"Is there any chance you'll forget I visited California? That I ever…said what I did?"

"No," he replied, and now he was deadly serious.

"I was afraid of that."

He frowned as she wiped away a fresh trickle of blood. "Come here. Let me take a look at that. I don't think it's too bad, but we should clean it up."

She glared at him. "I'll take care of it myself, thank you."

"I'm sorry," he said. "I feel terrible."

"Sure you do. Tell the truth, for crying out loud."

"What's that supposed to mean?" he asked, sounding offended.

"Since when have *you* ever cared about anyone other than yourself?" As soon as those words came out of her mouth, she thought of the boys ranch, but refused to give him any credit for that. She was too angry.

His lips parted in surprise, but she didn't regret what she'd said. Now that her system had gotten over the shock of her fall and that blow to the temple, the nausea she'd been experiencing when she ran in reasserted itself. "I really need you to go."

"Can't we talk first? Please?"

His stricken expression probably would've gotten to her, made her relent, but she was too sick. "Later."

"Why not now?"

She rubbed her churning stomach. "Because I don't feel well."

"You can lie here on the couch. I'll move out of the way."

"Not tonight. I—" Unable to hold down the contents of her stomach any longer, she ran to the bathroom.

Once she was done vomiting, she hugged the toilet because she was too weak to get up. "I need you to go!" she gasped.

When she didn't get a response, she tried to yell. She hated the idea of Hudson being out there, listening to her retch. Not only was her head pounding and her stomach churning, she was drenched in a cold sweat, couldn't help shivering as she summoned the energy to yell out a second time.

She never managed what she'd planned to say. She threw up again.

When that wave was over, she rested her cheek on her arms as she tried to catch her breath. "Hello? Did you go?" Her voice was a harried whisper. "*Will* you go? Please?"

"I'm right here," he said, so close that she dragged herself over to the other side of the toilet just to get away from him.

"Oh, God. Isn't what's happening to me bad enough? Leave me in peace. Go back to California!"

He didn't respond, and when she lifted her heavy eyelids to see why, she found him watching her, his expression concerned.

"This isn't because of the baby, is it?" he asked.

"I don't know. I've never been pregnant before." Her head was aching, her heart pounding. She longed to crawl into bed.

"Here," he said. "Let me help you."

"Don't," she told him, but he ignored her feeble attempt to swat him away and helped her up so she could brush her teeth and wash her face. Then he swung her into his arms and carried her into the bedroom.

The third time Ellie scrambled to the bathroom in the middle of the night, Hudson went from mildly concerned to downright worried. He'd never seen anyone vomit so much. He helped clean her up and put her back to bed each time, but he assumed that what she was going through couldn't be good for the baby, either. When he got her to drink some water, it came right back up. And she was listless and clammy, no longer had the strength to even beg him to leave. She didn't seem happy that he was there, but she'd accepted her fate.

After two o'clock, she slept for three hours without interruption. But that was almost *more* worrisome for Hudson. He waited as long as he dared before going in to make sure she was breathing. "Ellie?" he said, jiggling her shoulder, because he couldn't tell.

She didn't open her eyes. She did, however, moan and roll away from him.

"Ellie, how are you feeling?"

"Who are you? What do you want?" she groaned.

He could tell by the sound of her voice that she was being facetious. "If you're really that delirious, I'm taking you to the hospital."

"No," she said.

"Why not?"

"Because it's the flu. I'll be better in the morning."

She could also be worse… "You don't think you could have a concussion? I threw up when I had one."

"I'm sure tripping me didn't help, if that's what you're thinking."

"It was an accident!"

"Fine. If you leave now, I won't go to the media," she said and pulled up the covers.

"Aren't you funny" he muttered.

She didn't comment, so he assumed she'd gone back to sleep. Would she know if she needed to be hospitalized? Could he safely believe her?

He wandered around the house a bit more, hoping she'd improve over the next few hours. Most people didn't show up at the emergency room with the flu, but Ellie was pregnant. And this flu seemed particularly virulent. *He'd* rather be safe than sorry, but she was so resistant to the idea. She just wanted to be left alone to recuperate.

Once he reached the end of the hallway, he eyed the door to the room he'd peeked into earlier, when he'd first let himself inside her small, clean house. Seeing what was in there had taken him aback. He'd closed the door immediately and stayed away ever since. And yet…the memory kept beckoning him.

This time he did more than poke his head in. He walked inside, closed the door and turned on the light.

Ellie was in the process of creating a nursery. He saw a changing table along the right wall and a big box that obviously held a matching crib. Various shades of blue paint dotted the wall next to two different wallpaper samples, one with an animal theme and one with a sports theme. The wallpaper and paint—and the furniture, which was brown instead of white—made him believe she already knew the sex of their child. She hadn't mentioned that, and the room wasn't finished, but it sure looked like a boy's room to him.

He sat in the gliding rocker in one corner as he studied what she'd collected so far. She had a diaper pail, a car seat, a stroller and something he'd never even seen before—a breast pump, according to the box. He picked it up to take a closer look, decided he was glad to be a man and set it back down. Was he going to have a son? If he'd been given the luxury of choosing, he would've asked for a daughter. He felt a sweet little girl would somehow be easier to raise and harder to mess up.

"God, I hope I'm capable of being the kind of father you need," he whispered. He'd be working blind, in a way, because he'd never had a good example. Hopefully, he'd at least know what *not* to do.

A thud startled him. Ellie was up again. And she wasn't doing better. He could hear her bump into the walls as she tried to reach the bathroom. Only this time she locked the door behind her, and when she wouldn't open it for him, he understood that all the vomiting was now coupled with diarrhea.

He paced outside, waiting, until he heard the toilet flush several times. Then he said, "You done? You okay? Can I come in now?"

No response.

"Ellie? Will you let me know you're okay?"

Again, no response.

"Damn it, Ellie! If you don't say something I'm going to break down this door."

She still didn't speak up, but he heard movement and a soft click, signifying that she'd unlocked it.

He went in and found her lying on the floor. "That's it." After grabbing a blanket from her bed, he wrapped her up and carried her out to her car. It wasn't hard to find her keys; she'd left them in the front door when she got home.

"Where are we going?" she mumbled, her head lolling as he put her in the back seat. He knew it was illegal not to fasten the seat belt, but she was too sick to sit up.

"We're done messing around here," he replied.

"What does that mean?"

"We're going to the hospital."

"Don't! Please!" She shook her head feebly. "No abortion. I told you, I'll take care of the baby myself. This won't change your life at all."

He winced at the assumption but could hardly blame her when he'd acted as though he'd drag her out of the motel to a clinic. "I'm not taking you to get an abortion. I would never do that without your permission."

"So are you going to dump me in a ditch? Because there's no need for that, either." She was mumbling, so some words were easier to make out than others, but he understood the gist of what she was saying. "I won't ever contact you. And I won't tell *anyone* this is your baby. I swear it. No—no reporters. No one. I did tell a few people at my work, I admit, but…but only because they were there when…when I saw you on TV. I was shocked, you know? Stunned and…and reeling."

"Stop it. You're not making any sense."

"I'm not?"

She was, but he didn't care to acknowledge that, since he didn't like the fact that she thought he was so unhappy with the pregnancy he might want to kill her.

"I'm not going to hurt you. I'm trying to get you some help," he said, but she didn't believe him. She managed to scramble out and tried to run before he could start the car. That was when he *knew* she was no longer thinking straight. He had to get out, pick her up from the driveway when she tripped on the blanket and put her back in the car. This time he placed her in the passenger seat, where he could hang on to keep her from jumping out while he drove.

CHAPTER TWELVE

Ellie could hear voices—two of them, both female. They seemed to be buzzing around her like flies.

"Sakes alive, that man is gorgeous!"

"No kidding. I went weak in the knees when I walked in and saw him earlier."

"You hadn't heard he was here? The whole hospital's been talking about him, even the patients."

"I'd just come on, hadn't heard anything. Then there he was, big as life. Imagine how shocked I was to walk in and see the starting quarterback for the Los Angeles Devils sleeping in a chair."

"Yeah, I would've gone a bit weak in the knees myself. You should've seen how he charmed Lois to get her to arrange this private room. I've never seen her be so accommodating to anyone."

"She's a big football fan."

"She is?"

"You didn't know? Talks about the Dolphins all the time."

"To be honest, I try to avoid her if I can."

This was said in a low voice that gave Ellie a fairly good indication of how at least one of Lois's coworkers viewed her.

"I'm glad I was there when Hudson approached her this morning, though," the voice went on. "I thought she'd faint when he introduced himself and gave her that smile. 'Come on, now. You gotta have somethin',' he said when she tried to tell him we had no more private rooms, and that was all it took. We were busy cleaning this room in an instant."

The women laughed and one of them lifted Ellie's arm. The rhythmic whoosh of air sounded as a blood pressure cuff tightened around Ellie's biceps.

These women were nurses, she realized, summoning the strength to raise her eyelids so she could look around. She was in a hospital. She remembered hardly anything about the time she'd spent here so far—had no idea how long it'd been since she arrived, for instance—but she did recall the terrible plane ride from California, the jolting of the bus she'd taken to long-term parking and being sick at home.

Thank God the nausea was gone. She was only a bit groggy and weak. And her stomach felt tender from throwing up so often—

Adrenaline shot through her. The baby! Had she lost it?

She bolted upright, startling both the nurse who was trying to get her blood pressure and the one who was tucking her feet more securely beneath the blankets. "My baby! Is my baby okay?" she asked, appealing to one and then the other.

The nurse who'd been taking her blood pressure, a young blonde by the name of Amber, according to the badge on her uniform, shushed her and righted the cuff so she could start over, while an older, heavyset brunette by the name of Judy came up on the other side and patted her shoulder. "Don't worry, honey. The baby should be fine. You're scheduled for an ultrasound in a few minutes to confirm it. I wasn't here when you were first admitted, but I was told the doctor located a heartbeat, no problem."

Too weak and dizzy to remain upright without support, Ellie dropped back onto her pillow. If the baby had a heartbeat, he was alive.

She dragged in a gulp of air as that registered, calming her. "What made me so sick?" she asked. "What was wrong with me?"

Judy answered again, "A nasty flu, from what I understand."

Amber, intent on watching the blood pressure monitor, added, "It was lucky Hudson brought you in. You were almost completely dehydrated. Dr. Evans, the emergency room physician, said it wouldn't have been good if he'd waited any longer."

What would she have done if Hudson hadn't been there?

That was a scary thought, since she hadn't been capable of driving herself and had probably been too out of it to call for an ambulance. *He* was the one who'd insisted they seek help. "When did I get here?"

"Early yesterday morning, around six," Amber said.

"So it's been..."

Judy checked her watch. "Twenty-nine hours or so."

Twenty-nine hours. And she'd slept through all of them. As sick as she'd been, she was grateful she'd had a reprieve, but she felt disoriented as a result of losing so much time. Wasn't she supposed to be at the BDC today? "What day is it?"

"Monday."

"Does anyone at my work know I'm sick?"

"Hudson spoke with someone who kept calling your cell," Judy said. "Someone named Linda? I got the impression she was from your work."

"Did you say *Hudson* spoke with her?" Ellie clarified.

"Yeah. I heard him say you were in the hospital."

"So he has my phone, or..."

Amber, finished with her blood pressure, recorded her readings and folded up the cuff. "Isn't it right there, next to your purse?"

Ellie looked over at the bedside table. Sure enough. "I brought it with me?" She was struggling to fill in the gaps…

"Hudson went back for your purse and brought your phone, too," Judy explained.

Amber interrupted to say she had to visit another room and hurried out.

"Admissions needed your insurance card and ID," Judy explained when her fellow nurse was gone.

"Did they get it?" Ellie asked.

"I believe so. I remember Hudson going down to provide it."

He'd dug through her purse? Or had she told him where to find those things?

She couldn't remember. She'd been feeling so terrible, she supposed she should simply be grateful he'd handled everything. She *was* grateful, except it felt odd to have someone who was almost a stranger take over—and not just any stranger but *Hudson King.*

Because she wasn't quite sure how to react to his involvement in such practical matters—something a boyfriend, husband or fiancé would've done, which was obviously how the nurses viewed him—she changed the subject. "What time is the ultrasound?"

"Three," came the answer, but it wasn't Judy who'd spoken. Hudson had heard the question as he breezed in.

Ellie could smell french fries in the bag he carried. "What are you doing here?"

He blinked at her in surprise. "What do you mean? I picked up lunch and now I'm back to eat."

"He's had hardly anything all day."

Judy sounded defensive, but Ellie wasn't upset that he'd left. She was shocked he'd come back. Why was he still in Miami? He had her number. They could talk over the phone once she was out of the hospital.

Or was he afraid she wouldn't pick up? "You look like you've been out drinking all night," she said.

Not only was he wearing the clothes he'd had on when she first found him in her house, an abundance of razor stubble covered the lower half of his face, and his hair stuck up on one side. She couldn't say he looked like hell, because he didn't. He couldn't look like hell if he tried. Hence her problem. She didn't want him to appear *too* human. That made it far too easy to forget they really had very little in common.

He tried to force his hair to lie down by raking his fingers through it—to no avail. "Well, *excuse me*. I guess I've been busy taking care of someone who's sick as a dog. What do you think, I should've brought my luggage to the hospital so I could shower and shave after sleeping on that crappy chair?"

She heard Judy make a sound as if she was stifling a laugh, but when Hudson threw her an exasperated look, she cleared her throat. "I'll give you two some privacy," she mumbled and scurried out of the room, closing the door behind her.

"I didn't mean to offend you," Ellie said. "I just… I don't know. You're a public figure. Someone could take a picture."

"So?"

"So with you looking so unkempt, they could assume you're on a drug binge. Or worse. Word could get out that you're taking care of a woman who's in the hospital, which would naturally create the assumption that there's some kind of…romantic attachment between the two of us."

He grimaced. "That's worse than thinking I'm on a drug binge?"

"Well, it's not true."

"I'm not taking drugs, either."

"I'm saying the situation could be misinterpreted."

"Let 'em say or print what they want." He shrugged. "I can't live in fear of what people will make of every little thing I do."

Apparently, appealing to his public image wasn't enough to

get rid of him… "Still, there's no reason for you not to go on about your business. I'm fine now. Sorry for all the trouble I've put you through."

He scowled at her. "Oh, no, you don't."

"What are you talking about?"

"You're not sending me away."

"Of course I'm not *sending* you away. I'm merely…letting you off the hook. There's nothing worse than having to be around someone who's vomiting or…sick in other ways. Surely you've got to be *eager* for the chance to escape." She was certainly eager to finish recuperating without once again suffering from diarrhea while Hudson King was on the other side of the bathroom door.

"Everyone gets sick now and then. It's not a big deal. You should see how many guys throw up before—or after—a big game."

"I appreciate your understanding. That's very…down-to-earth. But I'm in good hands here. There's no need to waste any more of your time."

"I'm not wasting my time." He reached into the sack and stuck a french fry in his mouth. "You're about to have an ultrasound. I'd like to be here for that."

"Why?" she asked.

"Because I've never seen one. And it's my baby, too, isn't it?"

"Are you double-checking?"

"Just confirming."

"Yes. It's your baby. It can't be anyone else's. Sorry that I haven't been more promiscuous," she said sarcastically. "You've got to be hoping for a little doubt. The way I went to your hotel so easily was quite misleading. But what can I say? I'd had too much to drink."

He froze, an expression of concern on his face. "You were sober enough to make the decision. I was very careful about that."

"Sorry. You're right. That wasn't an accusation. I knew what

I was doing. So let me pick a different excuse—I was on the rebound. I shouldn't have gone out that night, especially with a handful of condoms in my purse. Anyway, the doctor checked for a heartbeat. The nurse told me the baby's fine."

He ate another french fry. "I know about the heartbeat. I was here when they put on the monitor."

She widened her eyes. "Was I dressed when they did that?" She glanced down at her hospital gown and realized that, of course, she wouldn't have been. "I mean…covered?"

He swallowed what he had in his mouth before speaking. "For the most part."

She pinched the bridge of her nose. "I can't believe a nurse—someone—didn't kick you out of the room."

He kept eating his fries. "Why would they? I told them you were pregnant with my baby. Obviously they'd assume I've seen it all, because I have."

"As I remember, we never even turned on a light."

"Semantics. I felt every inch of you."

"That was before!"

"Before *what*?" he said.

"Before I was pregnant."

He looked genuinely confused. "How does that change anything?"

"Just because we had a one-night stand doesn't mean… Never mind."

"You're taking it all wrong," he said. "We were afraid you were losing the baby. Like I said, I wasn't looking at you that way."

"I trust that's the truth. It just feels weird that I was exposed without my knowledge or control when there was a…a guy in the room." And deep down, she hated the thought that maybe he was comparing her to some of the perfect female bodies he'd seen in the past when she hadn't even had the chance to make sure she was presentable.

"A *guy*?" Losing interest in the fries, he put the sack on her rolling tray. "You mean the father of your baby?"

"Would you like *me* looking at *you* when you're naked and helpless?" she countered.

"I wouldn't care. I mean…maybe I'd have a problem with it if you were taking pictures you planned to sell. I have to worry about weird shit like that. But people see my body all the time. There's no privacy when you play professional sports."

"Yeah, well, I'm pretty sure you keep your pants on while female reporters are in the locker room. You at least have the choice. Besides, you spend your life honing your body. You probably live in a freaking gym."

"So this is about body insecurity."

"No!"

He gave her a look that made it clear he saw through her. "For what it's worth, I find you beautiful, or I wouldn't have taken you to my hotel in the first place."

"You took me to your hotel because I didn't have a clue who you were. You liked that. It made you feel safe. Otherwise, you would've told me."

"I might've told you if you'd stuck around long enough."

She ignored that comment. "Besides, I wasn't pregnant then. I wasn't throwing up, either. I'd just had a Brazilian, and I was wearing sexy underwear!"

"And you weren't yesterday? Because I didn't even notice! By the way, as long as we're talking about your body, the doctor expressed some concern that you haven't gained more weight. He was wondering if you've been dieting, and that made me nervous, too. You're not, are you?"

She rolled her eyes. "Of course not. I've been stressed out of my mind by an unexpected pregnancy. That's all. You think the surprise has been hard on *you*…"

He frowned at her.

"What?"

"We have to adjust, get you eating more."

How would he have any part in how she handled her pregnancy? "I've got it. No worries. Anyway, I'd rather you didn't stick around for the ultrasound."

His shoulders slumped. "Look, I agree that I didn't react well when you told me about the baby. I feel bad about that. But I knew hardly anything about you. What was I supposed to think?"

"You could've heard me out before rushing to judgment!"

"I was *upset*, okay? You don't understand how much..." His chest rose as he drew a deep breath. "Never mind. I'll apologize again. I acted like a complete jerk, and I'm truly sorry. I'm trying to behave better."

How had their lives become so entangled as the result of *one* chance meeting? What was she going to do with this six-foot-five-inch quarterback who took up so much space in her hospital room—who'd actually *arranged* for this hospital room?

Nothing in her life was turning out the way she'd thought it would...

"Are you listening?" he asked. "I'm being *very* nice, aren't I?"

Supremely conscious of the fact that she wasn't wearing a bra—and was now feeling well enough to care—she pulled the blankets higher. "Yes, you are. The nurses here are *so* excited to see you walking the corridors. It's a thrill for everyone."

"What do the nurses have to do with anything?"

That he created such a splash wherever he went reminded her that he wasn't a normal guy, and she didn't know how to deal with anything else. "You attract too much attention. I'm not comfortable being near you."

He reared back as if she'd slapped him.

"I don't mean that personally, of course," she quickly added. "But I'm someone who'd rather stay out of the limelight. A lot of women love that sort of thing. I'm just not one of them."

"Sucks for you that this is my baby, then, doesn't it?"

"Kind of," she grumbled.

He laughed without mirth. "How ironic."

"What?"

"I have hordes of women begging to have my baby. You should see the letters and pictures that pour in to my agent's address. And yet you wish you'd slept with someone else—*anyone* else."

She sighed. "That's putting it too harshly."

"How would *you* put it?"

"Your celebrity complicates things!"

"That's why I can't be included in the ultrasound? Because people know who I am? Because I play football? May I remind you that football's my profession and the fame that goes with it isn't something I can change? That'd be like me saying I can't tolerate that you wear a lab coat."

"That isn't the same thing at all! I can choose *not* to wear a lab coat. You can't do anything about the girls who scream when you walk by. And it's not only that. We don't have a relationship in the first place, so having you hang around *drawing so much attention* doesn't make sense."

"I'm the one who's been taking care of you. Isn't that what a friend does?"

She might've died without him—or lost the baby. Either way, he'd come through for her at a critical time. "Yes, and I appreciate your help. I do."

"And you've forgiven me for the motel. You said you would."

"Yes." If she was going to hold a grudge against anyone, it'd be Don. None of this would've happened without him, without his betrayal. Even so, in certain moments—when she had the objectivity to acknowledge the marriage would've been a mistake—she could see that, as conflicted as he was, Don had handled the situation the best way he knew how. He'd always put his own interests first, but most people did. "What happened at the motel is over. I understand why you weren't pleased by the news.

But remember, I thought I was getting married. I thought I'd be honeymooning in the Seychelles, a place I've always wanted to see. I wasn't expecting this any more than you were."

"We've both been caught in something that we didn't choose. Just…don't freeze me out because I overreacted—or for something that's beyond my control."

A regular Hudson was appealing; a penitent Hudson was irresistible. "Okay."

His grin slanted to one side. "Thanks. You hungry?" He picked up the sack he'd set on her rolling tray a few minutes earlier. "I brought you a blue cheese bacon burger and some fries. The food in this place sucks."

She couldn't even *think* about eating, least of all a greasy bacon burger. "No, thanks. I'm not interested in that sort of thing yet."

"You have to eat. You haven't had anything since you got home."

"I prefer liquids for now. I'll ask a nurse to bring me some broth later."

"No problem. I can polish off both burgers." He didn't seem at all put off by the prospect of doubling his caloric intake. Given his career, he burned off whatever he ate almost as soon as he swallowed it. But it didn't seem fair that he could eat so much and still look that good.

Adding jealousy to the list of reasons she needed to maintain some emotional distance, Ellie rubbed her forehead. She was trying to come up with a way to approach the subject of how involved he planned to be in the baby's life when she encountered a bandage at her temple.

The moment he noticed, he put his half-eaten burger back in the sack and lowered his voice. "I told them you tripped and fell—that's how you cut your head—and I hope you'll leave it at that. I'd rather not create any speculation about whether I *tried* to hurt you. You have no idea how closely sports figures can be scrutinized. If someone from California reports a shouting match between us at a motel, and someone from Miami reports that you were injured, and that *I* was the one who took you to the hospital…well, some reporter could claim that I followed you back to Miami to continue the argument and…and it got out of hand. In other words, they could make me look guilty of something I'm not."

He hadn't tripped her on purpose. He hadn't even been awake. He had no right to be in her house to begin with, but she wasn't going to quibble about that, since she or the baby might've died had he *not* been there. "I get it. I won't say a word."

"Great." He offered her a smile that somehow reminded her of when he'd pressed her up against the cab and kissed her.

With effort, she dragged her eyes away from his handsome face.

"So…what do you say about the ultrasound?" he asked as he went back to enjoying his burger. "Can I stay?" He lifted his right hand, burger and all. "I swear I won't look at anything I'm not supposed to."

She didn't get the chance to answer. The door opened and a man dressed in scrubs and a lab coat wheeled in a monitor and other equipment. "Hi, I'm Ed Tate," he announced as he pushed the cart to the side of the bed opposite where Hudson was standing. "I'm a diagnostic medical sonographer—or ultrasound technician."

Someone must've warned Ed that Hudson King was with the patient he'd be working on, because he didn't act shocked when he saw the Devils' starting quarterback. He did, however, come off as a little starstruck when Hudson, once again setting his food aside, offered his hand. "Nice to meet you."

Ed's face turned bright red. If he'd been hoping to pretend meeting Hudson King was no big deal, he'd failed. "Same here."

"So it's time for the ultrasound, huh?" Hudson said.

The technician, who'd been pumping Hudson's hand, finally

let go. “Um, yeah. Right. The ultrasound. Are you ready to see your baby?”

Hudson sent Ellie a glance, begging her not to make him leave. “I am. Are you, El?”

The shortened version of her name made it seem as if they were much closer than they were, but she supposed there wasn’t any harm in that. It wouldn’t be too difficult to maintain her modesty, not with the blankets she had at her disposal, so she didn’t really have a good reason to deny him. “I’m ready,” she said.

The ultrasound affected Hudson deeply, hit him much harder than simply hearing the heartbeat. Earlier, there’d been so many people in the room and so much chaos and activity as they’d hurried to get Ellie on an IV and check her vital signs that everything seemed to be happening at once. He’d heard the baby’s heartbeat, but he hadn’t been able to appreciate it. He’d been too afraid the baby would die and maybe Ellie would, too. That was how weak and sick she’d been.

Hudson had felt relief, for sure, but this was an entirely different emotion. When the baby’s image came up on the screen, and the technician proceeded to point out the head, the arms, the legs and even the male parts that revealed the child’s sex, Hudson’s eyes began to burn. He’d never had any blood relatives. Didn’t know of *one.* No grandmother. No aunt or uncle. No cousins. Other than his teammates, who created a rather loose family, since trades or cuts often moved players around the country, he didn’t even have an adopted family he could call his own. Not the kind most people had. He’d been raised piecemeal by this or that adult. A teacher who tried to take an interest. A coach. For the first time, he was looking at his own flesh and blood. He’d finally be able to lay claim to someone on a much deeper level than feeling gratitude for a kindness, resentment at unkindness or, more often than not, contempt for sheer neglect.

It was crazy to fall in love with someone so fast, but his heart seemed to latch onto this child immediately. And that frightened him. He had so little control over this situation. Almost everything that happened, at least in the first five to ten years, would depend on a woman who lived on the opposite coast, one he didn't know very well, who'd nearly kicked him out of the room.

"That's a strong heartbeat." Ed, the ultrasound technician, spoke as if Hudson should be proud. "You've got a future Heisman winner here."

Hudson heard what was said but the words didn't penetrate, not enough to elicit a reply. He was going to have a son. That was all he could think about. When he'd first learned about the baby, it hadn't felt real, but it was feeling real now, and instead of being filled with more of the anger that had sent him into a tirade at the motel, he was oddly...excited.

He would probably never have known this feeling if the baby hadn't been an accident. He'd been so busy avoiding romantic attachments, and was always so diligent about using birth control, that having a child hadn't been all that likely. He hadn't even realized he wanted one—until now.

He cast a surreptitious glance at Ellie. She didn't look back at him. She seemed to be transfixed by the monitor. But he was grateful to have a moment to observe her when she wasn't paying attention to him. His baby's mother was smart and attractive and seemed like a decent person. Maybe he should be glad *she* was the woman in this with him. Based on what he'd learned about her, he felt confident that she'd be a good mother.

That acknowledgment made him feel even worse about how he'd treated her in the motel. He wanted to take her hand, to feel those thin fingers curl through his like they had that night at Envy. He had no idea what they might be to each other—if they'd like or hate each other in the end—but, for better or worse, they were taking this journey together.

He was tempted to tell her how awed, overwhelmed and frightened he was, in case she was feeling the same. He thought it might encourage her to hear that she wasn't alone. But he didn't know how to say those words. And he didn't think she'd welcome any contact.

"Did you already know it was a boy?" Ed asked.

Hudson opened his mouth to respond. He'd guessed, thanks to the colors in the nursery Ellie was preparing at her house. But he couldn't get a response past the gigantic lump in his throat. He was going to have a lifelong connection to another human being, unlike any he'd ever had before...

Ellie interjected that she'd had an ultrasound a couple of weeks ago and had been told the baby was a boy, but when Hudson didn't chime in to show surprise or happiness or *anything*, a curious expression came over Ed's face, making it clear that it was Hudson's response Ed had hoped to solicit.

An awkward silence ensued as the ultrasound technician looked up at him expectantly.

"Hudson? Are you okay?" Ellie asked, once again attempting to fill the gap.

He couldn't answer. It was the craziest thing he'd ever experienced, but he felt as if he was going to burst into tears.

To avoid the embarrassment, he walked out.

CHAPTER THIRTEEN

After the ultrasound technician left, Ellie glanced over at her rolling tray, which had been shoved into the corner. Hudson's food was still there; he hadn't eaten much. By now it would be cold. Where had he gone? Even more pertinent—was he coming back? Perhaps the ultrasound had been too much for him. It was possible he'd decided he didn't want any part of having a baby, after all.

She didn't have time to wonder about that for long because several of her friends from the BDC came bustling into the room on the heels of the departing technician. Her boss, Dr. Carolyn Towers, walked in first, followed by Ned Pond, an associate who worked in immunology with her, Linda Staley, the receptionist at the BDC, and Dick and Diane DeVry from the foundation.

"I can't believe you're in the hospital! Are you *okay*?" Carolyn asked with a sympathetic frown. She was wearing her customary black pencil skirt and blouse. Although she had to be approaching sixty, she wore high heels almost every day and looked ten years younger.

"I am now," Ellie said. "Yesterday, however, wasn't so good."

Diane, who had her thick, sandy-colored hair piled up in a

messy bun, pulled the rolling tray closer to the bed and put a vase of tiger lilies next to Hudson's sack of abandoned burgers and fries. "I hope the baby's okay. Have you heard anything?"

"I just had an ultrasound. He's fine."

"He?" they echoed as a group.

She'd been so rattled by the odd way Hudson had reacted to seeing the baby that she hadn't been thinking when she spoke. "Whoops! I guess I let that out a little early. I was planning to do a gender-reveal party when I had the chance but…that won't be necessary now."

"A boy." Linda, who was shorter and heavier than Ellie, as well as twenty years older, smiled dreamily. "You're going to love being a mother."

Ellie had no way of knowing if that would be true, but there was no going back, so she hoped Linda was right.

"What made you sick?" Diane tucked a loose strand of hair behind her ear.

"The flu," Ellie told them. "Knocked me flat. I got dehydrated, needed fluids. I rarely get sick, but this virus really kicked my butt."

Her boss arched one delicate eyebrow. "You've been under a lot of stress."

Which compromised the immune system. She knew what Dr. Towers meant by that comment and couldn't argue. First she'd caught her fiancé in bed with his best friend from college. Then she'd gotten pregnant from a chance encounter with a man she thought she'd never see again. Recognizing Hudson—playing in the Super Bowl, no less—hadn't helped, because she'd been faced with yet more shock and uncertainty.

"How kind of Hudson to look after you," Linda said. "I about died when I called to see why you hadn't made it to work and he picked up. When he told me who he was, I wouldn't believe it at first."

"Several people have tried your cell since, hoping to get to talk to him," Diane added with a chuckle.

"And?" Ellie asked. "Did he ever answer again?"

"Don't think so," Diane replied.

"So…where is he?" Dick put his arm around his wife's shoulders. "Did he go back to California?"

No doubt Dick, who loved all sports, was anxious to meet him. "Not yet," Ellie replied, although she supposed he could've gone home. He didn't explain where he was going when he left. He'd simply walked out, leaving her and Ed, the technician, to stare blankly at each other.

Dr. Towers lowered her voice. "I'm sorry you're in such a difficult situation. What with the father of your baby living across the country and…and with him being who he is, I'm sure it hasn't been easy."

"No," she admitted.

"I hate to make light of the situation, but there's got to be worse things than having Hudson King's baby." Linda grinned as if she wouldn't mind trading places.

"Maybe so," Ellie told her. "But this isn't anything *I* would've asked for. As far as I'm concerned, Hudson's popularity only complicates the problem."

"At least he has the money to help with child support." Dick was clearly in awe of Hudson's fame and fortune, but Ellie preferred having control over her child's life to money. The more Hudson "helped out," the more say he'd expect in how their son was raised.

"I avoid the spotlight," she explained. "Don't want to be pulled into any of that."

Ned, who was about ten years younger than Linda but married with two kids he'd had late in life, jostled around the others to get closer. "Have you and Hudson been able to work anything out? Does he plan to be part of the baby's life?"

Ellie shook her head. "I can't imagine he will. Not in any *meaningful* way. As Dr. Towers said, he lives across the country."

Diane peered at her more closely. "But you don't know yet..."

"No." Saying that Hudson wouldn't be involved was only wishful thinking. The thought of sending her child so far away, over and over again, made her nervous. And what would happen as their son got older? Would he prefer his father, given everything Hudson could provide, including access to such an elite world?

She'd feel more comfortable if she was having a girl. "We were just starting to talk about it when I got sick." Perhaps it was euphemistic to describe what'd happened between them so far in such amicable terms, but she didn't see any reason to reveal that she'd argued with him in California and tripped over him when she returned to Miami.

"Is there any chance you'd consider giving the baby up for adoption?" Ned asked.

Ellie scowled. "*You're* not looking for another child, are you?"

"No, two's enough for us," he replied with an eye roll that suggested two was actually *more* than enough. "I heard Don say something about it. Know he's hoping you will."

"Don's not going to get his hands on *this* baby," she told them.

"Didn't think so," Dr. Towers said, and the conversation moved on to what was going on at work, when Ellie might get out of the hospital and return to the BDC, when she'd take maternity leave and whether they'd ever get to meet Hudson.

"I wouldn't count on meeting him," she told them. "We'll have an arrangement of some sort, but I doubt he'll be coming to our Christmas parties or anything like that."

They laughed, said it was too bad and probably would've visited with her a little longer, but Don and Leo showed up, and their appearance threw a damper on what had been an enjoyable chat.

"Whoa! The whole gang's here—or most of it," Don said.

"Why didn't you say anything to me and Leo? We would've come with you. Just because Ellie and I have a little…history doesn't mean we can't be friends."

Dick, Ned, Linda, Diane and Dr. Towers glanced uncomfortably at each other. Ellie had more than "a little history" with Don and Leo, and that history had been far too recent to treat it so casually. They hadn't been included because the others had rightly guessed she wouldn't want Don near her, but no one seemed eager to challenge his statement. "We didn't see you when we were talking about it," Diane mumbled.

"And we weren't planning to stay for long," Ned chimed in.

"Matter of fact, we were just on our way out," Dr. Towers added.

Although it wasn't the smoothest of exits, they said their goodbyes and managed to squeeze past Don and Leo, but Ellie wasn't happy to see them go. Now she was alone with her ex and his lover.

When Hudson heard voices, he paused outside Ellie's room. He expected to identify the men as doctors or nurses, but he soon figured out that they weren't.

"It's because you're holding a grudge. Otherwise, you'd see the sense in this."

"I said *no*, Don. I'm not interested." This came from Ellie.

"How can you be so sure?" Don asked.

"Because I've already made the decision."

"You're going to raise the baby alone." This voice belonged to someone other than Don, a second male.

"Yes." Ellie again. "And there's nothing wrong with that. I plan to do everything I can to be a good mother."

"Why tackle this by yourself when Leo and I would like to help? We can give this child *two* parents. And we'd never restrict you from seeing the baby. You could be a big part of his life."

Ellie began to sound exasperated. "I appreciate that, but like I said, I'm not interested."

Hudson almost walked in then, but the way Don lowered his voice made him pause again.

"You must've figured out by now that Hudson King's never going to take an interest. He probably has illegitimate children scattered across the US."

"You don't even know Hudson!"

Hudson was more than a little surprised that Ellie would stand up for him.

"You're naive if you think different," Don continued. "It was a one-night stand, Ellie. You've admitted as much."

"Please, I'm not feeling well," she said. "Can you go so I can get some rest?"

"Ellie, just let me say one thing." This was the second male again—Leo. "I've been trying to let Don handle this. I understand that you can't feel too good toward me, but—"

"You think I feel any better toward *him*?" Ellie broke in.

"I'm trying to apologize! I'm sorry for the pain we put you through, but don't let that make you miss a great opportunity."

"Since when did a baby become an opportunity?" she cried.

"Since you got pregnant with Hudson King's child!" This came from Leo, too—and made Hudson stiffen in anger. "Do you know how many baby-hungry parents would be eager to adopt his son? How much you could get for a baby with those genes?"

"Stop talking about money!" she snapped. "You're upsetting me."

"Leo, let me handle this," Don said. "What Leo means to say is that you might make a lot of money, but you'd never know how the child's being treated if you go in that direction. You wouldn't be part of the child's life. But if you go with us, you'll make the $80,000 we would've paid for a surrogate and an attorney *and* you'd get to watch the child grow up. It would almost be like…the three of us had a child."

Hudson couldn't tolerate any more. Shoving a hand through his hair in one final attempt to get it to lie down, he strode into the room. "Hey," he said when Ellie's guests turned to gape at him.

After setting the last of his milkshake on the tray—he'd gone to eat, since he hadn't had the chance to finish his burgers before the ultrasound—he held out his hand. "I'm Hudson King."

A slender man, several inches shorter with hair dyed black and styled like Elvis Presley's, reached out to shake with him. "Don White."

"Ellie's ex-fiancé." Hudson couldn't help squeezing his hand a little tighter than normal.

Ellie spoke up. "Yes. And this is his partner, Leo Stubner."

Leo was far more attractive. Even Hudson could see that. He was as thin as his partner but had a model's chiseled features.

"Nice to meet you." Hudson gave his hand a shake—harder than necessary, too—and started herding them toward the door. "I'm sure Ellie appreciates the visit, but she needs her rest now. So…if you wouldn't mind."

"No, of course." Don tried to look around Hudson at Ellie. "We'll talk more later, okay?"

Hudson didn't wait for her reply. "Not about my baby, you won't."

Don shot Leo a surprised glance that Leo returned with equal surprise. "You must've heard…"

"Listen, I can explain," Leo cut in. "We know you probably aren't too excited about this…surprising turn of events, considering how…how everything came to pass. So we're offering to step in. Ellie can vouch for the fact that we'd be great parents. And we'd sign anything you require to make sure you never had to worry about child support. We have solid jobs, will take excellent care of this baby."

"It'll be like the pregnancy never happened," Don added. "You'll be able to return to Los Angeles and get on with your life."

"Sounds great," Hudson said. "Except for one thing. I'm happy I'm going to be a father. Oh, and since you were speculating, this will be my first."

"You—" Don started but Hudson didn't let him finish.

"I want the baby myself," he went on, and only then did he realize how much he meant those words.

Don's mouth opened and closed twice before he managed to say, "Oh. Ellie didn't… Ellie didn't mention that."

"She did tell you no," Hudson said. "I heard her. I suggest you respect her answer, because I won't be nearly so polite if you ever bring this up again."

"Right. We understand," Leo said and grabbed hold of his partner as they scooted out the door.

Once they were gone, Hudson rubbed the beard growth on his chin as he turned to face Ellie. "I'm sorry if you felt I shouldn't get involved. But I can offer you a lot more than they can."

"*Offer* me?" she echoed skeptically.

"Yes, and there'd be no shame in accepting. Since we live on opposite coasts, it would be too hard to split custody, at least for the first while. Maybe once the child gets older, we can talk about changing things, but for the first five or ten years, it'd be better to keep him in one place, with one parent. Consistency is important." And was something he'd never had. He'd hated all the moving around, hated never being able to stay where he was already comfortable.

"You're suggesting that…*you* should be the one to raise him."

He could tell by her tone of voice that this wasn't going well, but she hadn't heard his offer. "I'm not saying I *should* be, only that I'm willing. And I'd make it worth your while."

Her eyes narrowed. "In what way…?"

His gut told him to back away from this. She hadn't reacted positively to Don's offer, but Don was her ex. Hudson would never expect her to give the baby up to him. Besides, Don couldn't pay nearly as much and, after seeing the ultrasound, Hudson was willing to make her rich in order to get what he wanted. "They were talking $80,000—I'm talking a million. And you could have contact, too," he said. "I'm not trying to pay you off to get rid of you. You could come out and visit whenever you wanted, send emails, texts and letters. I'd just like to have..." He'd been about to say *total control*, but those words had too many negative connotations. "Sole custody. To keep the child with me."

He held his breath as he awaited her reaction. He'd made her a darn good offer, one that *had* to be attractive, especially to someone who hadn't fully launched her career. With her education, she had decent earning potential, but right now she was working on a postdoctoral fellowship. According to Wikipedia, that paid only somewhere in the neighborhood of $42,000 a year; he knew because he'd checked as soon as he found out about the baby—to see how much incentive she might have to take advantage of him. After all those years of college, she was probably carrying a load of student debt, too. With the money he was willing to give her, she could pay off her loans, live far more comfortably and continue to devote herself to science until she was married and in a better position to start a family. And he wasn't cutting her off from *this* child, wasn't demanding she disappear from the baby's life.

She said nothing, simply turned her face to the wall.

"Ellie, I'm not trying to make you feel bad," he clarified in the ensuing silence.

"No," she said, looking back at him. "I realize that."

He would've sighed in relief except he could see tears swimming in her eyes. "This is hard. It's an emotional time for both of us, and I'm not the one who's pregnant." He smiled, trying to get her to smile, too, but that fell flat. "What could I do to be more fair?"

"Nothing," she replied.

He swallowed to ease his dry throat. "So…is that a yes? I could have the money wired into your account tomorrow, have the custody papers drawn up so we can get this over with as quickly as possible. Is that what you'd like?"

She closed her eyes, but a tear squeezed out anyway and ran into her hair.

"Ellie?" he prompted.

"No," she said. "I won't sell my baby even to you."

He caught his breath. What was he supposed to do now? "Ellie—"

She rolled away from him. "Go."

"Wait. Can't we talk about this?"

No response.

"What do *you* suggest we do?" he asked.

"The opposite," she mumbled. "The baby stays with me. If you ever want to visit you can—for free."

He dropped his head in his hand and attempted to rub away the sharp pang of tension hitting him right between the eyes. "Ellie, please," he said. "This will be all the family I've got."

Fortunately, the appeal in his voice—or maybe it was the sheer honesty—seemed to affect her more than any promise of money. She turned to look at him once more. "You can have other children. You know how easy it would be for you."

"Not nearly as easy as you think. I'm interested in *this* child. I want to be completely involved."

"That won't work. I won't give him up." She lifted her right hand. "And don't raise your offer. This isn't a negotiating tactic. I won't take *any* amount of money."

Of course he'd decide he wanted the baby and then not be able to have him. That was just his luck when it came to relationships. He clenched his jaw as he tried to think of something he could say that might actually be productive, but he couldn't come up with a single idea. "Is there *anything* I can do to make you change your mind?"

Another tear slid into her hair as she shook her head.

"Do you really want to tear this child apart by going to court and fighting over custody?" he asked. "That could take years. It could get bitter. It would cost a fortune. No one would benefit, least of all our son."

"You could choose *not* to take me to court," she pointed out. "I didn't *have* to tell you I was pregnant. I did it to be fair."

So twisted up he felt like punching the wall again, he let go of a long sigh. And then a thought occurred to him. "What if... What if I paid *you* to come to California? To live with me for the next year until we had the baby and could figure out the best way to go from there?"

"I can't move to California," she said. "I have a job here in Miami, a job I love."

"It's a job you'll have to leave, at least for a couple of months once you have the baby, right?"

"Yes..."

"Some women take a long break before going back to work."

"Maternity leave can differ. What's your point?"

"Since you'll be off for a significant amount of time anyway, why not...why not take a leave of absence and spend the rest of your pregnancy with me? I have a huge house. We'd hardly run into each other. But I'd be there for doctor's appointments and for when you give birth. I want to be part of that if you'll let me. We could share the first year of our son's life, which will go by fast—and then... Who knows? Maybe you'll love California. Maybe you'll find a job there you like just as much, and you'll stay. Or I'll get injured or something, which would make it impossible for me to keep playing, and I'll be able to move to Miami." He couldn't leave Aaron now, but after Aaron graduated it would be a possibility.

"You're kidding, aren't you?"

"No. Not at all. It's the perfect solution! I'll pay you $5,000 a month, so you can keep your house and pay your bills. That's more than you're making now, isn't it?"

When she didn't answer, he knew it was.

"Then we'll *both* get to experience having this child," he continued. "That's as fair as I can be. I realize it means you'll be leaving the BDC for a while, but maybe you could return in a year or so. Or I'm sure someone with your skills could find a way to be valuable in California. There're so many good research schools out there."

She wiped her cheeks.

"You don't have to give me an answer now." He didn't want her to say no just for the sake of saying no. "Take some time to think it over. There are a lot of positives with this solution. You won't have to work with Don and Leo anymore. That's got to be good, right?"

The expression on her face told him it was a point in his favor.

"And you'll have fun in California," he added. "I'll make sure of it. There's no better place on earth."

Her phone rang. He heard it rattling on the counter. He hated to be interrupted, since he felt he was finally getting through to her. And while he didn't want her to answer too fast if the answer was no, he wouldn't mind getting an immediate yes.

She tried to sit up to see who was calling however, so he handed her the cell.

"It's Amy," she said, checking caller ID.

"Amy?" he repeated.

"My best friend. She's the one who took me to the club the night I met you. I—I need to take this. She's probably wondering if I dropped off the face of the earth. The last time I talked to her was before I flew home."

"Two days ago?"

"I know it doesn't sound long, but lately...well, she's used to hearing from me more often since the pregnancy."

He took a deep breath to steady his emotions. He'd come up with the perfect solution. He felt it in his bones. Now he just needed Ellie to agree. He understood that might take some patience, which wasn't his virtue, but he reminded himself not to appear demanding or come off like a jerk. He'd already made that mistake once. "Go ahead and call her back," he said, since the phone's vibrating had stopped. "I've said my piece. Just... consider my offer, *please.* Think about how fair it is, how it allows us both to have constant contact with the baby. Meanwhile, I'll leave and give you some space."

"You're flying back to LA?"

He hated that she sounded so hopeful. "No, I'm driving your car to your place."

"*My* place?" she echoed.

"Why not? You aren't staying there. It's clean and comfortable. And I like the privacy. You don't mind, do you?"

She sighed. "I guess not. But how long are you planning to be in Miami?"

"Until you say yes."

Her eyes widened. "And what if I say no?"

"I'll keep asking." He winked as if he was joking—but he wasn't.

CHAPTER FOURTEEN

"So what do I do?" Ellie asked Amy over the phone. She doubted she should be trying to make such an important decision immediately after being so sick. She still felt weak, achy, rattled to the core. But it wasn't as if she could put this matter out of her mind and sleep, not with Hudson in Miami—at *her house*—waiting for an answer.

"Are you kidding me?" Amy replied. "Of all the options you've told me about, I'd take the million dollars! That's like hitting the lottery! You'd never have to work another day in your life."

"I doubt that's true. A million dollars doesn't go as far as it used to. Anyway, I love my job."

"So work when you want to."

"What about giving up the baby? *You* think that's a fair trade?"

"You can always have another baby when you're married and in the situation you'd like to be in before starting a family."

Despite the tenderness of Ellie's stomach, her son was hanging on. His heartbeat had sounded strong and true. He was tough—like his father. She hated that she admired Hudson so much, when he just saw her as part of the problem, but she figured she couldn't be too hard on herself. *Everyone* admired him. "I *can't* give up my baby."

"Even though he'd be with Hudson and well taken care of? Have everything he could ever want?"

She tried to imagine living in Miami with a child in California and couldn't. "Yes."

"Now you *want* the baby."

"You know I do!"

"I knew you'd grown accustomed to the idea and decided to make the most of it. I didn't know you'd prefer to keep the kid over $1 million!"

That was because Amy hadn't experienced the flutter of life Ellie had felt. Amy hadn't seen the ultrasound or spent hours trying to select the perfect shade of blue for the nursery. "This isn't how I would've chosen to go about becoming a mother, but...this child is part of me, part of my life, already."

"I told you not to start decorating."

But that was how she'd managed to recover from everything she'd been through—what she thought about in her off hours, what she spent her time doing whenever she wasn't at the lab. She'd enjoyed choosing the furniture, the color scheme, the wallpaper, the paint and chair railing. She'd also enjoyed shopping. She'd registered at various online sites to become familiar with everything she'd need, and she'd begun to acquire those items. Her baby had brought some sunshine into her life, had brought her pleasure outside work. "I won't let Hudson—or anyone else—have him. I know *that* much. I'm just not sure whether *I* should go to California."

"What do you have to lose?"

"I'd have to give up my postdoc."

"Won't the baby interrupt that, anyway?"

"I have twelve weeks of maternity leave."

"That's not as long as it sounds. A baby is still pretty small at three months. And isn't the BDC going to need someone who can be there during that time? They can't halt their research and wait for you, can they?"

"No. They'll need to get someone to replace me. They're already looking."

"Will they be able to do that? Get someone to jump in and stay for only three months?"

"It won't be easy," Ellie replied. "That's part of the reason I'm considering Hudson's offer. The BDC would be better off if I quit and let them hire someone else to take over. And I'd probably be better off, too. If I give up my job, the pressure will be off. I'd be able to stay with my son until I was willing to put him in day care and find something else."

"Especially if you had financial support from Hudson and weren't trying to live off your savings."

"True. He said if I came to California, he'd cover my monthly expenses—and then some."

"Perfect. Just put him off until closer to the delivery. Then you can work until the last possible minute. What about that?"

Ellie pushed the button that would move her bed into a sitting position. "Some airlines won't allow pregnant women to fly if they're past twenty-eight weeks. That means I'll be here for only a month and a half before I *have* to leave—if I go."

"So…what? You're thinking of going back with him now?"

"I'm considering it," she admitted.

"What's holding you back?"

Fear. She'd be giving up what was comfortable and safe and entering a completely foreign world. "What if I hate living there? What if I regret leaving? What if I feel useless without my job?"

"If you go now, you'll have time to come back if you don't like the way things are."

"True…"

"And who knows? It might be fun. Hudson lives a life very few people get to experience."

Ellie had considered that, too. She'd worked so hard, not only in college but after, that she'd had very little fun. She hated to see her best years pass without experiencing everything life had to offer. "What about my parents?"

"What about them? They're still in Europe, aren't they?"

"They are, but they'll be coming back. If I move to California, they'll hardly ever get to see their grandchild."

"Making sure you and the baby are happy—and that Hudson gets a fair shot at being a good father—is more important than anything else."

When she looked at it like that, Ellie had to agree.

"Besides," Amy continued, "that's several months away. Worry about what's going to happen later after you take care of now. If you wind up coming back to Miami, you'll be near your parents again. Problem solved. And if you don't, they can visit you in California. A lot of grandparents don't get to live close to their children or grandchildren. It's not the end of the world. But you're an only child, so I bet if it comes to that, they'll move out there. They have the freedom and the money to do it."

"True." Ellie rubbed her eyes. "So I should say yes?"

"Why not? Give something new and unexpected a chance. You're not making a lifelong commitment. You're trying to accommodate the father of your child—as long as it doesn't adversely affect your own life, and he's trying to make sure it won't. Fair is fair."

Ellie couldn't help smiling. There'd been times in her life when she wouldn't have taken Amy's advice on anything. "You've gotten good at solving other people's problems."

"What do you think I do all day?" she responded with a laugh. "Cut and style hair?"

"Thanks for your help, Aim."

"You're welcome. Except now I'm kind of mad at myself."

"For..."

"Talking you into leaving. I'm going to miss you."

They'd become closer than ever before... "You can visit me."

"See if he has any single friends once you get out there," she said, and Ellie laughed for the first time in several days.

"I will."

"I have to go. My next appointment's here."

Ellie said goodbye and pushed End on her phone. Hudson couldn't be all bad, not after the way he'd taken care of her while she was sick. That was a fairly reliable measure of someone's empathy and sense of responsibility, wasn't it? She should give him the shot he was asking for. Since the pregnancy would interrupt her work anyway, she couldn't see how it would hurt.

Before she could change her mind, she called Hudson.

"Hello?"

The rasp in his voice took her by surprise. "Did I wake you?"

"Didn't get much sleep last night," he mumbled.

She felt guilty, since that was primarily her fault. "Okay. Call me when you wake up."

"No, I'd like to hear what you have to say—as long as it's yes. Are you coming to California?"

She clutched the phone tighter. "Do you ever *not* get your way?"

"Let me think about that. No," he said immediately.

She had to chuckle. At least he was honest. "I hope I don't regret this," she said.

"You're in?" He sounded much more awake.

"I'm in."

"I can't believe it. What about your work?"

"It'll be better if I let someone else take over."

"Is that why you agreed?"

"That's what made it possible. Mostly I'm doing it for our son, so he can know you."

"I appreciate that. I really do."

"You're welcome. If we get along, I'll stay. If we can't—if it's not a good situation for me or the baby—I'll come home, and… and we'll work out some other way to share custody."

"Fair enough."

"Great. Get some sleep. I'll see you later."

"Ellie?"

"What?"

"Can I come to the birth?"

"Don't press your luck," she said and disconnected.

Hudson stared at the ceiling long after he'd hung up with Ellie. He was sleeping in her bed, which he preferred to being in a hotel, but living in her space, especially without her, felt weird to begin with. Now he'd be bringing a pregnant Ellie back with him to Silver Springs. That was sure to change a few things.

Would he regret handling the situation this way? What if he was wrong about her? What if she was difficult as hell?

The Ellie he'd seen so far made that hard to imagine. Despite her formidable intelligence, she seemed soft and sweet, and her room only enhanced that impression. He'd never been in such a frilly place. She *definitely* liked pink. What with the drapes and the bedding, he felt like he was swimming in a sea of it. The place smelled like woman, too. That was the best part. He could close his eyes and easily pick up the scent of her perfume on the pillowcase—and that scent was one he remembered well.

He should be able to get along with her, he told himself. Even if he couldn't, he had to try. He couldn't go on as if nothing had happened while Ellie gave birth to his child almost three thousand miles away. He'd lived his whole life feeling rejected by the very people who'd created him. He would not allow a child of his ever to feel the same.

His phone rang. Afraid it was Ellie—that she'd changed her mind—he checked caller ID.

Not Ellie. Aaron.

"Hello?"

"Hey, where are you?" Aaron asked. "You told Coach you'd

help with weight training at school today. Everyone's looking for you."

Damn it. Hudson groaned. He'd been so overwhelmed by the tsunami that'd upended his life, he hadn't even told anyone he was leaving Silver Springs, let alone checked his schedule. "Sorry. Something came up and I forgot. Is Coach there?"

"No. He got a phone call and stepped out to take it. One of the players told me earlier that you'd be here, so I came by."

"Can you apologize for me when you get the chance? Tell him to call me?"

"After he's done I can. But are you sure you don't want to drive over? It's not too late."

"Can't. I'm in Miami."

"Doing what? More endorsement stuff?"

"No." He hated to say he'd gotten a girl pregnant. He'd preached and preached to the boys at New Horizons not to be that irresponsible. But once he got home, he wouldn't be able to hide that he had a woman living with him, a woman who was expecting a baby. Within a few weeks, once Ellie was showing a bit more, the truth would be apparent. "I, uh, I've been dating someone out here." He cringed at the way he was stretching the truth. He'd also preached honor and integrity, and honesty was a huge part of that.

"You have?" Aaron said. "Who?"

"Her name's Ellie Fisher."

"You've never mentioned her."

"I should have." Except that he hadn't even known her last name until a few days ago.

"Why didn't you?"

"Didn't think it was serious, wasn't sure it would last."

"What's changed? Don't tell me you're getting married! Is that where this is going?"

"No, of course not. I mean…not yet. Maybe…maybe later.

Some day. But—" he felt he had no choice except to reveal the truth "—we *are* expecting a baby."

This announcement was met with stunned silence. "Wow. That came out of *nowhere*," Aaron said when he finally spoke. "How long have you been dating?"

"Six months or so," he said, stretching that, too.

"What about the women you've been seeing around here?"

Fortunately, he hadn't dated anyone in Silver Springs. "You mean LA?"

"Yeah. California."

"Ellie and I… We haven't been exclusive. She won't be upset, and neither will they."

"If you say so, but—" Aaron lowered his voice "—what's *really* going on?"

"What do you mean?"

"Something's up. You're acting weird. Don't tell me you're moving to Miami!"

"Stop! I wouldn't leave you. I'm coming back. Just wanted to give you a heads-up that I'll be bringing Ellie with me."

More silence. Then Aaron said, "How far along is she?"

Another uncomfortable question, one that would reveal how quickly they'd fallen into bed. "Four, five months," he replied.

"Oh, I get it!" Aaron said.

"What?" Hudson asked.

"You didn't *intend* to get her pregnant."

Hudson rubbed his left temple. He couldn't hide anything from this kid. Aaron was too savvy, too in tune with real life and what went on around him. "No," he admitted. "It happened despite my best efforts to be…safe." He hated to divulge too much, didn't want Aaron running around telling everyone the damn condom broke. But he also hated to have Aaron think he didn't take his own advice. "Doesn't mean I won't do everything I can to take good care of the baby, though," he added. "I'm excited to have a child."

"Yeah, you sound like it," he said, laughing.

"It's true!"

"You're totally freaked out!"

"It came as a surprise. That's all."

He sobered. "Sorry. I won't give you any more shit. I know you're sensitive about kids. Doesn't matter how she got pregnant. You'll make a great father."

Once again, Aaron had exhibited maturity and wisdom. He was a special young man. Hudson was so glad it seemed that, for now anyway, he was going to be okay. "Thank you," Hudson said. "I'll see you soon."

After he set his phone on the white, mirror-topped nightstand, he tried to go back to sleep. He was still exhausted, but he had too much on his mind. Now that he knew Ellie would be coming home with him, he kept thinking about all the adjustments he'd have to make. What would he do if he wanted to go out with members of the team or spend some one-on-one time with the boys from the ranch? Leave her home alone? Or take her with him?

She'd have to establish her own life in California, he decided. She couldn't expect him to hold her hand all the time. But would she understand that? And would she manage to accomplish it? She wouldn't be working, which would make it difficult for her to meet people…

A burst of panic had his heart pounding, and yet he couldn't devise a better solution. He couldn't leave her in Miami, but he had no idea how she'd fit into his life on the opposite coast, what role she'd play.

They'd just have to work it out. That was all there was to it. At least if she was living with him, he'd be able to ensure that she was gaining enough weight and taking care of herself. He'd go to her doctor's appointments and learn…whatever doctors imparted. And, provided he could win her trust, she might even allow him into the delivery room. If he was going to have a child, he planned to experience it all, do everything a father should do.

He climbed out of bed to use the bathroom and ended up wandering through her house, looking at everything a little more closely. A picture he'd noticed on a table in the living room showed Ellie graduating summa cum laude. Another picture showed her wearing a lab coat with several other scientists in front of the logo for the BDC. They looked like a bunch of thin, pale-faced intellectuals—but he found Ellie's nerdiness sort of endearing.

Yet another photograph showed her smiling at the camera with two older people who had to be her parents. Would her folks turn out to be interfering, annoying, heavy-handed? Would they ask for money or expect him to be available to their friends? Or would he envy her because she had the parents he'd always dreamed of?

His heart was still pounding, so he went into the kitchen, opened a bottle of cabernet he found in the cupboard and poured himself a glass. He was sure she wouldn't mind. She couldn't drink alcohol right now, anyway; he'd have plenty of time to replace the bottle.

Fortunately, the wine was decent. For whatever odd reason, it made him feel slightly better that she had good taste in wine. Perhaps it indicated she'd have good taste in other things. He'd liked her well enough in September; he just hadn't known, when he got into that cab, that he was essentially stapling their lives together.

Trying to talk himself down so he wouldn't have a full-blown panic attack, he carried his glass into the nursery and leaned against the wall while he drank it. The nursery wasn't bad, either. He liked her choices—except, of course, he preferred the sports theme to the animal theme. He hoped, now that she knew who he was and what he did for a living, she'd show enough consideration to choose the right wallpaper.

"Wow," he muttered. So much had changed—and in such a short time. But he supposed he should be grateful the situation wasn't worse. He hadn't known much about her when he took her to his hotel. What if he'd gotten another woman pregnant, a woman he couldn't admire in any way?

With a sigh, he pushed off from the wall and set his glass to one side. He figured he might as well take the crib out of its box and build it for her. He'd create a new nursery in California, wouldn't try to ship this stuff, but it gave him something to do. Maybe they'd come back here periodically and would need it then.

He was almost done when his phone went off and he had to go back to where he'd left it in her room. "Hello?"

"Hudson?"

Ellie. "How are you feeling?" he asked.

"Much better."

"Have you eaten anything?"

"They brought me some Ensure."

"Will you be able to keep it down?"

"Feels like it."

"I'm glad to hear that."

"What are *you* doing?" she asked.

He didn't want to tell her about the crib, preferred to surprise her. "Drinking your wine."

"Sounds like you're making yourself at home."

"Figured that bottle wasn't doing anyone any good sitting in the cupboard."

"I guess that's true. What happened to sleeping?"

"Can't. Too amped up."

"You're scared."

Absolutely *terrified*. "Maybe a little apprehensive," he allowed.

"That makes two of us. Are you convinced we're doing the right thing?"

"We're putting the baby first. Isn't that the right thing?"

"I hope so."

"We'll work it out. Don't worry."

"Easy for you to say," she muttered. "You're not the one uprooting your life."

But he'd be making plenty of concessions. "We'll set some ground rules, make sure the situation's tolerable for both of us," he promised.

"We should do that sooner rather than later, so we know what to expect."

In other words, she needed some reassurance, and he couldn't blame her. "Are you saying you want to do it *now*?"

"Not over the phone. Tonight, after you pick me up."

"Are they releasing you?"

"In an hour or so. I just saw the doctor."

"Understood," he said. "I'll be there to get you."

CHAPTER FIFTEEN

Hudson didn't have much to say on the drive home. Ellie took that to mean he was reeling as badly as she was. "How was the wine?" she asked, breaking the silence before it could stretch to the point of becoming awkward.

"Not bad."

"Did you get any rest?"

"Very little."

"Hopefully you'll do better tonight." Although she had no idea where he was going to sleep. She had only one bed—*her* bed. The couch would be miserable for a man his size, especially since he'd already spent one night on that couch while she was throwing up and the next night sleeping in an uncomfortable chair at the hospital.

Maybe he'd get a hotel. Lord knew he could afford it.

"Would you rather have our talk in the morning?" he asked. "You've been through a lot the past few days. Another night to recover probably wouldn't hurt."

She was tempted to put it off, but she wouldn't sleep at all if she still had that hanging over her. "I'd rather resolve everything, feel I have a plan. That should go a long way toward relieving my anxiety."

"No problem." With that, he let the conversation lapse, which gave her the impression he was waiting until they reached the house.

Sure enough, once they parked in her small garage and went inside, he poured himself a glass of wine, carried it—along with the entire bottle—to the couch and sat down. "Ready when you are."

She wanted a shower first. "Give me fifteen minutes," she said and hurried into the bathroom.

The hot water soothed Ellie and helped her gain some perspective. She told herself she needed to look at this as a grand adventure, needed to quit worrying so much. If she and Hudson could remain thoughtful and cordial through the coming years, all might end well. Perhaps their approach to parenting was a little unconventional, with all the negotiations, but they were facing an unusual situation.

She scrubbed and shaved and rubbed vanilla-scented lotion all over her body. After being so sick, she was dying to feel clean and as attractive as possible.

After she dried her hair, she slipped into her big, fluffy robe, made a cup of herbal tea and brought it into the living room.

Hudson was watching an action flick. He hit the off button on the remote as she perched on the wingback chair. "Feel better?" he asked.

When she noticed that his gaze flicked to where her robe came together, she set her cup down and tightened her belt. But she couldn't believe he had any *real* interest. There hadn't been anything sexy or romantic about the past couple of days. "Much. Thanks for waiting."

"No problem." He leaned back. "Where do we start?"

"I guess we start with…exactly how you imagine our lives once we hit California."

"Well, I realize you won't know anyone when you first get there. I'll do my best to entertain you, but I hope you'll make some friends soon, do what you can to acclimate. You'll be happier then, and it's important that we both retain our independence."

"In other words, you're worried I might get in the way of your social life."

"I wouldn't say *worried.* But I don't want to feel guilty for going places without you. That would put me under pressure to always take you with me, and I'm afraid I'd start to resent it."

"Understood. But just so you know, you won't have to feel guilty about that. I'm an only child, which means I figured out long ago how to entertain myself. Trust me, alone time is never a problem for me."

"You say that now, but what if I go out to play pool or poker with the guys? What will *you* do?" he asked, sounding uncertain.

She took a sip of her tea. The warm liquid felt good as it slid down her throat and eased her sore stomach. She was finally getting hungry but was still afraid to eat much. "Read. Study. Research. I have a whole library on my e-reader. Feel free to go out whenever and wherever you want."

Some of the stiffness left his body. "Okay. That's encouraging."

"We'll *both* be able to come and go as we please." She wrinkled her nose as she considered what they had planned. "Perhaps I should get my own place..."

"No. My place is plenty big. And I'd like to be part of everything that includes the baby, which will be harder if we have separate households. I can't see you calling me up in the middle of the night to tell me the baby's moving. Even if you did, by the time I got over there, I'd miss all the excitement."

Ellie gripped her cup a little tighter. "Wow. So you plan to be *intimately* involved in the pregnancy."

"I do." He stated that unequivocally.

"Then…you weren't joking about being in the delivery room."

"No."

"Not sure I'm up for that," she admitted.

"What would it hurt?"

"Besides the obvious—that I'll be completely exposed—I'll also be at my most vulnerable."

"You were pretty vulnerable while you were sick, and I didn't do a bad job. You'll need *someone* to give you support."

"Amy or my parents will come."

"Still. Your feelings could change once you learn you can trust me."

She couldn't imagine having him in the room with her. What if something embarrassing happened? She didn't want to be worrying about that at the same time she was giving birth, but it was too early to argue. "We've got a while. Let's leave that one until later."

"I'm fine with leaving it until we know each other better. But I hope you'll keep an open mind. So what if you'll be completely exposed? I wouldn't be looking at you in sexual terms. I'd be looking at you as the mother of my child."

She was more afraid of how he might look at her afterward—and not because she had any romantic designs on him. Whoever ended up with Hudson would most likely be fighting a constant battle to hang on to him, considering the amount of female attention he received. She wasn't cut out for such fierce competition, and yet…she wanted him to find her at least mildly attractive. But that was all. Letting him get any closer would be too real. The past few days had been real enough. She felt she was already working from a deficit. "We can talk about it when the time comes."

"Okay. Next?"

"What about dating?" she asked. "Are you seeing anyone who needs to be alerted to what's going on?"

"No. Thank God. I wouldn't relish *that* conversation."

"I'm relieved about that, too. I'd hate to feel there's someone in your circle who'd hate me on sight."

"No one will have any reason to feel that kind of jealousy."

"Well, if you start seeing someone who has a problem with me living in your house, we can make other arrangements. Communication is key. We'll have to talk, keep current with what's going on in each other's lives."

He raised his eyebrows. "You're saying we'll be free to see other people, even during the pregnancy?"

"I have seventeen weeks. That might not sound like a long time, but it is. We'd be much smarter to approach the situation practically."

"But…who will *you* date?" he asked. "You don't know anyone in Silver Springs, and that's where I'm staying during the off-season."

She shrugged. "I might meet someone."

"While you're carrying my baby?"

"I admit the pregnancy will interfere with my love life more than yours." That had to be the understatement of the year, but if she expected their arrangement to be successful, she felt he had to be free to do whatever he wanted, and that meant she should have the same right, even if she didn't exercise it. "I doubt I'll get a lot of offers, especially as I go into my…um… bigger months." She laughed but he didn't. He seemed more concerned with what she might say next. "We're just establishing some ground rules, and this is one of them. You can see whomever and so can I."

Surprisingly, he didn't agree as readily as she'd thought he would, even though that was the one thing she'd assumed he'd demand above all else. "If that's what you want," he said.

"That's what I want. So…what's left?"

He shifted on the couch. "Where we stand with each other. What type of relationship *we'll* have."

"You mean the financial arrangements? I hate taking *any*

money from you. I'd rather avoid the accusation that I did this on purpose, but—"

"I won't accuse you of that again," he interrupted. "I promise."

She fixed the lapel on her robe. "It's fine. I can see why you'd jump to that conclusion. And I'm sure there'll be others who think I'm after your money. But if I quit my job, I *will* need you to pay me what I was making. Otherwise I won't be able to cover my bills. And if I'm giving up my life here in Miami, I think that's only fair."

"I agree. I made the offer, and I'm prepared to stand behind it. I'll even give you a little extra."

"No. What you suggested is fine. That's enough. In return, I'll cook, clean and grocery shop—do whatever I can to contribute."

"I don't expect you to clean the house. I—"

"I'll do what I can," she repeated. "I'll feel better if I make myself useful." She took another sip of her tea. "Now, we should probably talk about timelines."

"I'm all ears."

"Most people get three months of maternity leave, but I plan to nurse the baby for at least six, and even though the baby will probably eat some other food by then, it'll be hard to be away. I'm hoping you're amenable to extending our arrangement until our child reaches half a year. At that time, I'll get a job in LA, if I can find something in my field of expertise, so you can remain close to the baby. If I can't find the right kind of work, we may have to talk about me moving elsewhere. In any case, we'll have a plan for the next eleven months to a year, which will allow you to be part of the pregnancy and the baby's early months."

He rested his arm along the back of the couch. "I'll pay you the $5,000 a month as long as you stay. You won't be cut off."

She breathed a sigh of relief to have that settled so easily. "Thank you. I'll just...focus on being a good mother until I can look for work in California." She stood up to signify the end of their talk, but he didn't budge.

"There's one more thing," he said.

"What's that?"

He leaned forward, clasping his hands loosely between his knees. "How do you see *us*?"

Hadn't she already answered that? She rephrased what she'd stated, trying to make it clearer. "I see us becoming good friends." She smiled. "I hope we'll always be kind and supportive of each other. I'll do my best to be your biggest cheerleader—come to your wedding when you have one, embrace your wife, your other children. That way our son can be part of it all, too. I hope you'll do the same for me."

"Of course. But...that's farther down the road. I'm talking about how things will be until we get to that point."

She sat back down. "I'm not sure what you're driving at."

He met her gaze. "What about sex?"

She swallowed hard. "Between us—or with other people?"

"We've covered other people."

"Between us." She hadn't been well enough to feel the kind of awareness he'd evoked in September. But now that she was getting back to her old self, she could tell desire would be something she'd have to contend with, maybe on a daily basis.

"I admit I go back and forth on it," he volunteered.

She hadn't expected him to be quite so candid. "Because..."

"Because I'd never want to get your hopes up that our relationship could lead to a long-term commitment. I'm not built for that. And yet..."

She still held her cup and tightened her grip on it even more as she waited.

"I feel it'd be a missed opportunity, since we'll be living together, anyway. And you said yourself that you might not find someone else to date, not right away, what with the pregnancy and all."

She cleared her throat. "You don't have to worry about me. I'll get through the pregnancy. And if I feel desperate, I'm sure there's *someone* out there who'd be willing to accommodate me." She laughed to lighten things up, but once again he didn't join her.

"That's just it. I wouldn't want you to feel as though you had to go elsewhere. Not when I'd be in the same house. We've already been together. We know we're…compatible." He paused for a moment. "What I'm saying is that I'd be happy to fulfill your needs in that regard and be happy to have you fulfill mine if you can accept a casual relationship."

Part of Ellie wanted to say yes—and suggest they start tonight—but she'd be foolish to put what she wanted now above what she'd need later, when she'd have a child to think about. "That's okay. I appreciate the offer, but we're dealing with such a…tenuous situation, we should avoid anything that makes either of us feel possessive—and sex has a way of making people feel possessive."

To her surprise, he looked disappointed. "If we go into it with the right understanding—"

"No," she broke in. "As generous as it is of you to make the offer… I think I'll pass."

His eyes narrowed. "*Generous?* Are you being facetious?"

"No! I'm being honest. I've never had a casual relationship. I'm the type of person who settles down, not the type who sleeps around. I'm glad you were willing to…to be so transparent about your…limitations, but you don't need to make any sacrifices for me."

He hesitated as if he wasn't sure how to interpret her response. "I didn't mean to make it sound like it'd be a *sacrifice*."

"I'm not offended. Truly. But considering the situation, we'd be foolish to let things drift in that direction."

It took him another moment to respond. Then he said, "Got it. I'll leave you alone."

That she could even be tempted to accept such an offer irritated her. But he was a particularly attractive man. And, as he'd pointed out, they'd already been together, which made it much easier to go there again.

Forcing another smile, she got up. "I'm going to get some rest. I'll bring out the extra bedding if you'd like to stay here, but… I can't imagine you'll be very comfortable."

"No, that's okay. I'll go over to the Four Seasons." He picked up the bottle of wine, which he'd set on the coffee table with his glass, and stared down at it. "Mind if I take this with me?"

"Not at all," she said. "You can take my car, too. I won't need it in the morning. I'll be here packing."

"I'll call a taxi. When will you be ready to leave Miami?"

"You can go without me if you have to get back. I'll join you as soon as I can."

"I don't mind waiting. Just give me a date and time so I can arrange the airfare."

"I'll figure it out tonight and let you know."

"That'll work."

After his cab arrived, she walked him to the door and they said a polite goodbye. Then she made herself some soup and managed a few spoonfuls. That cured her hunger but did little to alleviate the anxiety she felt about the future.

Sleep, she told herself. Sleep would help. But she didn't go to bed; she veered off down the hall. She'd barely grown accustomed to the idea that she'd be taking care of a baby here in Miami—and now that was no longer the case. Could she really give up her job, her house, the future she'd imagined in order to live on the periphery of Hudson's life?

No. Intent on calling him to back out while she could, she pulled her phone from the pocket of her robe. But then she stepped into the nursery, saw that he'd put the crib together—and hit End before the call could go through.

She couldn't renege. He wanted to be a good dad. For their child's sake as much as his own, she felt he deserved the chance.

Throwing back her shoulders, she texted him instead of calling.

I'll be able to leave the day after tomorrow.

★★★

"It's the middle of the night, Hudson. What's going on?"

Bruiser's voice sounded as if he'd been asleep. Hudson hadn't expected that. He squinted to see his watch and realized it was too dim in the living room of his suite, since the only light he'd left on streamed out of the bedroom. He put his phone on speaker so he could check the time. "Isn't it three hours later there? Aren't you going to the gym?"

"I go to the gym at seven. It's now *one.* Where are you?"

Placing the phone on his chest, he covered his eyes with one arm. He was lying on the couch, mostly because he couldn't get up. "Florida."

"That means *you're* the one who's three hours ahead."

"Oh. Damn. Of course. I wasn't thinking straight. Didn't mean to wake you. Tell Jac—Jacquel—Jackie I'm sorry. I'll call you later."

"Wait," Bruiser said. "Have you heard from the detective you hired?"

"He hasn't found anything. Got an email update from him tonight. So don't worry about it. We can talk later."

"Something must be wrong. Give me a minute."

Hudson heard rustling, guessed his friend was slipping out of bed so he wouldn't wake his wife, whose name Hudson had just butchered, and felt guilty for bothering them both.

He was trying to find End so he could hang up when he heard Bruiser's voice come back on the line.

"What's up, buddy? You drunk? You sound like it. I've never heard you slur your words this badly."

Dropping his phone back on his chest, Hudson studied the partially empty bottle of whiskey he'd had delivered to his suite once he ran out of wine. "I might be a *little* toasted."

"I think it's safe to say you're completely smashed."

"Yeah. Haven't been this drunk in a while." Maybe high school. He couldn't even remember the last time.

Wait, it wasn't *that* long ago. He'd drunk a lot at the going-away party when his previous left tackle was traded. He felt as if he couldn't hang on to anyone. The people in his life came and went…

"What are you doing in Florida?" Bruiser asked. "I wasn't aware you had any trips planned."

"Didn't. This was definitely *un*planned." He laughed as though that was the funniest joke he'd ever heard.

Bruiser remained silent, waiting for his mirth to subside. "What do you mean? Tell me what you're doing there."

"I'm picking up the mother of my child. Can you believe it?"

There was a slight hesitation before Bruiser said, "You don't have any children."

"Will soon. I'm going to be a father, like you. In June."

"How?"

Hudson tried to explain, but he knew he wasn't doing a very good job. He kept cutting in and out of the story. When he finished, Bruiser said, "Some woman is claiming to be pregnant with your child? Is that it?"

"*Is* pregnant with my child," he said, correcting Bruiser. "She's not just claiming to be."

"But you hardly ever sleep with anyone! You're so careful, you rarely go out with the other single guys on the team in case they lead you into trouble."

"Yeah, well, guess I wasn't careful enough." That was the thing. He'd let down his guard because Ellie was so different from the overeager groupies the other guys on the team—even a few married ones—seemed to enjoy.

"When did you sleep with this…*scientist*, did you say?"

Hudson tried to pour himself another drink and ended up spilling whiskey all over the table. "Damn."

"What is it?"

He used his sleeve to try to mop it up. "Nothing."

"Are you going to answer my question?"

"What *was* your question?"

"When did you get this scientist pregnant?"

"Name's Ellie. *Dr.* Ellie Fisher. Has a doctorate in immunology or something like that. Happened when we came down for the Dolphins game."

"Back in September."

"Yeah. She's due in June. She'll be showing in a couple of months. Sometimes you can see the curve of her belly now. Blew me away the first time I saw it—and realized what it meant."

"Coming out of nowhere, that would blow anyone away. But…before you go off the deep end, are you sure the baby's yours? That she's telling the truth?"

"I *think* so."

"Yeah, otherwise you wouldn't be drinking so heavily."

"This wasn't supposed to happen," he said. "Not to me."

"It's your worst nightmare. I know. You're in full panic mode. But listen to me."

The room started to spin as Hudson struggled into a sitting position.

"A child is a wonderful thing," Bruiser continued. "You'll love being a father—and you'll be a damn good one."

Hudson managed to get some liquor in his glass. "I can't be any worse than my own parents, right? There's nowhere to go but up." He tossed back another swallow and welcomed the familiar burn. "Why do you think my mother left me in that hedge, Bruiser?"

"Let's not go there tonight, buddy. You pick at the same old sore whenever you get drunk."

He picked at it when he wasn't drunk, too. He just didn't talk about it then.

"Whatever the reason, it wasn't your fault," Bruiser went on. "She couldn't have rejected *you*, because she didn't even know you. You've *got* to believe that."

"What are you talking about? I *do* believe that."

"No, you don't. That's what this boils down to, why you work so hard to keep everyone at arm's length. You don't trust love. But we'll revisit that when you're sober, since you probably won't remember any of this, anyway."

"I *can't* believe it," he muttered after taking another swallow.

"What'd you say?"

"Nothing. It's a boy, did I tell you that?"

"No, but that's cool. Maybe he'll play ball like us. So, how about you stop drinking now? It's time to put away whatever you've got."

Hudson pictured the crib he'd built in the nursery at Ellie's. "I'm going to love my son."

"You will."

"Doesn't matter that I'm not ready for him—or that this isn't the ideal situation."

"Exactly," Bruiser said. "You'll do what your parents *didn't*. Rise to the occasion. I'm convinced of that. But you have the money and you have the time. Maybe they had neither."

That could be true. But could anyone be justified in treating a baby like garbage? Couldn't they at least have taken him to a fire station or a hospital? Why hadn't they?

That was the question, what he was dying to know. If his mother lived in Beverly Hills, she'd most likely had access to money or to family who had money.

Hudson wanted to explain that, but after he heard Bruiser say, "If you could cut them some slack, maybe the rejection you feel wouldn't hurt so badly," he lost track of the conversation. Or he might've passed out, because the next thing he knew, the sun was shooting daggers through the blinds, stabbing him in the eyes, and his head felt like it was about to explode.

CHAPTER SIXTEEN

Ellie stretched as she woke up. She'd slept the entire night, hadn't had to get up once. All her flu symptoms were gone and her stomach felt normal. "Finally!"

She kicked off the covers and hurried out of the bedroom to get something to eat—she was happy to think she might actually *enjoy* a meal—but stopped halfway to the kitchen. This wasn't just another Tuesday when she'd head over to the lab as soon as she'd eaten and showered. Her colleagues didn't know she was out of the hospital, weren't expecting her quite yet, anyway. But now she had to quit her job, say goodbye to Amy and her work associates, pack her bags and close up her house.

Should she call her parents, too? Was it time to tell them she was pregnant?

No. She'd planned to wait until she was seven months, and she'd stick with that. She couldn't handle telling them today, not on top of everything else—especially because she'd also have to tell them she was moving to California so her son could live near his father, who happened to be the star quarterback for the Los Angeles Devils. Since they'd heard about Don's relationship with Leo and her broken engagement, but nothing beyond that, they'd be shocked about the baby. Shocked that she was giving up her postdoc and moving out to the opposite coast. Shocked that she'd somehow gotten intimately involved with a man she'd never even dated.

She wasn't looking forward to explaining how *that* had occurred. Until she was absolutely certain she'd be staying in California, there was no point in having that conversation, anyway. She'd probably wind up back in Miami. She had no guarantee that she'd like California, that she'd be able to adapt to it or that Hudson would remain interested in their child. Once she got out there, he could decide he missed his old life and ask her to leave.

Imagining that convinced her it wouldn't hurt to wait a bit longer to tell her parents—when she felt more stable and confident in the direction she was taking.

When she'd had some scrambled eggs and toast, she pulled out her laptop and settled at the kitchen table to compose her resignation letter. Leaving the BDC wasn't easy. But every time she felt she shouldn't do it, *couldn't* quit, she came to the conclusion that she really didn't have any choice. She couldn't be as committed as they needed her to be right now. They had so many great things going on. And a job with such long hours wouldn't be ideal for the baby.

After she'd finished writing her email, she reread it several times before summoning the nerve to send it.

After it was gone, she closed her laptop and buried her face in her arms. "I hope I haven't just destroyed everything I've built so far," she mumbled. She knew how hard it was going to be when she went in to gather her things and say goodbye…

Amy came over at lunch to see how she was doing and helped Ellie choose what to take with her. She insisted Ellie pack the dress she'd worn to Envy, but Ellie knew how impractical that was. Most of her clothes wouldn't fit in another month or two—and that dress would be one of the first things she'd have to put away.

"It could come in handy *after* you have the baby," Amy said when Ellie almost returned it to her closet. "He lives a more glamorous lifestyle than you do. You'll have to quit being so practical and spend some money on clothes if you plan to keep up with him."

But she didn't plan to keep up with him. He might not even want her to…

Rather than argue, Ellie shrugged and closed her suitcase. "Why not? Doesn't take up much room."

"You don't agree that you might need it?" Amy said.

"I'm not sure what I'll need." At least with Hudson paying her five thousand a month, she could buy a few things when she arrived in California. Shopping would give her something to do, since she would no longer be happily immersed in trying to help Dr. Towers bring her innovative islet cell encapsulation technique to clinical trials. As she'd told Hudson, she liked to read, liked to research. There'd never been a time when she hadn't been pursuing some new academic goal.

God, she was going to miss the lab. Now she'd be without her career, would simply be serving as an incubator for her baby. Would that be enough to keep her from feeling useless?

"You can handle a year. A year isn't that long," Amy assured her when Ellie expressed her concerns.

Ellie pretended to agree, but she still had misgivings.

"I'm going to miss you, El. I hope you know that," Amy said when she had to return to the salon for some late-afternoon appointments. "I'm sorry I ever took you to Envy."

"Don't be. This is an adventure," Ellie said, trying to remain positive.

Amy frowned. "One with far-reaching consequences."

"Life can get messy."

"Not *yours*. Yours has never been messy, because you never do anything wrong! Maybe that's why I feel responsible. I encouraged you to be bad."

Ellie laughed ruefully. "Amy, this one's all on me. I wanted

Hudson—and I acted on that. Now I have to live with the aftermath."

"Who wouldn't want a man like Hudson? That wasn't a fair test."

For a moment, Ellie remembered the way he'd undressed her and the feel of his strong body against hers, but quickly shoved that out of her mind. "It could be worse," she said, turning away so Amy wouldn't see her flushed cheeks.

"True. You could've gone home with some dirtbag instead. I mean...there are a lot of good-looking guys in the world who turn out to be losers or flakes, even drug addicts. You wouldn't want someone like that to be the father of your baby. They aren't all famous football players, you know."

Thinking of Hudson's tirade in the motel quashed the arousal she'd been feeling. "The only downside to Hudson being so rich and famous is that he has the money and power to *crush* me if he chooses to. Someone as indulged as he's been over the past decade might not be easy to deal with if I ever have to oppose him."

"He hasn't been bad so far, has he?"

"No." But, for the most part, she was giving him what he wanted; he had no reason to react negatively. Amy had conveniently forgotten what had happened at the motel.

"Good. Well, stay in touch. And let me know when you'd like me to come visit."

"I will."

After Amy was gone, Ellie looked around. She'd thought it would be difficult to get ready. She was moving across the country. But she led such a simple life, especially since she'd found out about the pregnancy, that there wasn't all that much to do. She'd already quit her job. Stopping by the BDC wouldn't take more than an hour or so. With Amy's help, she'd packed. Clearing her social calendar, alerting her landlord to keep an eye on the place while she was gone and forwarding her mail would take ten minutes at most. She didn't plan on having her utilities turned off or doing anything else even semipermanent until she'd spent a few weeks in California and felt safe about taking those steps.

At three, she checked her phone. She hadn't heard from Hudson all day. What was he doing? Did he have friends in the area? Perhaps he was out golfing with other NFL players. In September, he'd come to the club with two guys, hadn't he? She was almost certain he'd texted at least one friend when he led her out the back way at Envy. But he'd probably been with members of his own team that night, guys who were most likely in Los Angeles right now…

What was she thinking? Even if he didn't have any football buddies here, someone like Hudson would never want for company. She wasn't sure why she kept worrying that he might be at loose ends—except he'd been genuinely kind to her when she was sick. And he'd seemed so crestfallen when he left last night. She'd gotten the impression he'd hoped she'd go in a very different direction on the casual-sex issue. Why *wouldn't* he hope for that? Commitment-free sex sounded good to most men. Heck, sex with Hudson sounded good to her, too. She'd thought so much about the night they'd shared, fantasized about running into him again. But it was a risk she couldn't take. She had to protect her heart or she might not be able to tolerate their relationship at some point, and for the sake of the baby, she had to tolerate their relationship for quite some time.

She figured she owed him the offer of dinner, though. He was, after all, a visitor to the area, and he'd come because of her.

He'd turn her down, she told herself. Even if he wasn't out golfing, he had the money to eat anywhere, and there were so many top-notch restaurants in Miami. But, determined to show him the same courtesy she'd show any other friend who was so far from home, she texted him.

I'm not much of a cook, but the few things I make are decent. If you're not out seeing the city or doing something else fun, you're welcome to come to dinner. No pressure, though.

If he said no, she'd be off the hook. She could relax and enjoy one last evening in her home without feeling she was being discourteous.

His response was almost immediate, though. What time?

Eek! Was he seriously considering it?

Seven?

Sounds good. Can I bring anything? Maybe some nonalcoholic wine or dessert?

No. I've got it, she wrote back. Then she grabbed her purse. She needed to go by the BDC and then to the store.

Hudson showed up in a lightweight, V-neck sweater that made the most of his muscular torso. His well-worn jeans didn't hug his body quite as tightly, but they hinted at the assets he possessed below the waist. Ellie tried not to let her jaw sag when she answered the door. Physical beauty was just physical beauty, she told herself. She had her head on straight. But it didn't help that he was also freshly showered and shaved and smelled even better than Don always did.

"Hi." He seemed a little tentative. That wasn't like him, but they were both in uncharted territory, didn't quite know how to treat each other, and given who he was, she found that uncertainty boyishly charming.

"Thanks for coming." Somehow Ellie managed to sound normal, even though her mouth had gone dry at the sight of him, and her heart had started to pound. Her own reaction scared her, made her fear she was in over her head. How could she ever protect her heart from a man like Hudson?

She didn't have any choice except to try, so she opened the door wider to admit him.

He'd brought flowers—a huge tropical bouquet containing ginger, birds of paradise, some type of orchid and a couple of other flowers Ellie didn't recognize.

"These are *gorgeous*," she said, taking them from him as he stepped past her. "Thank you."

"You're welcome." He handed her a small Cartier bag she hadn't noticed.

"What's this?"

An eager smile curved his lips. "A small token of my appreciation."

"For…"

"For being willing to make the sacrifices you're making. I realize you're getting the worst end of the deal. I don't have to move, and I get to keep my job."

"I won't be able to work in a few months anyway, so it's logical that I should be the one to relocate. I'll get through it. You don't have to buy me gifts."

"I want you to know that this next year won't have to be miserable, despite what you're giving up. I may have come off rather…stingy at the motel, but that's not who I am. I'll be generous with you."

He'd purchased jewelry—at least, that was what Ellie assumed. "I appreciate that. I really do. But I can't accept anything."

His smile faded. "Why not?"

"Because I'd feel… I don't know…as if I'm cashing in on what happened in some way." She handed it back to him. "Thank you, though. I appreciate the gesture."

His eyebrows shot up. "You won't even open it?"

"No. Your money is your money. I don't want any of it—well, no more than I have to take to get through the next year.

I have the ability to make my own way, and I'll do that as soon as the baby's old enough for me to return to work. Until then, the amount we agreed on will certainly be adequate." She held up the flowers. "I'll take these, though. I don't see anything wrong with you making a small contribution to dinner."

He acted stunned, as if he'd never had a woman turn down a gift. "So what am I supposed to do with this?" he asked, raising the bag.

"Can't you take it back?"

"I didn't ask. I never dreamed I'd have to."

"If that's not a possibility, maybe you could give it to one of the women you're dating—if it gets serious enough. I know you said you don't have a girlfriend right now."

He gaped at her. "At least open it before you say that."

She wanted to—if only to satisfy her curiosity. But if she saw what it was, she might be tempted to sacrifice her ideals, and she knew Hudson wouldn't respect her in the long run if he felt she was capitalizing on his wealth or status. "Probably better if I don't."

"*Why?* I found the perfect thing. I think you're going to love it."

She was fairly certain she would. But she refused to put herself in the position of having to feel grateful to him. And why risk putting *him* in the position of feeling she was a little too interested in what his money could buy? Obviously he'd met a number of women who'd made him leery of that kind of parasitical behavior, or he wouldn't have reacted as he had when she'd told him about the pregnancy. "That's the problem." Giving him an apologetic smile, she took the flowers into the kitchen to find a vase.

When he didn't follow, she could tell he wasn't happy, but she didn't know what else to do. She *couldn't* accept his gift. Judging by the brand and the packaging, it was far too expensive. "Do you like seafood?" she called back, hoping they could just move on.

He appeared at the entrance to the kitchen. "Are you still holding a grudge?"

"For..."

"The motel?"

"Of course not. Don't mention it again."

"You know I believe you? Believe the pregnancy was an accident?"

"I do, and I'm glad about that, since it *was* an accident. But I still can't accept any gifts from you. Why give you any reason to doubt my motives? Besides, you can afford better presents than I can, and we need to keep things as even as possible, especially since I have to take a salary from you. What if you start to resent that?"

"I won't resent that." There was an edge of irritation in his voice. "It was *my* idea, the only way I could be part of the pregnancy."

"Well, what you're paying me is enough. Come in and sit down. I can't speak for you, but I'm hungry."

Shaking his head as if he couldn't believe her obstinacy, he tossed the Cartier bag on the counter.

She flinched as she heard it hit the granite but didn't comment. She figured it was best to drop the subject. "I made crab bisque," she said, attempting to cajole him out of his disappointment. "It's one of my favorite recipes, something I learned from my mother. I hope you'll like it, too."

"I'm easy to please," he muttered, but his heart obviously wasn't in that statement. It took most of the meal to get him to put aside the fact that she wouldn't accept what he'd bought at Cartier. But she felt she'd accomplished it by the time she told him about the encapsulation technique she'd been helping to develop at the BDC.

"Your eyes light up when you talk about your work," he said as if he reluctantly found that interesting.

She took a drink of water. After being sick so recently, she had to be careful; she wasn't going to eat anything other than the soup and pomegranate salad she'd prepared—and she'd gone light on the soup, since it was so rich. "What can I say? I *love* what I do. I believe immunology will change the world. I can't wait to see a cure for diabetes—and so many other diseases."

"You're nothing like the other women I've known."

"How am I different?" She grinned. "Let me guess. Less silicone? No spray tan?"

His mouth quirked. "Forget it. Now I'm not going to give you the compliment I was about to."

She sobered. "What?"

"You care about the things that really matter."

She hadn't been far-off, but she didn't point that out. From what she'd heard, LA was the most superficial city in the world—although she couldn't imagine Miami being far behind. "Thank you." She reached across the table to grip his wrist. "I'm sorry about the gift. I know my reaction seemed a little…unnecessarily strict. But it's important for you to be able to trust me *and* my motives. If you feel I'm after something or getting more out of the relationship than you are, it won't work."

When his gaze lowered to her hand, she grew self-conscious. She'd touched him spontaneously, the way she might've touched anyone in the fervor of the moment. She really wanted to convince him of her sincerity. But it was a bit presumptuous, and the level of energy that flowed through that single point of contact wasn't like anything she'd ever experienced before.

Suddenly self-conscious—and far too aware of him in a physical sense—she drew back.

"I should be able to give you anything I want," he said.

She took another drink of water. "Because…"

"That's my decision, not yours."

Hudson liked Ellie. She didn't always say what he wanted to hear, but her basic decency—her kindness and fairness—came through, despite the fact that she wasn't willing to give him whatever he wanted. He felt comfortable with her, normal in a way he couldn't feel normal when he was constantly being catered to and complimented and indulged.

He enjoyed watching her expressions and mannerisms while they finished eating—enjoyed the conversation, too. She knew so much about so many subjects. Academic subjects, anyway. She knew nothing about football. That was the great irony. She looked at him blankly whenever he brought up the game he loved—what most other people *wanted* him to talk about.

"What's a draw play again?" She held her glass as she sat across from him, awaiting his reply. They'd just had homemade blackberry pie—which was about the best dessert he'd ever eaten—and were finished with their meal but still talking. She seemed interested in what he was saying; he had to give her credit for that. But she didn't get certain nuances.

"Don't worry about draw play." He shouldn't have mentioned that when he'd been explaining how he'd hurt his knee four years ago. "It was a broken play, meaning the play never worked. I had to run instead of handing the ball off, and I couldn't slide to avoid the tackle. We were in a third down situation with long yardage, so I had to go for the marker. Even then, I would've been okay, except Jason Strombach came in with a late hit. I still don't know what the hell he was thinking. I was clearly out of bounds."

"He tore your meniscus."

"Yes."

"That's *terrible*." She looked concerned, but Hudson suspected that only the result—that someone tore his meniscus—made any sense to her. "So you had to have surgery? Were they able to repair it?"

"I missed most of the season but returned for the final two games."

"How many games are there?"

"Not including preseason, there are seventeen weeks. Each team—thirty-two in all—plays sixteen games."

"So you missed eleven games because of this... Jason guy?"

"Jason guy?" Hudson started laughing. "You mean Jason *Strombach*? The best safety in the league?"

When he kept laughing and couldn't seem to stop, she rolled her eyes and got up to collect their plates.

"Sorry," he said, trying to bring himself under control. "You could talk about a lot of things *I* wouldn't understand, so I'm not trying to make you feel stupid—if it's even possible to make someone so smart feel stupid. It's just that most people you meet wouldn't understand immunology—not unless they'd been trained in it—but they *would* understand the game of football."

"I'll learn it," she said.

He got up to carry the rest of the dishes to the sink. "I have no doubt. All you'd have to do is watch a few games with some interest."

She turned on the water. "When I asked if they'd repaired your knee, you didn't really answer me. You said you came back for the last two games of the season. That's not entirely the same thing."

He shrugged. "It gets sore and starts to ache now and then. I have to ice it after most games, but I'm fortunate that it hasn't impeded my ability to cut or run."

She turned off the water and looked up at him. "How do people who care about you watch you play?"

She was so serious, he wasn't sure how to interpret the question. "What do you mean?"

"It's such a dangerous game. Aren't they afraid you'll get hurt?"

"Oh, yeah. My agent. The owner of the team. My teammates. The coach. Any Devils fan. They're probably *all* afraid I'll get injured and won't be able to play."

She seemed to think about that for a moment. "*I'd* rather you didn't take the risk to begin with," she said and went back to washing up.

He leaned against the counter. "You don't want me to play."

"No."

He'd never had a woman tell him that. Most of the women he'd dated liked who he was in the world—and wanted him to maintain his status. "It's my job, Ellie. What else would I do?"

She cast him an assessing look. "You're smart. You don't have to play football. You could do anything."

She didn't understand. He hadn't been all that good in school, couldn't have taken the path she did. He'd been too busy rebelling. It was football that had changed everything, made him matter in life. "I love what I do," he said.

"Then I'm glad it's worked out for you, but… I don't think I'll ever be able to watch."

CHAPTER SEVENTEEN

Hudson wouldn't take his gift with him when he left. Whenever Ellie tried to give it back, he'd simply toss it over her head into the room somewhere. After retrieving it and trying to force it into his hands three different times, she gave up. "I won't accept it," she insisted. "I *can't* accept it."

"That's bullshit," he said. "You can accept it if you want."

"How much did it cost?" she asked. "If it was less than $100, I'll make an exception, but that's a nice brand."

"I'm not telling you how much it cost. It's not polite to even ask."

"You shouldn't have done it!"

"Why? I got something I thought you'd like to make up for everything you're going through. Why not leave it at that?"

"I told you why."

"Fine. If you don't like it, throw it away."

"Maybe I will," she said in an effort to overcome his attempt to strong-arm her. But he left without it anyway, and after he was gone she couldn't help finding that sack and digging inside.

She felt guilty when she realized he'd gotten her a card, too.

She hadn't even thought to check. The least she could've done was accept *that* part of his gift.

She sat on the edge of the couch as she tore open the flap.

The card had a beautiful peacock on the front. There was no preprinted message, but Hudson had written a few lines.

Ellie,

I look forward to the adventure that awaits us. Somehow, we'll get through even the hard times and be the best parents we can be.

If this had to happen, I'm glad it happened with you.

Sincerely,

Hudson

She smiled at the last line of his note. That was a nice thing to say.

As she put the card aside, she told herself to leave the gift alone. She'd be giving in if she looked. But her resistance lasted only a few minutes. Unable to quell her curiosity, she removed the tissue paper, opened a small box that held another box—this one made of smooth, polished wood—and opened it to find a gold necklace with a pendant representing a mother holding a child in her arms.

"Wow," she murmured as she lifted it out. He was right. She *loved* it.

She tried to make herself put it back in the box. But then she decided to try it on—and couldn't bring herself to take it off. He'd purchased this for the mother of his child. Surely she could accept one present. This wasn't something he could give to anyone else, after all, and if he couldn't take it back…

After wrestling with her principles for another hour, she finally picked up her phone and called his number.

"You win," she said when he answered.

"I win what?"

"I opened the necklace."

She heard him chuckle. "And? Do you like it?"

"It's *beyond* gorgeous. But you'd better not ever buy me anything else. This is all I'm going to accept."

"Fine. I'll respect your wishes. Just relax and enjoy it, okay? Your life is going to change a lot. You deserve something pretty—like you."

She told herself not to take the compliment too seriously. "It was very thoughtful of you. So was the card."

"Everything's going to be okay, Ellie," he said. "Thanks for trusting me enough to move to California."

"We're *both* taking a leap of faith. I realize that." After telling him good-night, Ellie disconnected. She was nervous—about everything—but she couldn't come up with a better plan.

A text came in. She thought it might be from Hudson—possibly more reassurance—but it was Don.

I heard you quit today, that you're moving to California with Hudson. Is that true?

He and Leo had already left the BDC by the time she'd arrived earlier, so she hadn't said goodbye to them. She'd been relieved that hadn't been necessary. But reading his words made the impending changes so real—and caused goose bumps to break out on her arms.

Was she crazy?

Maybe. But there was no turning back. Hudson had told her tonight that he'd purchased two first-class tickets to LAX. A limo would be picking her up in the morning—after collecting him from his hotel.

Yes, she replied.

You've got to be kidding me!

She didn't answer, but that didn't stop him from texting again.

Don't be a fool, Ellie. You're making a mistake. Whatever's going on between you two, it won't last. You don't even really know him!

Don't pretend you care, she wrote back.

That's the thing. I do care. Just because I love Leo doesn't mean I can't love you, too. Love is never an either-or. That was what made everything so difficult for me. I wasn't pretending when we were together.

She almost typed "You were still lying to me," but what was the purpose? They'd been down that road. I appreciate the kind words, she wrote instead. Regardless of what happened with Hudson, she was over Don.

But you're still going? he wrote.

Of course.

Ellie, please don't. This will screw up your life.

How do you know?

Do you understand the number of women who must throw themselves at him? Some of the most beautiful women in the world are probably vying for a marriage proposal. No one could hang on to someone like him—not for long. He's a dream, a mirage.

True. So she wasn't even going to try to win his heart.

I appreciate your concern and wish you and Leo the best.

There was a long pause before he responded. Then he wrote the classiest text she'd ever received from him.

You're a beautiful, smart, confident woman who's capable of doing great things. You don't need Hudson or any man, so hold your head high no matter what happens.

Ellie had never flown first-class. She'd been too practical to spend the extra money, but Hudson refused to fly any other way. He said he couldn't sit in the cramped seats of coach, that he didn't fit, and he wasn't about to subject himself to the onslaught of interest he'd receive if he didn't do something to separate himself from the other passengers.

She would've felt the same if she were him. He couldn't walk through the airport without people stopping to stare, point or give him a high five. One woman approached to ask for a picture, which Hudson was nice enough to allow—until other people started lining up. After five or six photos, when the swarm only grew larger, he excused himself, saying he had to get through security so he wouldn't miss his flight, and took Ellie's hand to make sure she moved as quickly as he did.

"I could've flown in coach," she told him after they'd boarded and were putting on their seat belts.

He'd taken the window seat to put some distance between him and the people filing past. "You told me that—about ten times."

"I meant it. This seems like an unnecessary extravagance."

"I'd never stick you in back while I sat in front."

"Why not? Coach is all I've ever flown."

"You're uprooting your life and coming to California because I asked you to. The least I can do is provide a first-class ticket."

Except that kept her right next to him, and she'd been hoping for a reprieve. The more time she spent with him, the harder it became not to touch him. The fact that she hadn't slept with anyone since their night together five months ago only added to that. After being so serious with Don, her body had grown accustomed to a certain amount of sexual activity, and she was feeling the long absence. She told herself that was why she kept remembering the taste of Hudson's warm, soft mouth on hers and the way he'd used his hands to excite and please her at the hotel.

You have to forget about that, she told herself and tried not to mind when an especially attractive flight attendant leaned across her to tell Hudson she'd be available if he needed *anything* during the flight.

"She was pretty, don't you think?" Ellie asked.

"Who?" he replied, although the woman had patted his arm before walking away.

"The flight attendant."

Hudson had his ball cap and sunglasses on in an attempt to blend into the background, but the flight attendant obviously knew who he was, and the people who'd recognized him in the airport hadn't been fooled. "Oh. Yeah. I guess."

Ellie got the feeling he hadn't really looked at the woman. "I wonder if I'm going to like California," she mused.

"I hope so." He sounded a bit worried.

She studied his profile. "Are you sure I shouldn't get my own place? Won't it feel odd for us to be…roommates?"

He kept his face turned to the window while he answered. No doubt he was afraid one of the coach passengers still boarding would get a good look at him and alert the whole plane to his presence. "Odd in what way?"

"Restrictive?" She had no interest in being privy to his encounters with other women, particularly while she was getting bigger and more unappealing by the day.

He risked pulling his gaze from whatever he was watching outside to give her one of his sexiest smiles. "I guess you'll just have to forget about other men while you're living with me."

She thought he was joking, but she was serious when she said, "And you will..."

He didn't hesitate. "Do the same."

She wished she could read the level of sincerity in his eyes, but they were hidden behind his Ray-Bans. "*Really?* You've invited me to stay for quite a while, so is that realistic?"

"It would be a lot *more* realistic if you'd change your mind about our...nighttime arrangements," he grumbled.

She glanced around to make sure no one was listening to their conversation. First class afforded them more room, but there could easily be someone who was trying to figure out if he was who he appeared to be. "I can't," she murmured. Not if she planned to survive the next year with her heart intact—to remain functional and independent enough to move on alone, if she had to. "But since we're back on *that* subject, I've been meaning to ask you something."

He yanked the bill of his cap a little lower. "What's that?"

"What are you going to tell your friends and...and the rest of the team about me?"

"Haven't decided yet. Why?"

"I hate to suggest you *lie*. But admitting that you picked me up at a club and took me to your hotel for a one-night stand doesn't show me in a very favorable light. I'd rather your friends not see me as some sort of...burden. Or jump to the same conclusion you did and think I'm trying to take advantage of you."

His eyes lowered to the necklace he'd bought her as she fiddled with it, moving the clasp around to the back. "I'm glad you're open to stretching the truth to a degree. Since sports figures are often unwitting role models for kids, I've been worried about that, too. I mentor quite a few boys at the boys ranch where I attended high school and would have some explaining to do—considering what I've told them about being responsible in their relationships with girls. Best to avoid that, if possible."

"Makes sense."

"So how do you suggest we handle it?" he asked.

"Why not say we met online? That we've had a relationship for at least six months?"

"I admit I've told a couple of people about the baby, but one of them will go along with whatever we decide, and I didn't get specific enough with the others that this would contradict what I said. So… I'm all for it."

She settled back in her seat. "Great."

"That gives us a history," he said. "But how should we characterize our *current* relationship?"

"That's a little harder," she replied. "I don't want you to feel I'm trying to stand in the way of you seeing other women, but since I'll be living with you… I'm wondering if, for the first month or so, we should pretend to be closer than we are?"

"How close?" He seemed all business.

"Together?" she ventured. "A couple? It would only have to be like that for a few weeks—not long at all," she added quickly. "Then we can 'break up' and tell people we're going to continue living together for the sake of the baby. Boom. Everything's explained."

He didn't hesitate. "Done."

She almost couldn't believe he was so amenable, but she was happy about it. Now maybe his friends and associates wouldn't be predisposed to hate her from the beginning. "*Really?* That'll be okay? Because if you're seen with someone else before we—" she used her fingers to create quotation marks "—break up, it could create a scandal. Make you appear to be a cheater, which wouldn't be flattering for either of us."

"You mean I'd look like the womanizer you're assuming me to be?" he said drily.

"I'm not assuming anything," she explained. "Merely pointing out that our plan would require some fidelity—if that's the right word—from both of us. It's just…that part will be easier for me, since it'll take time to get to know men I might find appealing."

The flight attendant started the usual preflight safety message, but Hudson spoke over that.

"I understand my responsibilities—and I'm sure I can handle them."

She heard the sarcasm in his voice. He wasn't happy that her expectations of him were so low. But it was important to be clear. Otherwise, why even start the charade? "Thanks." She smiled to show her gratitude. "I'll give my folks the same story when I tell them about the baby. That should make things easier all the way around."

"Your parents don't know you're pregnant?" he whispered in surprise.

"Not yet."

He pushed his sunglasses higher on his nose. "When do you plan on telling them?"

"In a couple of months."

"They're not going to be angry that you waited so long?"

She nibbled at her bottom lip. "They might be."

Ellie fell asleep almost as soon as they took off. Hudson wished he could do the same, but flying made him anxious. He hated the fact that he had no control over the plane. Although he tried to distract himself by using his tablet to get on the internet, the flight attendant wouldn't leave him alone long enough to sink into a movie. She kept coming back to ask if he'd like another drink, something to eat, Dramamine, a chance to join the Mile High Club. She didn't specifically make that last offer, of course, but the opportunity was implied.

"I'm fine," he told her for probably the tenth time. He was disappointed that having Ellie with him didn't seem to make any difference to the flight attendant. He would've thought the presence of a possible girlfriend would stave off some of the behavior she was exhibiting. But he'd seen women come on to other players while they had their *wives* at the same party. So he figured he shouldn't be too shocked. Fame seemed to interfere with some people's ability to think clearly. He was just glad Ellie didn't respond the way a lot of women did. His "celebrity," as she put it, didn't seem to affect her—except that she didn't like the attention he attracted, and he couldn't blame her. Most of the time, he didn't like it himself.

He chuckled as he remembered how strongly she'd argued for a coach ticket. She'd been hoping to leave him in first class, where he'd have to deal with his own fame, and she could relax and do whatever she wanted. But he hadn't let her off the hook, and not only because he was trying to be courteous. He enjoyed having her with him.

He glanced down to see her head sliding toward his shoulder. Generally she caught herself before settling against him. She'd wake up, realize she was too close and straighten—only to fall right back asleep, at which point her head would start to droop again.

He leaned closer, to offer her the support she needed before she could wake up in time to avoid contact. He managed to accomplish that, but it wasn't fifteen minutes later that the damn flight attendant was back.

"Would you like some more cookies—or any other snacks?" she asked eagerly.

Clenching his jaw so that he wouldn't snap at her, he responded with a polite and soft "No, thanks. I'm good." He was hoping not to wake Ellie, but almost as soon as the flight attendant was gone, Ellie lifted her sleepy eyelids, noticed she was leaning on him and drew back as if she'd encountered a snake.

"Oops! Sorry about that," she said. "I should've bought one of those neck pillows I saw in the terminal."

He took off his hat and settled it back on his head. "It's not like I mind. At least *one* of us is getting some sleep."

"It's that flight attendant," she complained with a grumpy scowl. "She's obsessed with you. Why don't you go into the bathroom and do her already?"

Hudson couldn't believe he'd heard her correctly. *"What'd you say?"*

She shook her head, looking flustered. "Nothing. I'm not quite awake."

He started laughing.

"What?" she said.

"I thought we promised to leave other people alone until we 'break up.'"

The way she stretched suggested she was extremely uncomfortable. "I'm willing to make an exception. Anything to get her to leave us alone." Her gaze flicked to his iPad. "What're you watching?"

"A documentary on India."

"Really?"

"Why does that surprise you?"

"I thought it would be sports related, I guess."

"I *can* think about other things—now and then—when I'm not out smashing female hearts, that is."

"A hopeful sign."

He shot her a dirty look but she merely smiled, as if she'd meant to give him a little grief.

"Is it good?" she asked and acted so interested that he ended up handing her one of his earbuds so they could watch it together.

"It was a long flight. Would you rather we stay at my home here in LA to rest up, or are you okay with heading out to Silver Springs right away?"

Hudson was driving the almost-new 4x4 truck that'd been waiting for them in long-term parking. Ellie was curious whether this was the type of vehicle he usually drove, but she didn't ask. She didn't want him to think she was too interested in his possessions—especially after insisting she wasn't. She was wearing the necklace he'd given her, despite what she'd said about *that.* "I'm not fragile. I can go on."

"Great. Since it's the off-season, I have more responsibilities in Silver Springs."

"No problem. It's barely a two-hour drive." Hard to believe she'd made that same drive just a week earlier, that she was now living across the country and had brought only two suitcases, both of which Hudson insisted she wasn't to touch, even though they had wheels. While she was in the hospital, the doctor had suggested she not lift anything, and Hudson was taking that to heart. He barely let her carry her own purse, since it was the big hobo kind that contained everything she could ever need or want. She'd been tempted to pretend it *was* too heavy to see what he'd do, but she knew how badly he'd be teased in the locker room if someone happened to catch a picture of him with a purse dangling from his shoulder.

"You hungry?" he asked. "Should we stop and eat before we set out?"

"That'd be nice," she replied. "Do you know a good place?"

"Babe, I *live* here."

She grinned at his response. "Does that mean you know *all* the great restaurants?"

"It means I know a lot of them."

The place he took her for lunch was an upscale, locally owned bistro with a private room, where the owner and chef greeted him personally. She accepted Hudson's recommendation on the hand-cut rosemary pappardelle, which was delicious, but insisted on choosing her own dessert. When she ordered two, because she couldn't decide between the bananas Foster and the carrot cake, he raised his eyebrows in surprise—then ended up eating most of both.

"You said you didn't want dessert," she complained as they left.

"Those were huge portions! You were *way* out of your league," he said, completely unrepentant. "Don't tell me you're going to order like that whenever we go out."

"Absolutely! Why not? I'm eating for two, after all." She was testing him to see what his response would be—if her physical appearance would embarrass him—but he never missed a beat.

"*Finally* a girl who'll be able to do justice to the food I provide."

"Whoa! You won't be providing *my* food. Take it out of my paycheck. Except for those desserts, of course. Those are on you, since I just got a few bites."

"You ate as much as I did!"

"Not even close."

He rolled his eyes. "Fine, if you want to quibble. Anyway, we've already made the financial arrangements. Don't try to change things now."

She whirled on him. "Since when did we agree that you'd pay for my food? We'll split groceries, as well as all the other household expenses. That's what roommates do—they buy their own stuff and share the cost of utilities."

"Really?" he said. "Because you don't make enough to pay 50 percent—and I should know, since I'm your new boss."

"You're *not* my boss. I have all kinds of skills. I could get a job anytime."

She had an education, but her skill set wouldn't fit in just anywhere. Fortunately, he didn't call her on that. "Manner of speaking," he said, and his laugh let her know he enjoyed getting a reaction out of her.

"Not the *best* manner of speaking. Anyway, this is your *vacation* house, right?"

"It's still big. Has to be in order to protect my privacy."

She slowed her step. "How big is big enough to protect your privacy?"

"The utilities are very likely more than your rent."

He lived a lifestyle she couldn't even imagine. "I see. Okay.

Well, *you're* the one who bought such a monstrosity. I guess that's your problem, then. Free room and board and five thousand a month. I'll consider it a raise."

"I can tell you how to get another one..."

His devilish expression revealed exactly what he'd suggest, so she steered clear of that comment. "I'm satisfied."

"Hopefully you won't remain that way."

She ignored that statement, too. "But since I always try to be fair—" she cringed "—I'll let you attend the birth. If everything goes well from now on, that is."

"Why is that so distasteful to you?" The question was serious, even though he followed it up with a more playful "After all, I'm *such* a nice guy."

"Have you ever seen a birth video on YouTube or watched a farm animal have offspring or...anything?" Her new ob-gyn would, no doubt, suggest they attend birthing classes. So he'd learn what to expect soon enough. But those wouldn't start until she was much closer to the end of her pregnancy.

"No. They had farm animals at my high school, but I didn't pay much attention to them."

"There you go. *I* know what I'm in for—and I don't want an audience," she said as she climbed into his truck. She didn't add "Especially *you*," but that was what she meant.

CHAPTER EIGHTEEN

Hudson's house wasn't the rambling Mediterranean Ellie had expected after seeing that so often in the wealthy neighborhoods of Miami. Although his home was spacious and new, it was built like a nineteenth-century farmhouse with white-beamed ceilings, hardwood floors, heavy-paned windows and tons of built-in cabinetry. The light fixtures, some of the best she'd ever seen, were as rustic as the expensive rugs. A theater room and an equally impressive gym took up most of the basement. She figured, worst-case scenario, she could spend her pregnancy down there, watching movies.

She could feel Hudson's eyes on her as they passed through the game room, complete with neon beer signs hanging from the walls, an antique jukebox in one corner and a bar, reaching an elaborate barbecue area, deck and swimming pool. "Not bad," she said as she ambled over to the edge of the property—the only place where the ten-foot perimeter fence was made of wrought iron so as not to obstruct the view—and gazed at the mountains beyond.

"You like it?"

She felt a bit intimidated, but she managed a careless shrug.

"I'm sure I can put up with it for a few months." She pointed to the far corner of the yard. "What's that little house over there?"

"Don't get any ideas," he said. "That belongs to the housekeeper."

"You have a housekeeper? And you've never mentioned it?"

"I didn't think it mattered. Maggie won't bother us."

"When does she come to the main house?"

"If I'm here, only when I ask her to—which means I'm desperate for food or laundry or both."

"You have her live in a separate house for the sake of privacy?"

He winked at her. "You got it."

He hadn't shown Ellie the bedrooms yet, just the basement, game room, gourmet kitchen—with its massive stone hearth, kitchen utensils hanging over a sizable island, copper-hooded stove and stairs leading down to a wine cellar—and living room, with its even bigger stone fireplace, enormous flat-screen TV, leather couches and ottoman.

"How often will I be able to use the gym?" she asked.

"Whenever you want," he replied.

"When do *you* work out?" She hoped to avoid showing up at the same time. She'd failed in her New Year's resolution to maintain a good exercise routine, didn't want him to notice just how out of shape she was.

"Are you thinking you'd like to work out together?"

She laughed. "The opposite, actually. I was planning to stay out of your way."

"How could you get in my way? There's plenty of equipment. I forgot to show you, but there's even a steam room you might want to use after you're done with your workouts."

"I can't get in a steam room or a whirlpool, not while I'm pregnant," she said. "Raising my core body temperature wouldn't be safe for the baby."

"Good information to have. You'll want to avoid those,

then—along with the wine in the wine cellar. I guess my house is fraught with danger."

He had no idea that *he* posed the biggest threat—maybe not to the baby but to her peace of mind.

"Should we go up to your room?" he asked.

"Sure."

He led her back through the house and up a wide, curving staircase. "There are four bedrooms, one of which is on the main floor, but I think you might be most comfortable here." He stopped by the double doors at the end of the hall to show her a room with a giant four-poster bed sporting an expensive-looking duvet and linen set, heavy furniture (something the room demanded since it was so big) and a bathroom with a walk-in shower.

"This is perfect," she said. "If we don't get along, we won't even have to see each other."

"Except my room is right next door."

She'd guessed as much. "Why don't I take that room on the main floor you just mentioned? I mean, with the size of the house, there's no need for us to cram ourselves into the same section."

He seemed surprised by the suggestion. "What if you need me?"

"I have a cell phone."

"This will work," he said as he carried her suitcases to the closet.

The problem was, she'd always be listening for him to come down the hall… "We can try it out, I guess. See if we need more space."

He shot her a curious look. "What are you planning to do in here?"

"Nothing. I'm just…used to living alone."

He shook his head. "Damn, you're skittish. Well, I'll try not to cramp your style."

Perhaps she hadn't sounded grateful enough. "This is beautiful, though. Really beautiful."

His expression said those words were too little, too late, but she couldn't believe she'd truly offended him. Surely he had plenty of other people to praise and envy him and his belongings.

"Do you have any preference on what I cook for meals?" she asked. "What types of groceries you'd like me to buy?"

"Other than organic, no. You can make whatever you want, but there's no need to shop. Just email a list to Maggie. She'll take care of it and stock the fridge and cupboards."

"Oh, because I won't have a car, right?"

"I have two vehicles here—the Porsche I drive to and from the city, if I don't have luggage, and the truck I use in town. Feel free to take the Porsche whenever you need to go somewhere."

"Did you say *Porsche*?" she asked.

"You can drive a stick shift, can't you?"

"My first car had a standard transmission. But I'd rather not be responsible for such an expensive vehicle."

"It's insured," he said as if she was crazy for worrying about that sort of thing. "I'll let you get unpacked and relax. It's been a long trip." He started for the door.

"Hudson..."

"Yes?" he said as he turned.

She couldn't stay here. She had no doubt she'd enjoy it, but... how was she going to feel when she fell back to earth? "I'm thinking I'll be more comfortable if I rent a small place of my own in town." Something that wouldn't be too hard to leave when the time came...

He frowned. "Why? You'll have everything you could possibly need here."

"That's just it. This feels...odd. I'd rather take care of myself."

He leaned against the door frame. "Give it a couple of weeks. If you don't like it, you can always leave."

She took a deep breath. He had a point. What was the rush? She could simply pretend she was on a fancy vacation. "Okay."

"Are you back?"

Lowering his voice, Hudson closed his bedroom door so there'd be no risk of Ellie overhearing his telephone conversation with Bruiser. "Yeah. Just got in."

"Did you bring *Dr.* Ellie Fisher with you?"

"I did."

"And? How do you feel?"

Hopeful, Hudson realized. He was looking forward to having Ellie around, which was unexpected. Thanks to his profession and the money he'd earned, he'd had to fend off so many women over the years, and yet she was the one who was always talking about putting more space between him. That made him feel safe. "Sort of…excited."

"Did you say *excited*?"

"Something wrong with that?"

"No, it's just…you were pretty upset when you called me from Miami. She's still pregnant, isn't she?"

"Yeah, she's still pregnant. I was drunk when I called you."

"Exactly my point. You were so upset you were drinking yourself into oblivion."

"Everything was new. I was working through the shock. But I'm feeling better."

"You must like her."

Hudson could hear the conjecture in his friend's voice. "I do. She's surprisingly easy to be around." He enjoyed giving her a hard time, enjoyed how she laughed at his jokes or came back swinging when he riled her.

There was a long pause.

"Bruiser?"

"I'm still here."

"What're you thinking?"

"To be honest? I'm concerned."

"Isn't that my job?"

"It is, but now that you're lowering your guard, I might have to step in. Are you *sure* she's not setting you up?"

"For..."

"Marriage? If she can convince you she's harmless, get you to trust her enough to marry her—to give the baby your name or whatever—she could get a lot more in the end."

He thought of how often he'd had to talk her out of renting her own place. "I don't think she's trying to set me up. She seems satisfied with what we've arranged."

"And what have you arranged?"

Hudson explained how they'd decided the rest of the pregnancy and the first six months of the baby's life should go. He also told Bruiser what they were planning to say about their relationship and asked him to go along with it.

"I won't give anything away. You want to say you've been dating for months? I'll stand behind that. But she seems almost too good to be true. Are you *positive* she's not trying to reel you in?"

"I've seen nothing to indicate that she's any less than she appears to be."

"Does she have any idea how much you're worth?"

"Doesn't seem to care. She'll hardly let me buy her lunch."

"Could that be an act? Hell, I try to get you to buy every meal."

Hudson chuckled. It wasn't true. Bruiser didn't lean on anyone. "If it's an act, it's a damn good one."

"That's it," Bruiser said. "I'm coming out there."

"When?"

"Tomorrow morning. Better if I get out in front of this thing, just in case."

"What about Jacqueline and Brianne? Are you bringing them?"

"No, Brianne will hate the long ride in her car seat, and Jacqueline's got a fund-raiser for the local hospital."

"She won't mind if you leave?"

"Not for one day. She'll understand that I need to meet Ellie, get a feel for her."

Maybe Bruiser would see something Hudson had missed. "If that's what you want to do, we'll be here."

"I'll leave first thing," he said, but as soon as Hudson hung up, another call came through—from the private detective he'd hired to find out who'd abandoned him the day he was born. Usually the guy sent an email update. A call was unusual, especially after business hours.

Hudson checked his watch. It was nine, so not *terribly* late considering the guy lived in LA—meaning they were in the same time zone. Still, nine was late enough. Seeing that name come up on caller ID sent chills down Hudson's spine. Something had changed; he could feel it.

His heart began to pound even before he could answer.

Once the PI ascertained that he had the right person, he said, "I've found a lead that might give us the answers you're looking for."

Would he learn who'd abandoned him at last? "How?"

"Digging. Doing my job."

"And this is hopeful?"

"It's not 100 percent, but it seems legit. Only problem is..."

The reservation in his voice made it difficult for Hudson to breathe. "Go on..."

"You need to ask yourself if you *really* want to pursue this."

Hudson's trepidation grew worse. "Why wouldn't I?"

"It's not something I'd ever want getting out about me—and I'm not famous."

When Ellie woke, she was a little disoriented. She still had her clothes on. The lights were on, too, and she was sleeping in a giant bed she didn't recognize...

Then it all came back to her, and she realized she must've fallen asleep after unpacking—and slept for several hours.

She got up to retrieve her purse so she could find her phone. It was nearly two in the morning. What was Hudson doing? She would've guessed he was sleeping, like most other people so late at night, except she heard the steady thump of bass coming through a set of speakers somewhere below. Was he in the living room, watching TV? The kitchen, listening to music while he made a midnight snack? She doubted she'd hear anything if he was all the way in the basement.

What was he doing up so late?

After brushing her hair and putting it back up, she changed into a pair of sweats and a T-shirt, washed her face, brushed her teeth and left her room to see what was going on. She hadn't meant to go to sleep when she lay down. She'd meant only to rest her eyes.

Had he come up to see if she wanted dinner? Or had he eaten without her?

She felt…left out, which was ridiculous. It was possible that he'd checked on her and she didn't know it. He didn't *have* to include her, anyway. She was the one who'd made such a point of telling him they'd act like regular roommates—the kind who lived entirely separate lives. Maybe he figured that should start immediately.

He wasn't in the living room or the kitchen. She found him in the game room, drinking and shooting pool. The music was so loud he didn't hear her approach, which gave her a moment to observe him undetected.

He was barefoot, wearing worn jeans and a cotton T-shirt that stretched nicely across his broad shoulders. But he looked tired, upset. What was going on? Why wasn't he in bed?

The power with which he sent the white ball crashing into a solid blue ball told her he *was* upset. Swearing under his breath when he missed the pocket he'd been aiming for, he turned to take another drink of whatever he had in his glass—brandy?—and saw her.

"What are you doing up?" he asked.

"I'm more surprised I went to sleep in the first place. I wasn't planning on it. I just...dropped off."

"You needed the rest. That flu took a lot out of you."

"I guess so."

He stood there staring at her for a few seconds. She got the impression he wanted to say more—especially when his eyes moved over her—but he didn't. He went back to his game.

"You okay?" she asked.

No answer. He sank two stripes—one in a side pocket and the other in a corner.

"Hudson?" Was this going to be where she learned he had an anger problem—that he was a mean drunk or insufferably moody? She was afraid she might discover something like that. The Hudson she'd seen since he'd come to Miami was totally normal, real, even kind. She'd forgiven him for punching the wall in the motel when she told him about the baby, but she hadn't forgotten it, especially now that she'd quit her job and they were back on his home turf...

Would that frightening Hudson reappear? Send her scrambling to buy a plane ticket home?

"I'm fine," he said.

She deliberated whether she should take him at his word and leave him to his music, alcohol and pool playing. He was obviously trying to cope with something the best way he knew how. But he didn't seem fine; he seemed troubled.

She ventured closer. "Have you had any dinner?"

"Not yet."

He had to be hungry. She was. They'd eaten lunch twelve hours ago. "Why don't I make us something?" He didn't seem to be drunk—he wasn't slurring his words, wasn't uncoordinated in his movements—but he was heading in that direction. She figured it couldn't hurt to get some food inside him.

"Don't worry about me," he said dismissively, but as soon as she'd eaten a quick bite, she made him a plate of bacon, eggs and toast and took it to the game room.

"Here you go," she said, as if he'd indicated that he *did* want to eat.

To her surprise, he accepted the food and sat down at a nearby table.

"Are you going to tell me what's wrong?" she asked.

"It's nothing," he replied.

"I can tell it's *something.* Are you having trouble adjusting to the idea of having a child? Or is it that you've had second thoughts about bringing me out here? I could leave…"

He stared at her as if none of that had crossed his mind. "No. I don't want you to go. What I'm feeling has nothing to do with you or the baby." He studied her for a few seconds before speaking again. "But if you're really concerned, you could be the remedy."

"The *remedy*?" she repeated.

"A temporary fix, for sure. You can't change reality. No one can. But touching you, I'd like that. It would be so much better than feeling—" he waved his fork for emphasis "—what I'm feeling now."

He wanted sex. He'd made it clear he wasn't satisfied with her stance on that issue. She had, however, believed they'd get past her first night in California before it came up again. "I don't know what you're talking about, what you're feeling now," she said, hoping to draw the information out of him.

"It's nothing I'm willing to share, nothing I'd ever want anyone to know."

"Why?"

"Because it's dark and ugly, and I wish I didn't know, either."

"Does this have to do with football?"

"No."

"Your childhood, then?"

"Yes." His past was such common knowledge, he didn't seem surprised by her guess.

"Sometimes it helps to talk."

He set his plate aside. "I don't want to talk. I want to take you to bed, Ellie."

He was too beleaguered—and he'd had too much to drink—to be anything other than transparent. She got that, but she didn't find his candid responses as off-putting as she wished she did. His honest appeal tempted her to ease his pain, help him feel better, be there for him. "We've talked about this—"

"Can't we make an exception?" he broke in. "Just for tonight? Because I never voted for no sex. My plan was the opposite, remember?"

"I remember, but you have to agree that abstaining would be for the best."

"When's the last time you were with someone?"

She rubbed her palms on her sweats. "In September," she said, suddenly feeling every one of the days between then and now.

"See? It's been that long for me, too. Don't you want a man? Don't you miss being held, caressed, kissed?"

She *did* miss that, especially by him. But she'd just landed in California. She needed to acclimate, adjust, get to know Hudson better before making such a big decision. "I'm trying to be smart..."

"Forget smart. Be greedy."

She would've laughed—except he was serious. "Greedy?"

"I must have something I could give you in return—for taking the risk."

"I'm not asking for anything..."

"That's just it! Most other people want *something* from me. Why don't you?"

"They're excited about meeting someone who's famous, I guess. Or they're trying to use you. I'm not."

"At least with them I have some leverage."

"Come on, you hate that."

He wasn't really listening, didn't respond to her comment. He was still talking as if she'd never interrupted him. "I can promise other people autographed sports paraphernalia, tickets to a big game, even money. But I don't seem to have anything *you* care about. You won't accept my gifts."

"I've been wearing the necklace you gave me ever since I opened it."

"You won't let me buy anything else, won't take more money than you absolutely need. You don't give a shit about knowing someone who's famous—or plays pro ball. You don't even want to stay in this house."

She wasn't nearly as ambivalent as he seemed to think. "Only because I'm not accustomed to such wealth. I can't let myself get used to living like this. I don't want to feel dissatisfied when I return to my small home and ten-year-old car."

"You're having my baby," he said. "No matter what happens, you'll never completely go back to your former life."

She supposed that was true. She'd always be connected to him—and he'd always be who he was. Even when he stopped playing, he'd probably become a Hall of Famer.

"We've made love before," he said, still trying to entice her.

Drawing a shaky breath, she walked over to collect his plate. "I remember." All too well…

"*I* thought it was good," he said, looking up at her. "I thought you liked it, too."

"I did." She picked up the plate, but he caught her wrist.

"Then don't reject me."

The warmth from his hand flowed up her arm. "I'm not *rejecting* you. That's a harsh word."

"You're saying no. It's the same thing." He took the plate and set it aside, then pulled one of her fingers into his mouth.

"Hudson—"

"I'll give you a massage every day for a week," he promised.

"We can't do this."

"Yes, we can. Let me feel you, let me bury myself inside you."

"You must be a little drunk."

"So? Sex isn't anything new for us. I wanted you before. I made that clear."

He took her finger back into his mouth, and the way he sucked on it made her nipples tighten and tingle. She told herself to move away, but she didn't. She couldn't even *look* away. "This is a bad idea," she said, but she could hear the breathless quality of her own voice, knew he'd heard it, too.

"No, it's not." He spoke so low, his words were barely audible. "I'll always be good to you. I promise. I would never mistreat you—or the baby. I'm excited about the baby."

She ran her thumb over his bottom lip. He never allowed himself to be this transparent when he was sober...

"You're thinking about it..."

"I shouldn't be."

He kissed the inside of her arm. "That means you're tempted."

She watched with bated breath as his lips moved higher, toward her elbow, which wasn't *that* far from her breast. "I am," she admitted. "You're not an easy person to resist."

"Thank God. Take off your clothes. Let me see you. I never got to see you in September." The hopeful, eager expression on his face was still overshadowed by whatever troubled him, and that made it impossible for her to refuse. She couldn't leave him to endure whatever he was feeling alone.

He watched, rapt, as she pulled off her shirt. "There you go, sweet Ellie," he said, pressing his lips to her bare stomach. "Our lives are already intertwined. And we *both* want this, don't we?"

She'd be lying if she said no. She raised his chin to tell him so, but he took her breast in his mouth and she moaned instead.

When he'd touched and tasted all she'd exposed so far, she felt him undo the tie at her waist and slide her sweats and panties down past her hips.

With her clothes out of the way, he ran a hand over the slight swell of her stomach. "Hello, baby," he murmured and lifted her onto the pool table.

"Are you sure you want to do it here?" she asked. "Under the light?"

"I'm going to do *you* here. I want to see you, watch everything." Spreading her legs, he kissed a path up her thighs.

Ellie tried to stop him. She was too self-conscious, felt she needed to know him better before she could enjoy oral sex. But he wouldn't let her refuse him.

"Relax," he said.

"I don't think I *can* relax," she said. "This is… This is pretty intimate—about the most intimate thing I can imagine letting someone do."

"It's also something I doubt your gay ex-fiancé was excited about doing—not very often, anyway."

"Never," she admitted.

"Great. Then it's something I can do that might make you glad you said yes."

"There are other ways to—"

"I want to do this," he said, and once his mouth reached its target, she nearly jumped off the table.

"Holy shit," she gasped.

His tongue moved against her. "I'm assuming that's a good 'holy shit.'"

"Better than you could ever dream. I've definitely been missing out."

She felt his breath as he laughed. "We can make up for lost time," he said and went back to work.

"Wow, you really… You really know what you're doing." Her words came out in a whisper. She couldn't seem to talk any louder. She was struggling just to breathe. She tried to grip the sides of the pool table but couldn't reach them, so she clenched her hands in his hair.

"That's it," he said. "Show me you like it. You're making me so hard."

"I *do* like it. I don't think I've ever liked anything this much."

He slid his hands under her to give him better access. "Then you're in for a treat."

"Oh, God," she moaned as the suction of his mouth caused every nerve to hum with anticipation.

When her legs began to tremble, she felt his strong hands squeeze her ass, encouraging her to succumb to the pleasure he was giving her—and it wasn't more than a few seconds before one of the most powerful climaxes she'd ever experienced made her whole body jerk.

"One down. Many more to go," he said with satisfaction. "*Now*, let's go up to my bed."

CHAPTER NINETEEN

Yes, this was what he needed, Hudson decided. A woman. Ellie in particular. He'd thought of her so often since that night in September. Hard to believe he had her back, and that she was once again naked beneath him. Although sex wouldn't change what he'd learned, at least he couldn't think about anything else right now. He was too consumed with desire. With touching her smooth, soft skin. With the small bump that proved she had his baby inside her. With hearing the little sighs that told him she was enjoying his body as much as he was enjoying hers. With the thrust of her tongue against his and, especially, the exquisite sensation of pressing inside a woman for the first time without wearing a condom. It was all so visceral and present that nothing else could get through.

Until it was over. Then, as he lay spent in her arms, everything he'd been hoping to avoid—the words the private investigator had spoken—scraped through his mind like barbed wire.

Shit. He closed his eyes in an attempt to shut out the memory. He wouldn't accept that version of events. He'd make up something else, a far more pleasing scenario, like the one he'd so often daydreamed about as a kid, in which some evil man stole him away from loving parents with whom he'd eventually be reunited. But as Ellie's fingers caressed his cheek, soothing him almost as if he were a child, he felt such an upwelling of emotion—and he was just drunk and exhausted enough that he didn't have anything left to battle it.

"Hudson?" she murmured.

Hearing the confusion in her voice, he blinked quickly, trying to staunch the tears that were dripping onto her breast.

He didn't answer. He hoped she'd assume the wetness was merely perspiration. But when another teardrop fell, and then another, he felt her kiss his forehead. "Are you okay?"

The concern in her voice was as soothing as her touch. She was so damn soft and kind. But the gratitude he felt to have her with him in this moment only put him at more of a disadvantage. He *wasn't* okay. He should never have hired a private investigator, should never have searched for his parents.

He opened his mouth to say something flippant and careless, anything to throw her off the track of what he was really feeling. But to his horror, more tears came instead.

Holding him tighter, she kissed his temple and smoothed back his hair until all the tears were gone and he was too tired to even apologize before drifting off to sleep.

Ellie listened to Hudson's steady breathing. She was blown away by what had just happened, never saw it coming. Hudson wouldn't even tell her what was wrong, which was why she'd been so shocked when those tears began to fall. Then he'd tensed, trying so hard to reel in his emotions that the opposite had occurred, and those few tears had acted like a crack in a dam that had suddenly given way.

At least he finally seemed calm. She was glad she'd come to bed with him, if only for the companionship and peace it had brought him. But the fact that his state of mind mattered so much to her indicated something she didn't care to face. She tried to tell herself it was natural to be concerned about the father of her child, but she'd had tears rolling down her own cheeks the entire time he'd been crying. She'd known that if this was happening to such a strong man, he had to be torn up inside, and she couldn't stand the thought of him feeling so much pain.

Earlier, when she'd questioned him about what was wrong, he'd admitted that it had to do with his childhood. Had one of his foster mothers or fathers died? Had he learned why he was abandoned? Or who'd abandoned him? *What?*

She was getting in too deep. She needed to go to her own room so they could try to start over in the morning.

Assuming he'd be grateful to forget tonight had ever happened, she inched away from him toward the edge of the mattress. But he must've felt the movement, because he woke up and slipped an arm around her waist to anchor her to his side. Whatever had hurt him still lurked under the surface, and he didn't want to be alone.

Turning so she could put her arms around him again, she kissed his lips, his cheeks, his forehead. "I'm not going anywhere," she whispered and knew she'd given him the reassurance and comfort he needed when she felt him relax a few seconds later.

What was he dealing with? He had so much—success, physical beauty, talent, money—and yet he seemed listless, empty, even broken. Despite everything he'd achieved, he hadn't outdistanced his early tragedy, his abandonment. She wanted to give the boy inside him the love he needed, but she couldn't do that without loving the man, too. And then how would she protect her own heart? Did she dare ignore caution and let go? Give him what she was holding back in the hope that he might one day be able to care for her in return?

God, that was a risk. But when he woke up a few hours later and rolled on top of her, this time for a slow, sweet encounter during which they didn't even speak, she knew she didn't have much of a choice.

★ ★ ★

Although Hudson had slept soundly, he felt a measure of reluctance when it was time to get up. Last night probably hadn't been what Ellie was expecting. Certainly nothing like that had ever happened to him before. He wasn't even sure *how* it had happened. One minute he was feeling the power of a strong sexual release; the next he couldn't staunch the tears clogging his throat and burning his eyes.

He wished he could forget breaking down, pretend it never happened. But Ellie was no longer someone who'd get up and leave and he'd never see again. She was the mother of his child, would be part of his life for the next eighteen to twenty years. He had no choice except to acknowledge his weakness and apologize for it.

Shifting onto his side, he propped his arm under his head. He was just planning what he needed to say when he realized her eyes were already open and she was looking at him. "Sorry about last night," he said. "I don't know what got into me."

She slid her hands, clasped in a prayer-like position, under her cheek. "So you're okay?"

"I'm fine. Like I said, I don't know what got into me. I promised you a good time, and then I ruined it. I feel terrible."

"Men have emotions, too, Hudson. Sometimes it's better to express what you're feeling instead of keeping it bottled up. Relieves the pressure."

Hot embarrassment burned through him. "Not when you're trying to make love."

"We were done."

"What a way to end it, huh?" He attempted a laugh, but she didn't even crack a smile.

"It was no big deal. I'd rather you be real."

"Well, I, for one, could live with a little less reality," he joked.

She continued to study him. "Do you want to tell me why you were so upset?"

"Definitely not. Are you going to push me to talk about it, anyway?"

"No."

"Good, because I'm not sure I can explain." It wasn't only what he'd learned from the PI; it was the accumulation of so many things—all the hurt he'd experienced over his life, especially in his early years. Why it had come pouring out last night wasn't clear, but he suspected it had something to do with the fact that Ellie was the first person who'd be somewhat permanent in his life. Since she was carrying his child, she couldn't decide he was too much trouble and walk away, at least not as easily as his foster parents had.

"Then we'll let it go," she said.

"Thanks. I'll try to make it up to you."

"You don't owe me anything." She rolled away from him, dragging the sheet with her as she got out of bed.

"Where're you going?" he asked when she headed for the hallway instead of the bathroom.

"I need a shower after last night."

"Last night was good—before I blew it."

"It was *all* good."

"You liked what we did in the game room."

"Yes," she admitted.

"Does that mean you'll be back for more?"

"Maybe. Maybe not."

"You're not committing?" he called out, since she was now out of the room.

"No, and I'm sure you aren't, either."

"I can't, Ellie. I'm not cut out for that."

No answer.

"Ellie?"

"I'm going to make omelets for breakfast, if you want one," she called back.

"Definitely, I'll take one." He started to look for his phone.

He hadn't bothered to plug it in last night, so it had to be in his pocket. When he found it, he'd just begun to text the PI, to tell him he'd made a decision, when the doorbell rang.

For a second, Hudson wondered who could've gotten through the security gate. Then he realized it was almost noon—plenty of time for Bruiser to have driven over from LA. The gardeners or Maggie must've let him in, because Hudson hadn't heard the intercom.

Before going downstairs, he took a second to finish his text. Don't continue to pursue the lead we talked about. If that's the truth, I don't want to know it. As a matter of fact, he wished he could *un*know what he'd already been told. It was too late for that, but maybe he could stop what he'd started before it got any worse.

Ellie could feel Bruiser sizing her up the whole time she cooked breakfast. She'd worn the only shirt she had with a high collar—she hadn't packed a turtleneck, hadn't expected she'd need to cover her neck—but she was afraid he could still see the red mark Hudson had left, and it made her self-conscious. She didn't want to come off like the average groupie; for one thing, she wasn't, and for another, she knew that wouldn't impress anyone. Bruiser was trying to figure out who she really was and whether her presence in his friend's life would be positive.

"Those were delicious," he said when she'd finally managed—after ten eggs and quite a bit of ham, cheese, spinach and onions—to fill him up. She'd never seen a more massive man. Not in real life, anyway.

She smiled as she started to clean the kitchen. "Thanks."

"Do you think you're going to like it out here?"

"In California? Don't know, to be honest," she said. "I haven't seen much of Silver Springs. But I'm trying to keep an open mind."

Hudson made no comment as he gathered up the dirty plates

and brought them over to the sink. He'd mentioned that Maggie, the housekeeper, would be stocking the pantry and the fridge today, but he'd also admitted that he preferred cleaning up after himself—at least dishes and that sort of thing.

"It isn't as humid in California, so you'll be pleasantly surprised come summer," Bruiser said.

Ellie took the knives and forks Hudson had gone back to retrieve and rinsed them off before loading them in the dishwasher. "That's what I hear."

Bruiser finished his milk. "Bugs in California are a lot smaller, too."

"Another plus," she said.

He let Hudson take his empty glass. "So you'll be having the baby in June?"

Ellie glanced over at Hudson. He hadn't mentioned that Bruiser was one of the two people who knew about the baby, hadn't even told her this person was coming over. She'd gotten out of the shower to learn they had company. "I'm due on the tenth."

He looked her up and down. "You're a tiny thing."

Ellie didn't know how to react to that comment. Almost anyone would be tiny next to him. "Considering I'm five months into the pregnancy, I won't stay this way for long."

"There's nothing like having a baby."

"Bruiser and his wife have a little girl named Brianne," Hudson cut in. "Cutest kid ever. They're head over heels—" he grinned as he jerked his head toward Bruiser "—as you can see by that dreamy expression."

They talked about Brianne for a few minutes and what it was like to be a father. Bruiser said Ellie had to meet his wife, Jacqueline. Then Hudson brought up the team. Apparently there were some changes taking place in management and rumors swirling about player trades. The two men were so engrossed in who might go where next season that Ellie finished loading the dishes without contributing to that part of the conversation. She figured they'd probably like some time alone—if only to be able to talk freely about her—so she started to excuse herself.

Just then, Hudson received a phone call.

"It's Aaron. I'm going to take it. Give me a few minutes," he said and stepped out of the kitchen.

Ellie could hear the drone of Hudson's voice as he walked away and wondered if everything was okay. He'd told her about Aaron and what the boy had so recently dealt with; she knew he was worried the chemo wouldn't be successful. Undoubtedly that had contributed, to some degree, to what had occurred last night. But there was something else going on, something Hudson wouldn't talk about.

"So you met Hudson at a club," Bruiser said when Hudson was gone.

Ellie hung up the dish towel she'd used to dry her hands. She could hardly excuse herself now. She needed to stay and entertain Bruiser until Hudson returned. "Yeah. Kind of ironic, since I don't usually frequent those places."

"Hudson told me you're a scientist."

"I am. Or I was—before I quit my job. I'll go back to immunology after the baby."

"You must be a little frightened of the future, given your situation and the fact that you don't know Hudson very well."

She *was* frightened. She hadn't anticipated her life taking such a drastic turn. The unknown, what might happen, worried her, but she was more concerned that every time she looked at Hudson it felt as if the floor was falling out from under her—and that sensation only seemed to be getting more pronounced. Hudson had apologized for breaking down last night, but holding him like that, feeling his pain and helping to soothe it, had made her feel closer to him than she'd thought possible.

She was falling in love with the unattainable.

"I'm tentatively hopeful." She was attempting to throw Bruiser off the scent of what was really going on in her heart and mind, but he was more intuitive than she'd expected.

"He's a good man, Ellie. One of the best."

"Thanks for the reassurance."

He gave her a look that said "Not so fast." "There is one thing..."

At the solemnity of his words, she took a deep breath to prepare herself. "And that is..."

"He struggles with trust. He had so many foster parents give up on him, send him back. He can't believe anyone will stick it out through the rough patches."

She'd read about his childhood, knew from last night that the rejection had left a lifelong impact. "Are you trying to tell me it would be a waste of time to...to hope for a meaningful connection with him?"

"I'm trying to tell you it won't be easy, but it'd be worth the effort," he replied with a wink.

Surprised that he'd taken her into his confidence so quickly, she moved closer. She was interested in learning more about Hudson's demons—those newspaper articles hadn't divulged nearly enough, and last night had whetted her curiosity—but Hudson walked back into the room at that moment, and Bruiser acted as if they'd been engaged only in small talk.

"How's Aaron?" he asked.

"Fine," Hudson replied. "They have a new kid at the school who's acting out. Aaron thinks I might be able to reach him. I said I'd head over."

"To New Horizons?"

"Yeah. I told him I'd bring you with me."

Bruiser got to his feet. "Let's go."

Hudson turned to Ellie.

"Don't worry about me." She raised both hands for emphasis. "I'm going to get settled in, maybe go into town to explore."

"Great. Keys to the Porsche are upstairs on my dresser."

"Thanks," she said, but she had no plans to drive his car.

★ ★ ★

Hudson ended up spending much longer at the school than he'd intended. The boy who was "acting out" threatened to kill himself, so Hudson had contacted Aiyana, who'd called in one of the psychologists under contract with the school. By the time the psychologist reassured them that the new student would be okay, off-season weight training for the New Horizons football team was about to start, and once the boys knew Bruiser was in town, they were begging Hudson to bring him.

The students loved interacting with Bruiser. He spent more time wrestling and play-fighting with them than he did spotting with the weights, but so many of the students needed the attention, especially from a man as well-adjusted and easy to love as Bruiser.

Bruiser talked Hudson into going to the field afterward to throw a football with the guys who were the most reluctant to see them leave.

Even after Bruiser went back to LA, Hudson didn't head home. He ran into Aiyana and spent almost an hour talking to her about the new kid and what they could do to help him settle in.

It was nearly eight and well past dark when he got home, which was why he was surprised to find that Ellie was still gone.

He tried to call her cell, but her voice mail picked up, so he texted his housekeeper, Maggie.

Have you seen my guest?

The woman? came her response.

Yes. Name's Ellie Fisher.

Since you gave me her name, I guess I'll be seeing her again?

Definitely. She's going to have my baby.

This is Maggie. Did you mean to share that much? Because you don't usually tell me anything about your personal life.

I have no choice with this. You'll probably read it in the tabloids soon. You might as well get the facts directly from me. She's five months along. She'll be staying with me until after the baby's born. She should've been here when you stocked the kitchen.

I saw her leave earlier, when I was at the mailbox.

What time was that?

Not too long after you drove off with Bruiser.

At one-thirty? And you haven't seen her since?

No.

Where could she have gone?

She took a few seconds to reply.

I have no idea. I've never even met her, remember?

"Smart-ass," Hudson muttered and searched the house again. Still no sign of Ellie. He tried texting her. No response. He called—and got her voice mail again. What was going on?

The Porsche is in the garage, so she must've come back at some point, he wrote Maggie.

You don't believe that I don't know where she is?

He scowled at her response. He'd hired Maggie because she treated him like her son—with no deference to his celebrity—and didn't put up with any shit. He appreciated her sarcastic sense of humor, but he was getting worried.

I am paying you, remember?

Not to hold women captive.

Funny. Is she with you?

No. I'm telling you I haven't seen her since she left. She never took the Porsche.

She must've taken the Porsche. It was the only vehicle I left her.

From what I saw, she walked off the property.

Walked? As in exercise?

I didn't stop to interrogate her, Hudson. I try to mind my own business.

Shit. He was dealing with the one person who respected his privacy.

I appreciate that. Protecting my privacy is always good. But now I need you to tell me everything you saw. How was she dressed?

Jeans. Sweater. Coat. Leather boots. She's a cute girl.

The outfit Maggie described suggested Ellie hadn't gone out for exercise. She would've been wearing tennis shoes, at least.

So where had she gone? She didn't know any of his neighbors; he couldn't imagine she'd be out visiting strangers. She'd mentioned a desire to go to town, but surely she wouldn't *walk* there. That trek was almost four miles each way.

Next time don't lose track of her! he wrote, just to give her a little of the hell she'd given him.

I'll buy a collar.

He couldn't even appreciate her comeback. He was too concerned.

He called Bruiser. "You didn't happen to see Ellie walking on the side of the road when you went through Silver Springs, did you?"

"I didn't. Don't tell me the Porsche broke down."

"No, it's still here, but she's not."

"Did you try calling her?"

"Of course. She's not picking up."

"Do you want me to turn around and help you look for her?"

"No. You stayed later than you intended already. I'm sure I'll find her—somewhere."

"Let me know the minute you solve the mystery."

"I will," he said and grabbed his keys.

The walk had felt a lot shorter on the trip *into* town, before she'd been on her feet all day. Ellie hadn't bought many things, but trying to carry even a few bags for three and a half miles was more of a challenge than she'd bargained for, especially since the boots she'd thought were so comfortable when she left the house had given her a terrible blister. She wished she could call Hudson to see if he was available to come and get her, but her phone had died two hours earlier.

Although the road wasn't terribly busy, there was a fairly constant stream of traffic. About halfway home, she grew desperate enough to consider flagging down a passing motorist to see if she could catch a ride.

After another quarter mile, she was no longer merely considering it. Prepared to do almost anything to avoid taking another step, she stuck out her thumb.

Several cars passed without stopping, but soon after that someone slowed. Although she couldn't see a lot of detail in the dark, she could tell from the headlights that it was a truck.

Hitchhiking wasn't a safe practice, so Ellie felt more than a little trepidation as she approached the lowered window—until she recognized the vehicle *and* its driver.

Hudson! Thank God.

She was so relieved to see him that she was taken aback when he snapped, "Get in!"

He didn't have to tell her twice. She scrambled into the passenger seat so she wouldn't hold him up any longer than necessary. Then she hung on to her seat belt as he raced off. She didn't question him about his excessive speed, however. She knew he was angry.

They drove all the way to the house in silence. Only after he'd pulled into the garage and turned off the engine did he face her. "What the hell were you doing back there?" he demanded.

She released her seat belt. "Back where? I went shopping. That's all. Found a really cute blouse and a more comfortable pair of pants. Now that my waist is expanding, I don't have much—"

He caught her hand to stop her from gathering up her bags. "I mean after that."

"When I was trying to get home?"

"When you were *hitchhiking.*"

If his stony silence on the ride hadn't already let her know he didn't approve, the acid in his voice would've made it crystal clear. "I was a little too optimistic about the distance."

"Do you realize what an easy target you were?" he asked.

"Some stranger could've stopped instead of me—and raped and murdered you and left your body to rot behind a barn."

She pulled out of his grasp. "That's a bit graphic."

"You need to think about it."

"The chances of being raped and murdered aren't…*great*. But I wouldn't want to be the exception, so I understand what you're saying. It's not something I would normally do."

"Then why'd you do it today?"

"My feet were killing me, okay? I couldn't walk anymore. And my phone was dead. I was out of options."

"I don't understand why you were walking in the first place. I left you the keys to my car." He gestured at the Porsche, which was parked right next to them. "What happened? Couldn't you find them?"

"I didn't even look," she muttered as she glanced over at it.

"Because…"

She turned back to face him. "Because your car cost… I don't know…$100,000, and I didn't want to be responsible for it."

"I told you it was insured!"

The fact that he hadn't bothered to correct the price told her she wasn't far-off. "I'd still feel terrible if I wrecked it. I'm sure it means a lot to you. Besides, it's very…"

His eyes narrowed. "What?"

"Distinctive," she replied. "I knew people around here would recognize it and assume we were together."

"Isn't that what we *want* them to assume? Isn't that what we decided to tell everyone?"

"For a month or so, yes. But we're going to be an item for such a short time, I didn't see any reason to start showing off."

His jaw dropped. "You think I bought that car to flaunt my wealth?"

"No. People know how rich you are. They'd expect you to be driving something like that. But *I* don't have that kind of money, and I'd rather not be driving around in a fancy Porsche one month, only to be tooling around in something I can afford the next—with our baby in the back seat—while some other woman replaces me in your little sports car."

"Seriously?" he said. "That's your answer?"

She rubbed her forehead. The issue was more complicated than she was making it sound. She didn't want to get too comfortable in his privileged world, didn't want to feel disappointed when she returned to her ordinary one. But she refused to admit that to him. "I guess I have more pride than I thought. I don't want the people I have to circulate among on a daily basis to think I'm enough of an idiot to believe that our relationship could be permanent, especially since you warned me from the start that you weren't interested in anything serious."

"Because I don't want to hurt you, or any other woman I might date!"

She spread out her hands in a conciliatory gesture. "Look, this is leading to an argument we don't need to have. Heading to town on my own seemed preferable at the time. That's all."

"You'd rather walk for miles and then risk your life by getting in with a stranger than be seen driving *my* car."

She opened the door. "Forget it, okay? Nothing happened. If these boots had turned out to be as comfortable as I thought, I would've made it home on my own without a problem. Three and a half miles isn't a big deal."

"It's a little more than that. And you're pregnant!"

"It's okay to walk when you're pregnant, Hudson."

"*That far?* And in the dark? Even if you didn't catch the attention of a psychopath, a drunk driver could've hit you. Hell, someone looking down at a phone could've hit you."

She didn't answer, but he didn't seem capable of letting it go.

"Don't you care that I was going out of my mind?" he went on. "That I couldn't imagine what'd happened to you? You tell me I'm about to be a father—that I'm finally going to have some semblance of a family for the first time in my life—*and then you go missing*!"

Ellie blinked as the real reason for his anger registered—she'd scared him, pure and simple. At first, he'd been so unhappy about her pregnancy, she'd never realized she had the power to do that. But the ultrasound had changed things, made the baby real for him. He hadn't seemed nearly as unhappy about having a child since then. He'd actually become quite committed. And Bruiser had told her he feared abandonment, that his childhood had made it impossible for him to trust in love. She should've thought more carefully before refusing to drive his car and just taking off. "I'm sorry. I never dreamed you'd care."

"If something happened to you?"

"The baby's fine, Hudson. Everything's fine."

"The night could've ended very differently. That's my point."

He got out and stomped into the house, leaving Ellie a little stunned. Hudson did everything he could to remain aloof and detached, to keep himself from caring too much about anyone or anything. But he *did* care. He'd let the curtain slip last night—and then again today.

Bruiser was right. Hudson had a scarred but tender heart. And she found that to be the most attractive thing about him.

CHAPTER TWENTY

After Ellie put away her new clothes, pulled on some sweats and doctored the giant blister on her foot, she went in search of Hudson.

She found him sitting in the theater room watching MMA with his leg propped up and ice on his knee.

"I'm sorry about earlier," she said as she stood in the doorway.

His gaze slid over to her before returning to the screen.

She moved a bit closer. "You're not going to accept my apology?"

"I'm going to buy a damn Toyota or Honda or whatever the hell you'll drive so you won't do that again."

"You don't have to buy another car, Hudson. I'll drive the Porsche if that's what you want, but if something happens to it, don't get mad at me."

"I was willing to take the risk! I told you that from the beginning."

"Fine. You win." She sat at the end of the couch and eyed his knee. "You're hurt?"

"It's nothing."

"What happened?"

"Same old injury flaring up."

"What causes it to do that?"

"I tweaked it today, playing with the boys."

"Did you see Aaron?"

"Of course."

"How was he?"

"Better than he's been in a long while. I'm so glad the chemo's done."

"Good." If Aaron was doing that well, last night really had been about Hudson's childhood. But what aspect? What had triggered those intense emotions?

He said nothing and just continued to watch the fight.

"You look tired," she told him, breaking the silence between them again.

"I *am* tired."

"Have you had something to eat?"

"A bowl of cold cereal."

"That's a healthy choice."

He reacted to her sarcasm by giving her a dirty look. "Someone went MIA, so I had to launch a massive search, which meant I was starving by the time I got to eat."

Ellie felt bad that she'd put him to so much trouble, especially because she'd had dinner at a cute little restaurant in town three hours ago. "I brought you half a sandwich from the place where I ate. Should I go get it?"

"I'm fine. Glad to know *you* had a nice meal, though."

She drew a deep breath. "So…are you going to continue to sulk—or will you let me make it up to you?"

He paused the TV. "By…"

"I could rub your knee, see if that would ease the pain."

"My *knee*? No."

"Because…"

He clicked the TV back on again. "Because I only want one thing—and that isn't it."

Stung—and more than a little surprised—Ellie straightened. "Right. Got it," she said and walked out.

Closing his eyes, Hudson dropped his head on the back of the couch. *Shit.* Now he felt even worse than he had before. Ever since he'd heard from Samuel Jones, he hadn't been himself.

He almost got up to apologize but stopped. He couldn't allow himself to grow accustomed to having Ellie soothe away his aches and pains—as she had last night. He took care of himself, didn't need anyone, and he was going to make sure that didn't change. That terrible hour when he'd had no idea where she could be, whether she and the baby were safe, had reminded him what it felt like to lose someone, to be emotionally vulnerable—and he didn't like it.

MMA was usually cathartic for him, especially when he was upset, but he couldn't get interested in the fights. Between what he'd said to Ellie and what the PI had told him last night, he couldn't concentrate on anything besides his own troubled thoughts.

He held out for another hour, tried to make himself leave things as they were. But as the minutes passed, he grew more and more afraid that she was packing her bags. And as much as he didn't want to care about her giving up and going back to Miami, he did—and not just because of the baby.

A few minutes later, he stopped trying to resist and went to her room.

"Ellie?" he called as he knocked on her door.

"What?" she replied without opening it.

"You're not going to leave now, are you?"

"I won't walk that far again. I already told you."

"I mean, you're not going back to Miami."

There was a slight pause. Then she said, "Do you want me to?"

"No."

She said nothing.

"Sorry I was such a dick," he added. "It's been a bad couple of days."

"Forget about it."

"Okay." Still not completely reassured, he scratched his head as he tried to come up with something else to say. "Thanks for understanding."

When she didn't come to the door, he went down the hall to his own room—and paced there for the next several minutes. He'd apologized, but he still felt unsettled. He'd lived alone for years—had to fend for himself since the second he'd turned eighteen. Maybe that was why, now that he had someone else living in his house, he couldn't quit obsessing about her, couldn't quit wondering what she was doing.

She was probably reading, he told himself. She liked to read. But that meant she could be in her room, content on her own, for hours and hours. It was possible she wouldn't come out for the rest of the evening.

He hated that thought, wanted a second chance to be better company. Last night had been the lowest he'd been in a long time. He wasn't sure what he would've done without her—and it wasn't just the distraction she posed. It was the comfort she'd offered. He could use a little more of that comfort, despite what he'd told her. So, after turning on the TV and flipping through the channels without really seeing anything, he went back to her door.

"Ellie? You're not sleeping yet, are you?"

"No," came her response.

"Any chance you'd like to watch a movie?"

"Not tonight."

She hadn't even taken a second to think about it.

"What about getting in the pool? Pregnant women can swim, can't they?"

"This time of year? The water will be freezing."

"It's heated. Not like a hot tub, but enough to take the edge off. I swim a lot. It isn't as hard on my joints as some other workouts. It'd be good for you, too. You should come out with me."

"You go ahead," she said. "Maybe I'll swim tomorrow."

He bit back a curse. What else could he suggest?

She'd eaten, and he doubted she knew how to play billiards. "Okay," he said at length. "I'll leave you alone."

He started to walk away, but turned back almost immediately. "Ellie?"

This time it took longer to get a response. "What?"

"I didn't mean what I said earlier."

"It's fine. I made a stupid offer to begin with. I'm sure you can hire a professional masseuse if you need a massage. You don't need me."

He was trying hard *not* to need her. That was the problem. He couldn't imagine a world where needing her, coming to depend on her, would turn out to be a good thing. "I was just… in a bad mood."

"We all have days like that. Hope you feel better in the morning."

He shook his head. Sometimes he was his own worst enemy. He'd had more than one foster parent tell him that, hadn't he? As a matter of fact, he'd heard every damn thing that was wrong with him—over and over. He was too aloof, too detached, too difficult to reach.

But he was who he was, and he didn't know how to change. He needed to stop caring so much about other people and what they thought of him.

If only he *could*…

"'Night," he murmured.

Ellie sat on her bed, staring at the door while she listened to Hudson's footsteps recede. She almost got up and went after him. She knew he felt bad for what he'd said. She could tell by the tone of his voice and how hard he'd tried to get her to come out again. But he had her twisted up in knots. One minute she was determined to offer him the love he so desperately needed—and consistently shoved away—and the next she was asking herself if she was crazy to think she could actually reach him. He was like a wounded animal, and wounded animals were dangerous.

She looked down at her phone. She missed Miami and her work. It used to be that she could throw herself into her research and let her work distract her if she was upset, lose herself for hours in something that could make a huge difference to the world. In the lab, her life was about so much more than her own problems. But now that she didn't have the BDC, every emotional bump felt like an earthquake.

Had she made a mistake in coming here?

Hudson had asked if she was going back to Miami. Maybe relocating had been a bad decision. She was falling in love with him when she'd promised herself she wouldn't. Should she pack up and leave before she could lose any more of her heart? They could work out custody issues like so many other parents who lived apart—because if she stayed, she had a feeling Hudson would devastate her in ways she couldn't even begin to imagine.

But she hadn't moved here for her own sake. She'd moved here for the sake of her baby. She kept coming back to that.

When the clock showed ten, she allowed herself to call her parents. Although it was early in France, she hoped they'd be getting up. She needed to talk to her father in particular, needed to remind herself how important he was and had always been in her life.

"Ellie?"

She smiled in relief at the sound of his voice, cheerful as ever. "Hi, Dad."

"How's my girl?"

Tears stung her eyes. She wanted to tell him about the baby and Hudson and ask for his advice. Should she give up and leave?

Or should she stick it out in Silver Springs and do the best she could—for both her child and the child's father?

She almost blurted out the whole story—the surprise pregnancy and everything—but stopped herself. It was too soon to reveal news of the baby. Her parents would fly home immediately if they thought she needed them, and she couldn't be that selfish. She wanted to give them a couple more months in Europe. She also knew she couldn't handle the complications that having them back would create for her and Hudson if she stayed in California. She needed to get to know him better first.

"Good." She cleared her throat, hoping to ease the terrible tightness. "How are you?"

"Fantastic! There's so much to see and do here. I know you're busy with work, and that what you do is important, but you've got to come across the pond before we head home."

She wiped an errant tear. "I'm glad you're enjoying your time there."

"What about you?" he asked. "Have you cured diabetes yet?"

"No." She wouldn't even be able to keep trying, not for probably a year. She felt certain the BDC would take her back if they could. They'd been sorry to see her leave in the first place. But she had no idea if there would be an opening when she was ready, and they didn't know that, either.

"You'll do it one day. If anyone can save the world, it's you."

When she couldn't respond because she'd just covered her mouth to stifle a sob, he said, "Ellie? You still there?"

After struggling to gain control of her emotions, she managed a fairly normal-sounding "Yeah. Sorry. I was, um, checking my phone. I was getting another call, but it's nothing important. I'm back."

"How're things with Don? Still awkward?"

"About the same."

"He blew it, letting you go."

She rolled her eyes. "He likes *men*, Dad. He left me for his best friend."

"So? He's missing out."

She laughed in spite of her tears. "Only a father could say that."

"I'll always be your biggest fan, Ellie Girl. There's no one as wonderful as you."

His unbridled love made her choke up again. "I miss you," she murmured.

"I miss you, too. When can you come to France?"

"I wouldn't count on that happening."

"Because…"

Rubbing the swell her baby was creating, she stared down at her belly. "There's too much going on."

"Can't it wait for a week or two?"

She decided to take a small step toward the truth. What she eventually had to divulge would be less shocking if she revealed bits and pieces along the way. "I'm in another relationship."

"That fast?"

It'd been five months since she'd caught Don with Leo, but she'd never jumped from one man to the next, so five months wasn't that long to her father. "Yeah."

"With who?"

"Hudson King. You recognize the name, don't you?"

"No. Why would I? Have you mentioned him before?"

She started laughing.

"Did I say something funny?" He sounded slightly amused.

"I didn't realize who he was, either, when we first met. Turns out he's the starting quarterback for the Los Angeles Devils."

"The football team?"

"Yes."

"So he's a professional athlete." He didn't seem nearly as impressed as most people would have been. He didn't value extreme wealth, fame or football any more than she did. He only wanted his little girl to be happy. "How'd you meet him?"

"Ran into him at a nightclub last September, when I went out with Amy."

"He's the reason you're not coming to France?"

She looked down at her stomach again. "It's not only him. I have…too many other things going on, can't travel at the moment."

"And yet you brought him up, this Hudson. Must be serious."

"Not necessarily. I'm thinking of bailing on the relationship. If a mere mortal like Don could crush me, what could someone like Hudson do?"

"You don't think he's gay, too?"

She chuckled as she said, "That isn't even funny. He's the straightest guy I've ever met."

"Then why not give him a shot? See what happens? You obviously like him if you're afraid of being hurt."

"It's not that simple, Dad. He had a difficult childhood, was abandoned as a newborn and tossed around from foster home to foster home as he grew up. So he's wary, to say the least. He pushes people away if they get too close." And he was freaking out because he'd let her get a little too close last night—and she'd made it worse by scaring him today.

"I'm sorry about all that."

"So am I, and… I'm not confident I can get through to him. I'd be smarter not to even try, right?"

There was a slight pause. Then he said, "How would I know, sweetheart? Only you can answer that question."

She sighed. "Really? You're putting it back on me? I feel most parents would warn their daughters away from professional athletes."

It was his turn to laugh. "I don't judge people by stereotypes. Everyone gets an equal chance. Maybe he's the perfect guy for you, and you're struggling because you're trying to see too far down the road."

"I'm trying to be careful. That's smart!"

"Careful *is* smart, but *too* careful can make you miss something magical. No one can foretell the future, Ellie. Just take it one day at a time. Go with your gut when it comes to Hudson. You'll figure out whether he's the one for you."

"And if I'm devastated in the process?"

"You'll pick yourself up and dust yourself off like you did with Don."

Although she winced at the memory, she knew her father was right. Any kind of love, especially romantic love, required risk. Besides, she couldn't give up on California *this* soon. By bailing, she'd only prove to Hudson that he couldn't rely on her. If she hoped to gain his trust, she needed to show him she could hang in, even when things weren't ideal. "Thanks, Dad."

He passed the phone to her mother, who told her more specifically what they'd been doing and seeing.

Ellie felt stronger, more like her usual self while they were chatting, but once she hung up, doubt crept in again. What was she going to do?

Go home, stay and try to keep the relationship platonic, or stay and return to Hudson's bed?

Returning to Hudson's bed was by far the most tempting option. Physically they were perfect together. She craved his touch, craved the opportunity to hold him as she had last night.

Problem was, she wanted more than his body. She wanted his heart—and he wasn't going to give that up easily.

The next six weeks or so were bittersweet for Hudson. Despite the fact that he'd called off Samuel Jones, the private investigator had sent an email, along with his final bill, to say that he was now quite certain he had indeed solved the mystery surrounding Hudson's abandonment. Obviously Jones had continued to pursue what he'd found. He'd even sent Hudson a DNA kit and told him that if he ever wanted to be sure, he should take the test. He also said he'd take care of getting a sample for comparison.

There were times when Hudson was tempted to move forward with that test. He wouldn't have hired a private investigator if he hadn't been dying to know who he was and where he came from. But not knowing was better than what Jones had dug up—except now that Jones had said what he'd said, Hudson wondered what he was really saving himself by *not* taking the test. Although he hadn't allowed the PI to give him any names or other specific details, the situation had been explained to him in general terms, and that was enough to tell him he didn't want to learn any more. Still, he couldn't help staring at that damn DNA kit, which he'd stuck in his medicine cabinet beside the mirror, every day while he shaved.

Maybe he would've been able to throw it out or send in a sample by now—do *something*—if he wasn't so preoccupied with Ellie. But she was driving him crazy. Since that night when he'd said he wanted only one thing, they'd spent a lot of time together watching movies, making dinner, playing billiards (he'd been teaching her), preparing the room next to hers as a nursery, even working out together. But she hadn't returned to his bed, and he couldn't figure out why. If he tried to touch her, she just sort of...slid away from him.

Was she worried about the weight gain and the other changes in her body? Was she afraid to let him see her now that she was showing? Because he wasn't put off by that at all. He was so captivated by the idea of his child growing inside her that, if anything, the pregnancy made her *more* attractive to him, not less. He wanted to hold her again, touch her, experience the wonder of creating a new life.

He planned to talk to her, to see why she'd backed away from him sexually, but everything was going so well otherwise, he'd been postponing that discussion for fear it might cause the relationship to take a turn for the worse. He liked having her around, even if she wasn't sleeping with him. That was the surprising thing. And he was hesitant to put her on the spot, since there was always the possibility that her avoidance of anything physical had nothing to do with the changes in her body. She could've decided that she wouldn't give him the opportunity to "use" her again—to punish him for what he'd said. Or she simply didn't care to be with him in that way anymore.

The thought that she might've lost interest gave him a sick feeling. But there were times, plenty of them, when he'd catch her looking at his mouth or some other part of his body as if she was feeling the same desire he felt. That was what confused him.

On the first of April, Bruiser came, sans Jacqueline and Brianne, since Brianne had a terrible cold, for New Horizons's big fund-raiser. Hudson always helped out by signing sports memorabilia for the live auction and attending the event to shake hands and sign autographs. He also auctioned off the opportunity to have dinner with him. And at the end of the evening, he matched the gross proceeds. It was a big night for him and Aiyana—for everyone who cared about the boys ranch—and it turned out to be even bigger with Bruiser in attendance, doing a lot of the same things to raise money.

"Ellie looked gorgeous tonight," Bruiser said as they played a game of pool after Ellie had gone to bed. She'd hung out with them for a while, but then said she was tired.

Hudson pretended he was too interested in chalking his stick to agree, but he'd noticed. On the way over, she'd made a comment about how difficult it was for a pregnant woman to look good in something fancy, but he'd thought she was the most beautiful woman there. She looked *so* good to him that all he could think about was how great it would be to get her back in his bed…

"Hudson?"

He turned when Bruiser said his name.

"Didn't you hear me?"

"Yeah. You said Ellie looked nice tonight."

"Don't you agree?"

"Of course. She always looks nice."

Bruiser folded his arms around his stick. "Cracked me up how she kept bidding on your dinner."

"She almost won yours," Hudson pointed out drily.

"Only because yours went so high. Why would she pay $25,000 to eat with you when she *lives* with you? Mine went for a fraction of that."

"She went up to five thousand before giving up on both of us. Good thing she didn't win."

"Her bidding kept the prices rising. She was a big help—although I know her bids were genuine."

Hudson remembered how often she'd put up her bidding paddle. He'd almost thrown her out of the event—would have if he could've figured out how to do it without embarrassing her. She didn't have the kind of money she was trying to donate to the school, and she wouldn't let him give her any extra. They'd already argued about money the day he'd taken her shopping for maternity clothes in LA, and she wouldn't let him pay for anything. "That soft heart of hers is going to get her in trouble one day."

"Has it gotten her in trouble already?" Bruiser asked.

Hudson felt his eyebrows come together. "What do you mean?"

"Never mind."

Hudson gestured at the table. "Are you going to play or what?"

"I have to leave in a few minutes, get back to my family."

"That's why we need to finish this game."

"I'd rather talk while we have the chance."

"I don't want to talk."

"You seem to admire Ellie," Bruiser said, ignoring Hudson's last statement.

"I do." That was honest.

"So what's going on?"

"Nothing."

"Something's off between you two. I ask about her every time we catch up on the phone, and you always give me the same story. You're getting along fine—nothing romantic going on but you're good friends. Yada yada."

"What's wrong with that?"

"That's what you *say*, but there's this deep…reservoir of feeling under the surface."

"Stop trying to create something that isn't there."

"Oh, it's there all right…"

"She got pregnant because of a one-night stand. You know that—you're the *only* one who knows it." Hudson bent over the table to take a shot, dropping two balls with a satisfying *clack, thunk*.

"The last time I came out here, she had love bites all over her neck."

"We messed around a little at first," he admitted.

"I'm wondering why that stopped."

So did Hudson—except he sort of understood. Ellie didn't want anything that didn't include commitment, and he didn't want anything that did. "I guess she's not interested."

"That's bullshit. She can't take her eyes off you. And you can't take your eyes off her. But you dance around each other as if you're afraid you might actually touch."

"She's pregnant, man! I'm not looking at her like that," he said, even though nothing could've been further from the truth.

Bruiser came closer and lowered his voice. "Making love doesn't hurt the baby. I was worried about that, too, when Jacqueline started showing. So I asked her to check with her doc, and her doc told her she could have sex up until delivery."

"There are other considerations."

"Like…"

"I said I don't want to talk about it. Can we finish this game before you go?"

Bruiser shook his head. "You're so damn stubborn. Ellie's special, Hudson. Don't let her get away."

He thought the same, but she demanded too much. "I thought you were leery of her—afraid she might be trying to trap me."

"I changed my mind. She's one of the most sincere people I've ever met."

"We're better off as friends," Hudson insisted, but it made him sad to say that, because he knew Bruiser was right. She'd make a great choice for a life partner. He'd never known anyone he liked as well. And she was already pregnant with his child. She just deserved more—more love and trust and devotion—than he could ever give.

And he was afraid if he let her get too close, she'd realize he wasn't worth loving after all.

The sound of someone banging on the front door dragged Hudson from his sleep. That wasn't a sound he heard often. He lived behind a security fence, which kept most unwanted visitors away. But he couldn't remember closing the gate after the fund-raiser last night.

Actually, no, he hadn't closed it. He'd left it open for Bruiser and hadn't even mentioned to Bruiser that he should take care of it on his way out.

When the banging continued, Hudson wondered if the gardeners needed something. They were the only people he could imagine having a reason to bother him this early. It was only eight. Maybe they couldn't rouse Maggie—or she was out, doing the shopping or whatever.

Intent on stopping the noise before it disturbed Ellie, he rolled out of bed and pulled on a pair of sweatpants.

"I'm coming, I'm coming," he muttered, taking the stairs two at a time.

What Hudson could see of his visitor told him it wasn't one of the gardeners. The tall man who waited on his stoop had to be in his midseventies. He was wearing a flannel shirt buttoned to the top, his gray hair slicked back as if he'd made an attempt to look presentable.

Who was this? The guy seemed nervous, kept fidgeting and glancing over his shoulder.

Some sports fan had tracked him down, Hudson figured. Perhaps one of the locals had bragged about having him in town and had given up the location of his home, most likely at the bar last night. This guy looked as if he lived in a bottle.

"What can I do for you?" he asked as he opened the door.

The man's rheumy eyes swept over Hudson—taking in his mussed hair, his lack of a shirt, his sweats and then his bare feet before rising to meet his eyes.

Whoever it was, he'd lived a hard life, Hudson decided. He had a scar on his cheek, was far too thin and reeked of cigarette smoke. Had he been drinking, too? Was that what'd given him the courage to approach the house and knock as if he had a right to barge in on someone who already received far too much attention from strangers?

"Hudson." It was a statement that seemed to stand in for "we meet at last."

Hudson dismissed his first guess about the stranger being a sports fan. This old man had a specific purpose in being here, and it wasn't to get an autograph. "Yes?"

"My name is Cort—Cort Matisson. I'm sorry to…to surprise you like this, but…do you have a minute? I *really* need to talk to you."

An impulse to back away and slam and lock the door shot through Hudson—which was odd, since this man had no chance of overpowering him and didn't seem threatening in a physical sense. "I'm sorry. I'm not in the habit of inviting total strangers in. If there's something you want from me, a donation or…or to ask me to speak at an event, you'll need to reach out to my agent. You can find his contact information online. I go over all requests with him. That would be the appropriate way to handle something like this." *Not* showing up, unannounced and uninvited, at his house…

The old man made no move to leave. "I don't think you want me to contact your agent."

A chill rolled down Hudson's spine. "Because…"

He patted the front of his shirt, where he had what looked to be a pack of cigarettes. Hudson could tell he was dying to light up, but he wisely left those cigarettes in his pocket. "This is a personal matter."

Hudson had the creeping sensation that whatever this man had to tell him wasn't going to be something he cared to hear, and yet he said, "You're going to have to give me *some* idea of what this is about, or we won't be having that conversation. We won't be having *any* conversation."

The man seemed unsure about how to continue. He glanced back at the circular drive, where he must've parked whatever vehicle he'd driven, as if he wished he could just go. Then he grimaced and scratched his neck.

"Well?" Hudson prompted.

"I'm the one who left you under that hedge," he said.

CHAPTER TWENTY-ONE

"How'd you find my house?" Hudson had let Cort Matisson in, but he hadn't invited him to sit. They were standing in the living room, facing off over the giant ottoman.

Visibly uncomfortable, Matisson swung his keys around and around one calloused finger. "Wasn't hard. I've followed you in the news. Saw the report when that pizza deliveryman turned you over to the authorities. Know every detail and stat of your career since you started playing ball. I even read about your volunteer work with the boys at New Horizons."

"That's how you found me."

"Yeah. A year ago, an article came out that said you'd bought a place in this area, so I knew folks around here would be able to tell me where you live."

Hudson couldn't help feeling betrayed by the locals. This, when he was just getting comfortable in Silver Springs? When he'd tried to contribute so much to the school? "Why would anyone give *you* that information?"

"I told them you hired me to deliver a load of firewood, but I lost your address." He hitched a thumb over one bony shoulder, gesturing at the driveway—if Hudson's fireplace hadn't been in the way. "Wood's in the back of my truck, so it looked believable. Don't be mad over it. The gentleman I spoke to was just trying to be helpful. He's so proud to have you as part of the community."

"In other words, you lied. You staged it all with that wood."

"I deliver wood. That's how I get by. But yeah," he admitted. "I knew I'd need to think of something if I was ever going to reach you in person. I figured I was doing you a favor by lying, though. Figured you'd prefer the lie to having me tell the truth."

If it was the same "truth" the private detective had given him in general terms—when the PI had asked, "Would you really want something like this coming out about you?"—Cort Matisson was right. "Who are you to me? If you're really the one who left me under that hedge, why'd you do it?"

A pained expression appeared on the man's heavily lined face. "That's a long story. And not a pretty one. I can't say I'm proud of who I was back then—"

"Spare me the regret and the justifications and just answer the question," Hudson interrupted. If this man had done what Hudson had been told, he had no patience with his excuses.

"I panicked, pure and simple."

So it was true. Cort Matisson might as well have slugged Hudson in the breadbasket. "I was your dirty little secret, so you tried to get rid of me," he said, his words coming out in a shaken whisper.

"I didn't know what else to do!"

This man—what he'd done before and after his visit to Bel Air that day—made Hudson sick. He was afraid he might throw up. "You're telling me that you're my father *and* my grandfather." He spoke in a low voice because he couldn't bear the thought of *anyone* overhearing, most of all Ellie, whom he respected.

Even Cort Matisson winced at those words.

"Isn't that true?" Hudson demanded. "Didn't you get your own daughter pregnant when she was only sixteen?"

He nodded. That was a yes.

"Then I'm the result of that filthy, reprehensible, heinous, *criminal* act."

He nodded again, acknowledging the absolute worst possibility Hudson could imagine. How could any man ever do such a thing to his own daughter? And how could that man live with himself afterward?

"I'm sorry," Matisson muttered.

Hudson's hands curled into fists, and it was all he could do not to use them. This man had nearly destroyed him—*had* destroyed certain parts of him. Thanks to his "father," he viewed everyone with distrust and tried to wall himself off to avoid more of the same rejection he'd suffered as a child. "You *sick* bastard. Rape is bad enough. You deserve to be beaten within an inch of your life for that alone. *But incest? Sleeping with your own daughter?* Someone should castrate you for that—or worse."

The old man started to shake and, once again, patted the cigarettes in his pocket. For reassurance? "It wasn't like that," he said. "I never forced her. There was no violence involved."

"I'm guessing that's because she didn't resist. She trusted you to take care of her, to be good to her."

He hung his head. "Yes."

"So *why*?" Hudson cried. "Why'd you do it?"

He lifted his hands in a hopeless gesture. "I don't have an explanation that you or anyone else will ever understand. My wife died in a terrible car accident not long before, one in which *I* was driving. I couldn't deal with that. I was lost, lonely and feeling like I'd never recover. And Julia was there, needing me and grieving, too."

"That makes it even worse," Hudson said with a grimace. "You took advantage of her when she'd just lost her mother!"

"I loved her more than anything or anyone. I didn't *mean* for that love to turn sexual—"

"Creeping into a girl's bed doesn't happen by accident," Hudson snarled. "Babies aren't left out to die by accident, either."

He finally looked up. "After I'd done what I'd done, I couldn't let her keep you. I knew the truth would come out if I did."

"So you made her have the baby at home and told her she'd given birth to a stillborn child, which you buried."

Matisson didn't answer, but Hudson didn't need him to confirm that part of the story. Although the PI hadn't named any names, he'd related the basic facts of the situation. How Samuel Jones had ever come across the newspaper article about this man being charged for molesting his own daughter, Hudson had no idea. Jones had said he'd been looking at every individual who'd had any reason to be in the area back then and found, through police interviews, that there was a gentleman who'd worked as a handyman for several of the families in the neighborhood. Although he was questioned at the time, he'd never been considered a suspect. It wasn't until some years later, when that man's daughter was in her thirties, that she went to the police with the allegations of abuse she'd suffered at her father's hands. Jones was a genius for putting it all together.

Hudson wished he'd hired someone a little less thorough. Or, better yet, never hired anyone at all. What a fool. He'd once mentioned Pandora's box to Bruiser. Well, here he was, staring right into it. "Isn't that what happened?" Hudson pressed when Matisson neither confirmed nor denied what Hudson had said.

"Yes," he replied, but he spoke with his head down. "That's what I did. I was terrified the truth would get out—knew my parents, my brother, everyone I'd ever known would think I was a monster. So I put you in the car and drove over to Bel Air, where I'd been working. I guess I was hoping one of the rich people who lived in that area would find you and take care of you. They had so much, far more than I could ever give you."

"How am I supposed to believe you cared at all when you didn't put me somewhere I was likely to be found?" Hudson asked. "You *wanted* me to die. Then your secret would die with me. You just didn't have the balls to kill me yourself. You were going to let hunger and cold do that."

"No..."

"Then why didn't you take me to a fire station or a hospital?"

"I couldn't. I was afraid I'd be seen!"

"Bottom line, you cared more about yourself than an innocent newborn."

No response.

Hudson cursed under his breath. The person he'd wondered about his whole life was standing in front of him. But it wasn't the joyous reunion he'd secretly dreamed of. His last hope for a positive resolution to the pain and neglect he'd suffered as a child had been destroyed. "You're disgusting."

"I'm sorry," he said again.

Hudson ignored the apology, could never accept it. "You knew I survived. You said so."

"Yes."

"And you've followed my career."

He nodded.

Hudson hoped that watching his son rise to the top of the NFL without being able to claim the connection had at least been some form of punishment. But that thought spurred another. Why was Cort Matisson risking a second prison term by revealing himself now? Was it because he was so old that getting put away didn't matter to him anymore?

Hudson couldn't believe his father's conscience had finally gotten the better of him. A man like that didn't *have* a conscience or he couldn't have done what he did in the first place. He had to want something.

"When they found you, it was on the news and in all the papers, like I said," Cort was explaining. "So I knew. The police even questioned me, asked if I'd seen or heard anything unusual in the neighborhood that day."

"And you lied, of course. But…they didn't question your daughter—even though she'd just had a baby?"

"They didn't know about that. She quit school as soon as she found out she was pregnant, hardly left the house. Right after you were born, we moved."

This was so surreal Hudson was tempted to think he was having a nightmare. He shook his head in astonishment.

"I was glad you were okay," Matisson added, "even though letting you live put me at risk."

Hudson barked out a humorless laugh. "Oh! How generous of you to be glad I didn't die! Am I supposed to admire you for that?"

"I didn't mean… No, of course not. It's just… I had nothing against you personally."

"Nice to hear, *Dad*. I've been worried all these years about what I could possibly have done wrong—at birth."

Matisson flinched at the heavy sarcasm, but Hudson didn't care. He wanted to lash out in worse ways, make this man hurt as badly as he'd hurt for so long. "Once your daughter came forward and told the police she'd had your baby, quite a few years had passed. Why didn't you do the right thing and confess—for her sake?" he asked. "If you felt *any* remorse whatsoever, that's how you should've handled it. Instead, you admitted there was a baby but told the police what you'd told her—that the child was stillborn and you couldn't remember where you buried it." Jones had said the police had been skeptical of Cort Matisson's story. But they'd never connected Matisson to the abandoned newborn in Bel Air. Matisson and his daughter lived in Arizona by the time she went to the authorities. Instead, they'd suspected he'd killed the baby, but without a body, they couldn't prove it.

Matisson shoved his hands in the pockets of his worn jeans. "Admitting anything else would've gotten me more time. I served ten years as it was."

Hudson sank onto the couch. "Why are you here now?"

he asked dully. "You have to know that what I'd like to do to you would be far worse than anything you might've endured in prison."

"I understand that, yes, sir."

"Don't call me sir, as if you have some respect for me. You don't respect anyone."

"I knew how you'd feel about me, Hudson."

Hudson didn't like this guy using his name, either. But what he *really* objected to was being related to this dirtbag in the first place. "And yet you came in spite of that."

"I wouldn't have come for my own sake. I'm here because I don't have any choice."

"Bullshit. No one dragged you here."

"You're my only hope."

Hudson jumped to his feet and grabbed the old man by the shirt collar, dragging him forward until they were nose to nose. *"You'd better not be here to ask me for money,"* he ground out.

The color drained from Matisson's face. "No. N-not for myself. It's for your mother."

His mother had been a sixteen-year-old girl victimized by her own father. Hudson had refused to let himself think about her, had refused to fully accept what the PI had told him. "This Julia person you mentioned that I've never met. You're here for her."

"Yes. She was married once. Has a couple of other kids—two boys, one ten and one eight. But she's divorced now, and her ex can't keep a job. *Won't* keep a job, I should say. She hasn't even seen him for over a year, doesn't know where he's at, so it's not like she can count on him for any support."

"You expect me to step in and fill that gap—knowing what I know? I realize she wasn't at fault, that she's as much a victim in this as I am, but what makes you think I'd ever want to claim either one of you?"

"I was hoping you might have some compassion—for Julia, not me," he said. "She has cancer. Can't cover her bills while she's off work to get treatment. With how well you're doing, I thought maybe you could help her out a little. That's all. She was just an innocent girl who…who trusted the wrong person."

Was this some kind of scam? Cort's daughter had eventually turned him in, but there was no saying what their relationship was like now. Had they reconciled and concocted this story between them, hoping to cash in on Hudson's success? "So she knows I'm alive."

"No. I haven't told anyone yet. I wanted to…to have some money to give her, so she'd at least talk to me. She won't answer my calls, won't let me in when I go over to see how she's doing."

"So money from me would be your peace offering."

"I only want to help her."

"But I'm sure she's needed things all along, things you knew I could provide."

"She's never been this desperate. When I caught someone going through my garbage, picking out the beer bottles, I realized the truth was about to come out, anyway. I'm not the smartest man in the world, but I knew what that PI was after as soon as I walked out to confront him."

"He told you *I'd* hired him?"

"No. Wouldn't say much, just handed me his card. But I knew it the second I saw he was a private investigator. I always expected someone to come knocking on my door—eventually. A person can't run from the past forever."

Hudson felt as if the atmospheric pressure had skyrocketed—and was threatening to crush him. "You ran for pretty long—and I wish you were still running. Or that you *had* killed me that day. That would've been better than learning what I've just learned."

Cort seemed shocked by the conviction in Hudson's voice. "You've had a good life," he argued. "Look at this place."

"You don't know anything about me," Hudson said. "Now, get out. Get out and don't ever contact me again."

"What about Julia? She'll die and leave those children motherless if she can't get some help."

"I said get out!" Hudson yelled, and the murder he was feeling in his heart must've shown on his face, because Cort scrambled for the door as fast as his spindly legs could carry him and didn't stop to look back.

That was when Hudson turned to see a shocked Ellie standing at the foot of the stairs, her mouth agape.

He was almost certain she'd heard everything.

CHAPTER TWENTY-TWO

Hudson couldn't bear the look of pity on Ellie's face. He'd been "that kid" his whole life. Different. An outsider. Alone in a way few people could relate to. If Cort Matisson was as desperate for money as he claimed, he could easily sell his story to the press. What was there to stop him? And if he did that, even Hudson's fame couldn't compensate for that kind of blow. Just when he was getting excited about having a child of his own, when he felt he might *finally* outrun his past and be almost like everyone else, the reason for his abandonment could very easily come out and be immortalized by his fame.

You've had a good life. Crazy thing was, the old bastard was right about that, at least for the past decade. Hudson had reached a pinnacle few people attained, even if they made it to the competitive arena of professional sports. He'd fought hard to fill the holes in his life, to make himself enviable if he couldn't be loved. It wasn't fair that something like this, something completely outside his control, could overshadow it all in the end.

He could only imagine what the press would make of Cort Matisson and his daughter—whose name Hudson didn't want to remember because it made her too real, too familiar. If and when the information got out that his parents had been found after thirty-two years, and the circumstances surrounding his birth were more scandalous than anyone had ever imagined, it would spread like wildfire. His name would be coupled with incest on every TV channel. That was what he'd be remembered for, no matter how many passes he completed, games he won or Super Bowl rings he collected. He could do nothing to compensate this time the way he'd tried so hard to compensate in the past.

"Hudson." Ellie, her voice full of compassion, came to meet him as he stalked to the stairs, but he circumvented her. He didn't want her to feel sorry for him. He wanted to be someone she could be proud of—as proud as he was of her.

"Can we talk about what just happened?" she asked as he passed.

What was there to say? His genetic contribution to their child was now tainted. He was beyond embarrassed, beyond humiliated. "You should go back to Miami, forget you ever met me. I'll still send you money."

"Hudson, stop." She followed him and stood in the doorway of his room while he jerked on his clothes. "Don't overreact."

Overreact? He whirled on her. "How could anyone overreact? Could there be anything worse?"

"It's a terrible thing, what that man did, a terrible thing to learn that you're connected to it—"

"I'm not just connected to it. I'm the *result* of it. I wouldn't be here if not for what he did."

"But *you're* not the act that created you! You're something special—with or without football. It was *his* actions that were depraved. You had no choice in any of it. You were simply a victim of his selfishness. So was your mother."

He tied his shoes. "Easy for you to say. I can't even think about it without wanting to throw up."

She looked worried. "So what are you going to do?"

"I'm leaving," he said as he grabbed his wallet and the keys to his Porsche.

"To go where?"

"I don't know."

"When will you be back?"

"I don't know," he repeated. "Maybe I won't come back."

Her eyes widened in appeal. "Don't leave, especially like this. You're so upset. If you stay, I'll do anything I can to make you feel better. We'll work this out between us—get to a place where you can live with it. I'm here for you. I'll *always* be here for you."

"There's nothing you can do. Nothing anyone can do." He headed back down the stairs but, again, she hurried after him.

"How do you know this man is even telling the truth? That your mother, if she is your mother, is actually sick? Let's check out his story—check *him* out—before we get too worried."

"Why waste the time?" he said. "The day we got here, Samuel Jones, the PI I hired, told me he'd found someone who'd impregnated his own daughter, and I might be the result of it."

"That's why you were so upset that night."

He wished he could throttle Jones. What'd happened was Hudson's own fault—for hiring someone in the first place. But why hadn't the private investigator simply walked off when Matisson caught him going through the garbage? Why had he given Matisson his card, for crying out loud? It was seeing the words *private investigator* that had caused Matisson to realize Hudson was looking for his parents and had precipitated his visit.

"Hudson, stop!" She grabbed his arm, but he shook her off.

"Let this go, Ellie. It is what it is. And there's nothing I can do about it. There's never been anything I could do."

"Let's get a paternity test, at least." She spoke in a tone that beseeched him to calm down and listen to her. "Make sure you really have to cope with this."

"There's a DNA test in the medicine cabinet. Jones already sent it. You think it'll change anything for me if I take it?"

She caught the door when he opened it. “Hudson, don’t go. I need you. Our baby needs you, too.”

He wished he could stop, but he couldn’t. He’d enjoyed her so much since she’d come to California, he’d almost convinced himself that he could overcome his childhood. That they might be able to make some sort of future together—the two of them and their baby. To extinguish that hope broke something inside him he doubted he could ever repair. “Go back to Miami, Ellie.”

After Hudson peeled out of the drive, Ellie paced in his big house, worrying about him—where he was, what he was doing—and stewing over Matisson’s visit. She kept hearing the old man’s voice spouting what had sounded like empty apologies. She didn’t believe he’d come for the sake of his poor daughter. That just didn’t ring true. Ellie couldn’t escape the sneaking suspicion that Matisson himself stood to gain something, and it made her angry to think he was attempting to use a situation as tragic as his daughter’s battle with cancer to manipulate Hudson into giving him money. It also made her angry that Matisson didn’t seem to even consider what such a terrible secret would do to a man as successful and proud as Hudson, how quickly it would knock him off his pedestal.

Ellie was tempted to text Hudson. To beg him to come back. She needed his help to do the research that lay ahead. He had the number for the private investigator who’d brought all of this to the surface. He was also the one who had to take the DNA test that should be performed first of all.

But she knew he wouldn’t text back. He was too distressed. He’d told her to leave and go back to Miami.

She thought of all the time they’d spent together, how much she looked forward to hearing his voice, seeing his smile, laughing at his jokes. She was in love with Hudson, and had slowly, over the past weeks, succumbed to the temptation of hoping and believing that he cared about her in return—that they might one day be a family. She wasn't going to give him up so easily.

Taking out her cell, she called Aiyana at New Horizons to get Bruiser's number—and had Hudson's best friend on the phone within minutes.

"You've got to be kidding me," he said when she explained what had happened.

She hated that she'd felt she had to tell him something Hudson would consider so private, but she knew he told Bruiser more than anyone else, that he trusted Bruiser, and she felt Hudson might need his help. "No, I'm not."

"Where do you think he's gone?"

"I can't even guess. But I've never seen him so upset."

"I feel terrible. I encouraged him to look for his parents. I thought finding them, learning some of the answers, might make it possible for him to find peace. I never dreamed it would lead to something like this."

"The weird thing is... I don't believe Matisson. Can't believe him."

"Why?"

"All his actions in the past indicated he didn't care about either of his children. Why would that suddenly change? He didn't admit the truth about Hudson, what he did with him, when his daughter came forward. Even then, he put his own interests first."

"But why would anyone make up such a terrible story?"

"Because he thinks he's going to get paid!"

"You don't believe he's trying to help his cancer-stricken daughter?"

"Maybe he thinks that'll be a side benefit. But I'm convinced he also thinks *he'll* get ahead in some way."

"Hudson isn't stupid. He'd never allow that to happen."

"I don't know if he's capable of being as objective as he needs to be in this situation."

"True…"

"Hudson isn't anything like Matisson," she said. "Doesn't look like him. Doesn't act like him. He's the exact opposite—too sensitive for his own good. I can't see them as related."

"Ellie, that could be wishful thinking."

"Or maybe it's my science background, telling me to check all the facts before drawing a conclusion."

"A DNA test will prove—or disprove—the relationship. We'll make sure he takes one before he gives Matisson any money. But won't that require time?"

"It shouldn't take too long. Hang on." She put her phone on speakerphone and used a search engine to pull up several links about paternity tests. "If we can get a sample from Hudson and the PI has a sample from Matisson, we can have an answer in two days."

"I'll try to call him," he said, "try to get him to go home and swab his cheek."

She knew Hudson wouldn't be eager to do that. Although he seemed to have accepted the worst—was certainly reacting to it—a small part of him had to be holding out hope, and could hold out hope, as long as he wasn't staring at proof. That had to be why the DNA test the PI had sent was still sitting in his medicine cabinet. "I'm not sure he *will* come back."

"He was *that* upset?"

She pictured the hopelessness in his eyes. "You should've seen his face."

Hudson drove slowly down the street. This was the intersection of Hudson and King, the place he'd been left to die. If not for a random pizza delivery—what if the family who'd ordered pizza that night had decided to cook instead?—and his own stubborn nature, which kept him clinging to life and crying for help, he wouldn't have survived.

After pulling to the side of the road within sight of that same privacy hedge, he turned off his engine and watched as various vendors came through the neighborhood to deliver furniture, put up shutters, mow lawns and clean houses. When he'd been a child, everyone had made a big deal about his being found here—in such a rich area. He'd always dreamed that his parents were wealthy and they would one day come and rescue him from the orphanage. That he'd have normal Christmases and birthdays, just like other kids. That his folks would put him in Little League or Pop Warner and come watch him play, eager to video the whole thing. That he'd have someone who'd come to his graduation from high school and then college.

Now, when he was thirty-two, his father had finally shown up. But Cort Matisson was a far cry from anything Hudson had ever imagined. He wasn't a man Hudson could be proud of.

All those dreams seemed silly now…

As soon as the road was clear, he got out and walked over to get a better view of the spot where he'd been abandoned and discovered a crudely lettered Los Angeles Devils sign posted there. "Hudson King—the best quarterback who ever lived—was rescued from this very spot as a newborn babe. Praise God. Go Devils."

He had to laugh, in spite of everything. Someone else, a Devils fan, must've bought the house since he'd been here last, because he'd never seen that before.

"Hey, don't you dare touch my sign!"

The sun was so bright it was tough to see, but when Hudson turned, he thought he spotted a little old lady standing in the house, peering out at him through a screen door.

"I'm not hurting anything," he called back, but he heard the screen door squeak open.

Sure enough, it *was* a little old lady with dated glasses and a white sweater over her dress, even though it had to be eighty degrees. The screen slammed behind her and her walker scraped the cement as she came out to defend her sign. "I'll just put it back up if you do," she threatened.

"I was only looking at it."

"So...are you here to replace the rain gutters?" She spoke loudly enough that he guessed she had a hearing problem.

"No, I was passing through the neighborhood." He started to walk away, but she called out to stop him.

"Are you one of Archie's friends? Because I baked a loaf of date-nut bread this morning, if you'd like to try a slice."

He couldn't stalk off without answering; the poor thing seemed lonely—and quite nice now that her sign wasn't in danger. "No, thanks. I'm afraid I don't know Archie."

"There he is now," she said as a black Cadillac SUV turned into the drive. "Archie's my son. You have to meet him."

Hudson wanted to get away before he was recognized, but this old lady seemed so happy to have a visitor—even one who hadn't actually come to see her—that he waited. He could say hello to these people; it wouldn't kill him.

"Archie, what took you so long?" the old lady asked. "You said you'd come for lunch, but that was hours ago."

"Sorry, Mom. Got held up at work." He looked harried as he climbed out, as though it was too much trouble to visit his mother but he felt duty bound to do it. Then he glanced over and spotted Hudson—and nearly tripped.

"Oh, my God!" he said. "How'd you get Hudson King to come here? Don't tell me he finally answered your letters."

"That's *Hudson King*?" The old lady nearly teetered over—had to grab hold of her walker to avoid a spill. "I need new glasses, but I thought there was something familiar about you! I'm Cecille. Cecille Burns." She gestured with one arthritic hand as she looked back at her son. "See that? There he is. I *told* you he'd come."

Hudson glanced from one to the other. "Was I invited here?"

"You didn't know?" Archie said. "My mother's been writing you for years. She's your biggest fan. Watches every game. I mentioned this house was available when she was moving up from San Diego, and she insisted I buy it for her, just because it's where you were found." He gestured to the sign with its handmade lettering. "And then she made this and put it up. The neighbors keep trying to take it down. They claim it's an eyesore. But she watches over it, won't let anyone touch the damn thing."

"That's hallowed ground right there," she said, as if they should follow up with an *amen*.

"God saved you," she went on. "He knew you were meant to do great things."

Hudson cleared his throat. "I'm not sure playing football can be considered great things."

She slid her glasses higher on her face and tilted her head back to meet his eyes more directly. "I'm not talking about football. I'm talking about what you did for my grandson."

"Your grandson?" Hudson echoed in surprise.

"Sean Parks. He was adopted when he was two, struggled with behavioral problems and depression and started taking drugs when he was only twelve. How he got them is beyond me," she said with a baffled shake of her head. "But by the time he was fifteen, we weren't sure he'd make it to sixteen. We were desperate for help when we got him into New Horizons—"

"I remember him," Hudson murmured, suddenly recalling a shy, dark-haired, dark-eyed boy he'd met almost a decade ago, just after he'd begun mentoring at his old school.

"He thought you could walk on water," she said. "The fact that you could overcome what you'd been through and do what you've done gave him hope. You were there at a critical time, and that's what pulled him through. Now he's graduated from college, married and expecting a baby." She smiled broadly. "You're his hero—but you're mine, too. I love that kid so much."

"I had no idea that my involvement in Sean's life had done anything at all." Hudson hadn't even focused that much attention on the boy, because he'd had a family who loved him. He'd spent more time with some of the others who'd had no support—and a decade ago his involvement was more limited.

"He never got along with his father, my daughter's ex. I think Drew was abusive, if you want the truth. Anyway, that man's no longer in the picture. But you were Sean's role model, someone he admired, right when it counted the most. I can't tell you how grateful I am for what you give to that school—me and his mother."

"I enjoy working with the boys," he said.

"And you can reach them, because you know what it's like to have a difficult childhood. It's made you caring, empathetic and willing to get off your ass instead of just sitting back and enjoying your money. That's why I won't let my neighbors take down this sign. I don't care if they like it or not. This sign stands for something. It stands for taking lemons and making lemonade. I, for one, am grateful that you were able to overcome what you've been through. You didn't let it break you—no sir—and that acts as a beacon for others. *That's* why football is important. It's football that put you up in front of everyone, so they could see your example."

Her words hit him so hard, Hudson couldn't speak right away. He'd been feeling sorry for himself, he realized, letting his pain and disappointment destroy him, as so many of the boys did. What he needed to do was overcome. Be the beacon this woman thought he was. He wasn't the only one who'd ever suffered—yet he'd been given a unique opportunity to make a difference.

"Thank you," he said. "Thank you for putting up the sign. I needed to see it."

"Oh, it's not going anywhere," she said, as if she'd gladly take on all challengers.

Hudson walked over to give her a hug. "You're an amazing woman," he murmured.

"And you're even more handsome up close. If I was forty years younger, you wouldn't still be single—not if I could help it," she said.

He laughed and waved at Archie, who was also laughing, as he walked away.

CHAPTER TWENTY-THREE

Ellie had gone to bed late. Even then she couldn't sleep. Bruiser hadn't been able to reach Hudson, either, so she had no idea where he was. She hated the thought that he was hurting and she couldn't do anything to help. She kept imagining him driving off the edge of Highway 1, a winding stretch of road hugging the California coast, because he was going too fast or being too reckless.

She wanted to call him again—but she'd tried so many times already. She was pretty sure he'd turned off his phone. Her calls transferred directly to voice mail and Bruiser said his did, too.

Hudson would get in touch with them eventually. He had to come back to his life, to her, at some point.

Didn't he?

"He'll be fine," she told herself, but nothing seemed to mitigate the worry that burned in her stomach like acid. As the minutes ticked by and she stared at her phone, hoping for some word on his whereabouts, the tears she'd held back all day began to fall.

She sat up and checked the alarm clock by her bed. It would be midday in France, which made it tempting to call her parents. They'd always been there for her, always given her love and support when she needed it most. Being so upset and frightened caused her to miss them more than ever. She wanted to talk to them—knew they were long overdue for a serious conversation, anyway.

She wasn't quite seven months, but she was close. It was time to tell them about the baby, about everything.

Hudson woke with a start. The sun was barely peeking over the horizon, and there was a highway patrolman peering in at him. Scrubbing a hand over his face, he collected his faculties and straightened so he could roll down the window.

"Hudson King?" the officer said as if he wasn't quite convinced he could believe what he saw.

A car whizzed by, and a gust of cool air ruffled Hudson's hair. "Yes?"

"What are you doing on the side of the road?"

"I was trying to make it back to my place in Silver Springs last night to surprise my girlfriend. But I got too tired. Had to pull over. And that's the last thing I remember."

The cop pursed his lips as he considered Hudson's excuse. "You haven't been drinking, have you?"

"Not a drop," he replied, but only after Hudson had taken a Breathalyzer test and the result showed zero alcohol in his system did the officer's attitude improve.

"It's not safe sleeping out here in the middle of nowhere," he said. "Anyone could've approached you, pulled out a gun, stolen your wallet or even your car." He whistled as he admired the Porsche. "You wouldn't want to lose this baby."

"I didn't plan to rest as long as I did."

"How are you feeling now?"

Hudson put his foot on the brake, ready to start the engine. "Fine. I'll be on my way."

"Will you do me a favor before you go?"

Hudson hesitated. "Sure. What is it?"

The officer gave him a sheepish look. "My son and I are big fans. Would you mind signing something I could take home to him?"

"Not at all." While he waited for the officer to bring him a piece of paper from his cruiser, Hudson searched for his phone. He'd turned it off to conserve battery power—he'd forgotten his charger in his truck—but he switched it on now. Bruiser and Ellie had left him many messages. He wanted to call them both, tell them he was okay. But it was too early. He didn't see any reason to wake them. He could reach out to Bruiser later. And he was only an hour or so away from Silver Springs.

He'd be home before Ellie even opened her eyes.

After a good cry while talking to her parents, who were too concerned about what might be going on with Hudson to be very angry at her for not telling them sooner, Ellie finally sank into a deep sleep. She kept dreaming about Hudson, though, so she didn't believe it was real when she heard him whisper her name, felt his hands slide under her and his mouth against her temple as he lifted her from the bed.

"Hudson?" she murmured, half-awake. "I've been so worried about you. Are you really back?"

"Yeah, I'm here."

"And you're okay?"

"I'm fine," he said as he carried her out of the room.

Reassured by his close proximity, she slipped her arms around his neck and pressed her cheek to his solid chest. "God, you scared me. I kept imagining you being too upset to pay attention to the road."

"I'm sorry."

She raised her head. "Did you get my messages?"

"I did."

"We're going to double-check every detail of what Cort

Matisson told you. Make sure it's all true. And if it is? We'll deal with it—together."

"We'll talk about that mess later."

"What are we doing now?" she asked as he put her in his bed.

"We're going to celebrate the fact that I have someone in my life who's worth hanging on to. That's what I need to focus on, because that's what matters most." He straightened. "If you want me as badly as I want you, that is."

She smiled up at him. "I've never wanted anyone more."

Hudson loved the swell of Ellie's stomach, the knowledge that she would soon give birth to their son. The three of them would be bound together for the rest of their lives by ties that could not easily be broken. Whether their relationship led to marriage or not, she'd always be the mother of his child, and his child would always belong to him. Barring something tragic, Ellie and their son would both be part of the rest of his life.

The feel of her naked body against his served as a perfect reminder that he was as lucky in some areas as he was unlucky in others. He needed to value the things that made him feel whole and happy, cling to the love she offered him and keep fighting to outdistance his past, regardless of the details of his birth or the humiliation he would suffer if those details were revealed to the public.

Being careful not to push down on the baby, he rested the bulk of his weight on his elbows and knees, then slid her beneath him. "What are we going to name our son?" She had a baby-naming book and had been highlighting ones with potential. She'd mentioned a few.

"We could name him after his father," she said, reaching up to smooth the hair out of his eyes.

"No, my name is a constant reminder of my past."

"It should also be a reminder of everything you've accomplished *despite* your past."

"I don't want to burden him with my bullshit—especially now."

"So what do you suggest?"

He kissed her neck, using his tongue so he could really taste her. He'd imagined doing this since he'd made love to her the last time. "Ryan has a nice ring to it."

"Don't you think there are a lot of Ryans in the world as it is?"

"*I* don't. I've never met a Ryan who's in an unfortunate situation. Ryans always seem to have everything. Ryan Gosling. Ryan Reynolds. Ryan Seacrest. Ryan Tedder."

"Who's Ryan Tedder?"

He chuckled to himself, somewhat surprised she hadn't asked who the other Ryans were, too. "Lead singer for One Republic."

"Oh. A band. But I was hoping to use a name that's more… unique. What about Cameron? Or, even better, Garrison?"

"Garrison King sounds good. Or there's Guido. I've never met a Guido outside the movies. That should be unique."

"Are you kidding?" she asked with a tinge of panic.

He laughed. "Yes."

"Whew! I'm happy to have your input, but whatever you do, don't choose Guido. That sounds like a member of the mafia."

"We'll talk about it later," he responded as he found her mouth. "You're all I can think about right now."

Her hands delved into his hair as she parted her lips. This was much better than the way they'd spent most other nights since she'd arrived. He should've carried her into his room long ago—and made love to her whenever she'd let him. The past six weeks suddenly seemed like such a waste of effort, trying not to love her. It felt good to give in to what he'd been feeling all along.

"You like California, don't you?" he asked as he kissed his way along her jawline. "You like living here with me?"

She took his face between her hands. "What are you talking about?"

"You're not suddenly going to tell me you're moving back to Miami? I can count on you being here at least until the baby turns six months, like we agreed? I have that long?"

"Hudson, I'm not going *anywhere*—not without you."

He watched her face as he spread her legs and pressed inside her. When she closed her eyes and arched her back as if their joining, especially in this moment, meant every bit as much to her as to him, he began to thrust with a possessiveness he'd never allowed himself to feel before. "This is where you'll sleep from now on," he told her.

She looked up at him. "What does that mean?"

"It means we're officially seeing each other. I'm done wanting you while you're in the next room."

She gasped as he lowered his mouth to her breast. "Careful. You're getting awfully close to a commitment," she teased.

"Whatever it takes," he muttered. "Just as long as I never lose you."

Ellie had thought she'd been in love with Don—and supposed that was a form of love, too—but it had lacked the ferocity she felt whenever she looked at Hudson, especially while he was sleeping, as he was now. The strength of her emotions overwhelmed and frightened her, made her fear she'd unleashed the dragon that would eventually destroy her. Although Hudson seemed to be doing better, he'd still struggle with the demons of his past. That type of thing didn't simply disappear.

Would he be able to recover? To put his abandonment issues behind him?

Maybe. Maybe not. She could still lose him to the dark thoughts that haunted him. He could decide to reject her love, to push her away, to insulate himself and make it impossible to feel pain. And if he couldn't feel pain, he wouldn't feel anything else, either. That was the thing.

She shifted so she could spoon him. "Don't let the past destroy what we could have together," she whispered, but she knew he hadn't heard her.

When Hudson woke, he kept his eyes closed for several minutes so he could savor the feel of Ellie's soft flesh and breathe in the smell of her silky hair. He'd found the woman he wanted to wake up with every morning. Thank God he'd been able to lower his defenses enough to realize it.

Actually, he *hadn't* lowered his defenses. The past six weeks were a testament to that. He'd fought what he was feeling from the beginning, but somehow Ellie had scaled his walls, and she'd done it simply by being herself. She calmed him, grounded him, *healed* him.

He moved his hand so he could feel his baby.

"You waking up?" she murmured, covering his fingers with hers as they moved over her belly.

"Yeah."

"Why? Are they expecting you at New Horizons?"

"No. It's Saturday." Sometimes he took Aaron or a handful of the other boys shopping, to the movies or out for pizza on the weekend. Or he played table tennis or video games with them in their game room. But he didn't have anything planned for today—and he was glad. As much as he enjoyed being with Ellie, having her back in his arms, he hadn't forgotten about Cort Matisson. He had to swab his cheek and get that DNA test sent to Samuel Jones. He also had to call Jones and ask for all the material he'd found on Cort Matisson. Hudson wanted to know *everything* about Matisson. He also wanted to know whether Julia was as sick as Cort had said and, if so, how he could make the most difference. Maybe she needed more than money; maybe she needed a better doctor, a better caregiver, a better place for her and her children to live. He'd decided he'd help *her,* but he wanted nothing to do with Cort, was going to make sure Cort didn't receive *anything*—not so much as a signed jersey.

Ellie covered a yawn. "So why are you waking up early?"

"It's nearly noon."

"But we didn't nod off until after eight. Four hours isn't enough. Let's sleep the day away."

He moved her hair to the side so he could kiss her neck. "I would if I could, but I have to get that DNA test in the mail."

"Oh, that's right." She turned to face him. "Can I make some suggestions on how we proceed from here?"

"You mean with Matisson?"

"How to handle the press that could arise from this."

"I think we need to prepare for the worst. The publicity will be embarrassing," he admitted. "For both of us. Now that you're connected to me, it'll reflect on you, too."

"I don't care—"

"That's easy to say before you hear the jeers and comments we're likely to get. Wait until you see the gross shit about inbreeding that'll be painted on posters and waved in the stands by fans of my opponents. It'll make you self-conscious about carrying my baby."

"That's terrible! Who would ever poke fun at something like that?"

"Believe me, it'll happen. Some people will find it funny. Because I'm famous, they think they can say anything they want about me. You've seen the 'Mean Tweets' segment on *Jimmy Kimmel…*"

"No."

He rolled his eyes as he laughed. "Of course not. Look who I'm talking to."

"Stop." She nudged him in the ribs. "I've been watching more TV since I came here. I'll get up to speed on pop culture."

"I'm not sure I want you to. I like you just the way you are—a little out of it." He laughed again to let her know his words weren't meant as a criticism. Then he sobered. "Even when I retire, this won't go away. It'll follow me for the rest of my life."

"I wish I could argue about that—"

"But I'm right."

"You might be. Some of the players on the teams you face will probably mutter comments—to try to get in your head—but you can't let them rattle you."

"Again, easier said than done."

She reached up to run her thumb along his jaw. "If the DNA test comes back and isn't what we hope, I say we hold a press conference."

"A press conference?"

"You need to make the announcement yourself."

"You want me to tell the world what I don't want them to know? What I don't want *anyone* to know?"

"It'll be better that way. If you make it very clear that what happened was terrible, reprehensible, but nothing you had any choice in, it'll set the tone for everyone else. You *can't* act as if you don't want it to come out, as if you're ashamed or hurt or whatever. That'll just hand your detractors a loaded gun."

"They're already holding a loaded gun, even if they don't know it yet."

"Still, that's your best play, the only thing you can do to control the fallout. Don't you think?"

He frowned as he considered her words. He hated the idea of going on TV to hang himself, but she was right. "Yeah." He started to get up, but she caught his arm.

"I did a little research while you were gone yesterday. Incidents of incest are woefully underreported. There have to be others—many others—who are in your situation. It's just not something anyone wants to talk about."

"Including me," he grumbled.

"I'm saying you're not alone. A baby doesn't result in every case, but I'm sure pregnancy occurs far more than it should."

"It should *never* happen."

"You know what I mean."

When she let him go, he got up to shower and dress—but heard his phone buzz from where he'd left it in the pocket of his pants. He almost ignored it. Because *he'd* learned the circumstances of his birth, he was afraid others were finding out, too, and this might be the first reporter. For all he knew, Cort Matisson had been so angry when he left, he'd contacted a journalist first thing and blabbed it all. Hudson wasn't going to check it. But as soon as he shut the bathroom door, he opened it again and went to get his phone.

Caller ID indicated it wasn't a reporter. "It's the PI," he said to Ellie, who was watching him with a concerned expression on her face.

He answered but didn't give Samuel Jones the chance to say hello. "Thanks a lot," he snapped. "You gave that douchebag Cort Matisson your card."

"I didn't tell him I worked for you."

"You didn't need to! Who else would hire a private investigator to go snooping around in his life? He figured out I was looking for my parents and showed up on my doorstep yesterday."

"I'm sorry," Jones said.

"I told you not to let *anyone* know what I was doing—least of all the people I was trying to find. You said you'd be discreet."

"I was afraid he'd call the police."

"Why would that matter? You would've been long gone by the time they showed up."

"He could've given them my license plate number, in which case they could easily identify me."

"Were you doing anything wrong?"

"Not really—"

"So if the police came calling, you could've explained that

you were working a case. They barely put rapists and murderers in prison these days. What could be the penalty for going through someone's trash?"

There was a long pause before he said, "You're right. I got what I needed, a beer bottle for DNA evidence. After that, I should've walked away without responding. I wasn't thinking."

Jones had seemed clever, had managed to do what even the police could not. That he'd been so obtuse at Matisson's house didn't make sense. "Why are you calling now?"

"I have what *might* be considered good news."

Hudson heard the emphasis Jones put on the word *might*, so he wasn't optimistic. "I'm listening."

"Cort Matisson just called me."

"He called *you*."

"Yes. He was upset that you threw him out when he tried to talk to you, but he said he'll give you one more chance."

Hudson felt his muscles tense. As far as he was concerned, Matisson had gotten off easy. "One more chance to do what?"

"Help his daughter. If you wire a million bucks into his bank account, he'll never contact you again. He won't say anything to the press about being your father, either. The manner of your birth and the details of your abandonment will remain a mystery, at least to the rest of the world."

Hudson felt his jaw drop. "He's *blackmailing* me?"

Jones cleared his throat. "He's...asking to be paid off."

How was that any different? "He can't come forward," Hudson said. "Not without risking criminal charges, maybe even attempted murder, for leaving me out to die."

"He's willing to risk it for his daughter's sake."

Tightening his grip on the phone, Hudson almost told Jones to tell Cort he could go to hell. Although Hudson wasn't unwilling to help Julia, he refused to be forced into anything.

The words were on the tip of his tongue when a flicker of hope stole some of the fire from his anger and made him think twice. *Could he buy his way out of this?* It was too late to escape the knowledge of his shameful conception. But it would be much easier to bear if only he and those who were closest to him—Ellie and Bruiser, whom he would've told even if Ellie hadn't—were aware of how he'd come to be born. With the amount of money he made, he could afford the loss. He'd originally offered that much to Ellie in exchange for custody, hadn't he?

"He's threatening to talk to the press?" Ellie dragged the sheet with her as she got up on her knees.

Hudson covered the phone. "Matisson claims he'll keep his mouth shut and go away—if I give him a significant amount of money to do so."

She scowled in obvious outrage. "You're not going to pay him, are you? Like you said, he *can't* come forward, not without incriminating himself."

"He claims it's for his daughter."

"What if she's not even sick? So far, all we have is his word, and I don't see him as reliable."

Neither did Hudson. He just wanted the whole thing to go away as soon as possible, wanted to return to enjoying Ellie and preparing for the birth of their son without this dark cloud hanging over him, making him feel worthless whenever his mind wandered back to the encounter with Matisson in his living room.

He uncovered his phone so he could agree to Matisson's terms. He'd be helping a dying woman, someone who had kids.

But after he wired the money, there'd be nothing to stop Matisson from selling his story to the press to get even more—or threatening to do it every time he needed a quick infusion of cash. Hudson would be a fool to believe someone like Cort—someone who could impregnate his own daughter and leave her newborn outside to die. If Hudson was going to help Julia, it had to be on his own terms.

"Try to buy some time," Ellie whispered. "If Julia's as sick as he says, you might want to help, anyway. And if she's not..."

"If she's not, this guy's the parasite he appears to be, and I can't let him get his hooks into me."

"That's the way I see it, too," she said.

He returned to his conversation with Jones. "I'll consider it on two conditions."

"I'm not sure you should mess around with this guy, Hudson," the PI said. "Imagine what your life will be like if he goes to the press."

"His will be worse, since he'll probably go to prison," Hudson countered. "Tell him I'd like to meet Julia, speak to her myself—and get her medical records to verify his story. Then we'll talk about money."

There was a long pause. "He doesn't want her to know who you are, what he did with her child. And you shouldn't want that, either. Then there'll be one more person who knows the truth and might let it out."

"He'll have to make up a story, then. Tell her he submitted her name to some charity where celebrities and sports figures help deserving people, and I'm coming out to meet her. Something like that."

After another pause, Jones said, "Okay."

Hudson could feel Ellie watching him as he disconnected. "What do you think?" she asked.

He tossed his phone on the bed. "I think I should've been satisfied with being rich and famous."

She chuckled, but he could tell she knew he wasn't entirely joking.

CHAPTER TWENTY-FOUR

Ellie rode over to the courier's with Hudson to mail the DNA test to Samuel Jones, who said he wanted to collect a fresh sample from Cort Matisson—rather than use the beer bottle he'd found in Matisson's trash. They had breakfast afterward at a little restaurant in town. She could feel the envious stares of the waitresses and the interest of the other diners, who kept glancing over because they were so excited to see Hudson eating in the same restaurant.

Hudson pretended not to notice the attention, but smiled and nodded at anyone who looked up as they walked out—which was pretty much everyone.

"You handle your fame well," Ellie told him as they reached the street.

He took her hand. "Believe it or not, I'm grateful for it."

"*Grateful?* I thought you resented the loss of privacy."

"Sometimes I do, but the only thing worse than being wanted too much is not being wanted at all," he said as he opened her side of the car.

She found it hard to imagine him in that kind of situation; there was so much about him to love. But of course, she knew his childhood had not been easy.

As soon as they got home and parked in the garage, Ellie asked him to pull out the original police file from when he was abandoned so she could read it.

"Why waste your time?" he asked.

"I know so little about what happened the day you were born and what was done to find the person who abandoned you. Who the police talked to, what those people had to say. I don't like being uninformed about anything I'm dealing with, especially something that has me frustrated, fearful or upset."

"But what's in the file doesn't matter anymore. It's down to DNA. Either my DNA matches Matisson's or it doesn't. There's nothing that'll change my fate, not if we're a match."

He sounded so fatalistic. "What if you're not a match?"

After letting them in, he tossed his keys on the kitchen table. "What are the chances of that? Jones went through every document in that file. You'll just be redoing work he's already done."

"I don't have anything better to do at the moment, and we might have a wait ahead of us. Who can say how long it'll take Jones to meet with Matisson, get a new sample and send it in? He's got to fly there, do the test, add your sample when it arrives, mail them both in and wait for the results. I'm guessing we've got a week to ten days, and that's if he moves fast. I don't see any reason *not* to put that time to good use."

Hudson looked as if he'd continue to argue, so she slid her arms around his neck and pecked him on the lips. "Please? Jones did what he did so he'd get paid. I'm sure he'll charge you more for jumping in and helping now—even though he's the one who caused all this by giving Matisson his card. *I'm* doing it because I care about you. Which of us do you think will be more dedicated to protecting your interests?"

He sighed as he locked his hands at her lower back, keeping her against him. "Fine. I don't see any reason why you *shouldn't* see the file. But I can't bring myself to read through it again."

She understood. He was too restless, too troubled. Watching

him was like watching a caged panther pace the length of a small cage, golden eyes staring out with anger and resentment—and the promise that things would not go well for whoever dared challenge him. Coping with such strong emotions was especially hard for him because he wasn't playing football right now, couldn't turn that anger and resentment into energy and unleash it. There were moments she felt he was coming to terms with what he'd learned. But more often, she felt him pushing it away, doing anything to avoid thinking about it.

"You don't have to," she told him. "You were talking about going to LA for a team meeting."

"I have to be there early Monday, so I'll have to leave tomorrow night."

"I'll study the file while you're gone. It'll give me a way to distract myself."

He tucked her hair behind her ears. "I was hoping you'd go to LA with me."

She could tell he'd been afraid to let himself lean on her. This showed that he was gaining trust. But she couldn't join him. "Unfortunately, I have a doctor's appointment here on Monday, remember?"

He frowned. "I guess I'll be going alone, then."

Ellie didn't mind being left behind. She wanted to dive into the file while he was busy doing other things.

She'd assumed she'd have to wait until he left to start on that. While he was home, he wanted her to play pool with him and swim and make love. But his agent called the next day, as they were having breakfast, and he went into his office to discuss his upcoming contract, which gave Ellie the opportunity to open the file a bit earlier.

She carried it, along with her laptop, into the dining room and was deep in a statement from the pizza deliveryman who'd saved the newborn when Hudson came to find her.

"You bored yet?" he asked, bending down behind her to nuzzle her neck.

"No."

"Once you've gone through it, you'll see how impressive it is that Jones figured it out. There's not a lot in there to indicate Matisson was involved. As many times as I read that file, I never thought twice about him."

Hudson had been on the phone for almost two hours, long enough for her to take a cursory glance at most of the documents. So far, all she'd found about Matisson was a one-paragraph statement that contained no information she considered particularly interesting. "So how did Samuel Jones connect him to your abandonment?"

Hudson took the chair next to her. "He made a list of all the people who were in the area that day and researched each one. Started with those who were viewed as persons of interest by the police—the neighbor down the street whose daughter had already had two abortions and the dog walker who'd gotten a woman pregnant and tried to run her over so his wife wouldn't find out. But those came to nothing, just like they had for the investigating detective. So he moved on to other people, even the obscure ones. Tried to figure out what had happened to every person who'd ever been contacted about the case."

"That's a lot of work."

"I paid a lot for it."

"How long did it take him?"

"Three, four months."

She picked up Matisson's statement. "So once he stumbled on Cort, who was in the neighborhood that day, he did a background check?"

"Basically. Told me he ran across a newspaper article indicating there was a guy connected to my case who stood trial about the time I started at New Horizons for sexually abusing his daughter when she was only a teenager."

"And he figured a guy like that might be the type of person who'd abandon a baby."

"He told me that's what made him dig deeper."

Ellie brought her laptop close. Sure enough, when she typed Cort Matisson's name into a search engine and sifted through the links that corresponded to people with a similar name on Facebook, she found a newspaper article from *The Arizona Republic.* The article covered Julia's complaints against her father and included a quote in which she mentioned her stillborn baby.

"Nice work." She couldn't help being impressed with Samuel Jones. The link was fairly obscure and yet he'd connected Cort to the neighborhood *and* an unwanted child.

But then Ellie read Julia's quote more carefully.

> I had a baby when I was only sixteen. The baby was his, no question. I'd never been with anyone else. He was freaky jealous of any boy who showed any interest in me. Anyway, all the police have to do is find where he buried my child, and DNA will do the rest. Doesn't matter that it's been fifteen years. You can get DNA from bones, you know. I've seen it on TV.

At first, Ellie was so wrapped up in the tragedy of those words and what Julia had been through that she didn't realize the dates were off. But just before she clicked on to the next article, it occurred to her. The article had been published fifteen years ago in November. If Julia had her baby fifteen years before that, the child would be thirty now. Hudson was thirty-two.

Could Julia have been speaking in general terms?

It wasn't as if she'd mentioned a date…

"What's wrong?" Hudson asked.

Ellie blinked and straightened to ease her aching back. "Nothing." Surely Julia wasn't being specific when she made that statement…

“Are you ready to give up yet?” Hudson waved at all the documents she’d spread out on the table.

“No. This is important.”

“The only thing that’s important is the DNA test.”

“Julia needs to take one, too. Maybe she isn’t really Cort’s daughter. Or you’re not really her son. Have you heard back from Jones? Will Matisson respect your demands?”

“Hasn’t called yet.” He stretched his neck in one direction, then the other. “For all we know, Cort’s already talking to *People* magazine, trying to sell his story for more than a million.”

The knot of worry that sat beneath Ellie’s breastbone grew tighter. She hoped that wasn’t the case. “Even though he’ll go to prison if he admits he left a baby to die?”

“With that kind of money, life inside would probably be better than what he’s known on the outside.”

“Would you rather just pay him off?”

He scratched his head. “If it meant I’d never hear from him again.”

“But…”

“I’m afraid he’d only be back on my doorstep after he blows through it.”

She let her breath seep out. “That’s what I’m afraid of, too. It’s hard to wait, but I don’t think we have any other choice.”

He nodded as he stood. “There’s no easy way out.”

During the next few hours, until Hudson left to have dinner with Bruiser in LA, Ellie couldn’t stop thinking about Julia’s statement in that newspaper article. Fifteen was a nice round number; it could’ve been a quick approximation. A lot of people talked in round numbers. But wouldn’t a grieving mother know *exactly* how long it’d been since she lost her child?

Ellie felt most mothers would’ve used terms more like “Seventeen years, two months and thirteen days ago, I had a child…”

Perhaps that was a bit extreme, but Julia should at least have gotten the year right.

Or maybe not. Everyone was different.

Ellie hurried back to the dining room as soon as Hudson kissed her goodbye. She was surprised by how many people she came across in that file—not only the people who lived in the neighborhood but all their extended family and friends and the hired help. Out of all the possibilities, why did Hudson's father have to be Cort Matisson?

With a sigh, Ellie returned to the statement given by the pizza deliveryman—a Stan Hinkle. He said he heard a faint cry and went to investigate. That was how he'd discovered Hudson. But Ellie wasn't sure how he could've heard a baby cry from two houses down. Perhaps two houses didn't sound like much in a regular neighborhood, but in Bel Air the houses were pretty far apart.

She called up Google Earth to take a look.

It was quite a distance, all right.

Unable to resist, Ellie called Hudson. "Do you stay in touch with the pizza deliveryman who found you?"

"No."

"Why not?"

"I don't know. He was only twenty-four at the time. Turned me over to the state and that was it."

"But he saved your life. You'd think he'd show some interest, even if it's just a Christmas card once a year."

"Never heard from him, but that isn't so unusual. Maybe he was afraid he'd feel obligated to do more for me than he wanted. Not many people took an interest—until I proved I could play football."

Once again, her eyes skimmed over Hinkle's interview. "Has he contacted you *since* you became famous?"

"No. I'll admit I've wondered why he hasn't at least hit me up for tickets. I'd certainly give him some. Why?"

"Just curious," she said. But if the DNA test Hudson had

taken didn't match Cort's, she was going to do a little more research on Hinkle.

Ellie's phone beeped to signal that she had an incoming call. She thought it might be her parents. Her mother was having a more difficult time forgiving her for not telling them about the pregnancy than her father. Ellie was still working on calming her down and making that okay, so she wanted to answer if it was her mother. Her parents were cutting their trip short, but only by a few months, so at least she'd succeeded in not ruining their entire year.

Caller ID indicated it was Amy, and Ellie wanted to talk to her. "Okay. Enjoy dinner with Bruiser."

"I miss you already," he said.

Surprised, she hesitated. He'd been so busy rejecting almost everyone that he'd starved himself of love. He needed her—needed someone. But she couldn't possibly know if he'd ever love her as much as she was coming to love him. "I'll drive to LA after my doctor's appointment. Maybe it'll be easier for you if we wait for the results of the DNA test at your house there. More distractions," she added.

"No. I'll come back to Silver Springs. LA was great when I was younger. But now that we're having a baby, Silver Springs feels more like home."

Fear that Hudson wouldn't be able to commit to their relationship as it progressed made Ellie wonder if, at some point, she'd regret letting go enough to reach for him. She'd once thought he was unattainable. Now that he was so responsive, she wanted to believe she'd been wrong about that, but only time would tell. "Then I'll be here waiting for you."

When they disconnected, Amy had hung up, but Ellie called her back.

"How's the pregnancy going?" Amy asked. "You haven't sent me your weekly pic."

"I'm getting bigger every day." Ellie stood sideways to get a new selfie that included her stomach and texted the photo to Amy.

"Nice," Amy said when it arrived. "I can finally see a baby bump. A little one, mind you…"

Ellie thought of the way Hudson touched her belly, so possessively and lovingly. "It's not small anymore, but thanks for trying to make me feel good."

"That's what friends are for," Amy said. "How's the famous athlete?"

He'd been better. Ellie wished she could discuss what they were going through, but she knew Hudson wouldn't appreciate it if she did. He was so private to begin with—and, understandably, he didn't want *anyone* to know about Cort Matisson. "He's doing well." She toyed with the ends of her hair. "Just told me he missed me, and he hasn't been gone an hour."

"Whoa. That says *a lot*."

Since he wasn't all that vocal, Ellie wanted to believe it did. But was she deluding herself? "I'm scared, Amy."

"Of what?"

"Of how strongly I feel about him."

There was a slight pause. "Sounds like you've fallen for him."

"I'm not sleeping alone anymore, I can tell you that."

"You're not?"

"No. He asked me to move all my stuff into his room this morning. I can't stop myself from loving him, not when he's always touching me, kissing me or making me laugh. I can't get enough of Hudson King, and that makes me feel so darn vulnerable."

"Don't freak out," Amy said. "Everything's going to be okay. You're just emotional because of the pregnancy hormones."

Ellie sat down and rested her head on the back of her chair. She wished that was all it was, but she had a feeling it had *everything* to do with Hudson. "I hope you're right."

"So do I," she said. "What happened to being cautious?"

"I can't be cautious and still give him what he needs."

"What he *needs*? Doesn't look like he needs anything."

"He's human, Amy. He has the same needs we all do. But he's so...contrary. Resists what he wants most."

"Yep. You've succumbed, all right."

Ellie slumped in her chair. "Completely."

"Maybe you should take a break from him, come out here for a visit."

"I'm already twenty-eight weeks along. I probably shouldn't fly." She couldn't leave Hudson right now anyway.

"I'd come there if I could, but I'm so busy at work, and I need the money."

"I'd rather you came after the baby's born. You'll want to meet him, won't you?"

"Of course. I'm the godmother, don't forget. Have you told your parents?"

"Just this week."

"Wow. A lot's changed, and you haven't even called me!"

"I've been too involved with Hudson. I'm sorry."

"I understand. I'd be pretty involved with him, too," she said with a laugh.

Ellie asked about her love life and how her parents were doing, and talked more about her own parents and their reactions to her news.

"They weren't happy to be left out of the loop, but they understand why I did it," she said.

"Are they coming home?"

"Not for a few weeks. They'll be here for the birth, but I told them I'm in good hands—and Hudson and I are in California and need some time alone to bond."

"That was a smart answer."

Considering Cort Matisson's visit, Ellie was especially glad she'd acted to protect her time with Hudson. He didn't need any more stress at the moment. "I think so."

"Well, don't forget to find *me* an NFL player," she said. "I could use a break from the salon."

Ellie wished they still lived close. "That'll be easier during the season. *I* haven't even met the team—only Hudson's best friend, who's already married."

"Do you think Hudson will ever find out who his parents were?" Amy asked.

Ellie caught her breath. "It's possible, I suppose. Why?"

"Just wondering. It would be so hard—knowing you were abandoned and having no clue where you came from."

The only thing worse was finding out—at least when it was someone like Cort Matisson. "I'd better go," she said. Ellie was afraid that if they continued to talk about Hudson's background, she'd blurt out everything she'd been worrying about.

"Okay, but before you hang up, I wanted to tell you that Don came in to get his hair cut, and he brought Leo."

Being engaged to Don suddenly seemed like a century ago—and almost insignificant now. "He did? What'd they have to say?"

"Not much. Just asked how you and the baby were doing."

"What'd you tell them?"

"I showed them the last picture you sent me, and Don stared at it for so long, I got the feeling he misses you."

Ellie shoved her hair out of her face. "I guess, when I think about it, there are things I miss about him, too. He understood my work and my love for it—shared that with me. In many ways, we were a lot alike."

"And you and Hudson are totally different!"

"That's true. But maybe that's why we work better as a couple. At least, in my mind we do."

"I'm so glad you're happy."

"Thanks," Ellie said. Problem was…nothing this good ever seemed to last. And—she drew a deep breath as she gazed at the papers strewn across the dining room table—she had a feeling Hudson would not take the news well if the results of that DNA test came back positive, even though he was expecting it.

CHAPTER TWENTY-FIVE

Samuel Jones called just before Hudson was supposed to go in for the team meeting. Bruiser glanced over when Hudson answered and must've been able to tell from the look on his face that this was the moment he'd been waiting for. He immediately stepped up to tell everyone that Hudson had to take care of a personal matter and would join them in a minute.

Hudson turned away. "So? What'd Matisson say?"

"His daughter's not doing well," Jones replied. "He won't wait, says he's desperate."

Tilting his head back, Hudson closed his eyes. "So...how fast is he talking?"

"If he doesn't get the money today, he'll go to the papers."

Bullshit. He'd sell his story to one of the gossip rags, capitalize on it. Why would he give it away for free? "So he's not willing to let me meet Julia? Speak to her?"

"No, he's too nervous about that. He's afraid she'll guess what's going on."

"How could she guess—if she thinks her baby died?"

"I don't know, Hudson. The guy isn't the easiest person in the world to deal with, okay? That's all I can tell you. He's a loose cannon. I suggest you pay him off and be done with it. You've got the money."

Hudson stiffened at Jones's last comment. "It's not just about the money. It's the principle. I don't like letting some lowlife blackmail me, especially when I have no guarantee he'll keep his word."

"I think he'll honor the agreement."

"How long will it take to get the DNA results?"

"A week or longer."

"Why? You'll have my sample today."

"I have to take it with me, fly to Arizona, get Matisson to swab his cheek and then ship it off. Who knows how long the lab will take."

"It shouldn't be more than two days. I've checked. There are labs with that turnaround time."

"Shorter might be possible. I'll try, but we've got to get this right."

"Yeah, I know." Hudson clenched his free hand, wishing he could plant it in Matisson's face.

"So, what do you say? Should we do this deal—get it behind us?"

Hudson walked over to the window and gazed out at the lush landscaping. If a million dollars could prevent Cort Matisson from selling his story, maybe Hudson was being stupid for resisting. And if the money was going to help a dying woman, he could even justify it.

But would the money really go to Julia? That was the question. And if Matisson was *that* desperate to help his daughter, why wouldn't he let Hudson meet her? "No."

"No?"

He heard the amazement in Jones's voice.

"What are you thinking, man? You have a public image to protect."

"If Matisson sells his story to some magazine, he'll incriminate himself at the same time. If he offers *me* the proof I'm asking for, we can keep the past just between us. Surely he'd prefer to avoid an attempted murder charge."

"This dude is crazy," Jones said. "He's willing to risk his freedom."

"Then tell him to go for it." Hudson hit End before he could change his mind. The thought of reading Matisson's story in the next issue of *People* magazine made him feel ill. But he wouldn't be able to respect himself if he gave in to this bastard's demands, not without doing his homework. He refused to be that big a fool.

Bruiser came out of the room where the meeting was taking place. Hearing his approach, Hudson looked up.

"Hey, you off the phone? That was the investigator, right?"

"Yeah."

"How'd it go?"

Hudson shook his head. "I won't give that no-good bastard a dime—not unless he's willing to prove who he is and why he needs the money."

Bruiser rubbed his big hands together. "I could've guessed that'd be your decision."

"The truth is the truth. Whatever happens, I'll just have to face it."

"You're a stubborn son of a bitch," his friend said with an affectionate smile. "But in this instance, I'm glad."

Ellie switched the phone to her other ear. "He did *what*?"

"He didn't tell you?" Bruiser responded.

"He didn't mention it, no. He called me after the meeting to let me know that the owner of the team—"

"Craig Thompson."

"Yeah—sorry, I'd forgotten his name." She'd been too immersed in what she was reading when Hudson had checked in. She'd grasped that he was staying a few more days to fulfill some commitments, but she hadn't paid much attention to the details. "Anyway, he told me Craig asked him to play some golf and then meet a friend for dinner tonight—but he didn't say he'd heard from Jones, and I didn't ask because I'd rather not keep hammering him about it. Matisson is weighing on his mind enough as it is."

"We talked about it during the meeting and then again after, while he was waiting for Craig. Now that he's refused to give Matisson the money, I think he's just holding his breath, waiting to see what happens next."

Ellie had been reading the file as quickly as possible, but it was thick, and she was being careful not to miss anything. She hadn't made it through all the material yet. "I hate that after doing what he did when Hudson was born, Cort Matisson is trying to hurt him again—even if he's doing it for the sake of a sick daughter. He walked off and left Hudson to *die*. He has no right to come back to him for help."

"While I pity the daughter—provided she's truly suffering—I agree. If that old man goes to the press..."

"It'd be a stupid move. Hopefully he'll hold off, continue trying to work out a deal with Hudson."

"Except Jones says Julia's not doing well. So Matisson's in a big rush."

"Then he should offer Hudson proof of her illness. That's all Hudson requested."

"Jones says he won't."

She bit her lip as she gazed helplessly at all the paper she'd organized into various stacks. There was nothing tangible in what she'd read, nothing that could help Hudson as things stood. "I wish there was something *we* could do to get the proof he needs."

"I do, too. But that's impossible. We'd need Matisson's DNA in order to establish whether they're truly related. Even if we had it, Jones told Hudson it'll take a week to ten days to get the results."

"Testing doesn't *have* to take that long. I've checked. And there's a lab in LA that's AABB accredited. If we had Matisson's DNA, we could drive it over there and still make it before five. That means we could find out as early as Wednesday."

"But if Matisson's out looking for someone to buy his story, even two days will be too late."

"Not necessarily. The man I saw was a bit rough around the edges. He might not know how to go about marketing the story, probably doesn't know who to approach. And negotiations could take some time. If he's trying to get as much as possible, he might try to start a bidding war, which could slow things down."

"I'm afraid that's wishful thinking."

She rubbed her tired eyes. Now that she was in her final trimester, the baby seemed to be sapping her energy. "Maybe it is, but I'm not willing to give up."

"I don't see that we have any choice. Hudson told me Matisson lives in Arizona now. There's no way we could get his DNA any sooner than Jones. At least Jones has his cooperation."

Dropping her head in her hand, Ellie massaged her forehead. She wished Hudson had offered Matisson a drink of some kind when he came to the house. Then they'd have his DNA right here in Silver Springs.

She lifted her head. Bruiser was saying something, but she let the phone fall from her ear. A memory had flashed in her mind. Cort Matisson had a pack of cigarettes in his pocket when he came here. She'd seen him pat his chest as if he was desperate for a smoke. And he'd walked in smelling like a chimney. She'd picked up the acrid scent all the way from where she stood on the stairs…

"Bruiser, let me call you back." She was in such a hurry, she set her cell on the table without even bothering to hit End. She doubted she'd be as lucky as she needed to be. After all, it'd been two days since Matisson's visit, so even if he *had* stood outside and smoked a cigarette before knocking on the door, the wind or the gardeners could've swept it away.

Still, she rushed out and searched the porch, flower beds and shrubbery. She even walked the long circular drive, looking at the edges of the grass in case he'd stamped on a cigarette as he got out of his vehicle and the butt had since fluttered to the side.

Unfortunately, she found nothing.

"Damn." She had no doubt a cigarette butt would be a good source of DNA. She would've been *thrilled* to find one.

Shaking her head in disappointment, she started back to the house. She was thinking she'd hire a different private investigator, one who had no contact with Matisson and would simply research Julia—her birth date and medical history—when she spotted a bit of white tucked up against the foundation of the house.

She held her breath as she went over to investigate—and felt a smile stretch across her face as she bent down. She'd discovered a cigarette butt, all right, and one that could easily belong to Matisson.

"I hear you're seeing someone," Craig said.

Hudson picked up his drink. They'd finished golfing—Hudson had lost to Craig for the first time since they'd started playing together, which hadn't improved his day—and were seated in the bar of a swanky steak and seafood place. The restaurant boasted five stars, but it was in Bel Air, not far from where Hudson had been found as a newborn. Normally that wouldn't be a big deal. Hudson was used to living in close proximity to that neighborhood. But with everything on his mind today, he wished Craig had chosen someplace else. "I am. Her name's Ellie Fisher."

"She's a scientist or something?"

"Yeah. Specializes in immunology."

"Sounds smart."

"She is. We're expecting a baby this summer."

"Congratulations."

He was sure Craig had already heard about the baby, too. Bruiser had likely mentioned it when he'd mentioned Ellie, probably when Craig had struck up a random conversation and asked how he was doing, but it wasn't a secret, so Hudson didn't mind. "Thank you," he said, forcing a smile. He had no problem doing favors for Craig—showing up at his house for parties and meeting his family and friends—but he wasn't in the mood today. He kept wondering if he was being foolish to refuse Matisson. Was he letting his pride get in the way of making a sound decision?

That would be like him. What would he do if he opened the paper tomorrow and saw the kind of headline he feared—Famous NFL Quarterback Child of Incest?

His phone buzzed. Although it was rude to reveal how distracted he was by focusing on that call at the table, Craig's friend hadn't shown up yet, so Hudson excused himself to go to the bathroom. Then he checked caller ID.

It was Ellie—as he'd thought.

"Hey, I'm still with Craig," he said. "Can I call you after?"

"I'm sorry to bother you," she responded. "But I need to swing by and have you step out for a second to swab your cheek."

"Whoa, wait. You're here? *In LA?*"

"I am. Will you be able to give me a minute?"

He twisted his head to see around a big plant that hid him from Craig. The team owner was standing and shaking hands with another man. Craig's friend had arrived. "I can make it happen. But why are we doing another DNA test? What about the one I sent?"

"This is for our own test, one *we* control."

"What good will it do without Matisson's DNA?"

"I'm pretty sure I have Matisson's DNA. I also have a technician standing by at a trustworthy lab."

Hudson stepped aside to avoid a waiter who was coming through. "How'd you get Matisson's DNA?"

"I have what I hope is one of his cigarette butts."

"From..."

"Outside, by the front door."

"You didn't mention my name, did you? When you called the lab?"

"No, of course not. I just offered to pay double if someone would wait for me. Figured you wouldn't mind the added expense."

"Not at all. Thanks."

"No problem. Anyway, I need to focus so I don't screw up and miss a turn. Can you drop me a pin so I can find you?"

"Doing it now."

"Perfect. We should get the results on Wednesday, Hudson. I've also hired a different private investigator—another expense I assumed you wouldn't mind."

"I don't, but...what for?"

"She's digging up everything she can find on Julia—so we don't need to wait for Jones to do that, since he's dealing with Matisson right now and getting to Arizona."

Since Hudson had been tied up all day and could only stew about his troubles, he was grateful for her help. "Do you really think all this will make any difference?"

"It's worth a shot—small beans in comparison to a million dollars."

Hudson lowered his head to stare at his feet. "I've never met anyone like you."

"I hope that's a good thing," she joked.

"It is. I'm glad I spotted you in that nightclub—and hit you up."

"So am I. I love you, Hudson—even though you warned me not to."

She spoke fast and hung up. He got the impression she was afraid of how he might respond, so she didn't hear him mutter, "Thank God you didn't listen."

CHAPTER TWENTY-SIX

When Hudson finally got to his LA house, he found Ellie asleep on the couch in front of a TV even bigger than the one he'd purchased for Silver Springs. Whenever he saw it, he had to chuckle. It reminded him of the pissing contest he'd gotten into with some of the other team members—which was what had compelled him to track it down and buy it. He loved that TV, and so did the other guys. They always came to his place to watch whatever fight or other sporting event they wanted to see together.

Some reality show was playing now, droning on although no one was listening or watching. Ellie looked as if she'd been asleep for a while. She'd mentioned that she was often fatigued in this stage of the pregnancy, and according to what she'd told him over the phone, she'd had a couple of long days since he'd been gone. She'd stayed up late with that file, gotten up early to return to her research and then jumped into action when she found that cigarette butt.

"Hey." He knelt down beside her and lifted up her shirt to kiss her belly. "I'm home."

She raised sleepy eyelids to focus on him, and a sweet smile curved her lips. "I'm glad."

He kissed her tummy again. "How do you like the house?"

"What I've seen of it is nice."

"You didn't look around?"

"I was afraid I'd get lost," she joked.

He put down her shirt. "Believe me, I would've found you."

She combed her fingers through his hair. "Actually, it felt a bit intrusive to let myself in and go snooping around when you weren't home. I decided I'd let you give me the tour."

"Only you," he said. "I don't know one other person who wouldn't have searched through everything."

She laughed. "Is that what you did to my house in Miami?"

He winced. "I glanced around. But then, I'm not as thoughtful as you are."

"Are you being facetious?"

"I wish I was." She always seemed to take other people into consideration, and that made him feel he could trust her. Maybe that was why he *did* trust her—more than he'd ever trusted any other woman. "Sorry I'm so late." Craig had insisted Hudson come home with him for after-dinner drinks and a visit with his family. Ellie had texted to tell him that she'd delivered the DNA test to the lab and found his house, and he'd called his housekeeper, who lived off the premises, to let her in. But he still felt bad that she'd been waiting for so long and hadn't felt she could make herself comfortable. "You should've gone up to my bed."

"This was fine. It's a huge couch. And I've never seen a TV that size."

He glanced back. "Yeah, I went a little overboard."

"Everything in your life is *big*. Your name. Your bank account. Your houses."

"Don't stop there." He winked at her, and she laughed.

"Is that what you're most proud of?"

"I'm a guy. What can I say?" He lifted her hand and rubbed her knuckles against his cheek. "So you got the DNA to the lab?"

"I did."

"And we'll find out day after tomorrow?"

"The guy who waited for me wouldn't commit, but he said it was possible."

All his levity vanished as he rested his head in her lap. "I spoke to Jones before the meeting today."

"I know. Bruiser told me."

"Did he tell you that Matisson threatened to go to the press if I didn't fork over the money immediately—without any proof?"

"He did. That's a concern on the one hand. But on the other… I see it as hopeful."

He lifted his head. "In what way?"

"If he's pushing that hard, maybe he *can't* offer proof. And if he can't offer proof, maybe it's because he isn't telling the truth."

"Don't I wish…"

"Even if he sells the story to a magazine, they're going to need substantiating documents, so he'll have to support his claims."

Taking the remote from the coffee table, he turned off the TV, then got up and sat next to her on the couch. "Tell me something."

"What's that?"

"You don't like the attention I attract—you'd rather I wasn't famous. You've made that clear in the past."

"It's true, but—" she grinned "—no one's perfect."

When he didn't smile, she put her hand on his arm. "Don't overthink it. You are who and what you are, and I'm willing to accept that."

He raked one hand through his hair. "But if you don't like the positive attention I receive, how will you cope with the *negative* attention?"

She took the remote away, set it aside and pressed him back

so that he was lounging on the couch. "I'll deal with it the same way you will. We'll pull through by focusing on better things."

"Like..."

He watched as she popped open the top button of his jeans and pulled down the zipper. "This."

Hudson wasn't in bed when Ellie woke the next morning. She pulled on a robe and went down to see if he was in the kitchen but didn't find him until she reached the gym. She stood at the door, watching him lift weights for a while. She could see the concentration on his face and the strain he was putting on his body and knew he was doing what he could to stay busy.

"Is everything okay?" she asked.

He glanced over once he realized she was there. "If you're asking whether Matisson's come forward—" he pushed himself to do another rep "—I don't think so." The barbell clanged as he dropped it the last few inches to the floor. "Not yet. I can't find anything new about him on the internet. So...we'll see what happens today."

"Is that why you're down here so early? You couldn't sleep?"

He walked over and, despite her attempt to fend him off, pulled her into his arms.

"What the heck?" she complained. "You're sweaty!"

"Exactly. My plan is to get you sweaty, too. Then you'll want to shower with me."

He looked as if he was about to return to weight lifting before their shower, so she made sure that didn't happen. Opening her robe, she brought his hand to her breast and tugged him in for a deeper kiss. "Where do you think you're going?"

"Nowhere," he replied as his hand slid lower. "I'm glad you're awake."

"Last night wasn't enough?" she teased.

"I could never get enough of you."

She felt the same about him, which was why the whole precarious situation with Matisson scared her so badly. She tried not to think of how rough the rest of the week could get—easy when Hudson urged her into the closest bedroom and onto the bed. But after they were both satisfied, reality intruded yet again. Shelly Gomez, the private detective she'd hired, sent her a text with pictures and a short video, which Ellie received the moment they stepped out of the shower.

"What is it?" Hudson had noticed she wasn't dressing. He'd put on his boxers and jeans but wasn't wearing a shirt when he walked over.

She lifted up her phone so he could see for himself. "Julia Matisson, who now goes by Julia Bowers, looks pretty darn healthy to me."

He slowly swiped through the pictures. "This woman is Julia?"

"According to Shelly Gomez, it's her and her two sons."

"How'd Gomez get these photos—and so fast?"

"She lives in Phoenix, not far away. That's partly why I chose her. I told her I'd pay twice her usual fee if she'd find Julia immediately and get me some concrete information."

"Apparently she took you seriously."

"She must've jumped on the case as soon as I contacted her."

"She has the two boys," he said. "That wasn't a lie. But Julia Bowers is severely overweight. And she has all her hair."

Those things weren't conclusive, but they were fairly decent indicators that she wasn't on her deathbed. "She'd be hooked up to a morphine pump or something if she was about to die," she agreed. "And did you see the video?"

He tapped the arrow and watched it play. "Damn. She also seems to have plenty of energy."

The video showed Julia screaming and fighting with some guy who looked like a biker dude in front of what Ellie could only assume was her house. "She seems almost as strong as he is, right?"

Hudson whistled as he watched the video again. "If this woman has cancer, there's no way she's at the stage Matisson claims. You're positive this is Cort's daughter and not some other Julia?"

"Let's find out." She texted Shelly Gomez and got an immediate answer.

It's the right Julia. She accused her father of impregnating her and had a baby thirty-two years ago.

Thirty-two years ago? What about the newspaper article I sent where she put her baby at age thirty?

She wasn't being specific when she made that statement. I checked first thing and was able to verify the date through her testimony at her father's trial. Her baby would be thirty-two.

Ellie sighed. There wasn't any discrepancy on the dates after all.

"What'd she say?" Hudson asked as he pulled on a shirt.

"She said it's the right Julia."

He gestured toward her phone. "Could that really be the woman who gave me life?"

She knew he was referring to the video and Julia's less-than-stellar behavior, which seemed especially bad since she'd been acting like that in front of her children. "We're going to find out."

"At least she's not sick."

"True."

He caught her arm. "You don't seem pleased by the news."

She'd been holding out hope that Hudson wasn't really Julia's child. "I'm relieved she's not sick," she said. And not only because of the money. After what he'd been through with Aaron, she was glad Hudson wouldn't be subjected to the difficult emotions of that struggle. Especially if Julia *was* his mother, which now seemed more likely than ever.

"I can't put Ellie through that," Hudson told Bruiser, using his Bluetooth the next day as he got onto the freeway heading toward Orange County. The results of the DNA test Ellie had delivered to the lab were due anytime. He wanted to sit by the phone with her. But since he was in town, he'd promised Craig that he'd do some media stuff, including a visit with some sick kids at a nearby hospital.

"Wait. You just said Julia *wasn't* on her deathbed."

"She's not."

"But I thought that was the only thing that could change your mind."

He accelerated as he switched lanes. "She doesn't look sick to me. But I have Ellie to think about now. And our child. I don't want her to be embarrassed, and I sure as hell don't want our son growing up with this story being bandied about in the press every time my name's mentioned."

"Things seem to have changed a great deal between you and Ellie in the past week or so," Bruiser said.

Hudson had to slow for traffic. "I'd rather not talk about Ellie."

"*Still?* Why?"

"I've never felt like this about anyone else. I'm afraid to jinx it."

"Stop being so superstitious," Bruiser said with a chuckle. "Nothing can jinx it. She's in love with you."

"All the more reason I should act to protect her."

"Ellie wouldn't want you to give him the money for her sake."

"Maybe she doesn't know what's good for her."

"And maybe she does. Trust her, Hudson. Her love is tougher than you think."

"That would be a pleasant surprise," he said, since he had no experience with love that could endure.

He and Bruiser talked about a few other things—his dinner

with Craig and how Craig kept asking him for favors—but as soon as he reached his exit, he got off the phone. He needed to use his GPS to navigate since he'd never been to this particular hospital.

He was just pulling into the parking lot when he got a call from Samuel Jones.

Seeing the private detective's name pop up on caller ID made Hudson wish he had the results of the DNA test with that cigarette butt. But he didn't, so he had to proceed without that information. After checking his watch to make sure he had a few minutes, he hit Answer. "What's going on now?"

"Good news," Jones replied.

Hudson angled his Porsche into a parking space and cut the engine. "Did you say *good* news?"

"Yeah. I made it to Arizona and spoke with Matisson."

"And?"

"I told him he can't expect you to part with so much money, not without giving you something in return. So he's agreed to provide the proof you requested."

"Are you saying he's going to let me meet Julia? Talk to her?"

"No, he can't do that. Like I told you before, he's afraid she'll guess the truth. But he said he'd email you her medical records. And I got a swab of her DNA, so we can test you against both of them."

Hudson rocked back in his seat. What the hell was going on? "You've *seen* her?"

"I have," he replied. "Left the hospital only a few minutes ago. That's how I got her DNA."

Hudson put his phone on speaker so he could scroll through the pictures Ellie had forwarded to him yesterday. "How long has she been bedridden?"

"I don't know. A couple of weeks or more. Pancreatic cancer is serious shit."

Hudson knew that. But how could they be talking about the

same woman? He had a copy of the video that was taken yesterday morning, which showed Julia striking a guy who was probably her boyfriend, given what she was shrieking about another woman.

"Hudson? You still there?"

Hudson scratched his head as he swiped through Julia's pics yet again. "Yeah, I'm here."

"I have good news on the DNA tests, too," Jones told him. "I'm going to deliver the kits to a lab here in Phoenix for testing. They've promised they'll put them first in line. We should have an answer by tomorrow."

Hudson pinched the bridge of his nose. Either *his* private investigator or Ellie's had to be wrong—and he had a sneaking suspicion that he knew which one was lying. "Sounds good," he said. "Call me as soon as you get word."

"I will, but...there *is* a bit of bad news."

Although he was still in his car, Hudson straightened his leg so he could shove his keys in his pocket. "What's the bad news?"

"Matisson's demanding $2 million now."

Hudson remained silent for so long, Jones cleared his throat.

"Did you hear me?"

"Yeah, I heard."

"That shouldn't be a problem, right? You've got the money."

Although Hudson felt his muscles tighten, he tried not to let his anger leak into his voice. "Yeah, I've got the money."

"Great. I'll email you wiring instructions. Once you receive the proof, you'll have twenty-four hours to move the money into Matisson's account. Understand?"

Hudson stared out across the parking lot, but he wasn't really seeing anything. He was remembering how much it had bothered him that Jones would be stupid enough to hand Matisson his card. "I understand."

"You'll have everything sometime tomorrow, so be ready with the money," Jones reiterated and disconnected.

Hudson sat still for several seconds. Then he called Ellie.

"Is everything okay?" she asked. She was obviously surprised to hear from him, since he'd just left her.

"Jones is in on it," he said.

"On what?"

"The blackmail. I believe he's the one who's behind it."

"Are you *serious*?"

He told her what Jones had said about Julia being in the hospital.

"He's lying. He's *got* to be lying. He's probably not even in Arizona."

"I'm guessing once he figured out who Matisson was, he realized how badly I wouldn't want that information to come out and decided to take me for more than his usual fee."

"So he set it all up with Matisson—they're in it together."

"Have to be. Can you imagine a guy like Matisson—someone who doesn't blink at sleeping with his own daughter and tossing her child away like trash—turning down the chance to make an easy mil?" Or *two*? Remembering how coolly Jones had raised the price made Hudson's blood boil. "I bet he's the one who gave Matisson my address in the first place. Not some poor local."

"Wow," she said on a long exhalation.

"He might even be the one who made up that part about Julia being on her deathbed as a way to twist my arm."

"But he has to know it wouldn't be all that difficult for you to check..."

"I'm sure he was banking on the fact that if I asked anyone to verify Matisson's claims, it would be him. He's a PI, after all. His plan might've worked if you hadn't hired Shelly Gomez. He didn't see that coming."

"Thank God for her."

"Thank God for *you*." A final glance at his watch told him he had to go or he'd be late.

"You would've found out," Ellie said.

"Probably not in time."

"So what kind of proof are they going to offer?" she asked.

He got out and hurried toward the entrance. "We'll see soon enough."

"Falsifying records—convincingly—wouldn't be easy for a low-level crook like Matisson," she said.

"But it wouldn't be hard for Jones."

"True. That means whatever they send will say there's a match whether you're related to him or not."

"I know—but because you found that cigarette butt, we've got our own test."

"*If* that butt really belonged to Matisson. We don't have any guarantees there."

None of his gardeners smoked. He'd never seen another butt around his house. But if the tests weren't consistent, they'd have to take a third one. "So we'll get the police involved and force an in-person test to determine, once and for all, if there's any relation between us."

"You do that, and this thing will go public for sure."

"Then they won't have anything to blackmail me with."

"You'll *still* have to deal with the humiliation you've been trying to avoid."

"Which is why I'm praying your test has the right sample *and* comes back negative."

"Yikes. I hope you won't blame me if this all blows up."

He thought of her in the shower with him this morning, the way he'd enjoyed touching her and kissing her even though they'd already made love. It reminded him that she was different from all the other women he'd known. He was going to ask her to be his wife. "I won't. We're in this together, remember?"

Her voice softened. "Yeah, I remember."

They ended the call, and he found the entrance to the hospital.

"Hudson, there you are!" Craig said as soon as Hudson opened the front door and the media reporters who'd been waiting with him came rushing forward.

CHAPTER TWENTY-SEVEN

Hudson didn't get home for several hours. "Sorry I was gone so long," he said as Ellie slipped into his arms to welcome him. "That was a bigger deal than I was expecting."

"It's fine. I'm glad you could visit those kids. I'm betting it meant a lot to them. And I've been busy, anyway."

"Doing what?"

"Working out," she said proudly.

"You?" he asked, joking.

"Yes, me!" She gave his arm a playful slug. "Why does that surprise you?"

"I guess there's a first for everything."

She rolled her eyes. "Have you heard from Aaron?"

"Just talked to him on the drive home."

"How's he doing? He can't be happy that you got called out of town so suddenly."

He tossed his keys from hand to hand. "He's doing great. He understands that I have my own life to lead and can't be at New Horizons all the time."

"Any more news on his condition?" Ellie was almost afraid to ask, especially today, when Hudson was already so wound up, but he'd said Aaron was doing better lately, so she thought it might be okay…

"I talked to Aiyana, too. She told me the doc thinks the cancer's in remission. They'll keep checking him, of course—once a year. It could crop up again."

"But for now he's in the clear?"

"That's the latest," Hudson said. "Any news from the lab?"

She glanced at her phone as she'd been doing all day. "Not yet."

"Have you tried calling them?"

"I have. They say they're working on it."

"Do they close at five?"

She nodded. That meant they had two hours before the end of the day.

"Let's go grab an early dinner. Maybe that'll make the time pass more quickly. There are a lot of good restaurants in LA I can introduce you to."

She went to put on her shoes and get her purse. When she returned, she was surprised to find Hudson looking at her with a strange expression. "What is it?"

"I've changed my mind. I'm not ready to eat—unless you're hungry."

"I had lunch a couple of hours ago, so I'm in no rush. What would you rather do?"

"Look for a ring."

"A *ring*?"

He took her hands and pulled her close. "If you'll marry me…"

Ellie felt her jaw drop. "You're *proposing*? Right now?"

"I should've waited. Planned something special, but… I don't know. I can't delay gratification on this."

She gently touched his cheek.

"Is that a yes?" he asked. "Because I'd really like to hear you say the words."

"That's a yes," she said. "I love you. I've told you that."

"Do you know what the next few weeks—what football season—will be like if Matisson *is* my father? The media storm if that comes out?"

"Doesn't change anything."

She saw his chest lift as he took in a deep breath. "Okay. Let's go buy you a diamond."

If she'd made a mistake by falling in love with Hudson, she was only making it worse by pledging the rest of her life to him. But she could no longer believe that loving him was a mistake. Sure, there'd be hard times, but every marriage had those. She felt they were meant to be together, that she was the luckiest woman in the world to have found him. "When would you like to have the ceremony?"

"I don't care—as long as it's before the baby comes."

"That only gives us a couple months! And it puts me in a wedding dress looking like this!" She pressed her hands to her pregnant stomach.

"You look gorgeous to me."

"This isn't how I want to be seen as a bride!"

"Do you really mind that much? Because I always wanted a traditional family, so that's what I'd like to give our baby."

"It's not just putting on a wedding dress while I'm in my final trimester, Hudson. Do you feel confident making this commitment? There's no rush. Don't marry me unless you're sure you love me. Why not wait until we've been together a year or two? See how it goes?"

He raised her chin with one finger. "I'll be honest, Ellie. I'm not sure what love is. I guess that's why I haven't said the words. But if it's feeling as if I can't wait to see you whenever we're apart, then I love you. If it's wanting to touch you constantly, even if we just had sex, then I love you." His voice dropped as he grew more earnest. "If it's feeling like I'd rather die than let anything happen to you, then I love you."

"That's all I needed to hear. The answer is yes," she said. "I'll marry you dressed in a tent, if that's all that'll fit me."

He couldn't help chuckling as she rose up on tiptoe to kiss him. "We can always wait to have the reception until later."

Ellie had gravitated to the side of the store that displayed the less expensive, modest-size diamonds. She'd said she didn't see any reason to waste money or buy anything ostentatious, but Hudson refused to let her be conservative about this. Now that he'd found the woman he was going to spend the rest of his life with, he planned to give her everything he could—and that included a giant, three-carat round-cut solitaire.

"Someone's going to murder me for my ring," she muttered as they left the jeweler's, but Hudson could tell she was secretly thrilled. That she would've been satisfied with less, that she didn't demand expensive things, made it so much more fun to splurge on her. She'd smiled shyly and blushed when the jeweler had encouraged her to try on the ring he'd ended up purchasing. But then she'd stared at it as if she'd never seen anything quite that beautiful before. So even though, once she heard the price, she took it off immediately and handed it back, Hudson had ignored her protests and bought it, anyway.

"Are you positive this whole marriage thing isn't just a reaction to the fear and stress you're feeling?" she asked as they drove home.

"I'm positive."

She kept glancing at the rock on her left hand as if she thought it might disappear if she didn't keep an eye on it. "Still, I don't think we should've bought a ring that costs as much as a house. What if you decide to give Matisson that ransom? You might need the money."

"Quit worrying. I've got this."

"But I'm not working. I can't contribute anything right now."

"You're carrying our baby. That's your contribution. Even if you weren't pregnant, you wouldn't need to work. You won't *ever* need to work."

She bit her lip. "What if I want to? That won't bother you, will it?"

His incredulous look told her she was crazy to even ask. "Why would it?"

"Because it might make me less available and unable to travel with you."

"I'm not going to demand that you sacrifice what *you* love just because we're getting married. Besides, I'm proud of what you do."

"Okay." She held her hand out. "Jeez, this is huge. It's hard to imagine being as rich as you are. Please tell me you won't spoil Garrison."

"Garrison? That's the name we're going with?"

"Do you still like it?"

"I do. But I can't promise I won't spoil him. I'll probably spoil both of you."

Her phone rang before she could respond. "Oh, my gosh, it's the lab!"

He pulled to the side of the road because his heart was beating like a piston. "Is it a match?"

She signaled for him to be quiet so she could hear the technician. "But you said you'd have it today... So when will it be?... You're sure? I can't tell you how important this is... I understand... Fine... Tomorrow, then."

"Well?" Hudson said when she was off the phone. "What'd he say?"

"One of their technicians went home sick this morning. This guy—Dane something—thought he'd be able to get to it, but he couldn't. Promised me he'd call with the results tomorrow."

Hudson let go of a long sigh. "Damn. More waiting."

"Just one more day." She was obviously trying to encourage him, but he could tell it sounded like an eternity to her, too.

★ ★ ★

It wasn't until eleven that night that Hudson received the "proof" and wiring instructions in an email from Samuel Jones. Those documents—and the fact that Jones would try to cheat him, especially in such a devious way—made him so angry he knew he'd never be able to sleep.

"Wait till I get my hands on him," he said as he paced in the living room where he and Ellie had been watching a movie. "Even if Matisson *is* my father, Jones is going to be sorry he tried to cash in on my misfortune."

"He sees you as having more money than you can spend. He probably doesn't even feel bad about it," Ellie said.

"I'm going to make sure he feels bad. I'll invite him over to get the money. Then I'll show him what happens to guys who—"

"Hudson," she broke in, "you can't touch him or *you'll* be the one who goes to jail. And you don't need that. You don't need the negative press you'd get from breaking his jaw, either." She made a fist with her small hand. "But I wish we *could* ambush him. I bet it would hurt if I hit him with this rock."

Hudson couldn't laugh, although he knew she was trying to get him to relax. "You stay away from him. With my luck, he'd kidnap you and hold you for ransom." He glared down at the DNA results he'd printed out that were supposedly from some lab in Arizona. "Based on testing results obtained from the analyses of the DNA loci listed, the probability of paternity is 99.9998 percent." He had one for Julia's supposed maternity, too. Those documents turned his stomach, even though he'd expected whatever Jones sent to signify a match—to both people. "We know Julia's medical records are bogus. But are these results real?"

"Anyone could make a document like that," Ellie told him, "and put whatever lab name and address on top, then turn it into a pdf file. There are samples of paternity test results online.

I checked earlier, while you were on the phone, hoping I'd be able to spot an obvious fraud when these arrived."

"And?"

"It's not that easy. He did a nice job."

"Good thing we're double-checking him."

"Yes, but I'm glad he doesn't know that. If he did, I doubt he would've sent these, since they'll provide strong evidence against him if he's lying."

That was probably why he'd tried to get the money without any documentation…

Hudson thumbed through the medical records Jones had sent along with the results of both DNA tests. "These look legit, too."

"I wonder if he had Matisson ask Julia to request her medical records. Then he added in the pancreatic cancer diagnosis, as well as the medications." She frowned. "On second thought, I bet he downloaded the sample medical record of a cancer patient from the internet and changed out all the personal information to make it coincide with Julia's. How else would he know the names of the medications—and the dosages and so on?"

"Bastard," Hudson grumbled.

"Julia might be involved. Have you considered that?"

"I have. But if she is, don't you think they would've had her call me? A teary phone call from a suffering woman would've turned the screws on me. It might even have made me give in."

"True. And she sent her father to prison, so chances are they no longer have any contact. That makes me think she's *not* involved."

"If she's not, but she is my mother, I'll send her some money, anyway. After what she's been through, I'm sure she could use a break."

Ellie smiled up at him.

"What?" he said.

"You have such a soft heart."

He gave her a mock glare. "What do you mean? I'm tough as nails."

She laughed as she stood, and he realized how much bigger their baby was getting as she walked over to him.

"Garrison is going to be enormous," he said.

"Don't scare me like that," she responded as he kissed her.

She turned off the TV and talked him into going to bed, but he was too preoccupied to do anything except hold her until she fell asleep. After that, he quietly left the room and went downstairs. So much had changed in the past six months. And so much more was going to change. He'd be married, become a father. He'd also become a son if Matisson was his father—not that he viewed *that* as a positive thing.

He paced and played some pool, watched TV, even swam, trying to galvanize himself for the results. He was up all night, so when he heard Ellie calling out to him the following morning, he was exhausted but prepared for the worst. Maybe that was why he could hardly believe it when she found him as he was coming down the hall, threw her arms around his neck and said, "The DNA test came back negative, Hudson! Whoever smoked that cigarette—and I'm 90 percent sure it was Matisson—is *not* your father. They're lying about everything! The fact that Julia Matisson happened to have her baby the same year you were born—and that it was a boy—was just a coincidence they capitalized on."

Hudson's knees nearly gave out on him. He'd been so sure he'd have to face the opposite. There'd have to be a third test, of course, one to confirm the results they'd received a few minutes ago. But now he had hope. Even with the uncertainty regarding whether that cigarette butt really belonged to Matisson, he believed the LA test to be more reliable than anything that came from Jones. "So what happened to her baby?"

"Who can say? Maybe he was stillborn as Matisson claims."

"Or Matisson killed him as the cops suspect. Smothered the baby before it could even cry."

"That's a sad thought, but a possibility."

He closed his eyes in relief.

"Hudson?" she said.

"What?"

"Do you still want to marry me? Maybe you should reconsider, now that—"

He caught her face between his hands. "Are you kidding? I want you to be my wife more than ever now that I don't have to worry I'll be an embarrassment to you."

"I'll always be proud of you, no matter what," she told him.

EPILOGUE

Hudson was sweating despite the fact that it was cold in the hospital. Ellie was sweating, too. He could see beads of moisture on her upper lip as he fed her ice chips—which was all the doctor would allow her to have. She'd been in labor for twenty-four hours, and the pains were getting more intense. Watching her suffer killed him, made him wish he could do more than stand idly by, worrying that something terrible might happen to her or their child before this night was through. Ellie had become such an integral part of his life. He'd never dreamed he'd like being married as much as he did, couldn't imagine having to go on without her.

He told himself he was overreacting. People had babies every day. And yet… Ellie's delivery was turning into a long, agonizing process.

"I think you should give her a Cesarean," he told their obstetrician, Dr. Billinger, when she came in to check on Ellie. Ellie's parents had been there with them until midnight. They'd returned to Miami a month earlier and had come to California for the baby's birth almost ten days ago—since Ellie had shot past her due date by a week. But when the nurse told them

Ellie hadn't even dilated to three yet, that the baby probably wouldn't come until morning, they'd gone home to his place to get some rest.

"I don't think that's necessary," Billinger said. "She's progressing a little slower than I'd like, but there's no need to panic. This is a first baby. First babies can take a while."

"I don't want to let this go on any longer," Hudson insisted. "Don't want to risk her."

"It'll be better for both mother and baby if she can give birth vaginally. Everything's fine, Hudson." The doctor patted his back as she'd been doing all day. Then she took hold of Ellie's arm to get her attention. "You're okay, aren't you, Ellie?"

Ellie didn't respond. She seemed to be somewhere deep inside herself, searching for the strength to endure. Hudson watched her muscles tighten as another contraction hit.

"This is too much for her," he murmured to the doctor.

"She'd say something if it was. I have monitors on the baby that'll let me know if he's in distress."

Hudson lowered his voice. "But if she's only at three, the end isn't in sight. And I'm afraid she wouldn't tell us if it was too hard on her. She'll keep hanging on. I don't want her to suffer anymore."

The doctor tried to speak to Ellie again, but Ellie ignored her. She hadn't been talking much during the past hour. She looked totally spent. Hudson wished he could lend her his strength. They'd decided to go with a natural birth, but he felt Ellie had already given it her best shot.

"Ellie?" The doctor spoke more loudly.

Finally Ellie opened her eyes.

"How are you doing?"

Ellie looked as though she might attempt an answer, but another contraction hit right after the last one, and she cried out.

Hudson felt so helpless. Angry that the doctor wasn't doing

more, he pulled Billinger into a corner. "Will you *do* something?" he demanded.

The doctor glanced over at Ellie, who was trying to catch her breath, and nodded. But as soon as she checked Ellie again in preparation for whatever she had planned, she said, "Whoa! That happened fast. She's in transition. She's going to have the baby any minute."

"What does that mean?" Hudson asked.

Billinger shot him a look. "It means you need to relax and let me do my job."

"Hudson," Ellie moaned.

He hurried back to her side. "I'm right here."

"I need an epidural. Get me an epidural, okay?"

"It's too late for that." Billinger answered for him as two nurses came in and raised the stirrups on either side of the bed.

"Should I get a mirror so you can watch?" a nurse asked Ellie.

Ellie was obviously steeling herself for the next pain, but she managed a weak nod, and the nurse rolled a mirror to the bottom of the bed.

From that moment on, everything went into fast-forward. Hudson didn't even have time to call his in-laws to tell them the baby was on his way before the doctor started encouraging Ellie to push, and the top of a dark head appeared.

"There's the baby. Did you see that?" Billinger asked.

Hudson *did* see it, but he could hardly celebrate. Not yet. So many things could still go wrong… "Is everything okay?"

No one answered. They were too busy. Ellie was bearing down, and the doctor was trying to ease the delivery using oil.

When Garrison's head finally emerged completely, tears filled Hudson's eyes. He dashed a hand across his cheek to get rid of them, but he couldn't stop more tears from replacing those. Although the doctor held the baby's head, Garrison looked purple—*dead*—and Ellie couldn't seem to deliver the rest of him.

Hudson stumbled back as several nurses crowded the room.

No one said anything, but he could feel their concern, knew something was wrong. One jumped onto the bed with Ellie and began to push right above Ellie's pelvic bone to help her get Garrison's shoulders out.

Panic made Hudson's blood run cold. He feared his worst nightmare was coming true, and there was nothing he could do about it. But the whole room relaxed the second Garrison's body slipped out.

The doctor suctioned the fluid from his lungs. "You have a son," she said above the sound of his baby's cry.

One of the nurses opened the front of Ellie's hospital gown and laid the baby on her chest, skin to skin.

Hudson released his breath. Now that Garrison was out and Ellie seemed to be okay, he felt light-headed but steadied himself by putting one hand to the wall.

After clasping the baby to her, Ellie looked around at the nurses who were blocking her view. "Hudson," she called. "Come meet your son."

He managed not to stumble as he moved to the bed and bent to kiss her forehead. "I'm so glad you're okay," he murmured. "So glad you both are."

She laughed. "I'm better than okay. You can stop worrying."

"Are you ready to cut the umbilical cord?" the doctor asked.

At that point he felt a little embarrassed, since his emotions had been so extreme. He should've had more faith. But everything that mattered to him in the whole world had been at stake. "Yeah," he said and wiped his cheeks again as the doctor handed him the scissors.

Later, when both Ellie and the baby were cleaned up, the nurses and doctor were gone from the room and he was holding his sleeping son, Ellie gave him a tired smile. "You have such a serious expression on your face," she said. "What are you thinking about?"

He wasn't sure he should tell her. He didn't want to bring her down when they were both feeling so euphoric. "Nothing."

"Tell me," she insisted.

He sighed. "My mother." They'd known for the past two months that the pizza deliveryman—Stan Hinkle—who "found" him had also left him in the first place. After Matisson's attempted blackmail hit the news, the police confronted Hinkle once again, at which point he admitted that he'd left Hudson under that hedge because his wife had gotten pregnant by another man, and he couldn't face the prospect of looking at someone else's child every day. He was leaving to deliver a pizza when she called to tell him she'd given birth in the bathroom. She'd wanted him to take her to the hospital, but he'd refused. He took the baby and left him at a neighboring house before driving down the street to drop off the pizza.

Hudson might've died under that hedge, except Hinkle forgot to deliver the bread sticks that were supposed to go with the pizza. When his manager sent him back, his conscience finally got the better of him. He'd picked up Hudson and turned him in to the authorities, claiming someone had abandoned him. Why Hinkle's wife—Hudson's mother—never stepped forward, Hudson didn't know. Once she and Hinkle had broken up three years later, she got involved with someone else, started doing drugs and was killed in a motorcycle accident. "I wish she wasn't gone—that you could meet her," Ellie said.

"So do I," Hudson said, but Stan Hinkle had denied him that possibility. Hudson thought he might be able to find his father if he hired another private investigator, but Stan knew only his first name, and after what Hudson had been through, he'd decided not to even look. He was happy with his life, happy with Ellie and Garrison. He didn't want to bring in an unknown element, especially when there was no guarantee about the kind of man his father would be.

"What Hinkle did was so grossly unfair," Ellie complained. "I hope he gets several years in prison."

"I doubt he'll wind up serving any time."

"What? Last I heard, the police were going to try to get him on something."

"I talked to the detective on the case a few days ago. It's been thirty-two years—a bit long to prosecute him for child endangerment. And because he rescued me in the end, they won't be able to make an attempted murder charge stick."

"There's always kidnapping!"

"But that would be tough to prove. With my mother gone, no one can say if she allowed him to do what he did or not. It doesn't appear she did much to stop him. She didn't even look for me after they broke up." Which made him pretty certain she wouldn't have been much of a mother in the first place…

"Still, it's hard to believe he can do that to a baby and suffer no repercussions."

Hudson ran a finger over the soft, downy cheek of his brand-new son. "What it comes down to is that my mother chose him over me. That's how most people will see it. So I went into the system. At least Matisson and Jones will be serving time."

She scowled. "Two years isn't nearly long enough in my book."

"You don't get a lot for a *failed* attempt at blackmail, especially when there were no threats of physical violence. Either way, they can't hurt us anymore."

She tucked her hands under her pillow. "So, are you really going to be able to leave your past behind you?"

"I don't want to hang on to that. I have too much to look forward to." Hudson smiled as Garrison opened his eyes and stared up at him with a somber expression—one that gave Hudson the feeling he was trying to make sense of his new surroundings. "Hi, son. It's your daddy," he said.

★ ★ ★ ★ ★

If you enjoyed Ellie and Hudson's story, don't miss the next book in Brenda Novak's SILVER SPRINGS *series,*
RIGHT WHERE WE BELONG,
coming soon from MIRA Books.
Turn the page for a sneak peek!

CHAPTER ONE

"You knew! You *had* to have known!"

The vitriol in those words caused the hair on the back of Savanna Gray's neck to stand on end. She was just trying to pick up a gallon of milk at the supermarket with her kids, had never dreamed she might be accosted—although, since her husband's arrest, it felt like everyone in town was staring daggers at her. The crimes Abe committed had shaken the small, insular town of Nephi, Utah, to the core.

"Don't you dare run off! I know you heard me."

Savanna froze. She *had* been about to flee. Her emotions were so raw she could barely make herself leave the house these days. She wished she could hole up with the curtains drawn and never face her neighbors again. But she had two children who were depending on her, and she was all they had left. Those children now looked up at her expectantly, and her son, Branson, who was eight, said, "Mommy, I think that lady's talking to you."

Gripping her shopping cart that much tighter, Savanna swung it around. She was determined to do a better job of defending herself against this type of thing than she had in the past. But then she recognized Meredith Caine. A video of Meredith—

clothes torn, mascara smeared and lip bleeding as the same sister who was with her now tried to comfort her—had played on the news several times while police searched for the man who'd attacked her as she carried a load of laundry down to the basement of her apartment building.

Savanna's house had been egged—twice. Someone had driven onto her lawn and peeled out, leaving deep ruts. And someone else had thrown a bottle at her car that'd broken all over the driveway. But she'd never been directly confronted by one of her husband's victims—only their friends or family or others in the community who were outraged by the assaults. Facing Meredith wasn't easy. Savanna wished she could melt into the floor and disappear—do anything to avoid this encounter. Meredith didn't understand. Savanna had watched her on TV with the same compassion and fear all the other women in the area felt. She'd had no idea she was *living* with the culprit, *sleeping* with him—and enabling him to operate without suspicion because of the illusion she helped create that he was a good family man. She'd thought he *was* a good family man, or she wouldn't have married him!

"Meredith, don't do this. Let's go." Her sister tried to drag her off, but Meredith remained rooted to the spot, eyes shining with outrage.

"Where *were* you, huh?" she cried. "How could you have missed that your husband was out stalking women at night?"

Abe had been a mining-equipment field-service technician for the last five years of their nine-year marriage, which meant he drove long distances to reach various mines and worked irregular hours. Savanna had believed he was on the road or repairing equipment, like he'd said. She'd had no idea he was out prowling around. Despite what Meredith and everyone else seemed to believe—that simply by being close to him she should've been able to spot such a large defect in his character—he'd never done anything significant enough to give himself away.

"I thought… I thought he was doing his job," she said.

"You believed he was *working* all those hours?" Meredith scoffed.

"I did." She hadn't been checking up on him. She'd been trying to manage the kids, the house and her own job working nine-to-five for a local insurance agent. Besides, Abe always had a ready excuse for when he came home later than expected, a *believable* excuse. Another piece of equipment had failed and he'd had to drive back to his last location. His truck wouldn't start, and he'd had to stay over to get a new battery. The weather was too terrible to begin the long trek home.

Were those excuses something a wife *should* have been leery of?

"Maybe you should've paid a little more attention to what was happening in his life," Meredith snapped.

Savanna began to tremble. "I wish I had. Look, I'd be happy to talk to you—to explain my side so that maybe you could understand. But...please, let's not do this here, in front of my children."

Meredith didn't even glance at Branson and Alia. She was too angry, too eager to inflict some of the pain she'd suffered on Savanna. "Your husband didn't care about *my* children when he put his hands around my neck and nearly choked the life out of me. Thanks to him, I haven't been able to have sex with my own husband since!"

"Meredith!" Her sister gasped, obviously more aware of the children and, likely, the attention this confrontation was drawing.

Alia, Savanna's six-year-old daughter, pulled on Savanna's sleeve. "Mommy, why did Daddy choke her?" she whispered loudly, her big blue eyes filling with tears.

"Your father..." Savanna's throat had tightened to the point where she could scarcely breathe, let alone talk. "He made some poor choices, honey. Like we talked about when he went away, remember?"

"Choices?" Meredith echoed, jumping on that immediately. "That man is pure evil. But keep lying—to them and yourself."

At that point, Meredith's sister managed to pull her away. They left Savanna standing in front of the cooler that held the milk and cheese, feeling as if she'd been slugged in the stomach.

"Show's over," she mumbled to those who'd stopped to watch the drama unfold and were still lingering.

"The kids at school say Daddy grabbed three women and ripped off their clothes," Branson said, his voice small as his gaze followed Meredith and her companion to the checkout register at the opposite end of the aisle. "That's true, isn't it?"

He wasn't asking. He was just now realizing that Abe wasn't innocent as they'd all stubbornly hoped. That her son would have to accept such a terrible truth, especially at his tender age, would've broken Savanna's heart—if it hadn't already been shattered into a million pieces. "They've been talking about your father at school?"

For the most part since Abe's arrest, Branson had clammed up when it came to discussing his father, pretended as if nothing had changed. Almost every day, Savanna had asked him how things were going at school, and he'd insisted that everything was fine.

This proved otherwise, which made her feel even worse.

Head bowed, he scuffed one sneaker against the other. "Yeah."

"Mommy?" Alia's lower lip quivered as she gazed up, looking for reassurance.

Savanna knelt to pull them both into her arms. "Don't worry. Everything's going to be okay. You aren't responsible for what your father did." She wanted to believe *she* wasn't, either, but part of her feared that maybe she had more culpability than she cared to admit. Had she been too gullible, too trusting, as everyone implied?

She must've been, or she wouldn't be in this situation. And standing by Abe even after the police searched the house had only made public opinion worse. She'd wanted so desperately to trust her husband above others, to protect her family, so that was what she'd done—until the mounting evidence had grown to be too much. But that process of utter shock, denial, crushing pain and, finally, numb acceptance wasn't anything others had witnessed her go through. They only saw her as being tied to him, loving and supporting the monster who'd raped three women, and since he was no longer walking around town, *she'd* become the target of everyone's resentment.

"Boys aren't supposed to hurt girls," a bewildered Branson said.

"You're absolutely right, honey," she told him. "You shouldn't hurt anyone."

"So...why would Daddy choke that lady?"

Tears burned behind Savanna's eyes as she hugged them both tighter. "I don't know." That was a question she asked herself every day, but she had no answers. It wasn't as though she'd ever denied her husband physical intimacy. Other than a few oddities she'd chalked up to personal quirks, she'd thought they had a normal sex life. Since this whole thing had come out, however, she couldn't help wondering if she could've been more alluring or adventurous or exciting to him. Maybe if *she'd* been satisfying, he wouldn't have gone searching for something else and none of this would've happened...

Straightening, she shoved her cart to the side, left the few incidental groceries they'd gathered and took hold of her children's hands.

"Where are we going?" Branson asked when she circled around to the far side of the store to avoid Meredith and her sister as she led them out.

"Home," she replied.

"What about the milk?"

"We'll get it later." She couldn't stay in the store another second.